"Near-perfect ... bristling with h ... an absorbing amalgam of the p
— D. J. Taylor, *The Spectator*

"Fiercely truthful, intensely funny. The novel brilliantly continues Mo's fictional enterprise."
— Peter Kemp, *The Sunday Times*

"Let me say from the outset that this is a terrific novel, one of the best ever written about the Philippines."
— Isabel Taylor Escoda, *Philippine Sunday Inquirer Magazine*

"Sheer excellence ... exquisitely written ... authentic, funny and revelatory."
— Alfred Yuson, *Philippine Daily Inquirer*

"Timothy Mo really is a brilliant writer."
— Peter Bradshaw, London *Evening Standard*

"Mo deserves applause for the quality of his prose. *Brownout* sees Mo in top condition again."
— Tibor Fischer, *The Times*

"There is no questioning the virtuosity of his style ... richly comic."
— Richard Tyrrell, *The Guardian*

Brownout on Breadfruit Boulevard

TIMOTHY MO

Brownout on Breadfruit Boulevard

*"When a society is cohesive, law-abiding and
productive, the source of its strength can invariably be
traced to the strength of its families."*
UN General Assembly Resolution, December 8 1989

Paddleless

This edition first published 1997
First published in Great Britain in 1995 by
Paddleless Press

Paddleless Press, BCM Paddleless,
London WC1N 3XX

Copyright © 1995 by Timothy Mo

The right of Timothy Mo to be identified as the author
of this work has been asserted by him in accordance
with the Copyright, Designs and Patents Act 1988.

British Library Cataloguing in Publication Data.
A catalogue record for this book is
available from the British Library.

ISBN 0 9524193 1 9

Printed and bound in Great Britain by
The Guernsey Press Company Limited

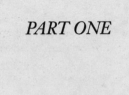

PART ONE

Prologue

WHEN THE SHOWER OF SHIT, which he welcomed, spattered over his chest and belly Professor Pfeidwengeler was thinking of his worst enemy, Dr Ruth Neumark. His tendency was to woolgather even, or rather especially, at moments of high and hardgained ecstacy. It was not every day such a situation could be savoured. He had his mind on the job, or jobs, he had paid Sunshine Abarquez to do for and on him, but the motion had been long coming and the strain was telling on both of them. Pfeidwengeler appreciated the effort it cost her, not so much from his own experience of constipation as precedent. Girls, even Germans, were shy, particularly the young ones, and the specimen squatting over him was both Asian and youthful, therefore doubly modest, doubly desirable. He touched her on the ankle – they were both naked, the Professor still in his socks – to indicate she should take the weight off her thin thighs, and relax crouched on hands and knees. As she tipped forwards, Pfeidwengeler guided her hand to where his own left fist was massaging his genitals. "Stop ngg-ngg, *Kuya*?" she inquired eagerly. Pfeidwengeler shook his head but of course she couldn't see him. "Noo!" he prohibited her with all the authority he could muster from the position. "If you want your money, you will do what I pay for. This is a break only."

"I just relax, *Kuya*, already? Making hand-job? OK?" She turned to smile at him, bright with temporary relief, happy to be able to do something she knew she did well, and in the sweetness of her expression Pfeidwengeler was reassured as to his original choice. His girls had to look absolutely virginal, no matter the reality, be becomingly reluctant without overdoing the nuisance, possess narrow backs, solid little breasts, and above all slim legs and delicate ankles with long toes. Otherwise it was in danger of degenerating into something gross. The vile harridans he had employed in Europe misinterpreted his special impulse as "degradation". One of the sows had done it on his face. His quest was for the beautiful and the unusual.

His large, uncircumcised penis dwarfed Sunshine's fist but there was no doubting the expertness of the manipulation. The Professor put his palms under the fold of her buttocks, looking up like a Jew or Mussulman entreating heaven, to push her rump higher and splay her legs for a better view. She squeaked, but didn't miss a piston's beat. In their familiar allure there lay before him the black slit of her hairless vagina, glistening slightly at the edge but the labia unparted and dry as a cock's comb, the dark splintered pit of her anus like the ventilation shaft of the rodent which lived in the next door brushy cave. Perfection for Pfeidwengeler! He looked for smoothness in the gulch, clean-ness of geological form. With a sigh he buried his nose in her soft buttocks, ferreting with his tongue in the round burrow. Sunshine gave a little scream – it tickled – but the way she wrig-gled was firmly in the direction of *Kuya*'s face. Professor Pfeidwengeler transferred his ministrations to the upper, rattlesnake part of the cleft, then lay back, kneading and patting the halves of her neat rump. She turned her head to inquire if she should also stop but he wanted the sensation to continue. She lifted her backside in the air and winked mischievously at *Kuya* through the tunnel of her legs, her head upside down. "*Ja, ja, fertig,*" the Professor groaned. Now he did signal her to wait. He didn't want his moment coming too early. Sunshine smoothed the inside slope of his thigh, then blew on his old man's scrotum, which spilled as extensively as a lava-flow. She was accustomed to the fat, the elderly, feeling no especial revul-sion from them, but she was sufficiently artful to hope that if Pfeidwengeler climaxed he'd lose interest in the deal but she would still be able to claim the HK$2,000 negotiated. "*Ja*, you stop that, my little pretty," said the Professor. "Now sit up straight again and try some more." Sunshine obliged, but getting into the squat, she checked, "Can like my dirty, *Kuya*?" She wrinkled her short nose. "Coming bad a smell."

"You do not worry your little head, just letting it come. Relax yourself."

"Easier is relaxing," Sunshine agreed.

Pfeidwengeler slid himself further under.

"Waiting, *Kuya*, hah?"

"Take your time, I said relax."

He stroked the honey moon soothingly. After half a minute the cords of the fleshy knot began to quiver. Professor Pfeidwengeler took a deep breath of satisfaction; the excitement stirred within him. Sunshine gasped, then shook her head vigorously. "Cannot do."

"*Ja*, you can, you can." He slapped the divine cheek hard enough to sting. He knew it was the time for coercion, at last.

"Shit, shit, shit," groaned Sunshine, straining. Professor Pfeidwengeler was sure the expletive was divorced from its meaning. Five drops of urine, startlingly hot, splashed on his stomach. Suddenly, the dark star split; burst, looking thin as sausage skin, the event not appearing normal, as if something must have ruptured. But he knew that was the way it was. The tip of her turd appeared, a shy brown toadstool poking its head out of the earth. "*Ja*, come on! *Weiter*!" Pfeidwengeler was of course the one underneath, being ridden, but Sunshine the one being spurred. She had a dizzying sensation, of letting go something she shouldn't abandon, of inappositeness, wrongness.

And then it was gone. The big brown one was out. Pfeidwengeler regarded it, athwart his sternum, glistening in the lamplight, caramel-coloured, fissured, looking ten million years ancient, not ten hours, some sixteen centimetres, tapering to a wick-like tip. Although little more than its own length separated it from his face, it appeared entirely odour-less. That, he knew from experience, was a matter of perspective, of relative position. The stink travelled upwards, was undoubtedly rich in her nostrils, but nothing presently affronted his. Sunshine looked back, panicking somewhat as to how much she had done, where it had landed and how it might sojourn or journey and, related to that, its composition, but she had to be careful not to lose her balance; besides, more was on the way. "Oh, *Kuya*, help, cannot stop."

"*Ja!*" cried the Professor in jubilation. "It gives plenty."

Three smaller pieces, the last really a pellet, shot from the hole. They always travelled too fast to see – one moment in the tunnel, the next already out. Pfeidwengeler touched the smallest piece, then going further than he had done in the past, picked it up and mumbled it between his lips first without the involvement of tongue, and therefore taste, before discovering it resembled papaya. The girl was so slim and fresh he felt no disgust, only extreme interest, but it spoiled papaya for him thereafter. Removing the shit crumb, he wanted to put it in his navel to prevent it rolling away but naturally Sunshine's rear intervened. She was sinking lower, her weedy legs failing. Pfeidwengeler could see her spinal column rising out of her back. Ruth Neumark was probably that emaciated, too. Old Gagool – bundle of bones and skin, sticks and hide. *Ach!* He'd like to give that one an infusion of liquid concrete in the rectum. Let her hear some Mahler while it dried and hardened. This was when Sunshine farted, giggled, said, "Sorry, *Kuya*," parped again, then to her horror heard a spray of matter explode from her sphincter all over Pfeidwengeler's torso. He nearly swooned with joy. "*Kuya*, sorry!" she wailed.

"You have been a very naughty girl," he said thickly. The matter was too sludgy to be called diarrhoea but definitely a loose movement, the result of a less than fresh pork *siu pao* bun Sunshine had snacked on. Now such solid matter as there was congealed on high ground while the coffee, pungent at last to Pfeidwengeler, ran away down the Professor's flanks and his domed belly. He was transported in time more than fifty years – he'd seen his hairless, skinny, boyish body like this as he lay back in the communal concrete troughs at Heidelberg, bruised and happily abrased, with another boy's toes brushing his outside thigh sexlessly after muddy games of football in the thirties. Already prone to intellectual flights, he'd thought then they were re-enacting the camaraderie of the trenches, with a fraction of the bloodshed and the only gassing the occasional hilarious fart bubble which earned the offender a prompt ducking. Carnal joy of the present moment mingled with nostalgic triste to produce a glassy look in the Professor's eyes.

"*Kuya*, you OK?" Sunshine inquired anxiously. Kindness – still abundant in her young heart – greed, and dismay at the prospect of finding herself alone in the shambles she had made, motivated her in equal measure. "Ah, *Kuya*, going on the sheet!" She had the extreme horror of dirt of the decent poor, Pfeidwengeler thought.

"*Ja*, let it. The hotel charge me fortunes already." In fact, Pfeidwengeler didn't begrudge the establishment its stiff fee, so long as it could guarantee to keep gatecrashers at bay. There'd been that distinctly forgettable episode with the Royal Hong Kong Police.

Sunshine found herself pushed forward again, then the Professor's stubby, (nicotine-) browned finger was probing in her *lobot*. "Ah no, *Kuya*," she wailed. It wasn't painful; it was eerie. After you'd done your big business the last thing you expected was the sensation of fullness again so soon. And it was just like the feeling of evacuation. As the Professor withdrew his finger a few inches, she panicked – it felt like more material was being expelled from her fundament to combine with the uncontrollable amount already in the world. "Stopping please! Cannot!"

The Professor's finger had travelled as far as it could without its tip leaving the ring's grip. As he paused, Sunshine felt relief flooding into her – it had been an illusion, she hadn't been compounding the pollution already on the bed. Then as the Professor thrust again, it felt like her insides were melting once more and staining the surroundings ineradicably. Shortly after, came the relief of reality, the waking from a bad dream, the cessation of illusory trepidation as the end of movement. She carried the still point of the Professor's questing finger deep within her. It was quite thrilling: like falling endlessly at terrifying speed, then finding a blossoming parachute suddenly arresting you. This repeated again and again, as many times as *Kuya* cared to poke. So when the Professor brusquely pulled out his satisfying digit, it was a shock.

"Now we go to bathroom," he commanded. Sunshine took some seconds to get a grip on herself. Then she cautiously swung her slender leg over what was on the bed; she was also nervous her *lobot* was leaking. "Washing now, *Kuya*?" she asked. "Just get in there," the Professor said. As Pfeidwengeler entered with a start-ling array of rubber pipes and bulbs Sunshine clapped her hand over her mouth in alarm. "Cannot do!" she said, eyes widening, already half-knowing she was coercible. It was the orangey colour of the rubber which was scary, like the processed and dyed intestine sold in Chinese cookshops, as if *Kuya* had pulled the bowels of previous girls inside out and was going to stuff them up her instead.

"*Ja*, you can," said Pfeidwengeler, fully versed in bullying those who desired chivvying.

"Cannot, *Kuya*. Not agree this."

"So you can make more money for your family at home, I can give you two hundred extra."

Sunshine put on a troubled look, as of deep inner moral perturbation which the Professor correctly interpreted as a communication that the deal could be clinched at a slightly higher price. "OK, three fifty." "Aw, *Kuya*, five hundred only." "OK – only because you're good girl. Now touch your toes." In addition to assholes, the Professor also had an interest in girls' feet. He would have liked to spend time adoring Sunshine's but this was not the occasion.

"It hurts, *Kuya*, *di ba*?"

"No, nothing I do will hurt you. But relax and it will go easier for you."

"OK, *Kuya*," said Sunshine with a confidence she knew was

not misplaced. "You doing."

Pfeidwengeler wondered whether to use the bulb or the gravity-fed hanging douche. On reflection, gravity feed. Pressure was easily controllable by raising or lowering the sac. He lubricated the first seven inches of hose, very solicitously, with KY jelly.

"What that, *Kuya*?" asked Sunshine, some suspicions ungovernable. The Professor didn't trouble to answer but pushed her shoulder down, parted her buttocks, and inserted the tubing. "*Ja*, pretty, now don't get scared of the sensation. You must keep in as long as you can. Keep in, OK?"

"Keep in, *Kuya*."

The water from the hot faucet was unmistakably cold, not tepid, probably from passing through miles of air-conditioning; the Professor had suffered more from chill in Asian bathrooms than those of Northern Europe, which was one of the century's minor but still noteworthy ironies. He knew it was better not to warn the girl.

"Aah, *Kuya*!" Sunshine half-turned, hands on knees, exaggerating her alarm because she sensed the customer might like it. Her prehensile big toe curled up almost vertically.

"Hold it now. Do not let go." Pfeidwengeler watched the level in the douche stabilise. "*Ja*, *ja*. We cleanse you now, my pretty. This will purge your poisons. It does you good, your skin, your liver. Everyone should do it. Get the bad from out of their system."

"It make my skin white, *Kuya*? Black already my skin." She found a strange desire within herself to chatter, it helped her concentrate on what she was retaining. She also had a desire to be filled, in the front. As if reading her mind, *Kuya* appeared before her and offered himself to her mouth. She didn't protest or bargain but put him in herself and commenced sucking. With what was in her rear, the sucking felt very satisfying, quite fundamental to her gratification. When *Kuya* left with a plop of suction, he was startlingly large from his semi-flaccid state on the bed. He straightened her – she took in her breath but kept control – then he negotiated the entrance to her narrow cunt with minimum clearance. "Ooh, *Kuya*! *Kuya*, you not like put your Junior in my *lobot*?"

"What do you think of me?" As they both laughed, the situation teetered; the Professor grew less stiff. "*Ja*," said the Professor. "You say some German for me: *im Arsch macht geil*."

"Hah?"

"*Sage*, I like to be fucked in my *arsch*." The Professor's eyes bulged; he spoke with fearsome sincerity.

Sunshine felt something uncontrollable about to happen. "*Kuya*, *Kuya*, cannot stop. I dirty early."

Pfeidwengeler pulled out; his organ throbbing. Don't tell him it was all happening together. He'd never been so lucky. The chances against it were monumental. With urgency, he clapped her hands on the washbasin – time to notice it was a professional manicure on such a young girl – and found his station against the opposite wall, all the time frotting himself at speed.

Like the car crash he'd been involved in, everything happened with extreme slowness and great clarity. The first pulse of the enema shot out in a rod, still a column even as it hit the wall twelve feet away, faecal particles staining the water and visible in themselves. In the pause, he felt his own orgasm begin. A few seconds later, Sunshine launched her second pulse – still forceful but the stream ragged by the time it reached the wall, though more aesthetic, like a fountain's spray and the water clear as crystal. The third and final pulse issued more weakly, only splashes attaining the wall as Professor Pfeidwengeler shuddered with the last wrenches of his climax. He was breathing harshly, one hand on the trickling wall as Sunshine came to him. Not troubling to avoid the semen on the wet floor – the Professor was as fecund an ejaculator as he was an ideas man – she skidded and nearly fell.

"Everything OK, *Kuya*," she said. "Come, sit down. You relax, then I bathing you."

Hi Dear Kuya *Detlef* (Kuya *is papa brother*),

Hi! Hows my kind friend today forever? If you the one to asking regarding me from my side just the same OK. Still can remembering me I'm hoping, I'm the one you meet me at the Lisboa coffee shop that before old year going. I'm the one to have three friends are pinay you talking us. One is Thai girl. She the domestic hilfer. Other dancer, me receptionist, but now dancer. Kuya, you know in my thoughts and prayers always. Regard to your family, your husband, your grandparent, all kids included. You know Kuya I sin give you name of Sunshine. Is name my friend Sunshine, the fat one. True my name is Rose. Easy remember my name being – Remember Our Sweet Experience, R-O-S-E You got wife, Kuya? How you like me? Joke only, Kuya. Ha, ha. Kuya, I have small problem, I rilly-rilly suppering in my life now have big troubles difficult. Maybe you can hilp me. Chinese not to give money when say. I know you generous me before Kuya not expecting big your tip plus plus. You are good man, Kuya. Is true. I telling my friend white your heart. Everyday you are in my prayer. So will finish now this letter excuse ashame my English. Regard your family. Remember distance is not a hindrance of forgetfulness.
Love your humble obedience is Rose (Sunshine don't forget)
PS God watch over us all "from a distance."
PSS Good your job and work I hope, Kuya.

Chapter One

THE COUNTRY WAS ON THE SLIDE, in the mire, had teetered on the brink of the crater so long no one suffered from vertigo any more. They were a nation as blasé as steeplejacks and as irresponsible as crows. Three hundred years in a Spanish convent and fifty in Hollywood had not proved an ideal apprenticeship for the technological exigencies of the modern Asia. That witticism was a world-class coinage, about the only first-rate thing the nation had ever inspired – one or two pugilists and all the entertainers apart – Boyet would think in gloomy moments. A more vulgar way of putting it would be that he found himself the citizen of a country that had been gang-raped by Dagoes for coming on four centuries and then put on the Yankee titty, or worse, for half the modern one. More than sixty per cent of the country existed below the poverty line. It was true the new President had secured some single digit growth after years of negative figures but Filipinos still imported virtually all their heavy requirements. "Nuclear plants?" an exasperated Taiwanese had said in his hearing in the cabin of a Sunriser 10,000 feet over the smoking cone of Mayon, "Shit! You guys couldn't maintain bicycles." Their major commodity was . . . people. They exported people – domestic servants to Kuwait, prostitutes to Japan and Lagos, nurses to Dubai, tailors to Jeddah, construction workers to Iraq: they were the lineal descendants of the galley-rowers of the Barbary corsairs, the Christian slaves of the Arab world, cheated and abused by employers who lived in another historical era and inhabited a different moral universe: the maids who were willing to lay down their lives for the Kuwaiti infants in their charge and who were in constant danger of rape by the fathers: the chauffeurs who had undergone circumcision in order to ride the ring road to an unsullied Mecca.

Boyet's part in all this was that of Greek chorus, free in his commentary but as powerless against the unrolling circumstances as the protagonists. He was a journalist. That was, when attractive women enquired as to the nature of his work, Boyet would say, with an off-hand pride all the fiercer for its casualness, "Actually, I work for a newspaper." He'd then admit that he was a writer rather than, say, a janitor, a vendor, or even in the advertising or sub-editorial departments. No, he was the publishing equivalent of a fighter-jock, Top Gun at the typewriter. (Computers were still rare in Gobernador de Leon – the voltage fluctuations and brownouts – that was the power outages – lobotomised their electronic brains in five minutes). Boyet's claim was not a lie. You could buy a copy of the rag – he hoped the girls did – and actually see his face above his column for the price of half a cup of coffee: his shock of jet hair without a trace of gray at 37, *en brosse* as a forest of pines; the strong eyebrows of his Catalan grandfather; the massif of the local jawline; the un-short but crooked nose which had not been broken in sport; the moustache of four years standing and the steady eyes; and a hint of powerful shoulders at the bottom of the 2x2 mugshot. Tall for a *pinoy* at nearly 6ft, he'd been on the basketball team of his college, UP. Touch of vanity – for the shot he'd removed his spectacles. He didn't know it but his nickname among the secretaries at *Citizen* was Clark Kent.

If Superman was his more flamboyant journalistic alter ego, the humdrum truth was that he made his living by the law. He was a well-paid attorney in the legal section of a large mining company with shadowy interests in logging, but it was his column which paid him a pittance and which, he felt, defined him. So he was a journo. "I'm a hack," he'd say, with a laugh, using the derogatory, outlandish word with pride.

Nestor Chavez, who was a full-time staffer, called himself a "media mercenary", and he didn't laugh, nor was he proud about it. Nestor wasn't above selling his services to anyone: speech-writer, producer of puffs or vitriol, propagandist, character assassin, you name it. He was also an accomplished cartoonist and said he knew how to make films, disposing of a formidable technical vocabulary. Boyet was in some awe of him. When Boyet first came to *Citizen* Chavez was already chief sub-editor. He'd ripped apart Boyet's initial contribution, lovingly crafted, written, and re-written at home, Boyet re-commencing pages two-thirds done if he transposed two letters of a word. Chavez read the piece in total silence before turning his back and walking to the subs desk. Boyet could see the others grinning. Chavez went to work with a red sign pen. Then he brought out a pair of blunt-nosed scissors and started cutting up Boyet's virgin piece. He frowned, flicked the tip of his nose with his forefinger; then re-arranged the scraps like a man doing a jig-saw puzzle before glueing each paragraph to a separate sheet. Boyet reckoned he was wasting paper. He clipped the sides together, then threw them at Boyet, who nearly missed the damp packet. "I think that's what you mean," Chavez said. Boyet would have liked to punch him out. Instead, he read the doctored article. It had been vastly improved. The guy was a wordsmith. Boyet could see that almost immediately. The "almosts" for instance were an almost extinct species on the territory of Chavez's sheets, though for Boyet that wasn't yet a noticeable improvement. What he could see was how much quicker and simpler the expression of his own thoughts had become in Chavez's hands. Also how Chavez had brought out what he really meant to say when he'd got confused or buried a point. Much of that was accomplished with the arrogant re-ordering of the piece, the juxtaposition of parts from wholly different original positions. "Put the most important thing first," Chavez said quietly, next to him now. "You're not writing an academic essay; don't lead up to it. Fire quickly. Also, don't link the paras with conjunctions because you feel you have to. The word "For" at the start of the para means the writer doesn't feel there's any connection with what went before. Just go for it, man. Bang, bang, bang. Get the stuff out of yourself. Next time leave a space between your lines; it makes my job easier, OK, buddy?"

That was the beginning of what was to become Boyet's bi-weekly column, *Up Periscope!* or Up Yours! as the sub-editors catch-lined it for internal consumption.

There was a lot going on in Gobernador de Leon. You couldn't say the place was dull. Sure, it was trivial but it was human interest. No shortage of news or commentary on it. For instance, the other month the chief of police had sent his body-guards round to *Citizen* after the paper's most controversial columnist, Kelvin Fugoso, had linked him to illegal numbers gambling syndicates. They'd thrown an armalite bullet on the subs' table with Kelvin's name, misspelled Kevin, on it. This was the chief of police who'd shot a car-park attendant the year before for denting his Mitsubishi Pajero. Only in the leg, but it had still caused a stir. Then the head of the city jail had just been discovered hiring out inmates, presumably the murderers rather than the necklace-snatchers, for hits. These assassins enjoyed, of course, the perfect alibi. Yes, people could still get outraged in Gobernador de Leon; they weren't so cynical yet. A well-known actor on vacation from Manila had a drug-bust case against him dropped for lack of sufficient evidence. The night shift at the police station had smoked the evidence. That was what Boyet implied in his second column. The first column had concerned a contract a "city dad" had helped to give his brother-in-law. Building contract, that was. This involved millions of pesos. The other kind of contract, the rub-out of someone you didn't much care for, only cost around US$10, dependent on the quality of your trigger-man. That would buy your enemy two bullets in the head from a .38 paltik revolver. A really professional hit with military weapons might cost twenty times that. Boyet got the peso equivalent of US$6 per 750-word column. It was surprising how much that could buy you in Gobernador de Leon – for instance, two columns, 1.2 human lives – but Boyet had to admit that by the standards of an internationally syndicated journalist it was no big bucks. He didn't know of any *pinoys* who were internationally syndicated journalists, not even Fortunato Natividad, the hot shot Manila novelist and queer who'd made the mistake of pinching Chavez's butt at a book launch in Intramuros, Manila. Quite a number of distinguished writers, musicians, painters, and what have you turned out to be homos when you got to meet them, Boyet thought, and the proportion went right up to 50 per cent with Filipinos. God knew what it was, maybe a sense of other-ness. Of course, the onlie begetter had been a guy if you believed the critics.

Boyet was a family man first and foremost. So strong were the bonds he could even make doubtfully feeble jokes. "I've been happily married to Miriam for two years," he could say to new acquaintances in her earshot and draw a quiet smile of complicity. "But married for thirteen," he would continue. She was a very good poet in her own write, Boyet would inform you early in your acquaintanceship. She'd been Valedictorian of her year at South Western in Cebu, assistant editor of the college magazine, and won a brewery-sponsored debating trophy. But she'd given it up for him, all but the poetry. Sometimes this could annoy people in strange ways, foreigners especially. A very nice dinner party was spoiled – almost – when an Australian woman took exception to Boyet's chaffing of his wife. At first Boyet didn't realise he'd made her mad. "Well, aren't you the lucky one," she'd said. Filipinos didn't employ irony much – not in that clever way of saying one thing when you meant quite the other, luring your defences down for the Sunday punch. Boyet walked right into it. "Yes, I'm a lucky guy," he beamed. Everyone else had continued on the diced franks and spaghetti with their white plastic spoons, talking ten to the dozen.

"What makes you men think you're each so special? You think your boring little lives are so romantic, don't you?"

That was when Boyet started to get just a little uneasy, but it was the tone, still not the words.

"Do you think your wife has to give everything up for you?

Why can't it be you?" She had red hair and green eyes, this lady.

Boyet just laughed, louder than he meant because he didn't like hearing nervous *pinoy* laughter, least of all his own. In retrospect, that was about the worst thing he could have done. She waded into him then, even called him a pig. That was when the quiet had descended.

"In this country a pig is a well-loved and valuable member of the household, so I won't take offence," he said, smiling at the red-haired lady and catching his host's eye to reassure him. The Australian lady said, "Don't try to be funny; it's not something that's funny for women." The Filipinos there tried to make the peace, Miriam sensible enough not to make things worse by rushing to her brave's defence. In fact, some of the *pinays* belonged to a women's sketching group. These were the ones working hardest to smooth things over. Unfortunately, Jingkee Zamora put her size 4 foot in it. "Well, we need the men, don't we," she said brightly, "or we would still be in the caves. That's if we're not tom-boys. You're not a tom-boy, are you?" Not for a moment had Jingkee imagined she was – she'd never met one in her life. Filipinas weren't, were they?

"What's a tomboy?" the red-haired Australian lady asked sharply, having more than an inkling.

"Oh, that's the Pilipino expression," Jingkee explained, "I know it means just a young girl who's like a boy but we're the ones here who'd use it to mean like 'lesbian'".

In the awful silence that followed, with Boyet realising the quickest, taking in the suddenly noticeable short hair and then the trouser outfit, the Australian said, "Yes, I am."

Their host whinnied.

Yes, Boyet loved his family. They had a girl and a boy, twelve and ten. They were good kids, studious, obedient, loving but full of fun as well. Miriam and he agreed there wasn't going to be any trouble with drugs and bad company in a few years time. They could be thankful for that. Engineer Rowell Sumilon, their neighbour, had a teenage boy who was a shabu addict, preternaturally skinny and of sullen mien. He didn't see his own

Dexter like that; the difficult age was just round the corner, but substance abuse wouldn't be part of it. The girl, Jennilyn, was very dark, like her mama, but with Boyet's calm eyes. The nuns had charge of her education, like Chavez's daughter, at St Monica's, the fashionable academy for the offspring of the liberal intelligentsia (fees per semester, US$50). Chavez's girl was a few years behind Jennilyn. He'd see the media mercenary there with his patient wife every five p.m., Chavez having knocked off – such was the chief sub's prerogative – at three p.m., after his return from lunch at 12:30 midday.

TOWN was a bustling place. New buildings were going up every-where. Not the wistful, deferential architecture of Europe but the space-age 2001 slabs of the New Asia rising behind classical skeins of poetic bamboo. All along the reclamation on the old harbour-front, in the filthy old Chinese downtown, over the demolished squatter areas, high-rise commercial blocks and hotels were erecting. A shortage of concrete had become felt; local suppliers couldn't meet the developers' demand. Instead, stuff came from the Bosphorus, Turkish cement. If a prosaic commodity like cement could be said to carry overtones, this did: nuances of bodies in blocks of it at the bottom of harbours; suggestions of *bastinado*, sodomy. So was it sub-standard? How had five weeks in the leaky brown bowels of Panamanian-regis-tered bottoms affected it? No one could say for certain. But the latest piles had survived the most recent earth tremor with hardly a crack.

Town had enjoyed a mini boom, like the bigger sister Visayan city of Cebu, leagues to the East. Give your helicopter pilot the co-ordinates of Paradise, a rather extravagantly pitched release from the would-be Tolstoys in the Tourist Office said, 8°5´N 119°48´E, and find yourself beachside in a Pacific Eden. Gobernador de Leon was not at all representative of the country as a whole, like an ornamental garden in the middle of the Gobi. The mayor, scion of a millionaire family, was in his official capacity nothing more nor less than a brilliant professional mendicant. Unabashed, he'd begged for aid and cast-offs in every major city in Asia. Rubbish carts too dilapidated to carry the neat and frugal household wastes of Osaka had come from Japan; schoolbuses no longer fit to carry Korean children from Seoul; traffic lights, too laconic to blink longer at the soldierly traffic of Wellington, would glare defeasance implacably red-eyed at the escaped lunatics behind the steering wheels of the Gobernador de Leon jeepneys. Traffic was absurdly heavy; there seemed a choke-point every three hundred metres of the town's major highways. Yet it was rare, nearly unknown, for movement to come to a complete halt. You would stay in the same place a maximum of five minutes before creeping on again, twenty feet or twenty inches. So what if it was only inches? Advance was cumulative; the achievement slow but palpable. In short, at the end of it you had made progress.

PROGRESS was Victoria Init's idol. She would sacrifice everything and everyone at the feet of that stern shibboleth, maybe even the Congressman and herself. That this concept of Progress encapsulated a large portion of self-interest would probably make such an ultimate gesture redundant. Happily so, for in large part Progress as a general social ideal was identical with the advancement of the Init cause. Mrs Init liked to measure progress in literally concrete terms: so many millions of cubic metres of grey Bosphorus powder poured. The mistake with Good Works – not that she was in any sense, you understand, against them – was you had no way of accurately quantifying their effectiveness. Better leave that kind of thing to His Holiness or His Eminence. Victoria had sat on committees herself (and no way you'd find her name among the Apologies); currently she was lending her presence to the Street Arabs Foundation (an unfortunate title which Filipinos often mistook for a Christian-Muslim Reconciliation Group, to Victoria's very great irritation for it would be dangerous to belong to such an organisation). Getting hit by some glittering-eyed, turbaned triggerman from the deep south was not progressive, it was a termination.

Mrs Init thought Imelda had got it right, mostly. She wanted to be Imelda, but Meldy without the eccentricity, Marcos without the mistakes. That stunt with the shoes! It wouldn't have fitted Victoria at all. What existed, what stirred consciousness of uneasy parallelism were a certain similarity in the face – give or take twenty years – emphasised by the circumstance that Victoria wore her thick hair in the same bob; a mutual penchant for handbaggery; the same air of demure brazenness, a Vestal caught douching. "That damn woman's got more front than Victoria Embankment," a junior British Council staffer had muttered at a chamber quartet's provincial recital sponsored mainly by the Inits. That evening had been exactly the kind of thing the Congressman didn't want repeated: a load of baloney with nothing to show for the trouble and expense at the end. It had been a whim of Vic-Vic's which he had indulged. The whole of the previous Administration had been a concert for him. What had Mrs A. left behind her? Nix. Some dying bars. At least Mrs M. could point to some decent architecture. To that extent she'd been a good home economist.

Mrs Init liked nothing better than to get a hard-hat on (say it carefully) and hie herself to the construction site; correction, she liked nothing better than a photo-opportunity in her hard hat. She had her own personal headgear, kept on the wardrobe shoe-shelf. Astute readers of *Citizen* might have deduced as much from careful examination of successive photo-stories. Mrs Init had learned that she didn't appear to best advantage with a grimy giant egg-shell over her ears, coarsening her face and shortening her nose. This one had been the provision of a young architect glad for the work and the chance of another commission (though the Inits preferred to spread the contracts, rarely giving the second promised bite at the apple). It was a perfect fit and, even better, pink. Not a spray-job; that was the real colour of the plastic, if plastic could be real. The Young Architect had it in mind for his girl-friend on the pillion of his Honda econodrive 70. Mrs Init had said, "But how charming! So they do have lady builders!" and, sliding it over bun with a care that was not in the least affected, "Well, it fits me perfectly!" To her chief bodyguard she called, "Get the photographers back," he forfeiting Uzi for cellular phone, and the subordinate goons joined in the spontaneous little ripple of applause that went up. To the beaming young man, provider of pink helmets, she said, "It's the best present anyone gave me this year," and being a *pinoy*, his smile didn't falter though it didn't broaden either. And that was how Victoria acquired the celebrated hat, as later captioned in *Time* (Asian edition).

With all the money that was doing the rounds of the city, it was difficult to see why so much poverty should exist: not just the peripatetic insane or the head-bombed glue whiffers, not just the black-toed jeepney conductors, holding on to their roof-ladders like monkeys in a dust storm, but the snowily dressed cashiers looking like starlets on $2 a day, the decent domestic helps on less than a buck. Representative Init had a theory, two theories actually. The leading one, which he held sincerely, was aired in the company of the like-minded, meaning mostly polit-ical cronies and adversaries construed as friendly, rivals who knew the score as well as the rules of the game. "Democracy and prosperity are not bed-fellows, not in Asia." This uttered as a secret piece of knowledge, a hazardous and esoteric piece of theology which might burn your fingers in the perilous arena of public debate. It was no more than the truth but the truth was dangerous. The addressed would nod and smile the occult smile, maybe having imparted the same information to the Congressman himself a while back. A complicit twinkle in the Congressman's eyes did not undermine the seriousness of his manner. "For a German, for an American, you know, even an American, affluence is what safeguards their democracy, *di ba*? Inflation is what the Germans are more scared of than anything and for our American friends, it's unemployment. Their soci-eties float on money. When there's no money, their democracies fail. But us . . . hah!" and the Congressman would shout with a fierce joy, "No way! An Asian can have his democracy or he can have his growth – but not the two together. We have to take our choice. Look at Singapore, Korea, Taiwan – strong government, that's what made them rich. Multi-party system – pah! Dragon economy – Dragon government!" And the two would grin at a joke shared by few.

The Congressman's other theory was for wider consumption and while it wasn't actually a lie it didn't bear the same self-conviction. "No, no," he'd intone from the platform *ex cathedra*, "that's not the way. You don't solve the problem of the poor by creating a new problem for the rich, hah? That way we all get poorer together, not richer. No, let the entrepreneur enjoy the fruit of his, hah, hard work. He's the guy who's making the pool of money for the little guy as well. What the big guy does will trickle down. We all move up together, *na lang*. One country, one people, all Filipinos." The Congressman could put his hand on his heart – he often did – and say he was telling the truth, but rather in the way of a physician prescribing an antique and inef-fective antibiotic of first resort to someone else's baby. The Congressman wasn't *certain* of the cure but he did believe it stood a fighting chance; he was happy to dispense the advice. Even placebos could be effective.

The Congressman, as he presently found himself, having held local government office in the past, was a battle-scarred veteran of the Philippine fray. With some justice, he regarded himself as the equal, if not a better pound for pound fighter than any US senator or British parliamentarian. Those guys had the resources to deliver the big smack but he felt they lacked the Asian finesse. You judged a politician by what he could accom-plish with what was available, his or her worth only became apparent when they laboured under a handicap. Third Worlders were the most sinuous, the most accomplished politicians in the world, just as the Japs and Viet Minh had proved the toughest infantry. Beating somebody with the A-bomb didn't prove you were the better soldier. Representative Init's ambitions and motivation were simple, unalloyed by any concept of public service or hypocrisy which might hinder an occidental: he was in politics for money, to safeguard his family's existing business interests and to lever open yet more future opportunities. That was all. He was brilliantly successful at what he wanted to accomplish on the national scene. Internationally, he still had something to learn but he had seen his cronies trip and tie up foreign politicians and aid reps like they were Christmas Turkeys. Like the little fellow in the black pyjama suit creeping up to turn Claymore mines right round to spew on the discharger, they used the enemy's own weapons on him. Or you could say it was like *aikido*. Guilt, compunction, naivety, laziness, insularity – the notion that the whole world was California – these were the tiny slots and fissures in the daunting granite features of the foreigner. And the cool operator only needed to insert a minute amount of potential energy, of verbal explosive, to send the whole massive face crashing down, when you might quarry the resulting rubble to your heart's content. Little words could carry the charge. Representative Init had heard the most effective and modern of these: empowerment, community, potentiate, sustainable development, social renewal, knock-on effect. It was amazing the things a modish and ever-burgeoning vocabulary could mask.

And it was here he could take lessons from Vic-Vic, Vic-Vic who'd actually written that speech of his on "protecting the flower of Philippine womanhood" against foreign insult that had gone down so surprisingly well with the Congresswomen and lady senators who normally gave him the widest of berths.

Yes, Mrs was a great help. On the domestic scene, she was the conduit to Mr. If you were scared of Representative Init, dismayed by the dead face and cold eyes, or worried to lose your dignity by encountering his direct refusal, why, Mrs Init, with her charm and grace, could be your intermediary, the bearer of your request, or the hinter that it was advisable, much more advisable, not to try the Assemblyman's patience by asking at all. It was an important role – ventriloquist to the voodoo dummy – but Mrs Init was as ambitious as any woman in the world, and the way she saw it her new and developing role – and therefore the Congressman's – was not at home but in the world: which was an international place, *di ba*?

Chapter Two

BOYET'S FIRST MEANINGFUL BRUSH WITH PHILIPPINE LAW – the textbooks not at all representative – had come when a Court of First Instance judge, acting in demi-official capacity, had smashed him across the forehead with a baseball bat. As the 19-year-old Boyet hinged at the knees out of deference and self-preservation (marvelling at himself for retaining the presence of mind to note that the bat was not nearly as formidable as it looked – or had sounded, *thwack*! – it lacked the weight to be a decisive street-fighting weapon, lacerating and stinging rather than depriving of consciousness or even stunning) the senior partner of a celebrated firm of Manila lawyers had swiped at the sinking victim with a set of brass-knuckles but missed, so that the kick in the kidneys received on the floor from aforementioned senior partner's Bally reptile skins could be regarded as a love tap. Boyet's third assailant, a law professor whose heart wasn't really in it, had pretended to pull his hair, slapping him very lightly across the face with a hand more famous for its ornate penmanship. Unfortunately, the CFI judge, an old sadist disappointed alike in family and professional life and whose sentencing was a by-word for severity, turned out to be a dour and unrelenting adversary, for reversing his grip on his rapist son's bat and utilising it less dramatically but far more effectively as pestle rather than samurai sword, he administered a rapid and debilitating series of pokes to Boyet's thighs and abdomen. Actually, it was fairly obvious he was aiming for the balls but Boyet, whose deference went only so far, was able to foil him with some adroit rolling and twisting. The guy was breathing quite heavily now – Boyet could imagine him a dab and mean hand with the gavil in sala, *order! order!* – with both his spectacles and what Boyet could now see was a rug starting to slide from their proper places when Dame Fortune took a hand, smiling on this neophyte aspirant to the Fraternity of Lex Iustitia Concordia MCXXXI, for as CFI judge and novice's eyes met for a milli-second of an embarrassment that was more excruciating than the stinging on Boyet's temples – no more role-playing, only an old bully walloping an over-ambitious young boy – Boyet had been dazzled by the instantaneous realisation of the imminent. His attacker's face had gone suddenly grey, greyer than the hair over his ears, he'd dropped his bat, now weighing one million tons, no longer Punch's laughable weapon, clawed his own left biceps and dropped to his knees. As he clutched his wrenching, treacherous heart, in a gesture of allegiance more perfervid than any he'd made to the flag, the look he had bestowed was one of appeal. Was it for help, for understanding, the offer of a bridge as well as the plea for rope? Boyet never knew. Attorney Kawatan took advantage of his moment's inattention to right hand him square on the nose with his knuckle sandwich. Boyet didn't see stars, he was witness to the glory of imploding super novae before tumbling into a black and crushing hole with no bottom, much resembling his remodelled face, he thought. When he regained his wits, he had the impression he was in a hammock on a banana boat drinking pochero soup. Shortly after he opened his eyes, he found he was being carried by his arms and legs down the corridor of the Frat House – Atty Kawatan's No 3 mistress's residence, loaned for purposes of the initiation – with the salt savour of his own blood in his throat. In the kids' bedroom he joined the heap of gory, groaning young bodies. He had got off lightly. He looked a mess – it was now he learned that even trivial scalp wounds looked spectacular because of the many minor blood vessels just under the surface – and his sister Lorna would faint when she saw him, but he could still walk unaided when he left and the nose even improved the more rugged good looks of his maturity. Others were less lucky; they'd drawn more skilled, fitter, or even meaner initiation masters. A couple of boys had shattered knee caps; these would never walk properly again. Teeth had gone, ribs submitted. But there were no comas; the ruptured spleen of the previous year hadn't been repeated. Above all, the death that no one – sincerely – had desired had failed to eventuate. Since the war, seven had been killed in this Fraternity – it wasn't a big deal frat. Joining something large time like Aquila Legis would be really risky.

"Drink this, Dodong," Atty Kawatan exhorted Boyet after the handshaking and congratulations, "It'll make a man of you." Boyet did his level best not to flinch as the Attorney put his arm round his shoulders – he was as big a man as Boyet, maybe a basketball player too once – but either he'd not been as successful as he prided himself or the Attorney retained vivid memories of his own induction, for he growled, "It's finished, Boyet. You are one of us. I am your older brother – you can ask me anything."

Smiling unsurely, for one because it hurt, Boyet drank the rum and water. The Tanduay Five Year Old stung his swollen lip unmercifully. "How is His Honour?" he enquired, with a solicitude that was not entirely genuine. The expression on Attorney's face changed from one of gruff benevolence to guileful subservience. Boyet suddenly had a glimpse of the Attorney as a youth; he saw how he'd been flexible enough to get on in the world: intransigent to juniors, accommodating to seniors. Now in the prime of life, Atty Kawatan bore the mien common to many *pinoys* in positions of middling authority (e.g. bank managers, customs officers) – stern but untrustworthy. What Boyet didn't know was that His Honour had also been an initiation master at Attorney's own induction twenty years back: haler by minus 10 beats on his pulse, heavier 20 pounds, but doubly mean for it. Young Kawatan had been in hospital five days. So it was with mixed feelings Attorney Kawatan now said: "I am afraid it looks bad, brod, bad. But let's not anticipate. The hospitals can do wonderful things now and I know the judge's brother is a director of Man Lee Infirmary."

Boyet said, "I'll send flowers," and thought "which covers my ass if he lives or dies." Atty Kawatan looked sharply at him; he hadn't arrived where he was by being anyone's fool, but the boy's face managed to be both battered and innocent. "Come and meet the big brods," he said, kindly for him.

IN fact, the hazing turned out to have been for nothing. Boyet never did enjoy fraternity advancement. Oh, the patronage network was all it was claimed to be, and more, but his time in private practice was so brief as to be ludicrous. For one, he didn't like it that much. Boyet had been drawn by the broad and majestic sweep of the law (only secondarily by the thought of the big bucks, which was his father's reason for supporting his third son so far); he'd borne an adolescent love for principles and generalisation on the academic side. Also he saw himself as a bit of a caped crusader, a *pinoy* Perry Mason as well. He wanted to help. He wanted to stand at the bar with his hands on his lapels and orchestrate the court's emotions; he wanted to give a hand to the inarticulate stumbling across the stone-strewn highway of words, he wanted to trip up the glib, the dishonest. In the junior assistant's tiny glass cubicle, listening to the droned spite, the wounded pettiness and self-righteousness of the litigating class of Filipino, he thought he'd go stir-crazy. Maybe by the time he had a paunch and no hair he'd at least represent big-time vindictiveness but the near term was one of wives sticking it to their husbands, neighbours tearing down each other's fences. Boyet didn't want to wait fifty-one million years. He had no conception of a long-term that went beyond weeks: 'sus Maria, he was a Filipino, he was twenty- three. He wanted to be an *attorney*, not an amateur shrink, baby's yaya, poison pen lettrist, and whipping-boy all in one. His direct experience with the courts had been disillusioning, too. *Justice delayed is justice denied*, went the motto above His Honour. Why was it Filipinos liked to crucify themselves on their own words? It was the intellectual's equivalent of the Holy Week flagellants who had themselves nailed to crosses. Shit, they'd still be pending in the Philippine courts when the Last Trumpet sounded. And someone would take a shot at bribing His Honour St Peter and if Pedro was a *pinoy* the fix would be in.

Boyet hadn't resigned; he'd been fired. Very politely, over a period of six weeks, so that he himself wasn't quite sure whether he was going of his own volition or being shown the door. "You'll be happier in another branch of the law," he was told. They even found him his next job (in the same branch of the law) which was the one he jacked in to join Evergreen Enterprises, Mining and Forest Conservation. He'd been nearly twenty-four, still a boy, when he arrived and here he was now, running thirty-seven and still at the same desk, with the same faces, including the secretaries. Except for domestic helps who transferred for an extra ten pesos or for change's sake, the provincial job market wasn't that mobile. Middle class people hung on to their positions; it would be scary to lose them. The work, anyway, was half-way interesting. There were only three of them in the section who were qualified lawyers (the company had been extremely profitable but the family corporation was too cheap to take on more hands), and Boyet had got important stuff early on in his career: dealing with tribal minorities, fencing with the union leaders (skilled duellists these guys and sharp amateur lawyers), evading responsibilities for damage to roads, villages, the watertable, the earth, the world, the universe. Nothing trite about these tasks, even if it was the devil's advocacy. A whole village had got wiped out once in a mudslide Boyet was personally sure had been caused by over-enthusiastic cutting. Unidentified armed men had also murdered a hutful of awkward Department of Environment workers, though nothing could be pinned on the company. In the last five years the logging side of Evergreen's operations had become more important than the prospecting. The wealth of the firm, and indirectly of Gobernador de Leon, had been built on a very rare mineral, otherwise found only in the USSR and the Republic of South

Africa, which was used in the manufacture of ultra-temperature heat shields. The Japanese preferred to obtain their supply of these pale purple or translucent green crystals – the chemical structure of both was absolutely identical – from the Filipinos. The principal purchaser was a Yokohama company called Sodo – no relation of the department store Sogo – and in a particularly unfortunate or felicitous moment, the mineral had been dubbed sodomite. Supplies of this were now exhausted, and Evergreen was into rainforest rape, as its own attorneys called it.

Under these circumstances it was his newspaper column which really satisfied Boyet's early crusading zeal. Those seven hundred fifty words were at once a pulpit, a Dr Schweitzer's clinic, and a courtroom to which the public might be admitted in infinite numbers to see him perform as prosecutor, public defender, plaintiff, clerk to the bench, witness, judge, and executioner. Not bad.

By the time he was writing his tenth column, he was already thinking of Evergreen as the sinecure. He wrote the *Up Periscope!*s at the office, rarely at home, sometimes devoting an entire morning or afternoon to the preparation and aiming of his sleek torpedoes – he had learned to motor fast with 750w. Many were the fat, smug bottoms he'd punctured below the water-line with a single well-aimed projectile. More agile or bigger targets got a spread of shots, follow-ups over the next issues. However, like any bearded, apparent young daredevil of a commander Boyet selected his marks with attention. "Careful target acquisition promotes mission longevity," Chavez jested at *Citizen*, but with a serious look only Boyet picked up. "There are old submariners, there are bold submariners, but there are no old, bold submariners." That had the subs table in stitches, and it became an office saying, like "Fire one, fire two," as Boyet's sheets got passed down table. Boyet lived for those trips to the paper. As the outsider, the visitor, for him the seamy offices were irradiated by a golden glow of romance and comradeship all the more alluring for the fact he could never quite penetrate beyond the penumbra. He loved the joshing – the journalists were wittier than the craftiest lawyers – the friendship (he was naive enough to think newspapermen weren't ambitious to the extent of knifing the other in the back), the easy professionalism, the technical vocabulary it was so wonderfully simple to pick up. It didn't seem like work at all, though of course the unsocial hours were part of the job's dishevelled glamour. He'd never know it either but he always stayed a little too long. The guys were either itching to get the pages to bed and be off or just to clear the decks; not that they were sufficiently uncouth to show it, admired and emulated though the brusque New York style was in that office. After always taking up the offer of the second cup of coffee, Boyet would swing his heels on a desk-top, suggest improvements to other writers' copy read on the tail-like galleys, stop just short of pinching the secretaries' butts (strict protocol ruled at Evergreen but Boyet felt such behaviour incumbent upon him at *Citizen*) before making his way out the squeaky swing doors.

"Amateurs," Chavez would grimace.

Chapter Three

THE QUICK BUCKS LAY IN TOURISM. Any fool – which Representative Init wasn't – knew it. The baggage porters, the taxi-drivers, the pumpboat-operators, the pimps in the Plaza, they could all have told you that. On the other hand it was a highly precarious source of income. All kinds of extraneous and unpredictable factors came into play: shifts in taste and fashion, that affluent part of the foreign public one courted as assiduously as a woman nothing if not faddish, with the traditional female prerogative of changing its mind; acts of God for Chrissake, with the vibrations of the last earthquake just subsiding as the next mega-typhoon swept in or one more volcano blew its top; politics, oh politics, with the Sparrows whacking another fat general or a Jesuit-led NPA detachment wiping out an entire infantry company, or the ultra-rightists bungling their fifty-seventh coup. For years, all the news had been negative; the country still had an image abroad that was even more dreadful than its due. Reality kept intruding into the crystal sea and sparkling sands bit. But export-led development, great expression, that was more solid, realer than the whims in Japanese and American heads. Your mosquito-coil plant, your hardwood and rattan furniture, your marble, your shell-craft centre, they were solid, not cushioned from world recessions but certainly independent from the subjective factor. Trouble was the returns were minimal and slow. If the country was to have a future it had to export something better than house-servants and whores. The Congressman could certainly see beyond his own nose. If his interests and the nation's coincided, then he'd do his best for both; he was a public servant when all was said and done. But if there occurred a contradiction, a conflict of those interests, well, he was no fool.

It was Mrs Init's idea, then. Credit where credit was due. The Congressman was always willing to give that. "You can trust a woman to find a middle way," he'd say, and her expression of cool mastery would not change.

Mrs Init's plan owed not a little to her heroine. She'd always admired the Cultural Centre and International Convention Centre in Manila, those contemporary tropical replicas of Hitler's bunker; the home of the Morlocks come to life, Imelda's Time Machine into the Philippine past. Wandering the Cultural Centre's huge halls, its silent escalators, its dumb air-conditioning, its lonely corridors, the aura of shattered greatness was inescapable. Mrs I's association was *Aliens* rather than H.G. Wells. Of course, the fact that it was a huge white elephant wasn't the fault of the constructor, merely evidence of the spite of her successor and rival who'd let it languish out of jealousy and vindictiveness. You couldn't ignore it, though. It was massively there. Nothing short of a tactical nuclear strike would shift it. Its day would come.

Then Mrs Init had travelled herself. She was no hick. She'd seen the Louvre; she'd stayed in the Gritti Palace (at first thinking it a sight on the itinerary rather than an hotel); she'd heard a public lecture at the British Museum, quite painless, well under the hour; she'd been jostled by Lions in San Francisco, had her feet stepped on by Rotarians in the elevator of the Siebel in Melbourne, seen IBM take over forty floors of the Westin in Singapore. At the balding boor who'd crushed her toes in Australia she'd directed her most winning smile. The Inits kept a low profile abroad. Mrs Init had been mistaken for a mail-order bride in Germany, the Congressman for a chauffeur in Paris (after which he junked the grey suit). In the face of ignorance and insolence, they'd exhibited the patience, the tolerance, the cheerfulness, the mildness of the poorer of their countrymen. The Inits were perfectly at home in alien cultures.

Correct behaviour could be ascertained simply by dropping themselves ten degrees on the social scale and pretending they were in the Philippines. They got place-jumped in the queue, quite failed to remonstrate with impertinent waiters and chambermaids. They demoted themselves on every possible occasion.

Seeing things as it were from the ground up, novel perspective, Mrs Init had noted the most insignificant company's propensity to consume easily outweighed that of the highest net worth individual. Even sheikhs only took a couple of floors of a hotel and Texans stopped well short of that. There was a limit to the wives and children even an Arabo could service but the sky was the limit for having employees.

The answer stared her in the face.

Combination package of business and vacation. Tap corporate wealth initially, but the icing on the cake could be personal spending at the day's end. There was a word for the package – it was on the tip of her tongue. What was it? The words rattled in the memory bag of recollections of abroad. Anyway she knew the thing, the concept, if not the word. Someone else would subtitle her dream for her.

The Congressman was not initially impressed. It was his inclination to be sceptical. And this smacked of high wackiness, bordering on the Imeldific. And it was some of his own money he was going to throw away? No way, Ray. Get out the door, Duane.

His wife was undeterred. She had that Presidentiable serenity, above the bickering, the small-minded parsimony, the negativity. She never lost her temper with the Congressman. That would have been a sign of weakness; but sometimes the Congressman blew his top with her. Always shortly before capitulation. Nevertheless, she could say this for him: actually, he was no sore loser when it turned out it was she who had been right. He'd quite graciously admit he'd been incorrect. And so it was this time as well.

She reminded him of what they'd seen outside the country and especially those "dragon economies" he had such a fetish about.

"The tourism is an extra, it's a luxury," he argued. "The manufacturing base is what created wealth for them." The Congressman was no fool; he was a subscriber to *Asiaweek* and the *Far Eastern Economic Review*. He was a reader. His wife wasn't, but she could draw conclusions from experience which she felt was the womanly way and, besides, generally more likely to be correct.

"But we," she said, "we can't do it from nothing, you know, Congressman." She called him Congressman in bed sometimes, too. "Where will the investment come from? Who wants, who actually wants, to put their money here, in Philippines?"

The Congressman was on the point of opening his mouth to give a public reply, reflex-action, then decided better.

Mrs Init said, "Much better we begin with this. It will make money itself – I promise you, Congressman. But it will *bring* money, it will . . . attract investment." She deliberately used one of her man's expressions. "We must put Gobernador de Leon on the map. We have to advertise it. And this is the very best way – by not paying for the advertising."

The Congressman blinked three times, a small mannerism of which he remained unaware but which Victoria knew constituted an infallible signal of an impending change of mind. Time to soft-pedal or even reverse. She knew better than to place herself head-on to that temper later. She made soothing noises, she extended the time-scale. For a *pinoy*, even a powerful one such as Representative Init, this provided the instant relief of decelerating the truck aimed against the man pinned to the wall from one hundred to one mile per hour.

"But it's a dream, Congressman, just a dream."

Madam's dreams tended to be detailed, structured more than other people's lives. They were as planned as a campaign; she dreamed like a general or mayhap she didn't dream at all.

That was to be the beginning of the Congressman's authentic firebreathing nemesis – he could actually date it – the VIP Multi-Media Resources and Dragons Convention Centre of Gobernador de Leon. But, as yet, still a glimmer in his spouse's eye, an egg needing more than two years in the hatching.

Chapter Four

BOYET HAD COME ACROSS THE INITS OF COURSE, as who hadn't in Gobernador de Leon: the *City Aide* T-shirted street sweepers (shamelessly Imeldific plagiarism of Victoria's), the barbecue stick sellers and the green mango and shrimp paste vendors, huge vagabond tribes shifted, deposited, scattered, swirled on again from their pitches on the breath of Victoria I's whim (depending on where she'd shopped and been inconvenienced on the sidewalk recently), the cockpit syndicates, trusting the Congressman's redoubtable roosters would prevail yet again – all these lower orders felt the Init influence, let alone the glitterati and mercenaries with their fingers on "the pulse of events". Chavez said the most accurate site to feel that was the groin.

The Congressman himself was known to go for the jugular rather than the femoral. He had a brisk way with rivals. Some years back, before he ran in politics, when he was still the one to manage his papa, that venerable warlord's, trucking business, a damn Chinese had set up in competition. The Chinaman's fleet was brand spanking new, in contrast to the huffing old monsters the Inits had been running for decades – and his prices were 30 per cent lower, not that – as the trinity of travelling public, Inits, and Chinaman knew – he'd have kept them that way once he'd put the Filipinos out of business. Still, his was the superior service, the better product. That didn't last long. Masked men with rifles, bandits, held up a couple of those shiny blue and silver charabancs, robbed everyone and shot the drivers in the legs. People took to riding Init. Also, later, someone started to assemble better electric fans than a major contributor to the

Congressman's war-chest. He ran into zoning problems which he had no idea of previously, such a shame. The Congressman had learned refinement. Some years back it would have been a fire. "Darn good fans," the Congressman would laugh. "I have three in the house. Pity you can't get them any more – the motors have lasted twice as long as Dodong's. My Mrs says we should have bought more when we had the chance."

Boyet, a father of two already but "still a cherry" according to Chavez, had attended Representative Init's press conference at the last election. He'd equipped himself with a notepad and ballpoint, which made Chavez smile. Prior to the Congressman's address there'd been a distribution of envelopes by the PRO, who had called the hacks into the men's comfort room. Boyet thought it a bit slim to be the information pack; the press secretaries usually went to town on that, if only to justify their pay packets to their puppet-masters. Never mind the quality, feel the width. Boyet began to slit it open.

"Shit! Not now dumbo!" Chavez snickered. "Where are your manners, buddy? Wait for Grace before you feed. Gimme!" Boyet smiled his frequent smile to Chavez, one of polite mystification. The journalists trooped out again from the john, the dirty business transacted. The Congressman's PR began his spiel, what the No. 1 man had already done, what he was doing, what he would do, a reply to critics, then an attack on same detractors. "Words not deeds," he concluded. There was a small pause, applause was not forthcoming. One of the corps, an old colleague of the PR's, prompted him. "You mean deeds not words."

The PR grinned. "Isn't that what I said? No? The other way round?" The meeting concluded in uproarious laughter. Chavez didn't join in. He said to the chuckling Boyet, "He did that deliberately." Boyet was plugged in to the general mood, one of good humour, not sourness. He looked at Chavez but didn't take his journalistic mentor's comment on board. At the office Chavez was still surly but his mood changed to a certain grudging cheerfulness as he remembered the envelopes. He threw one to Boyet. Boyet's contained P10,000, Chavez's P8,000.

"The definition of a professional," said Chavez without excessive bitterness, "is that he is prepared to work for less, just out of professionalism."

Boyet frowned, Clark Kent's innocent puzzlement, though he now knew perfectly well what it was all about. He asked sternly, "What's this?" Chavez didn't even trouble to answer. He was with the other subs at their table, Judas Iscariot presiding over eleven apostles. Boyet went over to where he was clearly not wanted. "I don't think I can take this," he said. Chavez smiled nastily; he had astoundingly bad teeth, crooked, black, 50% MIA or AWOL. "Oh, but how different of you," he said, looking at the fluorescent light fixture. Boyet persisted. He didn't think he was being insincere, it was just Chavez who was making him feel false.

"You might as well," said a friendly sub. "Everyone else does. What difference will it make? You can always write just the same as you were going to anyhow. Hey, it's only envelopmental journalism." Boyet gave the guy an interrogative look, his mind not changed at all, but wanting to be polite, not to rebuff a well-intentioned overture. It wasn't his ambition to be anyone's plaster saint. Chavez said, "It's not enough then?" With this Boyet didn't feel himself floundering anymore; there was a bottom, an uneven, treacherous bottom, below his flailing feet but still a platform to graze. In his warped way Chavez was being generous. He could just have said nothing at all and left Boyet bobbing up and down. "Even Charlie Zarate doesn't get thirty grand, and that's Manila prices, too," Chavez continued.

"It's not that; you know that, Nestor."

"Ah, I know what we have here. We have a virgin, we have a real live card-carrying virgin in our midst." His cronies tittered; Boyet didn't care. If the price was to be made a fool of, that was OK by him.

"But sometimes, as we all know, when the maiden says 'No', really what the lady means is 'Yes'. Not so?"

Boyet joined in this perfectly healthy laughter. "No means no," he said. "Come on, Nestor, give me a break, will you." Chavez seemed to have enjoyed his own witticism. Boyet could see him contriving to extend his metaphor in yet more cunning ways – typical damned sub, always looking to condense, snappy, going off at tangents with a crossword puzzle solver's weird logic, surprising you in the end with the appositeness rather than unexpectedness, brilliantly encapsulating. He was no good at it himself. 'Sus Maria, he'd had trouble naming his own children. Very quickly, then, he placed his envelope on the table. "You can donate it to the home for fallen women," he said.

"It's up to you, cherry boy," Chavez said.

Boyet proceeded to turn his own defeat into a rout when, unable to stand silence, he said miserably, "Sorry." Chavez waved him away. In the stair-well he heard a burst of laughter from the table. The whole thing was one of the sourer experiences of the month: Boyet knew he had taken the easy course. He had repudiated his first loyalty, to his own group, to his colleagues, his friends, his *barkada*, regular guys all, in favour of a private selfishness. It was like refusing to lend someone a bolo because it might get blunt and dirty. Above all, though, even if no one treated him any differently next time he delivered his copy (vehemently supportive of the re-electionist Representative Init), even if his column more and more just got marked up for type size, column width, and lits only, he knew he'd been incorrigibly, irredeemably amateur. Why the hell hadn't he just kept his mouth shut and given the dough to the Maryknoll sisters or even, ha-ha, made a contribution to the war-chest of the Congressman's opponent? The whole problem, he wouldn't dignify it with the term dilemma, had been this: lack of the imaginative dimension. He'd do better next time. That he promised himself – he owed it to his colleagues.

Like many professional stone-throwers, Boyet was in no way without sin himself. The difference was that he was conscious of this fact and hadn't tried to forget it. He felt a hypocrite. However, his way of justifying himself was that *Up Periscope!* was a public service. It didn't matter if the author was imperfect; he was just the instrument, the means of bringing abuses to the public attention. Did you care if your ambulanceman was an adulterer? The columnist's sins could be scarlet but his words were read. Still, Boyet tried to do something about his tone, the pitch of the prose, where he was coming from, as Chavez put it. To read some of those guys in the nationals (marked up fifty per cent for transportation costs by the time they reached Gobernador de Leon – he hoped people would have the sense to buy *Citizen* instead) Old Pomposity himself, Fonso Monzon, or Hard Nuts Butch Redondor, the heavy-drinking 250-pounder, you'd think they'd never had to wipe their asses clean. Boyet kept a check on himself. He went for the bad guys – within limits – but kept his cool: he tried not to boil over with righteous indignation – irony became him better than sanctimoniousness.

Second time the black cat – meaning Mrs Init this time – crossed his path, he knew enough to make the sign of the cross, at least mentally.

MRS INIT might not have objected to being called a black cat, did Boyet but know. Caprice, a certain liking for toying with prey, combined with a final ruthless speed of despatch, that was all her. She'd have been flattered by the comparison. The razor claws in the black velvet mittens – as Boyet would see later.

What Victoria had in mind was a roller-skating rink for the young of the town. She got many of her ideas just sitting in the back of her Corolla, watching the panorama unfold. She always had to be doing something, she told herself; that was the kind of person she was. Once, nothing particular suggesting itself from outside the environment of the air-con, she'd found herself prey to unusual irritation, in excess of the normal symptoms of her baffled creativity. After a while she realised it was the back of the chauffeur's neck. It was insufficiently differentiated from the shaggy nylon fur of the seats. She wanted a sculpted wedge, narrow at the bottom, the severe sides diverging up to the ears at obtuse angles of, say, one-ten, the whole phalanx bristling, the growth in varyingly ordered lengths, much like the hedges she and Representative Init had admired at Versailles. Instead, the one to do her driving was giving her a sight of disorderly, anaemic ferns, wispy, curling without organisation where they willed. That was a part of her day! She directed him to motor straight over the verge dividing the two lanes of the F. Init Sr. Super Expressway, causing two passenger-laden jeepneys to swerve violently – the drivers, if not the clinging conductors, taking it with surprising equanimity – and head back whence they'd come. Then she directed the barber as she might the driver himself: straight across, more to the left. As Victoria possessed an excellent memory and a good eye for detail the chauffeur was not too surprised to find the cost of the haircut deducted from his wages three weeks later.

The need for the amenity she'd surmised from the bands of the young lounging along the reclamation as she'd sped to a special mass. Usually she was well out of Downtown by dark, already in their sala, looking down on the twinkle. "That could be any town!" was the Congressman's frequent exclamation, as he nibbled at savoury delicacy on toothpick, meant as praise or the soliciting of it, a claim to normality and some kind of civic affluence. She didn't like the looks of those youthful legions at leisure, temporarily liberated from their textbooks. That the devil found work for idle hands was one of the few maxims of the nuns that Mrs Init had known to stand the truth test of adult life. What did young people like? What was wholesome? (She knew she was in jeopardy of the dichotomous). They seemed to like drugs, that was true. That had been something non-existent in her own time. But music, dancing, the concomitants of courtship. Sport even, the tennis of her teens – unhappily unavailable in public quantities, much as she'd have liked to: maybe later. Purgative exercise for the young males but also something the girls could join in; you didn't want a repetition of that basketball. But elements of the repetitious that soothed, pattern that appeased. Finally, the money. She couldn't justify something too big right now and, as the Congressman liked to say, "if it can turn a buck so much the better."

He was ready to come up with the necessary after she pinpointed youth. She knew and agreed with him that you didn't try to help the unhelpable. In its negative sense, what it wasn't, the Init philosophy was anti-lame duck.

"Hope is not for the hopeless."

Hope lay with the young, who also happened to be impressionable. "Seventy-five per cent of the population are under twenty-five, Congressman. These sixteen-year-olds can vote in the next election." That was the clincher. Victoria remembered hula-hoops, she recalled Coca-Cola sponsored yo-yos. Weren't there always revivals, wasn't that the way of fashion? She put it to the Congressman's niece, on a visit from Sarah Lawrence and loaned Corolla and driver. She learned what she had given the chauffeur was a Boston and that roller-skating was the passionate locomotion of the moment. "With a Walkman on your belt," the informative niece said. Mrs Init thought that was optional in the extreme, but she secured a lot of land – that was easy, the original lessor would only have rented it out as a car-park – shook down some downtown appliance stores for stereophonic equipment, and ordered fifty pairs of skates from Manila.

Citizen sent Boyet to the Ceremony of Blessing conducted by no less than Msgr Anecleto Ravoy. Mrs Init thought of the influential and rather worldly Monsignor as her private chaplain; he was usually "very available" for the Congressman as his secretary put it. Tall, austere, with a full head of grey hair and much given to wearing brown-tinted spectacles and a barong tagalog shirt rather than vestments, he didn't even look like a Filipino, let alone a Filipino priest. He reminded Boyet of a cross between Christopher Lee as Dracula on a good day and George Bush on a bad. His kids were too young to disturb with a comparison like that, unfortunately. He'd taken advantage of the opportunity to bring them along to one of the rare assignments they might appreciate. He wondered if he would get away with the Dracula-Bush crack in his column; the Monsignor hardly possessed a hit squad of his own. On the other hand someone else's goons might take it upon themselves. "Who will rid me of this turbulent hack?" They were in the VIP enclosure, not that it provided a better view or privileged access. In fact, they were all crushed together, unlike the public who had room to spread out. It was just a way for the organisers to make people feel they mattered. His kids loved it, the badges, the stewards. And if they were happy, Boyet was happy. Who'd turn down the chance to have his kids think he's a big shot?

Preparatory to the blessing, Mrs Init made a few remarks about Youth, Recreation, Opportunity, Discipline. It was apparent to Boyet that she didn't have a speechwriter. Her ideas were plainly her own – she spent too much time chasing detail and then losing herself for the address to be the smooth and impersonal handiwork of the mercenary and there was a touch of defensiveness, the voice changing pitch as it argued with a non-existent adversary, that would have been absent from the voice of the screed-reader. Boyet was surprised. The woman was a maker, an inventor; it might be a crappy one, but she was for real.

After Monsignor's blessing, a small masterpiece of unctuousness, patronising, it seemed, even God, the Congressman's wife cut a pink ribbon before carving a cake model of the rink. The Init niece, a very pretty girl, sufficiently like a white woman for the choosiest Filipino, skated a backwards circuit, slice of cake in the left, bottle of Mirinda in the right. "Oh, Pa," said Jennilyn, clutching Boyet's hand tighter. He was amazed, thunderstruck to see tears of happiness in his daughter's eyes. The contempt he'd have felt for someone else couldn't arise. What took its place he was unable to name.

Now a choir of what looked like hundreds but, consulting his hand-out, logic said had to be less than fifty, the number of available skates, swooped around the circuit trailing helium-filled balloons and giving the national anthem an even jerkier rendition than was its due. At a signal, the pink balloons, carrying INIT in white capitals, were released to come down in the northern part of the city, such was the prevailing wind, in a district held by a hereditary Init adversary, so that they mocked him from power cables and rooftops for weeks afterwards. Not by design – just one of the many instances where fortune, Mrs Init believed, abetted the daring, the strong. Handing his daughter a handkerchief, Boyet kept his eye on the woman. She had started to interest him. Not *qua* woman – 'sus Maria – but as public personality, political specimen. She was a whale of a lot more interesting than newspeak allowed her to be, that standardising mode of communication which bleached all power's aspirants to the same tone, relating big and small, eccentric and conventional to the same common denominator, mere enlargements and reductions on the same pattern. He could see straightaway she was an original. She actually believed fifty per cent in what she was saying. When Boyet thought about it later at the office – at Evergreen, not *Citizen* – he reckoned it was a weakness that nevertheless made her doubly dangerous. It made for a commitment, always a liability for a politician, particularly with the free-wheeling Philo power-brokers, ready to forge their fifty-fifth alliance at the notice of a moment or dishonour the compact of five seconds ago if it gave the smallest advantage; it made her less flexible than she should be and yet it conferred a zeal, a kick that went beyond personal ambition. It gave staying-power, that great *pinoy* want, and a consolation in adversity. As Mrs Init shook hands and beamed at the photographers, Boyet felt like a learned entymologist amid laymen, admiring a brilliant but highly poisonous creature perched on a pile of fruit in market, the only one to know the venom's capability but – he was forced to admit – as yet ignorant of an antidote. And also forced to admit that if he didn't respect her he was the possessor of an estimation capable of development.

So why was it his article came out so warped?

It was a good cause; at least, you couldn't knock it. The kids needed *something* to do. He might even let his own watch – under motherly supervision naturally. Jennilyn had mentioned an interest to Miriam, and then artfully let the subject drop a while. He didn't have anything against Mrs I. either; he wasn't automatically sceptical of her, the way he'd be with any other politician or their spouse. And yet . . . one by one the words issued innocuously enough but as the sentences wound into paras, the paragraphs uncoiling down the pages, the article as a whole writhed. It was positively serpentine in its venom, the obliquity of its purpose; it hissed its malice in the reader's ear. Even as he composed, throwing down his witticisms before the readers of *Citizen*, Boyet discovered he was appalled as much by how he was putting things as what he was writing. The whole piece had a nasty, sarcastic, smart-alec air about it, quite foreign to the standard *Up Periscope!* torpedoing. This was a little like machine-gunning survivors in the oily flame-lit waters. Chuckling the while. Boyet didn't mean to be snide, but everything he wrote came out that way. He started with a terrible pun, about how Amerikano kids went on bladed skates to the ice-rink but how the young of Gobernador de Leon, carrying blades on their belts, not their boots, weren't used to it and how they'd end up stunning themselves on ice instead (Boyet cognisant that was the ghetto word for shabu, metamphetamine hydrochloride, the poor man's cocaine that was rotting the moral fibre of Philippine youth, e.g. three-quarters of the country if you subscribed to Mrs Init's figures). From here Boyet devoted a couple of savagely intemperate paragraphs to Monsignor, his fashionable flock, clients other clerics might envy (Chavez felt obliged to take out the word "client" and replace it with "parishioners") followed by reflections on Monsignor's ambitions and some entirely unprovoked speculations about the condition of the Bishop's prostate. Wider references to Monsignor's contemporary, now a Cardinal, followed. Boyet described them as seminary "classmates", a term Chavez allowed, as he did the comparison with the influential class of '59 at the Military Academy, that seedbed of generals. Now Boyet commenced on Mrs Init, the heart of the column proper. He devoted seventy-five per cent of the space to a detailed description of her outfit, basically powder blue velours, in the language of the couturier without – to the best of his knowledge – a single ironic inflection creeping in. "The scarlet piping on the sleeves and shoulders and the repetition of that colour motif on the extra-large cloth buttons of the tunic were in the new spirit of resurrected detail being fine without fussy, an overdue reaction against the anti-colour chauvinism – the fashion for black – and fetish for simplicity of recent years. Nice." In short, Boyet concluded, "the queen of England would not have been ashamed to see her daughter-in-law Princess Fergusson presented to her at Ascot Palace in such an outfit." He decided to delete the bit about the piping picking up the red in Mrs Init's eyes.

"I don't think I can print this," Chavez told him.

Boyet smiled deprecatingly; he knew how to accept Nestor's praise, when it came, gracefully. The effect of the other's alarm was to cause him to behave more coolly than he'd felt a short while ago. Re-reading the piece in the jeepney down Guava – the headache of the eye-strain only now passing – the 4 p.m. school-leavers ignorant of the combustible freight they were sharing the ride with, he'd considered shredding the pages and putting them down the nearby blackwater ravine. But he wasn't the type who murdered his own offspring and floated the foetuses away. He was sentimental about his pars; he loved his word progeny.

And now Nestor did him the compliment of a third read. "Mmm, OK," said the terrible Chavez, bearing the radioactive matter to the operating table for implantation. Boyet grinned at the office, in the way of the newly hired gun at the saloon collectively. He had a tiny, advance inkling that the bravado he was prolonging would not survive the proofs of the outside world. He preserved elements of it in the jeep; the passengers were university students in the green and yellow check of Bonifacio U. and they conferred upon him something of their own sense of youthful invulnerability. But alone in the tricycle that bore him home over the last two km of dirt track, with only the ragged driver's back for company, his balls started to wither. Jennilyn was at her sweetest that evening, helping her younger brother with his math after dinner and beforehand assisting her mom and Leah, the help – her exact contemporary – in the outside "dirty kitchen" with its smoky wood fire because the rotating brownout had left the expensive modern appliances in the inside kitchen bereft of electricity. Boyet wanted to be a modern papa; he didn't want his kids so submissive, so self-effacing they couldn't say boo to a goose, still less joke with their Dad. That was how he and Lorna had been raised, in the traditional style, not daring to speak unless spoken to. He didn't want Jennilynn and Dexter scared to be initiators. *"Naulaw siya,"* his own mom – who so far from rebelling against the conditions of her own oppression hadn't even known she was being kept down – would say proudly at one more instance of preferably Lorna's – but also his – becoming reserve, modesty, shame, shyness, reticence. *Ulaw* meant all those things. You could have too much goddamned *ulaw*, though there was a side of Boyet which also craved this deep respect from his children and so what it was artificially inculcated. As he watched the two young heads touching in the pearl glow of the rechargeable lantern, all so unconscious of him in their innocent absorption in the difficult homework, Boyet felt the admonition of a powerful and insidious love. Not something he drew strength from; something weakening and subversive of resolve and responsibility. He went with it, the un-patriot.

Towards ten o' clock it was his custom to stroll over to the semi-rural subdivision's kindergarten, rich kids only, let himself in with the key he'd inveigled from the janitor and put into order his thoughts for the next *Up Periscope!* He didn't mind getting those thoughts into words in the hurly-burly of Evergreen but he needed tranquillity initially. Amateurs! He could almost hear Chavez's scornful voice. Tonight he drew no inspiration from A for Apple, B for Ball, C for Cat, and Project Rainfall (whatever the hell that was). The brightly coloured flash cards looked lurid by his stub of candle. He had already decided to phone Chavez when power was violently restored. He was alerted by the desperation clickings, like a geriatric being throttled by his own dentures, coming from the tired old ballast in the fluorescent fixture of the sari-sari store opposite. They were still selling fried bananas and canned sardines at this hour. As he crossed the road, he heard someone's TV set blow from the post-cut surge, followed by male cursing and juvenile and female lamentations. The store's phone was in order but his call was obviously not. He had to wait five minutes, three hundred long seconds, before Chavez was fetched from his place.

"This had better be good."

"Nestor, it's me."

"Who is me?"

"Boyet. Listen, Nestor, you can't run the piece. Not the way it is at the present. There are some rough edges I'd like to trim. Hello!"

After a long pause Chavez said, "You were brave enough this afternoon. Why the cold feet now? What happened?"

"Nothing. I'd just like the chance to put things in order."

"We're your hired helps. Leave the tidying up to the pros. It didn't need much, as I recollect."

"Listen, Nestor, I'm asking as a friend."

"You're not a friend. You're not even a colleague. Now get off the phone."

Assailed by feelings of chagrin, guilt, and disappointment, Boyet was as much baffled as anything. He just wasn't on the right wavelength to Chavez. Why couldn't the guy behave like a Filipino? Get the context, the silent agenda, his cue to conciliate? He was playing an Amerikano newspaperman, one out of the movies at that. Boyet took a deep breath. "Look, I just need to look at it again. Is that too much to ask? You thought it went too far at first. Maybe it'll look different to me on the galley."

"It won't."

Chavez had obviously been waiting for an effective moment to hang up. This was it.

Boyet said his "Hallo? Hallo?" into the receiver as dutifully as an actor; he knew what had happened.

Under the funerary drapes of the mosquito net he slept pitifully. At Evergreen, perusing the rival rag, he thought it typical that he'd got the worst of all possible worlds for himself, securing the wrath, or at the very least the ill-will, of the powerful while forfeiting the respect of his most senior colleague. Darn it, Nestor was his colleague. Queuing for his martyr's crown at celestial quartermaster's he'd been issued a dunce's cap instead. He was too proud to go to the lengths of physically intercepting the article at *Citizen*, although that was certainly within the realm of the volitionally accomplishable, much like running stark naked through traffic lights. But after hamming it up in the offices yesterday he'd rather take his chances than go abase himself. Boyet operated on the principle that nothing personal was so sacred it was confidential – with a journalist! – with a Filipino! – but in fact Chavez hadn't divulged any part of their short conversation, not even to his wife. Word at *Citizen* was that Clark Kent really was Superman, the guy with nerves of steel.

Up Periscope! appeared Friday. Boyet bought it from his usual vendor – the ragamuffin still marked it up 50 centavos from its official cover price of P3, as he did with everyone else – and he winced as he opened the rag. A dearth of hard and/or juicy local news had ensured the piece appeared on an early right hand page – five – and the uneven two deck headline ran – The lady wore blue velvet. Sub-head – Victoria skates rings round her rivals. Boyet read the damn thing fast, face half averted, back hunched, flinching from the specimens of his own hardihood in the posture of the pack's subordinate baboon. In cold print it looked even worse than in the fevers of his night imagination. His playful quips appeared as unadorned insults, his irreverent pleasantries like unprovoked attacks, and the pet asides to the reader like cheap sneers. His face got even hotter than the fierce sun was making it already. He was no longer nervous; he felt ashamed.

Chavez never alluded to their telephone conversation. It was as if it hadn't happened. Boyet wondered if he had dreamed it. As every day passed he felt better, much like the first time he'd used a prostitute at the age of nineteen, standing with dread at the urinal for days after, waiting for the razor blades and molten lead he'd been told about, counting the days with increasing insouciance until he knew after a month that he was unscathed. And so it was this time. No notices for libel, no excommunication from the Church, no goon squads bursting in to *Citizen* to spit on typewriters or throw cartridges around as they had after Kelvin Fugoso chronicled the chief of police's extra-mural sources of income.

Seventeen days after the relevant issue *Citizen* received a reader's letter, posted in anger on the same day of the story, accusing Boyet of being in the pay of the Init camp.

"Shucks!" Boyet exclaimed. "I don't believe this!" He laughed as much from the bliss, figuratively speaking, of a provenly painless piss and this latest unexpected testimonial to his urinary health as at the idiocy, the terminal obtuseness of the letter-writer.

"It's from a Bugnaw patsy," Chavez said sourly, referring to the hereditary Init enemies, chance recipients of the emblazoned pink balloons, "if not old Bugnaw himself. Surprised the gorilla can read, man."

"What the hell is going through these people's heads? Anyone could see the piece was hostile to the Inits."

"Think they actually read your deathless prose, Boyet? All they see is the headline, that and how much space. Think again."

"I'll keep this letter for the album. It's priceless."

"No. You are."

As for Victoria, Boyet had to wait two and a half years, not seventeen days, to know what she thought of the piece. That was at the time of the Symposium. By then he'd compounded his original felony so many times that he never thought of the first Init piece anymore. He considered himself a hardened recidivist. He was standing in that stunning lobby of the MMR and DCC by himself, waiting for his appointment with Dr Neumark – he was never to get that interview – kicking his heels for forty-five minutes, listening to the amplified voice of Professor

Pfeidwengeler hectoring in the main hall and regarding the dirty coffee cups when Mrs Init and Chavez appeared like footloose demons in that empty cavern. Chavez steered his principal Boyet's way; she'd been headed upstairs.

"Mum, may I introduce Mr Boyet Dinolan, one of our columnists from *Citizen* and my right-hand man."

Mrs Init smiled dazzlingly and offered her hand in a cooler gesture. Boyet found himself wanting to please her, to say something nice about the event but she spoke first. "I know Mr Dinolan well. He is one of the first writers I read when I open the *Citize*n."

Boyet knew how to accept a lying compliment as gracefully as anyone. "I'm sure Mum doesn't mean that. She has more important things to read than my scribblings," he said, patting the back of his neck. He found he was sweating, what with the air-con the delegates had masochistically denied themselves.

"No, Mr Dinolan. I mean everything I say. You can rely on my . . . what is it, Mr Chavez?"

"Quotes, mum?"

"Quotes. I hope you are enjoying the Symposium, Mr Dinolan?"

"Very much, mum. It's really a privilege to be here."

"I'll tell Representative Init. Nestor, ask the girls to give Mr Dinolan an ID badge; they must have forgotten to give him one."

Boyet smiled glassily. He also knew a rebuke when he heard one. Just as Mrs Init and Chavez headed for the stairs she turned again, as if something had only just occurred to her. She touched Boyet on the chest lightly, then straightened the pen in his shirt pocket. "Oh, yes. You should know, Mr Dinolan, the Queen of England does not have a palace at Ascot. It's just a horse-race there. Just a horse-race, you know."

Chapter Five

WHICH WAS THE BIGGER HIGH? Cars or guns? Crescente would have been hard put to answer that one. "Speed kills," he liked to say. Those who listened didn't understand exactly what he meant by that – maybe he wasn't too sure himself – but they laughed, some more nervously than others. Privately, there were those who thought he was a greater public menace sober behind the wheel of his Mercedes Benz than drunk waving a Colt. "Shit, if I hit anyone," he'd say with a roar of fat man's laughter, "if I didn't kill them first time, I'd be the one to go back and run them over again. No witness, no crime." That was family policy – it had been the standing instruction of his grandfather to the drivers of his line of buses. As for himself, Crescente wasn't sure of the answer to the question. He loved his fleet of automobiles and his collection of firearms equally well. At last count, he owned seven cars, all in the colour red except for the white British Range Rover which was such an unusual vehicle that any but the plainest livery would actually have detracted from its uniqueness. Currently, the BMW coupe was his darling but before that it had been the Lamborghini. And he found he had an affection for the nippy little Japanese Datsun that surprised him – the one with a better standing start than the broad-shouldered German vehicles. In fact, countries produced cars and arms according to their national characters: the immaculately machined, one hundred per cent reliable HK's, Walthers and SIGS (OK, stretch a point, the latter was Austrian), which were the handgun world's equivalent of your Merc and Audi. And then there was Beretta, the stylish and ingenious counterpart of

Ferrari and Alfa. His nickel-plated Smith and Wesson .44 magnum, the Colt Commander .45 auto, the Ruger Blackhawk, he thought of as the equivalents of his Ford Mustang: gutsy, durable American classics beyond time, and with one helluva kick too. It was a crying shame the Japs didn't have a small arms manufactory to compare with Sony and Nikon. Or how about a Saturday night special by Casio? It was a restriction imposed on them for sure. Those bowing monkeys could copy anything. It was probably just as well, he was already spoiled for choice. Most times now he'd still dither what to wear but in the end plump for the Colt .45: only seven shots to the Beretta's sixteen, a design nearly eighty years older but, shit, the .45 ACP round would send a man right across a room where the pissy 9mm cartridge of the European autos would leave a wounded foe standing, firing back at you. Gun love, surpassing the love of women. In fact, Crescente had never had cause to lament the ballistic ineffectiveness of 9mm parabellum in other than an academic sense. No one had ever fired back at him. They hadn't survived the first bullet in the back of the head or spine. Of the five men he'd killed, four had been trussed or held kneeling while he performed the honours at arms length, his own participant goons flinching at the coup de grâce. The German chef had got it upright. Crescente still remembered the foreigner, the other four were a blur, the same emptying faces, the same cold rage in himself. They'd been planned, those items of revenge. The hits – that was the word he used to himself, professional-sounding – had been self-contained episodes in themselves. But the foreigner had been unplanned, the shooting the climax to a whole evening that had proceeded uncontrollably from good to bad. He'd begun in For da Guys bar, the only place he could safely resort to in Breadfruit, tucked away down a cul-de-sac, having left his own morons, the merrie men, posted in the street so a gunman, Sparrow or paid assassin, would have no chance of making a successful get-away (he hoped). He reckoned that constituted a substantial deterrent: Filipinos were no fanatics. It was as safe and snug for a guy in his position as you could get.

'Sus Maria, it wasn't a 100 per cent world anyway. The barman, a one-armed wonder called Jun(ior), had greeted him with his standard "Hi, Boss," and taken down his initialled bottle of Black Label. The usual girls had been gyrating in their bikinis, their knees at the customers' eye-level. Crescente's favoured chair faced barman, not chicks. He didn't want anyone thinking he was there to look at chicks. The disc-jockey saw him as he came in and without further ado faded out what was on to replace it with the Boss's favourite song of the moment: *Dangerous*. The girls liked it – it was nice to dance to, far better than the "sophisticated" Manila crap no one had ever heard before and with which the DJ justified his job. Something catchy that would cheer the place up – and it worked this time as well. Crescente raised his tumbler to the DJ, the girls grinned, called down "Hi, Boss!", and the customers found themselves laughing and talking louder without knowing why. Architect of mood, Crescente smiled with satisfaction. He didn't want or expect praise or thanks, not he. He had contented himself with a magisterial wave of dismissal the night he had paid the bar-fines of the four girls left in the place at 1:30 a.m., miserable night turned memorable for them. All the others had been taken out for screwing by customers – it was the week a Spanish training frigate had been moored in harbour – leaving the biggest dogs in the place reclining their fat heads moodily on their forearms. Even the dancer – they were getting up to do their stint to an empty house every seven minutes – was lying on her back, one bare foot up in the air on the brass pole that normally had snatches sliding on it, not soles, her stilletos by her head like the ears of a giant rabbit. Crescente counted out the twelve hundred pesos matter-of-factly, no flourishes, and told the chicks they could go. Shit! he was the hero for weeks.

But this night, smiling quietly to himself, things started to go sour. The tourists who came to Gobernador de Leon were ninety per cent male and looking for action – Japanese, German, and Australian in that order. The Japs preferred Karaoke to the bikini bars; they had their own places, mostly owned by Tokyo gangsters, girls in uniform, the latest in laser disc technology and high, high prices. Not that Crescente cared about prices – he'd blown $500 US one night at For da Guys. The clientele of the place was foreigner, not a *pinoy* in sight, and this night was no exception. The Germans got drunk quietly – as a rule they were middle-aged to elderly – the Australians noisily. Near the Boss six or seven Australians looked well into their evening. The dancer had just removed her brassiere in an effort to drum up some custom, her health card only just returned after a positive swabbing. One of the Australians, who for a change was a handsome young fellow, was wearing the head-band she'd thrown at them. Crescente grinned. Entertainment was a co-operative venture; they'd all amuse each other. That was why he came out on his ownsome. Forget the merrie men; they were no company for anyone. That afternoon he'd drawn them up for an impromptu parade of inspection, checked the new Ingram MAC 10 sub-machine guns he'd got them from the US, then noticed something. "It's raining. Why are you all wearing sun-glasses?" The chief moron had pulled in his belly, drawn back his shoulders. "Boss, because it makes us look professional!" No, their job was to sit outside until he was good and ready to move on. He decided he'd befriend the Australians. Surprise them by picking up their tab. He enjoyed showing foreigners there were Filipinos richer than they were, that it was wasn't just bananas and monkeys. Laughing heartily, he called to the guy in the girl's headband, "Hey Joe, you look like a *bayut*!" The Australian seemed not to have heard him, though the last bars of *Dangerous* were fading away already. The Boss never forced his company on those who didn't desire it. Not when he was sober, which he still was. So he'd turned his attention to the excessive number of ice-cubes in his tumbler – Jun happy to be scapegoat – when the Australian asked in a loud voice of nobody in particular, "What's a buy-out when he's at home?"

The Boss didn't like the tone, aggressive foreigner, but he wasn't one to pick fights with total strangers, so he kept his back turned.

"I'm going on a diet tomorrow, anyone want to join me?" Sniggers from the Australian's companions. The Boss sat very still. Even when the foreigner stood behind him, sashaying his hips. The manager and the disc-jockey, hovering nervously behind, tried to get between the Australian and the Boss without success. It was a narrow space and the Boss's 220 pounds took a lot of it. Another Australian, slightly more sober, grabbed his friend by the belt of his shorts and swung him away, like an Olympic hammer-thrower. The swung continued his momentum over to the rest of the party, going "Oink, oink, oink."

"Sorry, mate," the thrower said. "He gets a little carried away."

"OK, my friend. No problem."

"Can I get you a drink while I'm at it?"

At what, Crescente wondered? "I have my personal bottle there, friend. It is not necessary for you."

Manager and DJ piled in as the grey-haired foreigner left. The Boss was as curt as they were effusive, but that was part of the whole game of pluses and minuses for the self-esteem and they knew it too. A trio of girls arrived to pour additional oil on the waters, refusing the ladies drinks the Boss offered. They draped themselves around him, mermaids paying court to a sea-elephant – the Boss usually wore black, for the effect and in order to minimise his stoutness. All looked settled when the first Australian appeared again.

"You called me a poofter, didn't you?"

With real reluctance the Boss turned to face him. He didn't want trouble; it was the last thing he desired tonight.

"A buy – what you called me. That's a queer."

"I don't know what you are talking about."

"Yeah, well I know what you were talking about, fat boy."

The manager was ready to tear his own hair out if he could somehow get the foreigner into his seat again and Mr Crescente left to himself, safely blocked off into a corner by half his hospitality girls if he had anything to do with it. He dreaded the thought of pistol play in his bar, the squeeze from the police, the screaming from the girls, the danger to his own life as a principal witness, the mess. Blood on the walls and ceiling – he knew that. 'Sus Maria – he'd make football of the girl who had interpreted for the foreigner. The six Australians were around the Boss now, not all of them as drunk as the one who was still wearing the dancer's headband.

"Wayne, this overweight ratbag called me a poofter."

"No, he didn't. Drop it, John."

"It's not worth it, John."

"Come on, fellers, let's sit down and act our ages."

"Not till Billy Bunter apologises."

The Boss knew he had bad eyes. He really did. He knew he didn't look like a Filipino, more Spanish, maybe like a Mexican bandido, El Jefe from a Sam Peckinpah movie. Now he gave the foreigner The Look. It spoke of power, absolute and fathomless in its utter corruption; of a tired but still virile experience; of having seen his like and disposed of it before; of a piercing shrewdness, unclouded by anger; of mastery and a total disregard for consequences.

The Australian took the Boss by the throat. "Who the fuck do you think you are, cunt?"

The Boss stared at him in utter disbelief, too amazed even to contemplate the Colt inside its velcroed holster in his trouser band.

The disc-jockey just beat the manager to the Australian's hand, and a lugubrious struggle began between the two Filipinos and the burly foreigner. It was the Australian's friends who succeeded in pulling him off.

"Who am I?" the Boss managed. "Who am I?" He nodded to the DJ – yes, slip outside and get the merrie men. He moved his neck like a turtle, regaining composure with every second's anticipation of the dénouement of the scene, the arrival of reinforcements. "No. I will not be the one to tell you who I am. You find out for yourselves very soon."

Not that he cared, he could see this failed to win him friends and influence among the other foreigners. Their mood was changing to a group solidarity where they'd not had their hearts in backing their touchy companion until now. Crescente found himself ringed; there were more of them behind him, so it would be risky to draw without a good distraction. "You motherfuckers had better be careful," he enunciated slowly. "I'm trained to kill."

This statement was greeted with howls of laughter. The grey-haired peacemaker said, "Who the hell is this comedian?" The cause of all the trouble, the one with the girl's headband, wasn't so mad as before. "I'm buggered if I know," he said, "but he should fire the script-writer."

Where were his morons? Shit, he'd pistol-whip the newest. After they'd shot the Australians. As his attackers – that was how he thought of them now – hemmed him in more closely, he saw something very disappointing: the DJ held by the largest foreigner, not violently, not painfully, but with massive control as if the foreigner had restrained thousands of people before.

"So what do you do in your spare-time, sunshine?"

The Boss swallowed. He wasn't scared, just very angry. He wasn't the one in jeopardy of death. He was perfectly aware nothing very bad could happen to him. Foreigners knew limits; he didn't. "You ask," he said, pointing with pursed lips to the manager.

"You've got a mouth, fat boy, use it."

The Boss now had an entirely new experience. Nobody, but nobody, had ever twisted his arm in his life.

"Shit, John, chummy's tooled-up."

Crescente found himself looking at a beer puddle on Jun's otherwise immaculately kept counter. His pants waistband became looser without the Colt.

"Goodness, Mildred, it's a big one."

"Naughty, naughty boy."

"There's no wallet."

"Who are you, boy?"

"Tell them," Crescente gasped. "Tell them."

The girls chorused, "You are our Godfather, *kuya*."

"That's right. The Godfather."

"Thought he was in the movie business, didn't you, Wayne?"

"What's your name, joker?"

"I just need to tell you my rank and number."

"That's a different film, mate. Ve haf vays and means to find out vot ve vant to know, *jawohl*."

"A little birdie tells me chummy'll have some tiny friends outside."

"Yeah, it wouldn't surprise me at all. Where are your side-kicks, fat boy?"

"I am Special Forces. Don't expect me to talk."

"Jesus Christ. He don't give up easy, do he."

"The best place for chummy is the khazi. Got the front door key, have we Mr Manager? All right, Wayne, lock up and we'll piss off out the back."

The Boss found himself propelled in what he thought of even then as a highly professional manner towards the gents Comfort Room, a tiny Augean stables that called no cleaner master. He had his head driven against the door-frame on the way in and only speedy anonymous intervention from behind foiled the attempt to continue the momentum and ram his head down the filthy bowl. The door slammed and he heard the scrape of a chair being tilted up under the knob. He knew they wouldn't trouble to open it again, so he called out, "Australian pigs, I'll kill all of you."

"Australian?" said a voice outside – he thought it was the one with the headband – "They're Poms, mate. RHKP. Ta ta. We're pissing off at sparrow-fart, so don't bother."

Later, much later, several nights, in fact, when he was shaking the hapless Jun by the collar, both of Jun's feet off the ground on the barman's side of the bar, Crescente was able to fix the time he had spent in the CR as slightly more than fourteen minutes, or the length of two of the sets the girls were dancing that night. One of the permanent legacies of the encounter was the destruction of his Rolex Oyster helium diver's watch, guaranteed to 20 atmospheres absolute pressure, for which he had paid the full-blooded US$10,000, now shown to be a Hong Kong fake. He had congratulated himself on his coolness, his presence of mind as he'd consulted the instrument comparatively early in his immurement only to discover it had stopped. After that it became difficult to keep track of how long: of course, it had seemed like an eternity in the hole, waiting for his morons; on the other hand, psyched up like that, it was as if you were speeding on the hormones rushing round the bloodstream. Two sets. Fourteen minutes, give or take.

"You mean you kept the girls dancing?"

Jun nodded. That was all he could do. Head back, toes of shoes scraping floor, hand at side still holding the polishing towel.

"While I was in there? That place?"

Jun gurgled. Amidst the rushing in his ears he wondered if his own face was suffused as the Boss's. Crescente relaxed his grip a little, not out of charity; he just wanted to hear what Jun had to say; he wasn't a monomaniac.

"The show has to go on, Boss, does it, *di ba*?"

Crescente began slapping him about the face, just short of hard but the smacks loud enough to be heard over the music (*Air Supply* tonight).

"What time I left here that night, Jun?"

"You leaving, Boss? Maybe 12:30."

Smack. "No, Jun." *Smack*. "You must improve your memory, Jun." *Smack*.

"I don't understand, Boss."

Smack. "Yes, you do, Jun." *Smack*. "I left at 4 a.m." *Smack*. "And all the time between 12:30 and 4 a.m. I was the one talking to you." *Smack*. "We were having a pleasant conversation, just like now." *Smack*. "Remember?"

"No, Boss. You were leaving much earlier but we still had a nice conversation like always."

"I'll be the one to say what happened, Jun, and how long."

Smack. "It was 4 a.m." *Smack*. "Remember now?"

"Yes, Boss. 4 a.m. I remember now."

"Good already, Jun. This is just five hundred. Get yourself a new polo."

"Yes, Boss. Thank you very much your consideration, Boss."

Making his exit from For da Guys that night of the incident (at 12:41 in fact, Jun's sense of time proving basically accurate like his instinctive appraisal of liquid volume, though inclining slightly to the short measure in both cases) Crescente had scrutinised the extensive street and doorway hangers-on for minutest signs of complicity and/or levity. He'd been ready to blow the whole bunch away, taxi-drivers, blue army security guard, cigarette vendors, barbecue hawkers, child door-openers for the cars, dope-pushers. All was usual. No one over-did it; no one ignored him, which would have been a yet more blatant sign. A pity almost. Very quickly he'd decided not to punish his morons. They'd be a better posse for it. Besides there was no time to lose. They stopped only to pinion the security guard while the Boss whopped him twice in the gut, right-left. Then they charged through the bar, guns drawn, making the girls scream, though the shrieks were probably just dutiful. Crescente could see how the Australians had escaped – the backyard adjoined a thriving outdoor restaurant specialising in roast pig on one side and on the other a cinema parking-lot. He hesitated: to the left brightness and noise, to the right quiet and shadows. It was obvious what escape route would be preferable but that was why he thought twice – he didn't consider himself anyone's common or garden adversary. No. He led the merrie men across the carpark, one group covering the other in turn as they scampered from objective to objective, in this case Lancer to Corolla, to VW Beetle, to Pajero, to Lancer, to Tamaraw. He'd told his morons the opposition was armed. Which was only true. They were in possession of a fully loaded, cocked and locked, ready to go .45, weren't they. His.

Standing at the front of the cinema, looking like they were a trailer for the show (the routine shoot-out that was the staple of the Tagalog movie) the merrie men turned to the Boss for direction. They had not the faintest idea what the quarry looked like; other than that they were foreigners. "There, Boss!" the head thug gestured with his Ingram. Crescente winced – he hoped at least the safety was on, what with the cyclic rate of fire exceeding a thousand rounds a minute – but it was merely a Danish septuagenarian with his teenage Filipina penpal. The dotard nearly passed out as he registered the interest of the armed men. "No, idiot," Crescente said, "you think *lolo* there could disarm me and lock me up by himself?" Uproarious laughter from the merrie men. The butt scowled, not at the Boss of course, but for the benefit of the other goons. In general, all goons hated being laughed at. It probably damaged earning power. Crescente sent three men for the vehicles. In the meantime it was not unpleasant to be stared at by elements of the public. He decided they'd check out all the bars in town, a taller order than it sounded. He led the way in the BM, the merrie men trailing him in their ancient jeep. Just to be mischievous, he'd blip the accelerator now and then, especially as the lights were changing, purely to keep the morons on their toes. He could hear the ludicrous dismay and swearing on each occasion and once, in their zeal, when they shot the lights a jeepney nearly struck them side-on. The Boss thought that was a hoot.

The drinking-holes yielded no prey. These were places Crescente hadn't been able to enter since he was a student. He resisted the temptation to drink at the first four or five but gradually the boredom got too much. He seriously doubted the possibility of seeing the Australians again that night. The kind of downtown mousehole they had worked their way round to didn't stock whisky, let alone Black Label, so he was resorting to beer and rum chasers. Later, he would lay the blame on mixing his drink. "Makes me ugly. I get violent once I start cocktailing it." He said this not very regretfully but both ruefully and proudly, as if he was the inventor of the demon drink, the libation that turned quiet Dr Jekyll into .45-brandishing Mr Hyde. It was actually with a full glass of beer still before him that he remembered Odyssey's. How had he omitted the swankiest hotel in town from their itinerary, the goons' stations of the cross? Shit. The prices weren't that crippling for a foreigner, even if there were no go-go dancers, just hunting girls. He bet that was where they'd gone first – probably moved on by now. No time to lose. He was already parking while the merrie men were crunching down from third to second half way up the hill.

Odyssey's was empty, not one customer. There hadn't been anyone all night, the doormen told him. That put him in a foul mood for a start. Inside the hotel proper was Mimi's Owlerie, the 24-hour coffee shop and games room. He transferred his presence there. Darts, pool, bar football, a contraption involving a ball suspended on a string and some miniature skittles which looked interesting but not worth the trouble of learning still less mastering, and a wheel of chance. The merrie men found the Boss occupying himself by throwing peanuts into the firebucket. He considered making the newest goon stand against the wall while he blocked in his shape with the available flights of darts but decided against it. They were his morons but the bottom line was he shouldn't abuse their loyalty; he might really need it one day. He called up a line of beers for them; those who tried to refuse he ordered to drink. They obeyed with wide grins. Crescente knew he was an unpredictable and difficult boss but he was also pretty damn sure he was a popular one.

It was now 2:30 a.m., all solid citizens unconscious, only vampires around. A man came in through the hotel side of the Owlerie, wearing small check blue trousers and a white tunic. He was a foreigner but not, Crescente signed to the merrie men, one of his Australians. He had one of those European-style moustaches that twirled up three inches at the ends, like bulls horns. He began to corral the pool balls with the wooden triangle. Crescente saw he was wearing clogs, which meant he was probably a chef. "Who's feeling like a game?" the man called, holding up a cue. "You?" he gestured at the newest goon. A frisson went through the air, an inaudible collective goon sigh. They could smell trouble impending. That came when someone didn't know their proper position in the hierarchy and the difference between that slot and the one occupied by the Boss and, therefore indirectly, themselves. It was like the physical laws of nature. Some force would always rush in to fill the space left empty by another. Nature abhorred a vacuum. What caused thunder? Air pouring in to fill the sky's breaching. The roar of an indignity justly repelled. The guy waved his pole at the Boss, which was about as wise as holding a lightning conductor during a storm. He was stirring all the suspense in the room, gathering the static of expectation around the tip of his rod. The Boss nodded. He took up the challenge, moved in on the table like an elemental force of nature, an act of God. "Twenty pesos a point, my friend?" the foreigner said, a hustler then as well as a fool. The Boss ignored him; sharing a game of pool didn't constitute the right to conversation.

It was a pity the Boss had to go and play such a good game; it really was. For it made the losing all the harder. Like a lot of fat men he was agile round the table, could cock his short leg as easily as a dog. He liked to poke the cue between two of his fingers in the unschooled way but could still shoot crisp and straight. He got off to a marvellous, a truly marvellous start, an awesome break, ball following ball into the pockets. The merrie men grinned. Damn it if the foreigner didn't do the same. He scored exactly the same as the Boss. And all the time he kept up this imbecile commentary. Worse, he continued when it was the Boss's turn again, not even stopping when the Boss was setting up his shots. They could see the muscle in the Boss's cheek twitching as he gritted his teeth, and all the time the fool was unaware of the effect he was having. It was almost painful to watch. Despite the distraction the Boss ran off another headlong break. "Bad luck, ha-ha," said the nincompoop in clogs as the Boss finally miscued. "Now watch the master." This time he bettered the Boss's score by one point. To watch him, you'd have thought he imagined that the best joke ever. Then when the Boss missed this very, very difficult shot by just a whisker, the clown roared with laughter. With tears in his eyes, he said, "A miss is as good as a mile, my dear sir." He then proceeded to fluke a couple of outrageous shots, bellowing like an elephant as they dropped into the net. He twirled the points of his moustache, chalked the end of his rod. As the Boss concentrated on his comeback, scowling at the balls remaining on the table – he could still just win – the asshole started whistling. It was no tune you ever heard before, some foreign ditty. He'd told the Boss he was Swiss. The Boss, you could see, had just about reached breaking-point. He put down his cue, looked up from the table and asked, "Could you stop whistling?" Mr Shit-for-brains looked surprised, pointed at himself – you could be sure no one else was whistling – and did a jerk-back of the head when the Boss nodded. He even looked offended. And then the Boss had to go and accidentally move a ball with the edge of his hand. He realised he'd done it – the Boss never missed much – but was still continuing with his shot when Shit-for-brains put his hand on the butt of the Boss's cue as it was moving back. "You make a foul shot," he said. It was touch and go whether the Boss hit him with the cue, you could see it in his face. But he stood aside and gave his opponent his turn. That was the Boss's style – he gave you enough rope to hang yourself. Shit-for-brains now tried shooting with the cue held behind his back. There was no need for it; the balls lay easy. He was just trying to be clever. He missed the cue ball completely and laughed. The Boss was deadly serious. Maybe he was trying too hard, because he miscued – and he wasn't goofing off. "Ho! You need spectacles!" Shit-for-brains said. His next shot saw him miss a sitting duck, parked right on the verge of the pocket. The merrie men wondered if he was trying to lose, like they would in his place. But no, he didn't have the brains for that. After a few exchanges it became clear he was trying to be obstructive – he was no longer aiming to pot balls, merely to contrive awkward predicaments for the Boss. He guffawed as the Boss hit the wrong ball, then set up an even more impossible play, with the target ball all but concealed by the others. He jabbed the edge of the table with his forefinger. "Aim here, partner, bounce it off the cushion."

The Boss ignored him – how could he do anything else? – and hit the wrong ball. "You lose points, ha-ha," said Shit-for-brains. "In fact, friend, I don't think you can win anymore."

The Boss looked him over. "Is that so?" he asked quietly.

"That is so. So pay up, ha-ha. You have lost . . . one hundred fifty. So the children will not eat tomorrow. Ho, ho!" For the merrie men the spectacle was akin to watching a man throwing explosives on to a fire. Why the Boss hadn't gone off yet was a mystery to them. It seemed he had been endlessly provoked all night. He'd displayed the patience of a saint. Now he just turned and walked to the door.

"Mister! A gentleman will pay his gambling debts!"

It seemed each word was a nail hammered into the Boss's broad back. He began to turn and as he did those of the merrie men behind the asshole foreigner scrambled to get out of the direct line. They'd seen all too often how dangerous strays could be. Sometimes it was safer to be the target than a stand-by.

"I beat you fair and square. If I had lost, I would pay you. So you pay me. It's not so much for you, I think."

The Boss didn't look so much mad as disgusted. You could see him on the horns of a dilemma, wondering which way to turn. If he hadn't had his earlier problem with the Australians he would probably have just left. "So you like me to pay you something," the Boss mused. "How do you like to be paid what you deserve?" The merrie men could see it coming now, nemesis looming with a fatal inevitability.

"Hey, what do you think you are doing?" The foreigner's voice had risen to a squawk when he saw the Boss draw his back-up piece, an unglamorous .38 borrowed from the newest goon. "You're not going to be a sore loser, are you?"

The Boss got a ball, the No. 8, and balanced it on the foreigner's head. "Did you say you were Swiss?" he asked.

"Ha, ha," said Shit-for-brains, "I hope you are a better shot with a gun than a pool cue." If he thought he was going to get himself out of trouble with a line like that he was wrong, very wrong. The Boss's face clouded. He cocked the revolver.

"Shit!" the foreigner said, the ball dropping and rolling over the marble with a whirring sound. "You're going to shoot me because you lose a game of pool?"

"No," said the Boss, "because I don't like you."

"For God's sake, Mister whatever your name is, it's just a game. We pass the time, we joke, we amuse each other. Look, if you are not having the money, forget it. Take my money – here. Consider I'm the loser. Take all my cash."

"You think I'm a robber or what?" the Boss asked, rising to the full majesty of his wrath – no inglorious sight for the merrie men.

"I don't know what you are or who you are – just please leave me alone." The man's voice cracked with the last words, for the Boss had put his revolver barrel to his ear.

"On your knees," he said, with the grimness only he knew how to muster. By now Shit-for-brains didn't know who or where he was; probably he soiled himself a long time ago. Funnily enough, his moustache ends still stuck up jauntily enough, though his eyes had that watery-panicky look.

The Boss pulled the trigger. Click. For a moment he looked as surprised as the foreigner. Then he guffawed. The merrie men joined in, nothing sycophantic, genuinely tickled.

They left him there on his knees.

In the car park the Boss recollected something. He'd left his car and house keys on the edge of the pool table – even the Boss had to have house-keys; he led a human being's life, didn't he. He hadn't lived as long as he had without being cautious either, so he took three of the merrie men back in with him. They were able to tell the others what happened – outside they heard nothing, of course.

Shit-for-brains hadn't had the wit to leave and they found him having a well deserved and probably deeply desired beer with his back to them at the bar. The tender never betrayed by word or movement their arrival. They heard him say, "OK, that fat pig has money and he can buy himself what do you call them

. . . hoons, but in Europe we have a word for him. He's just a coward. One on one, he is a fat coward."

They reckoned he never knew what hit him. The Boss grabbed the new Ingram from Lito and just slashed Shit-for-brains off his stool with half the magazine. The suppressors they'd all been so anxious about on full auto in a real situation, the suppressor worked beautifully – just a series of big pops, while the gun stayed steady as rock in the Boss's grip of iron. Even as the body hit the floor – only a few bottles broken – the Boss had put the gun on safety and was picking up the shell cases from where they'd been ejected. He made them stay a minute, hunting down each last cartridge – maybe also to show he hadn't blown his cool. He was sensitive sometimes, the Boss.

Afterwards they drove at a steady thirty to the hospital. His hospital, the one he'd inherited from his late papa, the one which made all the fun possible and sustained the high jinks. That hospital car-park had provided sanctuary to them after many an escapade. Like the Sherwood Forest had to Robin in the film.

Chapter Six

THE OLD EDITOR WAS GOING. Rumours of his impending departure had been prevalent for years – ever since he'd passed his sixtieth birthday which had been perceived as a symbolic milestone of sorts. But old Cesar had stayed, and stayed, and then some. Finally, just when all his staff had begun to accept him again as the fixture he had been for fifteen years, he'd made his move. An international computer company had funded a new chair in investigative journalism at a second division Manila university. It was designed as innovative – computers being nothing if not novel and always renewing their own capabilities: investigative journalism the subject, an un-posh college, and a non-Tagalog incumbent from off the metropolitan patronage network. "The only thing Cesar ever investigated was my expenses," Chavez commented, "and then he didn't get to the bottom of them." This from the man whom the editor had assiduously favoured, promoted; from the man who always called Cesar, "Sir." The newsroom and secretaries were shocked. It was as un-Filipino as potatoes. How could he?

Cesar came in. "Sir," said Nestor, "Belated congratulations. But how can you be a Professor of investigation when you never queried my expenses?"

Old Cesar roared with laughter. "You'll see just how big a fool I am," he said. "Just wait."

Formal applications for the vacancy had to be submitted. An advertisement to the effect appeared for one week in *Citizen*. Chavez reckoned they'd give the job to a Tagalog, just to be different. A case of musical chairs, what with the old ed going to the North.

Boyet wondered if the new broom would sweep away his column. He had doubts about its viability. They were no longer novelties, his articles, but had yet to become institutions on the pages. He wondered if he should try the rival? He knew he could get an utterly disinterested opinion from Nestor. "Ask the new ed, man," was the disappointing response. At the time he thought Nestor could have done better than that.

Cesar was to go without fuss two weeks hence. Betting was that they'd get a complete stranger. Then a rumour began that it would be the deputy ed of the rival, the guy who'd been Nestor's predecessor as chief sub: that way management would get the advantage of old and new combined. Chavez stayed cool. The guy had been no friend of his but he stayed cool. Finally, he came into the newsroom first one morning. One by one as they arrived the others turned to those already in the office, pulling expressions of surprise. Chavez didn't look up from his paper, the Manila Chronicle ("only decent paper in the whole RP," Chavez would say to howls of protest – "No way, sir! They just reprint articles from foreign papers!") but as the last came in, Nestor said "Cesar has sent up white smoke, folks." Shortly after the proprietor arrived and announced that their new editor was none other than Nestor Chavez.

"Yay!" shouted every single one of the subs spontaneously. Jingkee Zamora kissed him. Roel Jiminez punched the air. Boyet was told Nestor managed not to betray himself by the smallest smile, though he had too much to drink at lunchtime. By three o'clock which was when Boyet arrived, Chavez was mellow.

"Congrats, brod, congrats. They couldn't have found a better guy." Boyet meant it; he was full of genuine pleasure for the appointment.

"Bush after Reagan. The Veep doesn't often get to step into the big guy's shoes."

"Don't put yourself down. You taught me everything I know – and you're my age. No, younger a little, hah?"

"Get lost. We're having a few beers in Breadfruit later.

Come along."

"I can't. I have to collect the kids."

"I already told Maribeth to get yours for you. She'll drop them off."

"You did?"

THERE were to be no big changes. Chavez called a meeting in the newsroom to say all their jobs were secure. "The syndicates can relax," he said. "Your scams are safe." The prop laughed the loudest. It was a profitable paper with plenty of fat. The ads department carried all of them. "We know what happened to John Paul I," Nestor said. "No, but seriously, people, just carry on as before. We're a good team and it'll go on that way."

There were some small changes. *Up Periscope!* was increased to 1,000 w. "Thought you'd prefer that to an extra column a month. It'll seem like less work this way, and we're paying by the word now so same effect money-wise as two extra columns."

Boyet didn't know what to say. He didn't want to be effusive, he didn't want to be ungrateful. So he nodded and said nothing.

And, of course, neither the old Chavez nor the new one were saints. Despite his reassurances, Nestor terminated two columnists he'd always disliked – professionally, not personally – and he took the two youngest subs off the desk and turned them into reporters, garnering more stories and making the remaining subs work harder. All good management stuff – productivity the name of the game. He chose not to move into Cesar's room but placed himself unscreened in the centre of the room, the open-plan office, no defence against the innate factionalism of Filipinos. Then life went on.

It had become apparent to Boyet that Nestor Chavez was what you might call a coherent personality. He was consistent in his bile. He wasn't a different person depending on the company he was in. Despite the cynicism, the abrasiveness, he was a regular guy, but not a typical *pinoy*. The fact that he'd spent so much of his youth in Hawaii explained a lot. At least people said it did. In only one respect was there a fracture in this geologically hard and homogeneous personality – Nestor was a different person with his kids. You had to know him a while and have the opportunity before it struck you.

The barbed, ambiguous quality that was the most unsettling thing about Nestor to his fellow Filipinos – he would never have been caught napping as Boyet had by the Australian lesbian: he was already attuned to that mental wavelength – unravelled and simplified when he spoke to his daughters Myrlinda and Marilou. He was quiet and direct with them without Boyet's own tendency to dote on Jennilyn. Nestor spoke to the kids as if they were adults, a difficult thing. It wasn't in the vocabulary he employed, which was tailored to fit the less than fully developed, so much as in his range of expectation, which was both extensive and demanding. The kids, of course, took it for the norm. Maybe they thought their Poppa was the same at the office, which begged the question of what he was like with their mother Maribeth at home. Boyet remembered his uneasy telephone call to Chavez about the Init article. Nestor had reverted to his non-domestic manner quickly enough. Going out the school gates one afternoon Boyet had heard a tantalising fragment as Chavez passed with a brief nod of acknowledgment: "Then, maybe," Nestor had said to eleven-year-old Myrlinda, "sensible people will conclude that Mother Superior lacks the most important virtue of Christian charity." He'd never seen the Chavez girls at the Init skating rink. Probably they were at home in the brownout playing the Truth Game by candle-light or going thorough some other foreign psychological callisthenics. No, he mustn't backbite. He was just jealous of Nestor's success as a father. It was something worth admiring in a man. He remembered that line of Marlon Brando's from *The Godfather* (Part 2, *di ba*?): "A man who don't spend time with his family, in my book he's not a man." Amen.

LBC WAS how Mrs Init mentally referred to that time, her girly days. Not LBC, the message despatchers. Life Before the Congressman. When she was Victoria Humot, pretty Vic-Vic whom all the other girls hated and the boys were always chasing. Such a problem she'd been for the sisters of St Monica's. She smiled to think of it now. Sister Annunziata of the Five Wounds (was it?) taking her aside on her seventeenth birthday – August 7 1957, an era, a world away, might as well be 1857 – to tell her she was telling her for her own good, for her own sake purely, with no other motives, she was a girl with remarkable qualities, great natural or God-given endowments, and more in this vein while Vic-Vic listened with a polite attentiveness that nobody would think assumed. On went Sister Annunziata, no one was saying Victoria couldn't change, you weren't predestined to an end, no, by no means, unless you were, heaven forbid, a Calvinist and to the best of her knowledge there weren't any in Gobernador de Leon though she'd met one in Cork once, but you could leave things too late, great good could turn into great evil, all the more dangerous.

"What exactly are you trying to say, Sister Annunziata?"

Well! Well! Sister Annunziata's pink, downy face (so bland and broad-cheeked it reminded Vic-Vic of a backside) turned even pinker. She spoke in a flustered way – Vic-Vic couldn't understand why. She was the one being told off, if this was a telling-off. Strangest scolding she'd ever had. Sister Annunziata was telling her she was an ungrateful minx (grateful – what for grateful?). She was sure now she'd come to a bad end, Sister Annunziata said. All the wealth in the world, all the power the devil could give his lieutenants wouldn't help you.

Now Vic-Vic knew where she was. Sister Annunziata was where she wanted her, on firm ground. She knew how to deal with this. She'd learned, from precept and example, not just Papa's, that allusion to family standing, envy, still less disparage-ment were not to be tolerated. You sat on it, squashed the obser-vation or recalcitrance very firmly, very immediately. It was not a subject which admitted of articulation, still less debate. It wasn't just a teenage girl, then, who stood before Sister Annunziata so much as ex-Mayor Koyaw, that old feudal magnate himself, his father (Vic-Vic's great-grandfather) and his long dead minions. "I do not understand, Sister Annunziata. Were you the one to call Papa the devil's lieutenant? I will have to tell Papa. And ask Mother Superior for guidance."

Sister Annunziata opened her mouth, then shut it. Vic-Vic continued, "As for money, sister, I don't know about these things," (she lied, even then, with some facility) "my Papa never discusses it with us," – that was certainly true – "and I think that you should not be the one to discuss it either."

"It is easier," said Sister Annunziata breathlessly, "for a camel to pass through the eye of a needle than for a rich man to enter the gates of Heaven."

"It is also," said Vic-Vic, quoting the older brother of a senior girl but considerably startling Sister Annunziata who was not to know that, "quite difficult for the poor to pass through the gates of St Monica's. I am very confused, Sister. You were the one to confuse me. Now I must seek the illumination of my elders and betters." O, the beauty and economy of using an enemy's weapons against them!

Sister only just prevented herself from saying, "Wait!"

Even then Vic-Vic was as good as her word, not in the sense of the abrogated promises or, better, deferred fulfilments which already littered her path so much as in never making an empty threat. Mother Superior listened with what could easily be construed as respect but was what she considered no more than a fair hearing for a pupil whose progress was one to watch. Mother Superior was an adroit and experienced politician, a formidable proposition, so 17-year-old Vic-Vic just inclined her head meekly when she said, "Sister Annunziata has your best interests at heart, just as I do. As all your teachers do. For your part, it would be appropriate for you to be grateful for any guidance you could receive."

"Oh, Mother, this is why I have come to you. For guidance, *na lang*. I did not understand Sister so well."

"From what you have told me, my child, I also do not understand Sister so well. Maybe it can be that she will explain better to me personally."

"That is what I hoped, Mother. Thank you so very much."

"Perhaps your parents should be the ones to give you counsel. I mean, when you are perplexed as now."

"You are so good to me, Mother. I think I will not trouble Papa. You only have helped me so much already."

"That is good, child."

BOYET and Nestor had discovered a mutual predilection. Like all the best discoveries, it had necessarily taken some time. This wasn't something you broached early in an acquaintanceship like, say, a passion for golf, an interest in the fortunes of the Chicago Bulls, or a hankering after rare stamps. Nor was it something that became apparent – the sight of Jingkee Zamora with a tennis racquet, leaving work forty-five minutes early, showing off her nice legs in shorts. You didn't flaunt this too much. And to have encountered the other *in situ*, after the awful initial surprise, would not have opened the subject but imposed a permanent mutual censorship. The information had to be volunteered freely; that way there was something heroic about it. Otherwise it was just too embarrassing for words.

Three months before Nestor got the editorship (Boyet hoped he didn't regret it now – would he have come clean after the promotion?) he'd said over his third Super Dry at Erlinda's Eaterie, "I hear our friends at . . ." mentioning the rival rag's name, "are thinking of an article on vice in the city."

Boyet couldn't forebear grinning. Was there a wryer than usual twist to Nestor's complicit mirth? "Plenty of scope there," said Boyet.

"Uh-huh," said Chavez, "they're talking of eight to ten thousand girls involved."

"What?"

"That's what they're saying, I hear."

"In a population of under 300,000? It's not possible." Boyet stopped to work it out. "A female population of 150,000. Say, 100,000 nubile. Shit, are you telling me one in ten of the chicks in Gobernador de Leon is a prostie?" He found he was wearing the same broad grin as Chavez. " 'Sus Maria, what have I been missing?"

"Well, it's not just the ones officially registered with the municipal health department. I mean the ones in the bars, or the massage joints; you got to count the hunting girls and the semi-pros too. Then there's the student prostitution. I heard there was one girls' dorm where they were charging the boys a peso a peek."

"No, Nestor. That sounds like one of your alliterative head-lines."

"I'm not joking. That was the girls' game. They'd undress, pretend everything was normal, the boys would be hidden behind a hanging blanket, that way the girls would get to keep their self-respect."

"Sounds like hell for the boys."

"I don't know so much about it. Anything would get an 18-year-old cherry boy going."

"That's what I meant. The frustration."

"Well, you could always beat your meat afterwards on the strength of the memory."

"Sounds just like journalism."

"Actually, I always think a co-ed is overrated. Give me a barrio girl every time. She'll be clean, no disease. Smooth skin. Fresh responses – screw you like her boyfriend."

"A friend told me Momo's casa specialised in that kind of chick."

"Oh, you been there, too?"

"Who hasn't?"

Then and later Boyet was glad he didn't come out with something lame.

Nestor said, "Uy, who hasn't. Too true. Last time I was there it was, what, one thou the hospitality and the high jinks all."

"Hoy! You're paying too much! Foreigner prices! Seven fifty, seven fifty all in."

"Oh!" Nestor didn't look to put him down; the guy's basic competitiveness wasn't engaged. "Better you're my bodyguard next time. You're the one to conduct the negotiations."

"Well, it had better be soon if we don't want our faces in the rival."

"Shit, they won't be doing Momo's. Not unless they want to catch their own ed with his pants down. Old Wenceslao's been going there for years. Years."

"I never believe these stories anyway – you know, the ones ending our reporter left with an excuse at this point."

"Hey, our reporter came with an excuse."

THE two heroes sit in the diffused submarine twilight of Momo's sala, relaxing over the San Migs which on this occasion are prophylactic as well as refreshment. Alcohol, Nestor tells Boyet, in case he'd never happened to notice during the sixteen years of his legal majority, is a diuretic, makes you piss like a fire-engine. "Take in a litre of this half an hour before and you'll urinate so much directly afterwards you'll flush out all the bugs and microbes."

"Take in a litre of this and you won't be in a position to get infected by the bugs and microbes."

They guffaw, tipsy and still dizzy as well from the three o'clock sun outside. They were probably dehydrated even before the beers. The room is neat; furnished, decorated, and maintained to a standard well beyond what might be considered acceptable or necessary from the customer's point of view. Who hasn't come to admire the décor, after all. But that's typical of the pains of Momo who has the best stable of girls in town. The lacy curtains billowing in the air-con's icy spill, the richly beaded cushions with minute mirrors of glass sewn in, the kalachuchi flowers, contribute a feminine touch to this place of male needs. Momo, as all his customers know, is a queer. The TV, a 20" Sony

Trinitron, is on at low but audible volume. This is not the cute Danish teenies or hard-faced Texas Roses getting it in snatch and asshole simultaneously from vicious-looking bisexual white boys or huge-donged blacks (such as plays at less exclusive joints like the Pistol n' Holster) but merely the afternoon news. Momo's girls don't need help. Boyet and Chavez find themselves sharing the large room with a group of three Filipinos, attorneys, suspects Boyet. The news story shifts from the arrest of the capital's superintendent in charge of the anti-kidnapping squad (his arrest for heading a ring of kidnappers) to a hotel fire in Seoul. Tiny but still human figures perched on sills thirty, forty storeys up, horrible tongues of orange flame and filthy smoke solid enough to eat, reaching towards them. The first to stand it no longer jumps and plummets, the arms and legs waving; you can see the consideration and deliberate intent of the act, it was no accident. The men in Momo's sala murmur, shake their heads. The two groups, who have sedulously avoided looking at each other until now, catch a glance between themselves. "How terrible! The pity of it!" is the gist of their unspoken communication. The sentiment is perfectly genuine, not in the least affected, but they are also glad for the chance to say, "Look! We find ourselves in a house of prostitution, but we're not bad guys. We have feelings; we're the type who are kinder than others, we blades."

One of the girls, fussed in by Momo, a lot brighter than the others, a student of chemical engineering, one of the co-eds whom Nestor affects to scorn, notices, sums up the situation in a glance and thinks, "Anyway, they have bigger hearts than small girls, even if they're stupider." No one will choose her, by the way: too short, too dark. The other seventeen girls, each wearing a round red and white number badge ranging, Boyet notices (with what he thinks of as a journalist's eye) from 3 to 86 – is it policy not to make them even loosely consecutive, does Momo want to inflate the potential range of choice in his customers' minds? – line up in room centre with serious faces. In this casa the girls aren't allowed to giggle. The men look at them, not so much hungrily as sceptically. Boyet included, they're all old hands at this game. Chavez nods at the other guys – Boyet now damn sure they're partners in a private law practice, run out of secretaries to screw – to say: go ahead, you're the ones to take first pick. But, no, in the unspoken code and ritual of the player, they indicate their own polite determination to relinquish. OK, thanks, guys. Chavez points an inky forefinger at 37, a sultry hoyden with frizzed dark-brown hair, a snub nose, big mouth, long legs, and no butt worth speaking of. She's the only one in bare feet, scarred on the instep, undeniably cute feet but the toes widely splayed from a childhood without the restriction of shoes, the nails clipped short right to the quick but even so – is it imagination? – edged by a thin line of grime, the biography no manicurist can suppress. Yuks! thinks Boyet, he wasn't joking, he likes a village girl. The attorneys on their fortnightly spree make banal, uninspired choices, plumping for the whitest, longest-nosed, deepest-busted chicks they can get. Boyet selects 14, who has very likely been allocated the number because it's her age. There's about a year at the most between her and Jenilynn, but here resemblances end. This girl is dark, long-haired, skinny legged, where Ilynn has a pageboy and her ma's plumpness. She also has painted nails and when Boyet gets her into the cubicle she reveals a mentality of fourteen going on forty- four. Boyet says conversationally, "You're young," speaking in Tagalog as he usually does in the casa, the pretence being he's a Manila businessman on a trip but, perched on the edge of the bed, the towel wrapped round her torso though she's still wearing her T-shirt, she replies in English, "I am young, but my pussy very old."

As he listens to the patter of the shower Boyet wonders if he will be wasting seven hundred and fifty pesos. He likes some give, simulated or not, when he's using a girl; he doesn't like them hard. 14 returns, her long hair up. She sits on the bed edge, back to Boyet. When he puts his lips to her neck the nape is damp. As he pulls her back on to the bed, tugging at the towel knotted between her insignificant breasts, she requests "Off the light, sir."

"No," says Boyet, pulling the damp towel end to roll her towards him.

"Sir, I ashame."

She won't let him put his tongue in her mouth, the first of Momo's girls to resist this trespass. Instead she pushes him away, ducks down, and with her fragrant hair brushing his face, commences sucking his nipples with ardour. This is a move common to all the girls Boyet has ever used here; he reckons Momo has instructed them in this little dodge which has the advantage to them of being impersonal, hygienic, and, they would fondly imagine, original. However, it is also intensely pleasurable. Boyet arches his back. 14 moves down to the region of his navel, tongue flickering. "Give me sing along," he beseeches. "I like *um-um.*" She ignores this request, returning the way she came, rubbing her toes along his shins. Not put out – it's rare though not totally unknown to get a buckshee blow-job – Boyet flips her on to her stomach. The subdued globes of her junior Miss's butt prove firm as mini-basketballs when he pats them with something of his former guard's touch. They are darkly scarred with antique scratchmarks, the intolerable itches of the poor. Boyet parts the worlds with his thumbs, then rubs the head of his dick over her tiny black ass-hole, leaving a snail's trail. No objections from 14. He takes a deep breath, putting pressure on his dick with thumb and forefinger. It's not going in easy. 14 mumbles something into the pillow. To their mutual benefit, he'd like to rim her but he's heard on the customer grapevine that city health check them for all kinds of clap and hepa B but not hepa A. She says it again into the pillow. Now he hears it. "Coondoom."

"No," he says, splitting the sphincter at last and getting his full length up her in a hurry. Would you know it, she's a spelunker's dream inside, tiny opening acceding on to cavernous kingdoms. Not so perfect for screwing. Has her uncle been giving it to her there from age nine? No complaints from complaisant 14. Loose though she is, he's going to shoot all too quickly. He stops a second but she knows – a mind-reader or consummate professional – and touching his thighs with her rough soles, she puts her hand under her crotch, pretending to masturbate and levitating his eggs at the same time. As she quickly moves her buttocks against his groin, Boyet lifts himself, pins her down by the neck, like a snake in a forked stick, and comes, flatly.

He lies a while. She is in no hurry now – astute little chick. At length he withdraws. He sneezes – like his junior just has – and laughs. "Thank you, 'day," he says.

She smiles faintly, then wraps the towel round herself – the intrinsic modesty of the Filipina, hooker or nun – and goes to shower a second time. "For a while," she excuses herself. Listening to the patter of the water, he gives himself a once-over. Four folds in his stomach now – none at twenty, two at thirty. He'll be lucky to have a vertical view of junior at fifty, please God he live so long. Mixed with whatever, there's a trail of his slime on the edge of the bed. Incentive to join 14.

He towers over her, blocking the faucet. She begins to soap his back, not part of the regular service. Probably angling for an extra tip. Her hands feel so small. "OK," he says more sharply than he intended, "that's enough." Feels like Ilynn's hands. He takes care to wash the neck and the hollow of his jawbone just under the ear; scent, he has discovered, lingers there.

Drying in the bedroom, 14 asks, "How many the girls you use here? Many chicks?"

"Few," Boyet lies.

"Better same chick," she advises him.

"You'll be the one," he says. It can be a sweet experience with these girls; you'd think the money was secondary. He's left without paying more than once and never encountered remonstrance. Of course, he's shelled out heftily next time, making it more than worth the girl's while. Still, to get a Filipina to think of a term of maturity more extensive than the inconsiderable length of her own nose is no mean achievement. "The girls are looking to fall in love, too, you know," Boyet will tell an unsceptical Chavez. Unfortunately 14 whines, "I got big problems, sir. Making many credits this month. All paying now." Silently, Boyet counts out his money. He pays the bare minimum. He had been planning a decent if not spectacular tip. With dignity 14 says, "Thank you, sir." She stands on tiptoe to smooth down Boyet's collar, picks a long hair off his shoulder. She starts to brush her own hair with confident strokes. She's not hassling him to go. Boyet feels cheap and smaller. At the door they head in their separate directions. Many times Boyet has walked down this dim corridor as if he was on air, feeling proud and happy, as if he's accomplished something, happy to have made someone happy. Today, not so.

Nestor is waiting in the sala. "Hoy, animal, what took so long?" Boyet starts to feel better already – that's what male gregariousness can do. They take a cab from this suburb to Senhor Donut to have coffee and butternut munchkins before looking in on the paper's progress. Nestor treats. While they enjoy their relaxed conversation Boyet mentally re-writes the afternoon's history. It is now he makes his remark about the girls always hoping to fall in love with the next customer. "O-o," says Nestor, nodding reassuringly, "o-o," agreeing for smoothness and friendship's sake, not a sceptical hack or an ersatz Amerikano for the duration of this break.

"We must do it again," Boyet says as they rise. "Yeah," agrees Chavez. "It's more fun this way."

Chapter Seven

YOU DIDN'T VENTURE YOUR OWN CAPITAL – not under any circumstances. That was something Representative Init had imbibed along with mother's milk. To do so wasn't business, it was gambling, and gambling was better left to Chinese. That was their style – it was no strain for them; they actually enjoyed the risk. They hit the jackpot or wound up flat on their faces. Without the possibility of flat on their faces they wouldn't have savoured the reward so much. In their personal relationships it was compromise and moderation; with money, on the other hand, it was a ruthless all or nothing, devil take the hindmost. Other way round for the Congressman: timid in business, tough with people wholesale. He shed blood easier than he spent cash. What he looked for was not the entrepreneurial opportunity but the dead-sure set-up, a guaranteed killing whether stock-market flotation and privatisation or climbing on the back of an already profitable operation. So who was right and who was wrong? Well, sure as hell it wasn't the Congressman and his like getting kidnapped every day by scallawag police and military in Manila Chinatown. You could keep visible wealth so far as he was concerned, cash without kudos, without clout. Sure enough financial riches translated into political influence but not directly; there was a big idler wheel between the two, someone like the Congressman. You could be rich but still victimised, in need of a protector. Money was not always power but power always made you money. Init's theorem. The best ideas were always the simplest, the greatest truths the most self-evident. The Assemblyman was not frightened to appear simpler than other people. In that, he'd like to think, consisted his essential genius. Some really were smarter than others, but the truly smart didn't point that fact out.

These days, local debts of honour discharged in the electoral aftermath – and from earliest days it had been ingrained in him that the national political picture was essentially a mosaic of local power bases – the correct palms greased from his pork-barrel in the just proportion – the Congressman spent five days a week in Manila, coming home at the weekend. Victoria spent less and less time there. She didn't like the capital. Dirty, chaotic, and actually dangerous even for them. Also she liked to be Queen Bee, not just another metropolitan drone. They had their own house there, of course, with its permanent staff. That was in Forbes Park. She'd had to surrender a point. She'd have preferred Teacher's Village, less assuming but more tranquil, a touch of the artiness she wasn't averse to. But the Assemblyman had got his way. She was large-minded; she'd furnished the house for him with as much thought as she had invested in what she thought of as their "own home". Up North the Congressman busied himself on a joint Senate-Congress committee – the statesmanlike side of the job – and filed his applications on behalf of Gobernador de Leon.

Meanwhile he let his better half cover his back at home, sit on the eggs he wanted hatched, act as his request-receiver, advise on who should receive his allocation for public works. There was always the telephone. Long distance direct dial had recently come to Gobernador de Leon. You didn't go through the goddamned inane operators any more – "Long distance call for Mrs Victoria Init from Cherry Pie Humot. Will you take?" – with the attendant hassle and chance of the telephone company's employees listening in. Mrs Init had always been reluctant to accept in-coming calls; it was never entirely clear what their tariff basis was. A caller might sneak in a collect one, more likely the operator's scam was to charge *both* parties. A very uncomfortable feeling for Mrs Init; it was the principle, of course, not the cost. Now the Congressman was just at the other end of the line with no chance of billing errors.

Not long after, Mrs Init was the recipient of a poison-pen campaign – not victim, she never thought of herself as victim. The first one took her by surprise at the breakfast table, though she was still able to do justice to her longaniza sausage and two cups garlic rice. The writer informed her that Representative Init had acquired a new mistress in Manila. "New" was interesting; she wasn't aware he'd had one before. The writer thought she ought to know it because she deserved unhappiness of the extreme variety, the revelation was not to be construed as in the nature of a favour. The Assemblyman was tired of her tantrums and no longer interested in her withered looks. The author had broken into Tagalog for this sentence. The girl – whom he loved, far, far more than anything in the world, he'd told her so himself – would soon carry the baby she – meaning Mrs Init – had been unable to give him. Probably because of the venereal disease which had ravaged her insides.

Mrs Init burst out laughing. She wished the sender was there to hear her. At the very least she'd have liked to show the letter to the Congressman at the other end of the table, share the joke while it was fresh (and observe his impassive face for smallest signs of discomfiture).

Mrs Init re-read the letter, without a laugh break this time. She'd have been interested to know, had there been a conveniently placed mirror, she was frowning frighteningly. She reckoned 1) it was true, not like the filthy letters she got after Sister Annunziata was sent to a remote dispensary in the mountains; you wouldn't have thought a nun knew such words and 2) it was from the girl herself. First of all, the letter had been sent to the home address. Hardly anyone knew that; she must have purloined it from a letter in the Congressman's pocket, because Mrs Init didn't imagine Representative Init had been stupid enough to give it out to her. The phrases vented in Tagalog implied she was a Northerner, not a Visayan – nearly all Visayans knew Tagalog but nearly no Tagalogs knew Visayan. Unless she was double-clever – which Mrs Init took leave to doubt, one clever woman was quite enough for the Congressman to handle – and was a Visayan trying to hide her origins, she had reverted to her native language under pressure of high emotion. It figured. The stuff about loving her far, far more could only have come from the horse's mouth. Actually, it was desperate. She could imagine the Congressman selling the line. And the bit about the baby "soon"? Not already. Mrs Init Xeroxed the letter herself, not in the office but at a 30 centavos a sheet stall she knew of; then destroyed the original. Other than to be tricky for the sake of it, there was no particular purpose to this. She had no plans to take the issue up with her husband, unless it helped with something else. She wasn't at all mad with him. Not she.

MRS INIT fully endorsed the Congressman's ideas on capital-raising. She, too, was damned if she would contribute more than a token of her own funds to all but the surest-fire project.

So where could the money come from?

In general, she knew.

Hot money was the newspaper expression. You weren't supposed to use it in polite conversation – better to cuss and swear than to describe your partner's money as hot. A dirty word was also "launder". But that was the only backing you could realistically expect. Even a multi-national looking for a loss-leader was too much to hope for. There was no way big Philippine capital or developers like the Ayalas, the Sorianos could be duped into throwing their money into grandiose pipedreams like this. In a place that was already a success story, like long-ago Makati, or a city like fabled Cebu where the boom was still under way, they'd invest there on the strength of the name. The problem was to get the name in the first place. Well, when you went fishing you had bait. You dug up the worms and maggots. What Victoria was in need of were the requisite creepy-crawlies, and to do this you turned over stones and poked and pried into darkest corners. She could just hear the Congressman saying, "Don't fool around. We're the ones to go dynamite fishing!

Throw the bottle in. *Ba-woom*, but only underwater *na lang*! No one hears a thing on the surface. Float up all the dead fish already! That's collection time for the smart." He did have this aggravating habit of extreme literalism, which sometimes accidentally capped your own expression more aptly than the original. After thirty years of married life, looking into the dead-set of his professional mask, she was still uncertain whether he was cognisant of the inspired effect of his crassnesses, their occasional serendipitous wit and relevances. The Congressman had more or less no sense of humour, which in his circles was not a weakness but a strength. When speaking publicly, in perfectly grammatical English, but a heavy native accent and terrible slowness, without a flicker of participation from eyes in what was issuing from mouth, he really did resemble a voodoo doll. When he turned his head in that stiff way, such that you expected the movement to continue all round 360 degrees, his dead eye upon you, the similarity became overwhelming.

When Mrs Init thought about it, really it suited her not to have him around at the moment. It was much less effort to push the Congressman in the small of the back with his toes already curled over the precipice (that would be the equivalent of signing on the dotted line) than to drag him screaming and struggling one mile to the cliff (the bargaining) over a period of months. Also, there was an unfortunate lowest common denominator effect to negotiation between the Congressman and this type of potential client/sponsor/mark. How could she put it? (After all, she was talking about her own husband, a Philippine Assemblyman, to boot). They brought out the worst in one another, angler and worm. After the initial formulaic civilities, there was a distressing no holds barred aspect to things, civilities particularly formulaic on the Japanese side – the bowing and scraping meant sweet nothing at all. Ugliness confronted intransigence with appropriate results. After wrestling for advantage, no hold too foul, they proceeded to live down to each other's expectations. There were the karaoke bars where the Congressman had a small piece of the action. The Japs had learned it was better to cut him in – and more cost-effective in the long run – it put a cap on the bureaucratic obstructions and police shakedowns. With the guys who funded and ran those places it was face-to-face stuff. Mrs Init got most of it second-hand from Representative Init but she'd been in on one of the meetings: a very big Japanese – she didn't think they came in that size – wearing a loud floral polo. Her image of Japs was tiny men in suits, meticulously polite. But this guy barely hid his insolence. He had a permanent sneer on his wide, unshaven face. He was too wise to say it outright, but his manner proclaimed the thought – I can buy any Filipino. The Congressman was the one to make allowances, refusing to rise to provocations but still driving a hard deal. The Japanese kept his hands in his lap but when he reached for a document Mrs Init could see why. He was missing two fingers. 'Sus. She'd seen the films on TV – the guy was probably decked out with tattoos underneath louder than the design of his shirt. Communication on his side was mostly through grunts. But he certainly had the wherewithal. Gorilla was loaded, wasn't he. The attaché case had appeared; he'd sprung the catches without noticeable difficulty despite the digits missing on both hands (Mrs Init not quite quick enough to catch precisely how many he was missing – didn't they do it in front of the boss and other gang members as a public atonement?) and he'd raised the lid to reveal the sheafs of bank-notes. He hadn't had the case locked. It wasn't chained to him, he didn't seem particularly careful of it. Mrs Init could only assume the last thought in his tiny brain was that anyone would have the effrontery to mug him. Even then she thought the confidence misplaced. This is Philippines, dong, she thought; watch your back. She marked down the trait, as she marked down most things, unconsciously, instinctively. They made good cash cows (phrase heard from Representative Init), the karaokes. A karaoke was about the perfect haven for individual Yakuza money, what you might call non-institutional funds (Representative Init knowing from the mags what institutional money was but incapable of understanding its use in the context of a pleasantry). By

Jap standards, the sums involved were trifling – the dusty lot, the light building with its GI roof. It was surprising (though not to Mrs Init) how pleasant an unprepossessing exterior could be made inside. The furniture had to be little more than adequate – the deeper than usual cushioning giving an impression of comparative luxury; a little ingenuity with the lighting worked miracles with mood; some strategically placed mirrors (even a whole wall in one place) opened the joint out; and a fish tank stocked with the local cyanide-stunned exotic species could be spectacular. The Congressman's brother down south of the island did a nice line in this illegal trade. Only the sound systems were on the expensive side. But the Japs had to do *something* – other than providing cash – and this was where they came up trumps. The most fabulous laser-disc systems arrived straight from the land of the rising sun. The Congressman reckoned they had some way of getting them cheap – stolen, or slightly spoiled goods failing quality control, a clandestine lien on the manufacturers. Needless to say, they didn't pay Philippine duty. Don't make the Congressman laugh.

Stock the joint with local girls in smart uniforms to complement the fish, lissom, long-haired, college graduates all; bright, sweet ladies who could sing in Japanese and screw the customers afterwards Nippon-style, with plenty of fake appreciation. Pay the commission to the Jap tour-operators, and you were ready to go.

Mrs Init's lip curled when she thought of it. Not how she thought of herself at all. It was squalid. Not the music joints with their fabulous prices, a ladies drink coming like clockwork every fifteen minutes; she didn't mind standing up and singing *Matud nila* herself. It was the level of Jap which was the distasteful aspect. You knew a man – woman, for that matter – by their associates. At the moment she found herself being thrown bananas by a tribe of tattooed primates.

Mrs Init brooded about it. Bowling along in the Corolla, contemplating the perfection of the chauffeur's neck; flicking through the Assemblyman's periodicals in the sala; listening to the mayor's wife droning at one of the charitable committees they took turns in chairing; just standing under the shower, she attacked the position from every angle. At a certain point – she already knew – dirt was no longer black; it was transmogrified into something quite other. The disreputable became hallowed. It was a matter of size, proportionality. Daring and scale sanctified the enterprise. Someone with a misappropriated million was a thief; someone with ten billion was above the law. She remembered one of the Assemblyman's no doubt borrowed sayings: "If I owe you a hundred, I'm the one to have a problem. If I owe you a billion, you're the one with the problem." Too true. However, no one toted ten billion – ten billion anything, US bucks, Singapore or Hong Kong dollars, Swiss francs, even Philippine pesos – in a case. It was a different order of instrumentality. Even the Imeldific hadn't put that much on the flight from Clark to Hawaii. Even the Colombians put that kind of money into respectable institutions, where it ceased to be grubby or greasy – that smell of worn bank-notes, as of failed lives – and became something abstract, a kinetic potential.

The Congressman should not have been conversing with common criminals in the first place – would he even think of mixing with the equivalent native riff-raff – but dealing at his own level with his own kind.

What were his own kind? Statesmen, financiers; or at least, parliamentarians, bankers.

Mrs Init decided that if the mountain would not come to Mahomet, Mahomet would go to the mountain. She knew she was being naive, she was aware she was doing the undreamt of, or at least the unheard of. You approached through channels, begged for delegations. But she wasn't bound by protocol; she wasn't scared of rejection. Unlike the Congressman she had no dignity to lose.

Mrs Init was old enough to know herself; experience had displayed to her both her follies and her strengths. "I am impulsive," she'd admit, but she also regarded this as a virtue. It was particularly so in her marriage to a chronic dilly-dallier – ruthless when a course was set, but beforehand indecisive in the extreme. She now executed the big-time equivalent of a Corolla's screeching U-turn over a freeway verge. She bought herself a business-class ticket to Tokyo. Not for the next day, of course. She might be impetuous; she wasn't stupid. Some elementary preparations were required. You didn't jump into the bland bafflement of a Japanese city without at least some names and telephone numbers. She went to the police. Rather, she instructed the police to come to her. The Superintendent, who had also been in the Marcos-era Philippine Constabulary, barked out his "yes, mum's,", "no, mum's" and "no problem, mum's" in a way which didn't give Victoria great hopes for his intelligence or promotion prospects (the two not necessarily linked). Strictly a triggerman, he. The trawl of the city's hotel registers yielded no vacationing Dietmen. She hadn't supposed so either. The typical Jap holiday was only four days anyhow. She looked for someone who needed a favour, the bigger the better. But no Japs currently in clink in Gobernador de Leon. She extended her sweep, to Davao in the south (pomelos and assassins), to Zamboanga (grenades and Muslims), to Cebu (civic order and growth, an economic explosion – Ceboom!), to Iloilo (Miriam Defensor Santiago's place, how the Congressman hated her and her corruption crusade), Cagayan de Oro (trying to emulate Cebu). Nix. Only a handful of visa over-stayers and some Neanderthal idiotic enough to try to smuggle a hand-gun through customs. Exactly the circumstances she wished to shake off. Well, she'd have to make do with what came to hand. She had the pistol-packer (only it turned out to be a micro machine-gun) sprung from his hole.

And it was actually the people he mentioned who led her indirectly to where she wanted to get. In Japan she was to find out she'd been wrong all along! Sitting in her tiny hotel-room (smaller than the CR of the Gritti but half as much again in price) reflecting on her conversation with Hanabishi-san, she learned she'd applied a Castiliano's hieratic sense of caste and class to a pragmatic society that knew only a division of functions to a common end. She was stunned. It was *Planet of the Apes*. What she'd thought of as the troglodytes, tattooed troglodytes, were full members of the governing class. Heavens, they were running the country! The powerful, the respectable were scared witless of them! A trio of the primates in blue suits, sunglasses, and metalled white shoes picked her up in a large *American* car, then drove to a division of a financial institution so mighty that even she had heard of it before she took to perusing the Assemblyman's money comics. Their interpreter sat with the chauffeur and one of the gorillas in the front, a very informal and – Mrs Init used the word to herself in a complimentary way – *Westernised* young man with a head of permed hair who probably did scientific conferences as well as gorillas. The division of the institution was housed in premises a few streets away from the monstrous HQ, but was still larger than the Makati PNB. Superb polished marbles – maybe Romblon marbles which, Victoria reminded herself, were as good as Italian: she had first-hand experience of both – a huge abstract modern painting probably worth more than the marble, a system of waterfalls and cascades large as life which she was able to recognise as on the vulgar side to the occidental eye, and at the six-strong reception unit (divided into teams of two per visitor) a computer or electronic service system so spartan, so light-free and button-less, that its internal sophistication and complexity were probably such that it could defend an aircraft carrier. There was no security whatsoever, not a gun in sight. No bars, no grilles, not even bullet-proof glass. And at this Victoria marvelled the most.

She parked herself in the maroon tweed sofa the smiling girl indicated to her. It was of a comfort and quality commensurate with the surroundings. As she surveyed the hall, to stop herself from being intimidated Mrs Init reminded herself it was only a large-scale version of karaoke design. The gorillas seemed perfectly at home, to the extent of smoking. After a wait of two minutes a man came for them. Victoria knew the Congressman liked to manicure his nails, sink putts on the carpet while you paid him a tribute of your hours.

Mr Yamaguchi did not need the interpreter. For a senior officer of a great Japanese financial institution he spoke startlingly good English. At least it startled Victoria who, brought up on sagas of Nip insularity, had been informed that the higher you went the less English they were capable of, seniority in inverse proportion to this particular proficiency, while deep suspicion attached to anyone who had spent sufficient time abroad to acquire a good command. The stigma was not grasp of another language in itself but time spent abroad. It polluted, de-Nipponised. There was a special insulting word for this class of degraded Jap. How come the gorillas spoke zilch English? Mrs Init was at a loss for a moment before grasping it as the proof positive of her new theory of gorilla hegemony.

"Welcome, Madam, to Japan," Yamaguchi smiled. He shook hands, with the briefest suspicion of an inclination of the head, so minute there was no need to interpret it as a bow requiring reciprocation. Mrs Init, however, did interpret it as such. Yamaguchi then gave her ninety degrees of salute. Mrs Init, all her life, had been used to living in a man's world and to getting her own way in it. She'd learned and refined on her papa the techniques she'd applied to the Congressman and others in mature life. The insidious assumptions, overweening egregiousness, partisan selfishness, and generic exclusiveness of her own male countrymen were a submerged minefield to which she had long ago charted the solution and the institutionalised supremacy of the Japanese man was simply the same waters with the hazards more conspicuously marked. She thought she started here with an advantage over the Assemblyman and his like, and she intended to preserve it and to exploit it.

"Thank you so much, Yamaguchi-san, for receiving me at such short notice. I expected to see your subordinates first, not such a high officer of your house. I am very grateful."

"No, no, no," Yamaguchi said, fluttering his hand and tittering.

"I think I had better explain who I am." A long time ago Mrs Init had learned it was best to presume nothing. You started from the very beginning – it was actually quicker that way, with no need to go back and correct misapprehensions. She laboured under none of that false pride which afflicted Representative Init and his ilk. Why should she expect Mr Y to have the faintest notion of her own self-importance?

"It is really not necessary, good Madam. Of course I already know."

Victoria persisted, though. "Representative Apolinario Init, my husband, is a Congressman of Gobernador de Leon City in the central Philippines. I think you would call him a Dietman. At the time of the election he did not stand as a member of the President's party but he has already changed his affiliation."

"Ah, ah," breathed Yamaguchi-san.

"My country is a poor one," smiled Victoria, "but, sir, you must understand not all Filipinos are poor. There are people in our country who possess great wealth. The rich in our country are as rich as the richest American or German," – she decided not to say Japanese – "maybe some of them richer even."

"Ah, so," Yamaguchi actually enunciated, "like your late President Mr Marcos."

Mrs Init decided that this was an impertinence to which it was incumbent to respond if she was to acquire or retain the respect necessary for any potential transaction. "That is so," she said, shooting in the dark, "and I understand the late President accumulated and maintained a portion of that fortune with the assistance of Japanese banks and securities houses, including chiefly your own." Bull's eye. "Chiefly" was good – she congratulated herself on that: Mr Yamaguchi almost certainly didn't know whether it was true or not but couldn't admit to not knowing. He smiled more widely than ever. Mrs Init determined it an opportune moment to display him, as an evolved gorilla relative, the nape of her neck. "I must also tell you, Yamaguchi-san, in case you may have an anxiety on the subject, I have the confidence of my husband. In my country many people will prefer to approach my husband through me – that is how a favour will be requested. I understand the Japanese style of business, maybe it is not suitable to deal with a woman. I understand. But just feel confident that you are not already conducting with an intermediary. I am a principal. Any agreement I make would be binding on us."

Yamaguchi was no longer smiling; but he allowed himself to say, "Of course, you do not have to explain yourself Madam Init. It was Mrs Marcos who was the strong one also."

Mrs Init let that go. She now passed Yamaguchi the be-ribboned, bound, presentation of her proposal, professionally edited and corrected by the new editor of *Citizen* newspaper at no notice at all. Mr Yamaguchi took it with both hands, bowing over his desk.

Leaving, Mrs Init said, "Please allow me to congratulate you on your excellent English. Have you lived in America?"

Yamaguchi did grin now. "Very bad English. But I'm learning in Berlitz school here. One week total immersion course. Ask for food in Japanese – no food comes. Very cruel." He roared with laughter. Mrs Init wondered if he'd also learned that at Berlitz.

The gorillas remained expressionless during this final exchange as they had for the duration of the interview. The interpreter had not been running a simultaneous translation for them, so far as she could make out, although she had been speaking for effect, in slow and measured tones. Like an actress in a Japanese play, she thought.

Driving she wasn't sure where – there were no landmarks at all, each street looked exactly the same as the next – perhaps to another meeting, perhaps the hotel, something to be seen in retrospect as fortunate happened. The front seat ape jerked to attention with a burst of fast, low-pitched Japanese which, had Mrs Init not once been given to understand the language contained no swear words, she would have called curses. He was excited by the activity of five or six young men around a car which had stalled or broken down on a corner in the worst, that was to say most obstructive, spot conceivable. Simultaneously, all of them commanded the driver to stop. Without a word to

Victoria the entire trio got out. A moment later the car drove on. Mrs Init was unable to forebear looking back. The gorillas had gathered round the broken-down car.

The interpreter smiled at her.

"It's their friend broken down," she hazarded.

Again the interpreter smiled. Surprisingly shortly afterwards they came to the hotel. The interpreter jumped out and opened her door. She held her handbag in front of her. The interpreter hesitated. Tip? Surely not.

"I may accompany you a while, madam?"

"Of course." She walked with extreme slowness, as if it might hide a brain going in top gear. "You would care for coffee, no, tea, I think?"

"I can drink coffee, Mrs Init. Thank you."

In the coffee-shop she offered a snack to go with drink – all Filipina she, but to her relief he declined. She didn't press him twice. Those prices! You could have bought a first-class dinner in Gobernador de Leon for the cost of the two coffees. "You're working many times for these people, Mr . . . I don't know your name."

"Hanabishi is my name, Mrs Init. Just call me Bish, will you. The answer is no, the first time." He smiled his open Caucasian's smile again. "Maybe the last also?"

"I am sure they must be very satisfied with your work."

"I would not dare to give them reason to be dissatisfied, Mrs Init."

"It is not your fault Mr Yamaguchi happened to speak such good English."

"Oh, my work was not to translate for Mr Yamaguchi. I will report back on what I have heard and seen to someone else."

Mrs Init felt a fool for having been surprised. Hanabishi said, "Always a second opinion, you know, Mrs Init. Spying and spies are part of being Japanese."

Victoria realised she had just put three spoons of sugar into her coffee, instead of one. Perhaps it would be better just to concede control of the conversation. "Where have," she couldn't think of a word for the gorillas – guides, escorts, warders, body-guards, hosts – "our friends gone?"

"Ah, so. You did not understand what you encountered to see. Of course not. They went to deal with a competitor, an interloper in their market."

Mrs Init smiled encouragingly.

"The car put there so you could not get past without hitting it or the boys complaining you scratched it? It is, mmm, an unofficial tax post."

Mrs Init understood immediately. But: "Can't you just drive away? I mean escape?"

"They have your number. They will visit your house."

"They will know?"

Hanabishi said, "They will look on the police computer. Of course, they are great friends with the police."

There was a silence. Mrs Init said, "Mr Hanabishi, please be candid. I am working on a big project. What you say to me is confidential. Am I wasting my time with the people I am seeing?"

"I want to help you, Madam. But, to be honest, I do not know. Decisions are made by them."

"No, Hanabishi san, I mean do they have the connections, do they have the ear of the people who matter?"

"Ah, ah. Yes, very much so. I promise you. This is not because they are paying me."

"And Mr Yamaguchi? His company's decision?"

"Mrs Init, our friends own maybe a quarter of the stock of the company. And of nearly all the other securities traders and banks. Outstanding to themselves in loans on favourable terms will be a large portion of the, mmm, questing, no, venture capital the institution is managing. It would be a small exaggeration to say they own half Japan."

Mrs Init had the pleasure of a gratification afforded few: that of seeing an eccentric personal hunch validated by an insider. There was a silence as she took a sip of coffee, and pondered. Hanabishi was unabashed by silence – like words part of his job

– and he allowed her the interlude. She said, "These Yakuza, there aren't attempts to control them. I mean by your military and your politicians? The difference is our senators and congressmen want to keep the power for themselves."

"No, madam. We have no military influence – it's in the constitution."

"Of course, how ignorant I am to forget that, Hanabishi san."

" . . . as for Dietmen – they have a problem. It's not just the money our friends pay the LDP factions. Who can a Dietman choose for a bodyguard? Yakuza, of course. Very difficult for them. Very difficult."

Arriving by Mrs Init's elbow with assassin's stealth, a waitress poured her a second cup of coffee, so solicitously, with such matter of factness and lack of inquiry that Victoria imagined it must be free. What had it been in the San Francisco Best Western, the "bottomless cup"? In any case she lacked the resilience just at the moment to be bothered to refuse. She wondered if Representative Init had known the score all along; actually, maybe not. It wasn't in his magazines, not even hinted at between the lines. The lobby muzak died suddenly. As a group of swarthy, moustached Latins swaggered through the swing doors, it was replaced by a scratchy, jaunty, unmistakably national anthem of what she had once overheard an Australian diplomat call the all cock and no balls Italian or Philippine variety. The Spanish colonial inheritance: certainly all form and no content, the rolling phrases, the elegant script of the will but only blind moths in the iron coffer. Mrs Init thought she was probably hearing the song of the Medellin cartel. She was jarred by another reflection; standing outside her immediate situation, even momentarily, had made it possible.

"Why are you doing this?" The words jumped out of her mouth, without a palliative Hanabishi san.

"Doing what, Madam?"

"Why are you helping me, Hanabishi san?"

"Please call me Bish. I am helping you because I need your

help."

All made clear. Mrs Init's suspicions vanished as quickly as they had arisen. "Sure. Just ask." That was her standard reply. If her answer to the request was going to be "yes" anyway, the graciousness delighted even further. If "no", they wouldn't be much more disappointed in any case and the initial openness made the refused favour look an impossible grant. She was used to making the Congressman the scapegoat anyhow.

"Your husband is a powerful man. And you," Hanabishi added, "are a powerful lady. I think it is not too much to ask. The favour is not for me but my sister's husband. My brother-in-law encountered to have a Philippine wife. As usual, the marriage was not successful. But there was a child. My brother-in-law supported this child but the mother abused her privilege. She took up with a Filipino, spent her allowance on shabu and the man. Now my brother-in-law wants his son but cannot get him. Maybe you can help him."

Mrs Init was surprised and pleased with the simplicity of the request, the banality of the situation, but she hid this. "Mmm." Perplexity replaced openness on her face. "It's not so easy. A mother always wants to keep her children . . ."

"I am sure another woman could be all the more persuasive."

"I will not be the one to see her," Mrs Init said with a touch of sharpness. "He met her in a karaoke? I hope she is not a bargirl."

"Does it make a difference?"

"Maybe. OK – I will see what I can do. Give me the name, if it was her real name; they use assumed names in the karaoke, did you know? Oh, and also her home place."

Hanabishi pulled out his wallet. "This is my card. I will write the information on the back."

"Thank you, Hanabishi san. Oh, your name is Harold Hanabishi?"

Hanabishi laughed. "I spent six years in Britain, my father's posting. Six years in Wales to be precise. I am a graduate of

Aberystwyth, if you ever encountered to hear of it."

"I think so."

Mr Hanabishi smiled once more. Mrs Init saw his training had been as a marine biologist and, on the flip side, that Liliosa Morales lived at Km 19, Cotabato Road, Tacloban City. Hanabishi rose. "Anything I can ever do for you, Mrs Init, let me know. It's better I leave now."

"For a while, Mr Hanabishi." It was Victoria's turn to fumble in her bag. "*My* card." He clicked his heels and bowed.

The chit came for her signature. She saw she had been charged exactly the same price for the second cup of coffee as the first. A five star hotel run on the same principles as a clip 'em quick karaoke. No, the whole country.

WELL, she waited, and she waited. This was back home in Gobernador de Leon, in the relative comfort of her own sala where, of course, she could drink as many cups of tea or chocolate as she desired without getting mugged on the way to the cashier. She knew very, very much better than to write to Yamaguchi san, however long the wait. Three months, six months, a year and a half, or the 32nd of never – still you didn't jog them. It was, in fact, sixteen weeks later, nine and a half if you discounted the six weeks logjammed in the Christmas post up in Manila. Someone indecipherable, not Yamaguchi, informed Congresswoman Init that her plan had been carefully considered by a committee. It was an interesting proposal, which would require further careful consideration, and it would go before another department before being submitted to a funding committee. The final paragraph added that Yamaguchi san had been transferred to another department in Yokohama. There existed, Mrs Init reflected without excessive bitterness, three or four ways of saying "yes" while meaning "no" in Pilipino/Spanish but one hundred and three in Japanese/Japlish. She was not one to waste time on regret or energy in vain endeavour. Without conceding defeat – for she flattered herself she was not known to be a quitter – she put the idea on hold in a frontal compartment of the brain, ready to be reactivated on the smallest cue.

This was more like standing next to the peal of the cathedral bells while firecrackers exploded. The danger was not so much of missing the opportunity as of being deafened. The interval between hearing from Japan and the arrival of the Formosan delegation was less than three months. Was there a connection? Not the kind of question you could really put. It breached etiquette; it was rude. Also it put you at a tactical disadvantage, having been rejected by the Japs. The timing could, of course, just be co-incidental. But this was about the right time for news to reach the right people, decisions to be made, and proposals concocted. She reckoned it was Jap and Chinese double-bluff, part of their elaborate business poker, but she could never be really sure.

The cards of a Mr Mao Sung and a Miss Miranda Lai arrived via the wife of the mayor, from the honourable lady's own charities office in city hall – Victoria on passably cordial terms with her, despite the Congressman having a distinctly cool relationship with the mayor's older brother, the Provincial Governor. The visitors had asked at city hall to be put in touch with Representative Init, not knowing (naturally) his address. Victoria decided she'd remind him – nicely, of course – that they'd come to his own backyard, not via Manila.

What they wanted was a one-sided rout; they wanted to scalp the poor Filipino, the poor Inits. It was a good thing the Congressman wasn't around. He'd have blown his top. A ten year tax holiday – not within the Init purlieu. The Philippine developer to deposit a sum equivalent to thirty per cent of the foreign investment in an escrow account abroad, in case of the future non-possibility under Philippine law of repatriation of profits or original capital, the interest on the principal (how generous) to be enjoyed in the meantime by the Philippine guarantors. She had never, never heard of that one before. A provision whereby it was not possible for the developer to ask the sponsor for more funds to bridge a short-fall, but was contractually obliged to meet the liability himself. An option to develop other projects on the same terms. Finally a lot to be released by the local developer from its land bank at 25 per cent of its open market value.

"Would you," the Congressman had lyingly told Victoria he was in the habit of rebuffing Amerikanos – she didn't believe him capable of this level of open confrontational vulgarity, of assassination, yes, "like to screw my wife as well as myself?"

Mrs Init looked at the three flinty Chinese faces before her, hoping she hid her dismay, and forced herself to smile. It demanded some effort of will. If she only knew it, she succeeded admirably. What she did not want was a deterioration of the general climate of negotiation to Assemblyman-Yaki level. She wanted to preserve her style, show her class.

"These terms are very onerous," she said, putting it the mildest way she could. Not a flicker. Sometimes – she knew it was demeaning especially as her maternal grandfather had been one – she could succumb to the ordinary strain of anti-Chinese prejudice. There was no give in them, the home ones domiciled here generations, let alone the undilute vintage before her now. Cane vinegar in their souls, sour fermentation of the spirit.

"Honourous because we respecting," said the younger man of the trio. Mrs Init had taken an instant dislike to Lam, Ricky: his flashy watch, glittering 18K Singapore gold medallion and chain (vulgar on a man even the sober but more precious 22K Chinese gold), his half-open polo, his sharp guttersnipe's face. You can't hide your origins, she thought, and new Chinese money was a particularly brazen coinage.

She said, "What I meant is it is hard, you are *strikto*, we say here."

They let a silence descend, which Victoria exercised all her considerable mettle not to break first, this being peculiarly uncomfortable for someone of her upbringing. Finally, Mao (surname or first name? they reversed this at will it seemed) the older man said, "These are not make-or-break clauses.

Everything can be subject to negotiation. But we give you an idea of what we expect from you."

"In that case I may feel free to tell you clause two and the final clause are unacceptable to our side. The others maybe we could meet you half-way though we still consider it severe on us." Again no response. She was starting to think of them as the three wise monkeys. Of the simians, the full-blown apes were in retrospect much easier to deal with, there existing a more or less complete pattern of approach posture, controlled aggressive display, and appeasement behaviour, even if all purely formulaic. Here, heaven knew what. She was now seriously regretting the tour of the city she'd arranged in the mayoress's luxury coaster (the Honourables having to be cut in on any action in town, the Congressman and she somewhat exceeding themselves but the result would justify everything). 'Sus Maria – two hours of batting a ball against a stone wall!

The woman, whom Victoria could acknowledge without chagrin as a beauty, said in a cut-glass English accent, "There is not much room for bargaining. We are the ones with choice – capital is mobile. Labour and the site are not. There are many cities in the Philippines hungry for investment. With respect, you must take it or leave it."

Bastos! Despite the fact that she still couldn't believe her ears – you should be ashamed to talk like that to anyone, let alone the wife of a Congressman on home base – Mrs Init's eyes flashed. Neither her age nor her position had protected her from this girl's naked assertiveness.

Mao, the oldest, said, "Let us not be hasty, please. It is in all our interests to co-operate with each other."

Mrs Init said, "It is good to talk frankly. Then we all know where we are standing. I would say it is better to treat your Philippine partner – wherever you find him, here or you are free to choose elsewhere – as a partner and not a servant. That way you have more interests in common – your partner will defend you because he is defending himself."

"Your law say foreigner can only own property through

Filipino," Lam contributed; he grinned inanely. What was this? Victoria wondered. A display of resentment against the discriminatory investment laws? She hadn't drafted it. Another proposal? Or showing he wasn't as stupid as he looked? She smiled brightly. "So you know our country quite well already, Mr Lam. Actually there is a new law pending for fifty year leases, extendible."

"First time here."

Mrs Init had decided she would be right more often if she disbelieved everything Lam said. He was probably a regular visitor. "In that case I would be so happy to show you some of our country and particularly our beautiful city. We have transportation arranged . . ."

"Seeing police chief now."

If the woman, Lai's, abrasive speech had come as an unpleasant surprise this resembled a slap in the face. Lam had that, not so, foolish grin on again. Even Mao couldn't stop himself smiling faintly. Mrs Init fought not to show her anger or her unease but succeeded only in the latter. "Well, of course, you are quite free to do that, but you may be wasting the short time you have here. He is responsible for law and order but not economic development."

"Important man," said Lam with the implication that she was none of those two things.

"Maybe," said Mao, "he is in the position to help us with some import business."

For a moment Mrs Init thought he'd mispronounced "important business". "A policeman?"

"We are the agents for some people in pharmaceuticals. They could always use friends in the law."

"I don't understand. But I'm sure Representative Init could help you better."

"Also," said Mao. "We shall talk to him as well. But it is a separate matter."

She called for tea; she poured for all of them; knew that much about Chinese etiquette.

Another appointment was scheduled for the day after next, Victoria needing time to regroup. She resisted the temptation to hot-line the Congressman in Manila. That was her equivalent of having a cigarette; it might soothe your nerves temporarily, but there was a longer term price to pay.

It wasn't, as it turned out, necessary. The Taiwanese left town the next evening, heading (she discovered from the police chief) to Cebu for two nights before taking the Cathay flight to Hong Kong. After that, God knew where, for there her power ended. A strong grasp but a short reach. Interesting point: the police chief said the older man knew Mandarin (Tagalog the equivalent) while the others spoke Cantonese (or the equivalent of Visayan) among themselves.

Back to touch homebase, the Congressman also had something interesting to say next week. His bun of a face displayed unusual animation when he heard of the visitors. His wife had tended to disparage them but then he became quite vehement. "No money? Hah? You must be joking –" Mrs Init resented this: joking was a bad word in the Congressman's lexicon – "they're overtaking the Japanese if they haven't done it already." He had a nugget of wisdom. "You know who have the most bucks, the biggest dollar reserves in the world?" Mrs Init thought about it. Although it was clearly a rhetorical question which Representative Init would relish answering, it was quite interesting in itself. Plainly, it was a trick question, so it wasn't the Americans themselves in Fort Knox (that was bars of physical gold?). "The Taiwanese?" she hazarded. Representative Init's face fell. "How did you know that?" he asked crossly.

"Just only guessing, my darling," she said. He had this ability to be blind to a context; sometimes it was a strength.

"They are making one in ten of every computer sold in the world, one in ten! Did you know it?"

She shook her head, militant disengagement from the disturbing prospect of besting her man. The Congressman looked better pleased with himself. She didn't want him making disadvantageous comparisons with the effortless superiority of his life in Manila, its domestic non-jaggedness. "You can't keep a good Chinese down," he said. "That's just one island. Can you imagine if the whole of China goes that way? Watch out, America!"

Victoria murmured her surprise and pleasure at the information coming her way. She somehow doubted if her Formosans had been in computers.

"You already took their address?"

Victoria shook her head. Representative Init just restrained himself from saying something angry; he knew he'd get paid back later, find himself figuratively bleeding before he even knew he was wounded.

"There's no address, Congressman. Just a letter box in Taipei. I didn't press them. But if they're as rich as you say they are, we should have no worries."

"I did not say these particular people. Just the Taiwan economy in general."

"Then we don't need to concern ourselves too much about them."

This, the Congressman thought gloomily, was what they called feminine logic. His wife really was wired up a different way. He moved on to what he'd been able to do for his constituents in the metropolis, allowing himself to brag a little. If you couldn't boast to your Mrs who could you boast to? He'd managed to get an allocation out of disaster funds, following some flooding in Gobernador de Leon. Not exactly a king's ransom – to be accurate about the size paid by well-to-do Chinese families for the release of a kidnapped daughter to (if you believed the rumours and the Congressman was shrewd enough to do so) the very police and army generals who were meant to protect them but found the need to supplement their salaries in this way. The Congressman had visions of mini-ambulances running round the town, prominently legended *Thanks to the contribution of Representative Apolinario Init.* This from the pork barrel, the Countrywide Development Fund. Actually, what was needed was not more vehicles on the road but the filling in of the holes in the "road improvements" the Congressman had taken a hand in starting prior to the election and abandoned half-completed the day after the polls closed. Someone had already broken a leg. But if you thought it out, a peeling sign stuck in one place would not be seen by nearly as many people as a brand-new vehicle blaring its siren up the boulevards. No need to carry patients even. Victoria told him it was a simply wonderful notion, which he must accomplish at the earliest opportunity.

"Perhaps you could be the one?" he suggested – give his Mrs a participant role, keep her happy, while he controlled the expenditure, specified the make and equipage of the vehicles: loud sirens, strong lights, nothing too pricey inside. She smiled very brightly. "That is kind of you, Apolinario."

He was Manila-bound at the time the Taiwanese got back to her. There'd been no delays (PAL – Planes Always Late), so she conceived of him masticating his pork bun and slurping the guyabano juice out of its box somewhere above Romblon islands, Romblon source of fine marble for Japanese banks. She walked on air herself for some time afterwards. Finding the money was OK no problem from the point of view of her partners. However, they'd already costed the building project and would not pay a centavo more. They would also have their own quantity surveyor on site. In short, they were unwilling to have their pockets picked by the Congressman and his cronies, subcontinental politicians being the finest short-change artists in the world but some Filipinos no slouches either. Mrs Init's part was to get the investment up and working. Not the day to day running of the place – the Taiwanese would negotiate a management contract with an established Hong Kong group – but pulling to it the influential, the rich, the glamorous. "Just leave that to me," Mrs Init thought. Sharon, Richard, Robin, maybe even little Lea – she'd do her damnedest to get them down for the opening. Maybe not at the same time – hadn't they supported rival politicians or were each other's ex's, or what already? She'd ask her niece Cherry Pie. A fashion-show – for charity, of course, with the local elite in attendance, some foreign models (maybe she could pay pin-money to a few of the less dowdy tourists). Then it also needed a touch of, what was the word, gravity, Roman gravity. Serious but contemporary, an intellectual fashion-show, eclectic consensus, electric discussion. The media loved that kind of thing. As she directed the polishing of the antiques in the sala, she could barely contain herself. It was like being a schoolgirl again but this time knowing in advance you were going to be the one to win the junior piano competition. A touch of class, that was going to be her contribution to what would otherwise – she suspected – be a spectacle of unbridled venality. She'd be the one to ice the cake, the heroic confectioner.

Chapter Eight

A GET-TOGETHER, A WEEKEND OF FAMILY SOLIDARITY – those were the words Nestor Chavez had used to Boyet without ironic implication contained therein. "Oh," said Boyet, registering polite interest, surprise, approval, none of them feigned. It became clear Nestor had been planning for some time. The excursion would take the form of a night and two days by the sea for selected members of *Citizen*: those important enough to qualify for Nestor's consideration but not so functional their absence would impede the production of the Sunday issue. As personal friend – he flattered himself – and mere columnist Boyet qualified on both counts. Also going were Jingkee Zamora, as representative of the subs desk, and her daughter; the assistant editor Sherwin de Leon (shrewd stroke on Nestor's part: nice for Sherwin and also serving to show the rag could appear without him); Jimmy Boyar, another columnist; a junior female reporter, Cathy – Boyet had forgotten her last name; and some people from the production and advertising side of things. Nestor had chartered a jeepney at a startlingly low rate to take them the 30 km north and back. He'd also negotiated a massive discount with the owner of the beach cottages they were to stay at; the accommodation was going to work out dirt cheap. They'd also bring their own soft drinks and beer, depriving the owner of revenue on this head as well, besides BBQ-ing for themselves. "What did you do?" Boyet asked, "promise him a full-page spread?" Nestor pretended to look surprised. "Oh, how did you guess it? I said you'd be the one to write that." "Over my dead body." "Maybe."

They boarded their transport outside Senhor Donut, everybody vivacious and chattering ten to the dozen, despite the fact it was five a.m. only. Boyet had never seen any of the staffers' kids before, except of course Nestor's Myrlinda. They were all dressed in the ragamuffin finery that was the best occasion uniform of the young, its comfortable sloppiness belying the expense to which the parent had been put. In general, the kids were wearing stuff more appropriate for a birthday party or Christening than running round a couple of days on the sand. Boyet feared his kids in their rubber slippers and old shorts were bringing down the collective tone. He said as much to Miriam, who laughed, but Jenilynn didn't look too happy herself.

During the trip she made friends with young Charina Zamora, Jingkee's daughter – the strangeness of kids and parents. He'd never said more than a few casual words to Jingkee, yet here their daughters were, bosom buddies by the time of the first comfort stop. On the other hand Jennilynn had no interest in Nestor, Boyet's pal's, daughter. Charina and Ilynn wandered past the sari sari store, munching their rice bibingkas out of the banana leaves, giggling about Sherwin de Leon's sixteen-year-old son, Darwin, who had inherited his father's appalling complexion and mother's scrawniness, rather than Pa's decent height and ma's skin. Darwin stayed in the jeep to tinker with his CO_2 pellet pistol. He was apparently a proficient massacrer of rats. "Reminds me of me," said Sherwin indulgently. Boyet expressed polite interest in the toy, which to his surprise had a satisfyingly heavy feel, like a real gun. The girls walked slowly back to the vehicle, all the time in the world before them.

It was surprising how quickly you could leave town behind. Within forty-five minutes the outlying crowded suburbs were but a memory, the houses lining the road thinning from an unbroken line to clusters and then twos, threes, and ones. Now it was papaya trees, banana palms; then coconut groves as they followed the line of the sea. From Nestor's behaviour it had become obvious the junket was a total freebie. He'd loaded in the Eskimo containing their meats and veg, paid the few pesos for the rice cakes and cokes at the stop. The odd bus overtook them but this route was not heavily trafficked, thanks to the highway constructed in the Marcos era. In under two hours they were pulling up at the Lasang Beach cottages where the warmth of the owner's welcome bore no relation to the minuscule profit he stood to make out of their presence. They prepared to eat at once, Jingkee getting the coals going within minutes of arrival. Soon, the barren, unpopulated, boring strand with only the dismal sound of the breeze in the fronds and not a soul in sight was full of their conviviality, the odour of roasting meat, the cassette player going at full volume and Sherwin de Leon – recovered from a slight giddy spell on getting out of the jeep – strumming his guitar. Miraculous change! Uninhibited *pinoy* joy! Jingkee had whipped together a marinade of calamansis, chili, soy, and palm toddy vinegar and was now skewering more dripping strips of pork. Nestor followed Boyet's gaze. "That's quite a girl," he said. Boyet nodded, participating in the banality. Jingkee wasn't exactly pretty, but for a woman of thirty-five she still had a nice body. Boyet looked appreciatively at her slim legs. "No, I mean really," Nestor said. "You know she used to give writing workshops to rebels?"

Boyet was startled. "*Jingkee?*"

"The same you see. She'd go up to the mountains with ballpoints and paper. And there was a safehouse in Bacolod City. She's a Negrense, you know. I remember she said staying in the town was more dangerous than the mountains."

"I can see how that would be." Boyet looked at her; still the same old Jingkee. To him she'd never been more than a tennis-player, if a good one. Charina, Myrlinda, and his own Jennilynn were assisting with the BBQ, while their mothers turned the sticks. Now they brought full plates for their papas.

"Thank you, 'day."

"You're welcome, pa."

After "lunch" – it had been about an hour early at half past ten a.m. – they took what Sherwin de Leon referred to as "advance siesta". Under the influence of sea air and fatigue this seemed much funnier than it might actually have been in, say, the environment of the office. Boyet was still chuckling as he stood in his briefs by the low bed with its darned but clean linen. Miriam had surprisingly allowed Jennilynn to stay outside with young Darwin and Charina. It became apparent why when she put her hand on his waist as they lay on their backs looking up into the high roof. The strangeness of the environment, the simple rustic appointments, the crude but snowy bed, the breeze, God knew, maybe the fresh bloody meat and the spectacle of her own daughter's latent sexuality had combined to awaken Miriam's modest appetite. Jesus Maria. Boyet loyally overcame his spasm of irritation. It was about the last thing he felt like. "I will be the one," he said, removing her hand from the elastic waistband, shucking the briefs over his knees and ankles. He rubbed his dick over her vulva, sure way of getting it hard and then maintained his precarious interest by thinking first of Jingkee Zamora's painted toe-nails and when these lost allure – God forgive him – by picturing young Darwin screwing Charina. At length he climaxed. This was in itself sufficient gratification for Miriam, who rarely did. She put her head on his chest as they rested without speaking. Miriam knew men needed the act, desperate creatures that they were; they were as desirous as a thirsty child. And about as grateful! she thought, listening to Boyet's snores.

Waking alone two and a half hours later and going outside with faint disappointment, as of having missed out on irreplaceable times, Boyet found all the females in the sea. Fully clothed, down to his town shoes, Jimmy Boyar was sitting on a rock reading with utter absorption a paperback on the Silva method of mind control. I need to borrow that, Boyet thought. Boyar was a familiar figure to him, as doubtless he was to Boyar, though they had never met before. He knew the mugshot above the column, of course, and their mutual bi-weekly ruminations afforded particular insights into the other. No one read the columnists more closely than the other columnists. You could get a reference point on your opinions, what was the fancy Eng Lit word – an objective correlative. Or was that the wrong meaning? Basically they were all working on the same raw material, the identical core of events and facts; they knew the distortions, the exaggeration of some aspects, the suppression of others, which had been necessary to the shaping of the piece and therefore the true opinion of their rivals was more apparent to them. Boyar, for instance, had a bark worse than his bite. He had a rep for outspokenness among the readership which was entirely undeserved. His accusations were never quite specific enough to sting, to bring real wrath on his head from the mighty of the township, although his language tended to the unbridledly extravagant. "Kamikaze" Kelvin Fugoso, the columnist who'd taken on the chief of police, didn't toss insults and denunciations around but he named names and gave times and places and amounts. Boyar operated a big machine-gun, spewing impressive smoke and flame but those in the trade knew it was blank ammunition, whereas Kamikaze Kelvin, much like a Sparrow assassin, crept up behind you to point-blank range with his ancient single-action revolver and let you have it in the head. Or – Boyet thought of his utterly favourite author from sophomore days until now, Ernest Hemingway – one was a bullfighter working at a safe distance, all flashy capework and deceptions, the other a torero of clean lines standing right up to the razor-horned bull of truth. He'd like to see a bull-fight one day.

Boyar closed his book, with a charming smile.

"Don't let me disturb you, er, Jimmy."

"Ha, ha, no. I can read any time, but not meet the famous Boyet. You're not going to risk bathing?"

"Perhaps later, Jimmy."

"Maybe we can get a thrashing from Jingkee on the tennis court."

"Uy! I'll get my bathing briefs."

Charina and Jenilynn arrived with a large blue starfish. They'd dumped Nestor's Myrlinda, Boyet was sorry but not surprised to see. Even six months closer might have been OK; it made all the difference at that age. "Uncle Boyet, Jennilynn says we can eat this."

"She does? Let it be her dinner then."

"Pa, what do starfish eat?"

"Shellfish. Scallops are their favourite."

Boyet looked at Boyar in surprise.

Boyar continued, "They use their arms to open the shell-fish."

"Pa, can they grow new arms?"

Even Boyet knew the answer to that one. "Very easily, 'day."

"Uncle Boyet, do they reproduce sexually?"

Boyet saw Boyar's grin as as he turned his face to look out to sea. Sure as hell he wasn't going to pop up with the answer to that one, know-all columnist. "I am not sure, Charina. Maybe your mother could be the one to answer that."

"Oh, pa," said Jennilynn scornfully, if Philippine daughters, imbued from birth with *ulaw*, could ever be said to speak scornfully to their papas, "starfish reproduce assexually. Everyone in Grade 2 knows that already."

The look Boyar exchanged with Boyet was one of twinned helplessness. Times moved on. Boyet just about kept his face straight. It was *nuns* teaching this to twelve-year-olds?

"Will it live, pa, if we put it back?" Loyal Jennilynn re-bolstering the old man's authority.

"I am sure it will. It's, er, wrong to . . . to destroy God's creatures without, er, just cause. Hah? Just put it back where you already found it."

The pair waded back out through the hot shallows, the weed tugging and slithering through their toes. The moon was nearly full and the tide was in huge recession – they'd learned that as well in school.

Boyet accepted Boyar's offer of a cigarette – he didn't know a columnist who wasn't a smoker. They could see what seemed like way out but was probably nearly five hundred metres – a small land distance – two black dots of heads, in all likelihood Jingkee and press-ganged companion, Boyet trusted not

Miriam. "Maybe we will take a dip tomorrow, Jimmy?"

"Maybe you. I'll be returning tonight."

"Already? We only just arrived. You're bored so quickly?"

"Ah, ha, ha!" Boyar had a laugh that got falser the longer you knew him. He was not, definitely not, a regular guy in Boyet's book. You could never, for instance, go to the casa and trust him not to split on you. Probably in his goddamned column. As if reading minds also lay within his power, Boyar said, "Perhaps I'll jump the gun and get a column in about a day at the beach. Beat the boys to it, ha, ha. No, but seriously, Boyet, it's the birthday of my Mrs. She will kill me if I'm not there."

"You should have brought her."

"Unfortunately this is not the kind of thing which Mrs Boyar likes." Boyar did not appear to use the expression "Mrs Boyar" ironically. I should make allowances, Boyet thought, maybe it's not just me in particular. Maybe he talks to everyone like they're his domestic help. "That's a pity, I would very much have liked to meet your wife, Jimmy. Maybe some other time."

"Maybe some other time, Boyet."

Charina and Ilynn were returning, having torn an arm off the starfish to see if it would regenerate by night-time. They had decided not to tell Boyet this. Boyar excused himself and made his way to his hut. "I'll leave you to handle the questions," he said. Boyet had decided by now he disliked Boyar very much. "Sure. It was nice to meet you at last, Jimmy," he said, "let's stay in touch. I'll ask Nestor to give you my phone number next time you're in."

"Likewise, *amigo*."

Charina and Jennilynn were evasive about where they'd put the starfish but agreed at adult behest to let Myrlinda accompany them to buy lanzones fruits. Boyet really didn't like to see the daughter of the organiser left out of things.

He would have liked to have been left out of some things himself. As predicted by Boyar, Jingkee had brought her tennis racquet – steel and carbon fibre – and her old one – mere wood – as well as a couple of sets of snorkelling equipment. The second items could wait till later or tomorrow but, she said, you needed the light for tennis. Everyone went up to the busted old court, grass growing through the top covering – whatever it was, not "clay" for sure. The ludicrous state of the surface should have benefited the unskilled (Nestor, Sherwin) or tyro (Boyet) but Jingkee still slaughtered everyone. Overhead service (that was the warning signal) as opposed to the swiping underarm two out of three misses from Boyet; top spin; swerving shots; ferocious volleys at the net – Jingk could do it all. When this palled, they played doubles. Not mixed, but reporter Cathy and sub Jingkee against permutations of men. Cathy hardly needed to lift her warped old resort racquet, Jingkee routed their opponents single-handed. "Anyone for another game?" she enquired brightly, encountering a chorus of groans from the vanquished. Sherwin led the way off court for the generality, but Nestor remained to get some coaching. "Let the racquet-head do the work, sir," Boyet heard Jingkee calling. "Just relax and hit through the ball, Mr Chavez." Pock, pung. You didn't have to look behind you; you could hear the difference between their strokes.

Later they all saw Boyar off on the ordinary (as opposed to air-con) bus, everyone waving, Ilynn and Charina even their handkerchiefs as the celebrated columnist was borne away in clouds of dust.

It was a good departure. They were all sorry to see him go, even Boyet. But it was good for the group: the loss of Boyar drew them all closer to each other – they could discuss him, say nice regretful things – and it conferred the sense of survivorship upon them. It put a feature, a landmark into the weekend. "*Party*," said Sherwin de Leon, "*c'est mourée un peu*." Charina and Jennilynn, who were the only ones to comprehend, gave each other fish looks.

THE roar of the engine, the slap of the waves on the fibreglass bottom, the wind running its fingers through your hair like a lover, the aggressive sharp smell of the little engine's fuel, the bubbling of the exhaust underwater as you slowed and manoeuvred – all these as well as the glorious sensation of speed – magnified from the same rate of land mph – made the Boss feel more alive, more of a man, when he was astride his new love, his latest acquisition. He almost liked just sitting on the comfortable cushion and twisting the throttle with the clutch in neutral in full view of watchers as much as howling along way-out from shore. That throaty gurgling – it sent the adrenalin rushing already! Like all vices the vice of speed was no cheap hobby. It was Jap, of course, the invention, or at least Jap makes dominated the Asian market and – who knows – probably the North American. He'd got his first taste on rental at five thousand the hour, fuel and tax plus plus.

He had soon realised it would be more economical to own than rent – the case with nearly everything – and acquired his very own personal jet-ski. Lovable monster, the *Urgent Orange*, lettered in that shade on a powder blue and white trimmed hull. He really had a sense of freedom on her, much more so than in the Lamborghini, even on a clear road (how often did that happen?) where you had to proceed in more or less linear fashion. With the aqua-cycle it was like you owned the whole world, writing your signature on the ocean's face. He'd have liked to take out one of the shotguns, maybe the Mossberg combat, or even a magnum revolver, and browned away on the move – so tempting the buoys and floats – but had to forego with regret. He wasn't a vandal. Even if he hadn't turned turtle, the salt spray and damp would have been terrible for the firearms.

You did need a little variety after a while. Not having had the experience, you might think one stretch of water was pretty much the same as another – just something to speed over, a rush of grey alongside you. But that wasn't so, it was nice to have a different shoreline and islands, pleasant to be an explorer in virgin territory, and it conferred more than curiosity value on the Range Rover. He had known it was going to come in useful one day; he really had.

THE last day began clear and burning-hot, and stayed that way. The visibility was prodigious. You could actually see the peak of volcanic Mt Otot more than 75 km away. The sea looked like it had a plastic lid put upon it. The wind of the previous day had dropped completely. Boyet knew as much from the silence in the palms, the bars of light on the floor of the cottage. Even so he was surprised, going outside, by the nearness, the clarity and immediacy of things. So much variety – it seemed like they'd been there a week, rather than under 48 hours. It was truly a shame for Boyar to miss this. He knew it was going to be a memorable day; it already had that feel of you having lived in it in another lifetime. Breakfast was piping hot rolls and honey, compliments of the owner, and salt eggs and dry fish, the provision of Nestor. The kids were already splashing in the sea before the food was on the table and, having been summoned half-way through the meal, were in the water again while the adults were lazing over their second cups of native chocolate. Boyet indulged himself in the first cigarette of the day – he didn't normally start so early – causing health-conscious Jingkee to move away, apologising to him for her extreme rudeness. Boyet fanned the smoke from her direction, and stubbed the cigarette when he was half-way through. "Oh, please finish it, Boyet. I feel terrible now."

"It's good for me – I don't need the whole cigarette." He went round with the jug of chocolate for everyone, Jingk first. Strange, the day was only just getting under way, yet it already possessed the mellow quality of a beautiful culmination to something perfect. Nestor's camera clicked, taking the words right out of Boyet's mouth.

"Miriam forgot ours."

"Hoy! You were the one!"

Mostly veteran married couples, they laughed louder than the stagey exchange warranted, including single Cathy.

"You make sure you give back your Mister as good as he dishes out, Cathy, when the time comes," said Mrs De Leon.

"Just don't get married," Jingkee said.

"Very available up till now," said Cathy, setting them laughing again with the pleasure of their own company.

"Was that your flash going off?" Boyet asked. "In sunlight like this?"

Nestor grimaced. "That's Jap over-kill for you. This little thing eats batteries like a shark."

Boyet examined the sturdy yellow little box on its rubber lanyard. "It's waterproof?"

"That kind of thing, splash-proof they call it. It'll go to three metres without flooding, but who wants deeper anyway? My ears give out just under the surface."

"It's because you don't clear them, sir," Jingkee said. "Just pinch your nose and blow. I'll be the one to show you."

"Maybe you can take mercy on me, just this once, Jingkee."

Then they were all cackling again.

In fact, it was little Myrlinda and Ilynn whom Jingkee took out first, with Boyet tagging along as supernumerary adult lifeguard. Some lifeguard. It was he who needed saving, not they. The implausible looking yellow flippers – far too small for him – were astonishingly effective. The girls just wiggled their legs and they were already ten feet in front of him. Within two minutes he was so far behind he'd already reconciled himself to a solo swim. Jingkee, doing crawl to his breaststroke, was managing to keep up, though even she was ten yards behind. Boyet stopped and turned to look at shore, they seemed way out, though no one appeared to be giving themselves concern on the beach, all backs turned to examine a gigantic, smashed jellyfish, defiled with sand. Boyet had trodden on it without getting stung. Jingkee was now taking her young charges – thank God – parallel to the coastline instead of out to sea, along the only piece of fringing coral reef for twenty km to survive blast fishing; although Boyet was not to know that or to have an inkling of the green, black, and white moray eel the young girls had sighted (far more interesting and suggestive than a mere, and now heartily despised, star fish amidst the ruby and emerald jewels that were anemones). He headed in and half-way back had to fight down a rush of panic at his surprising tiredness. The girls overtook him without a word, heads down, boggling and flipping, oblivious to what was above. But as Jingkee passed him, she inquired, "OK, need help?"

"No," he gasped indignantly. A little later, she said, "It's OK. You can stand now." He swam as long after this admonition as he could bear, then knelt in the waist-deep water, trying to hide the heaving of his chest. Now he knew it for a fact that he was no longer twenty-three. Somehow he'd thought time had moved on for everybody else but not for him – the pair of eyes scrutinising the foibles of others: the greying of his friends' hair, the sudden inelasticity in the women's throats. It was like suddenly finding oneself implicated in a crime to which one had only been a bystander.

On the beach he lay flat on his back, no longer caring whether people could see the rise and fall of his chest. He was on the hard, wet sand which was still pleasantly cool, despite the climbing sun. The indefatigable Jingkee was gathering another duckling party, which this time included her own daughter and teenaged Darwin de Leon. A model Philippine child, Charina had given no hint of impatience as she waited on the shore for her mother, but now she was in her mask and fins in five minutes flat with time to advise skinny, pimply Darwin whom she was plainly sweet on (the tastes of women even at this age opaque and baffling as ever – what did this ravishing nymphet, chip off Jingkee's elegant block, see in the youth?) to spit in his mask.

"Why?"

"Because if you don't the glass will mist over and you will see nothing at all."

"Why?" Darwin was clearly being deliberately aggravating, probably resentful a girl could do something capable of a macho construction better than he. He had only wanted to take the BB pistol with him, hand above water like in the film *Excalibur*.

"Because," said Charina, parroting with the obligingness of one who has had scientific principles drummed into them by parents very much unwillingly but against appalling odds has fought through to mastery because of the delightful potential for practical application, "the water temperature will chill the outside of the glass, while the heat of your face on the other side will warm the glass, thereby causing condensation to form."

Boyet loved the "thereby causing condensation to form" – the authentic complacent tones of the adult preceptor describing something inevitable to someone young.

"Shit," said young Darwin, out of the hearing of all adults except the prostrate Boyet.

Charina smiled seraphically. "Here, let me do it for you." She worked up a mouthful of saliva, then dribbled it slowly, rather than spat it, into the mask. "See, the spit warms the glass already. Put your finger in and spread it. That's right. Yi! Don't put it on already – without rinsing it. Yuks! You've got my spit all over your face."

Boyet decided he'd better lie on his stomach. He heard the group splash off, Darwin's breaking voice incomprehensible and suddenly guttural as he asked an, obviously essential, question through his snorkel, for the next event was his uncontrolled spasm of coughing.

Something Boyet was to regret – it could be said for the rest of his life – was that little barrel roll from back to stomach – a matter of an inch or three but diametrically altering his whole perspective, his entire viewpoint. He no longer faced the sea but looked inland. And what had prompted that turn of a crocodile? He cared not to formulate it: an illicit desire followed by shame of discovery. He remembered reading in *Citizen* – long before his voice swelled the chorus – an account by one Ka Rambo (no irony intended in the name, Boyet knew), a burnt-out NPA guerrilla in whom the only fire that still flared was the beacon of personal survival, about how the propeller-driven ground-attack Tora Toras were not a problem because you heard them droning in, whereas jets were a menace because they over-flew you before your ears ever got a warning.

It must have been the same now, on the water. Jingkee probably didn't realise at first what was upon them because, swimming breast-stroke now, her ears were out of the water most of the time. Using mask and snorkel, with faces submerged, the kids would have heard the engine noise amplified over a great distance but in the excitement of the chase – that muscular, writhing moray flushed out of its hole by a wildly duck-diving Darwin de Leon – it would just have been another distraction on the periphery of their concentration.

He must have been doing well over thirty knots. (You measured nautically or in mph? – crazy irrelevance prompted still, Boyet thought, by the journalistic habit).

On shore, it was Nestor who noticed first. Boyet saw his pointing finger, the alarm slowly building on his face of a vacationing *pinoy* without a care in the world. It was the end of the jet-ski's long parabola that Boyet saw, the second and a half before an impact that was not quite visible, heads so small, so low in the sea. The scooter jumped fractionally, about a foot maybe, though difficult to judge at the distance, maybe more, then skimmed its own length before flaying the water's green rind again. The rider looked back, maybe alerted by the bump, as of striking a bobbing coconut but Boyet could imagine whatever it was lost for him in the spray of his passage. Without losing speed, he heeled and tight-turned to retrace the hundred fifty metres or so of overshoot. No one on land had uttered a sound so far but as the jet ski closed in to the original point of impact, they began to shout at the same time. Boyet found himself on his feet, waving his arms, desperately bellowing. He felt his a special urgency: he was nearest. If anything, the ski seemed to be travelling faster. One of the swimmers was also waving arms. Just as it seemed too late, a pair of yellow fins went up in the air, submerging as the craft rushed over. The jet ski slowed to turn, this time returning at a more modest clip. Then it reared as the rider throttled forward, the subdued roar reaching shore as the wake widened once more. He passed over the swimmer this time – obvious from the lack of fins, unless they'd been knocked off, in which case it might not be Boyet's surmise of Jingkee after all. The starting and slowing, the repeated passing – it was difficult to believe, but the driver, rider, pilot, whatever you cared to call him, wasn't trying to rescue the individual he'd hit. He was bent on striking the remaining two. The same realisation had come to the others; they'd stopped shouting. Everyone was standing together now, knee-deep in the water. The rider was having difficulty accomplishing what he wanted, although on the face of it all the cards seemed to lie with him. His problem was if he moved off to get up sufficient speed to do damage, the swimmers had time to dive under and elude him, as well as always closing the distance to shore and, presumably, safety. If he stayed now and manoeuvred around them, he could eventually touch but not with enough force to hurt – and the pair in the water could either pull him in or climb aboard: Boyet wasn't sure which would be best. He'd already seen someone (Jingkee, or Darwin, the young male? Probably Jingkee – but Darwin's idea of taking his pellet gun with him didn't sound quite so foolish now) grab the rider's foot but have it wrenched away with a kick. The rider was giving it up as a bad job; you could see his frustration in his throttle work – *rrr, rrr*. At length he turned the ski on its side, coming perilously close to falling over, and went full tilt southwards, citywards, on a curve which had to take him probably nearer than he would have liked (always assuming him a sensible person) to their spit of land. And as he gunned the throttle to full, planing on the white mane of his bow wave (Boyet had seen the chariot-race in *Ben Hur*) he gave them (it was difficult to believe but they had the evidence of their own eyes), driving one-handed with the other held aloft, he gave them the finger.

"*Bastos!*" exclaimed Cathy.

The closest part of the jet-skier's course took him around eighty metres from shore and although the spray and flying hair made it difficult to recognise or remember him, it could be discerned without doubt that the rider was corpulent. In fact, his thighs were huge. In his white briefs he resembled a giant, manic baby, the folds of flesh shuddering with the vibrations of his runaway perambulator. Within a minute he was gone from their sight.

The swimmers, their friends, their children, had made half the distance to shore. Boyet looked at Nestor, considering swimming to help. But what help? Look how he was just recovering. And if the jet-ski came back, wouldn't he just add to the trouble, inconsiderately making a casualty of himself?

Maybe there was a rope. How did the lifesaving jingle go that they'd had on the kids' page – throw, then tow, don't go? Quiet rippling to the right.

Boyet saw Miriam slide herself into the water, still in her halter top and city shorts. Her buttocks floated higher than her head, or appeared to, that enviable positive buoyancy of the other sex. He didn't trouble to expostulate with the back of her head or her ass. The snorkeller, who was in front of the swimming Jingkee, lifted their head, and they all saw it was Darwin. Sherwin de Leon crossed himself, guiltily. There were huge sweat patches on his shirt. It must have been hell for him. Boyet hadn't considered the parental aspect of things until now. Poor guy, Sherwin. Jingkee was pulling what must be Charina, towing on her back and scissor-kicking those athletic legs. Miriam reached her, taking Charina's left arm. Things didn't look so good. The women didn't waste time speaking to each other, but kicked energetically, Miriam a lot cruder than Jingkee but their joint efforts bringing them in much faster. Boyet behind and Nestor in front waded out to their chests, issuing instructions. "Get her head, Miriam," Boyet commanded. "Watch it, it's going underwater – she can't breathe."

"Just get her legs," Nestor instructed. "It's OK now girls, we've got her."

They took Charina from the gasping women, Jingkee more breathless than the less athletic Miriam because of her longer swim. Boyet was shocked by the blue-grey pallor of Charina's face. She felt light as a bird – not that he'd ever held one – better, weightless as polystyrene. And as lifeless. He had her by the feet, Nestor the head. The other man, the organiser, his superior, shook his head discreetly – as if he was privy to something Boyet couldn't know yet. To Boyet's horror, Jingkee caught the gesture. She seemed content, however, to relinquish control to Nestor, certainly possession of the body. *The body.* He'd better stop thinking like that. Desist – you might make it happen. Jingkee said, "Excuse," as she squeezed past the men and blew into her daughter's mouth, pinching the short nose. Nestor nodded in approval. He came round to Boyet's side to whisper, "The head's smashed at the back, buddy. The little girl's head, it's like someone hit a boiled egg."

"You could feel it?" Boyet inquired, whispering also in his horror.

"Mmm. Even when I was careful. Don't stop, Jingkee. Just keep going."

Charina's mother was also now pushing on the girl's chest with stiff, straight arms. Like you saw on TV hospital dramas, except surely they were doing it with bent arms? Should someone tell Jingkee? No, it was useless anyway, according to Nestor's earlier information.

But after five minutes Jingkee had restored her daughter to a passably normal colour. "Go on, Jingkee. Keep doing it," Nestor exhorted her. His eyes slid away from Boyet's. Not wanting to acknowledge his earlier mistake. If so, very human.

The front of Charina's head and her face looked OK, no visible sign of injury but there was something over and beyond salt water in the hair, encroaching its stain on the sand behind. Boyet noticed recalcitrant strands of pubic hair peeping out of the crotch of Jingkee's swimsuit. She was careless of appearances now, really the last thing she was concerned about as she arched her body over her daughter's, passing the breath of life from herself to the cold clay. Young Darwin de Leon was talking to his father and Cathy a few yards back from these resuscitation attempts. Boyet stole slowly backwards, as if turning his gaze away would jeopardise Charina's chances by subtracting from the collective desire to will her back to life. Doing so, he trod on Cathy's bare feet. She smiled at him, all the more gloriously for the utter inappropriateness of such an expression at the present juncture: it was like a secret sweetness between them, some unspoken and unspecifiable agreement about the others.

"You could hear the engine really loud," young Darwin was saying, "I looked up and saw it when it was way off. But Charina dove down to the coral and the boat, the thing, *koan*, whatever you call it, was moving so fast it hit her just after she came back up again. Shit."

"You don't use language like that, young man," Sherwin rebuked his son.

"He's a very good boy," Cathy corrected her superior. "He has done very well to remember what happened, so brave. Don't be so hard on him, sir."

"I am too hard on him, but that's why he's a good boy."

Darwin grinned foolishly, twenty-three-year-old Cathy's praise sweet as candy. Even being called "good boy" by this sexy, older sister-type was strangely exciting rather than diminishing as it would have been coming from a man.

Boyet reckoned the kid was in serious danger of a hard-on in those skimpy briefs. Maybe his old man had a thing going with the cub reporter – lucky guy if he did.

"For a while," Cathy said, thereby immeasurably increasing her potential for promotion, "I'll be the one to get a notebook."

"Good thinking," Sherwin said. "Boyet, we've got to catch that madman. I've never seen anything like it. Did you see – he came *back* to hit the others after Charina. He's got to be crazy."

"Or very sane." This was Nestor joining them. He explained: "No witnesses that way. Finish them all off and cover his tracks."

"*O*," exclaimed Boyet and Sherwin simultaneously, Nestor's analysis bearing the cogent simplicity of truth, its blatancy immediately triggering the reflex of "Why didn't I think of that before?" Darwin, who'd been on the receiving end of the cold-blooded stratagem, didn't look so surprised, either because he'd seen the rider's face or because conspiracy theories of reptilian deviousness were standard teenage entertainment fodder.

"Did you get a good look at him?" Sherwin asked.

"Not so, Pa."

"Well, could you recognise him if you saw him again?"

"I think I could."

"You think."

A cry of sheer anguish interrupted them. Jingkee's magnificent self-control had cracked – only temporarily it was to prove – but she'd thrown herself across Charina's chest, clasping her unconscious daughter's head to her own breast. Nestor opened his mouth – probably to tell her not to compromise the resuscitation which only she appeared to know how to give – but a moment later she was again administering in a ratio of six pulses of external cardiac massage to one of oral ventilation.

"We've got to nail that crazy son of a bitch."

"She hasn't got a chance."

Sherwin and Nestor had spoken simultaneously.

Cathy had moved down to stand next to Miriam, with her notebook tucked into the side panel of her swimsuit. "Can I help, mum?" she asked. "I'll be the one to give the kiss of life if you show me. I've forgotten from school."

Jingkee didn't look up, but down the line of Charina's nose and chin to check the chest was deflating and dropping correctly with no obstruction to the airway from the tongue. She came back to compress the sternum and on the second pulse said, "OK. Pinch the nose – remember? – and don't blow too hard – it will go to the stomach. Thank you, 'day."

Nestor lit cigarettes for the men off his own. He smoked Philip Morris, a brand Boyet regarded as having a glamorous identification but overly expensive. He therefore smoked the long cigarette he was given with appreciation. They had turned their backs on the distressing tableau of Jingkee's grief and labour, but by unspoken accord faced the sea again after a short interval – that prospect inspired a greater contemplative ease.

Sherwin de Leon said, "We'd better report this as soon as possible. In fact, one of us better had go right now." Boyet looked to Nestor. It seemed like pretty good advice from the assistant ed but you never knew. Nestor took a while to speak.

He said, "I think there's greater safety in numbers. Maybe two or three of us."

"It'll be dark in three hours," Sherwin said. Boyet was unable to determine whether Sherwin considered this bad (they could be stolen upon unaware) or good (they could all effect their escapes in the darkness).

"We'll stick it out here for tonight," Nestor said, "I'll go into the town meanwhile with the owner. He knows the score here, whatever it is."

Boyet could read nothing in Sherwin's face but didn't argue, offer to make it to town himself, for instance.

"Nestor's going to get help in town," Boyet informed the women. He'd become Nestor's unofficial lieutenant, Sherwin seeming to be more of a rival than anything else. He added, "So just, er, hang in there, girls." No one said anything to him. Jingkee and Cathy were gleaming like bronze statues. It was obviously harder work than the short, abrupt movements looked; in the tennis court Jingkee had hardly broken sweat. Cathy took a sharp intake of breath and shuddered. Boyet was immediately hopeful for Charina but it turned out he'd been the one to drop hot ash on her shoulder. Fortunate the perspiration really.

"Just give them some room, Daddy," Miriam requested him quite mildly. Jennilynn was standing next to Miriam, looking with big eyes at her new found friend laying on the ground next to the smashed jellyfish. In his fatherly role Boyet wondered if it was OK for her to watch; actually she seemed just fascinated at the moment rather than shocked. That wouldn't last. He hoped it wasn't going to be a trauma, turn her off – what? – swimming, men, meat, in some quirky, unpredictable way. At that moment young Darwin de Leon said very calmly but chilling all the men, "There's three guys with guns up by the trees." Boyet saw them flitting by the coco trunks. Sherwin said with a touch of asperity, "Don't point at them, son." Jingkee looked up from her work of revival without breaking the rhythm of her compressions. Boyet was frozen in the sunshine, his bowels melting like ice-cream.

Young Darwin broke for his father's cottage, the nearest. Taken by surprise, Sherwin called, "Come here this instant, young man." He hesitated, then as Darwin emerged with his BB gun, ran clumsily up the sand before tripping on a root. Jingkee put Cathy's linked palms on Charina's chest, "Like this, one every second," and sprinted over the beach, stopping to grab Nestor's camera from him. Boyet had not moved at all. In Nestor's eyes he read a communication, akin to the ones they'd shared in the bordello. The only recklessness they'd ever show would be on those visits. After Jingkee had made about forty metres on them, Nestor began to pursue sedately, Boyet alternating his calls of "Come back!", "Wait, Jingkee!" A gun-shot went off, sending a startling number of birds out of the grove. Boyet had forgotten how loud shots could sound. The man had fired in the air. Darwin, somewhat in front of a closing Jingkee, dove behind a trunk. Not the most observant guy in the world or maybe just a father, Sherwin shouted in dismay.

"He's OK!" Boyet reassured him.

Quite undeterred, Jingkee had not even broken stride. Reaching the cowering Darwin, his toy pistol dropped heedless in the sand, she found herself too short to hurdle the bent tree but hopped the obstacle like a steeple-chaser, with one foot levering her over the top. Faced with this Valkyrie, the armed men wavered.

Afterwards, Boyet, Nestor, and Sherwin all agreed the men – whoever they were – hadn't actually wanted to kill Jingkee. "They could have blown her away anytime," Nestor rationalised. "It wouldn't have been difficult. And what did she have in her hand?"

But at the time, and for the women ever afterwards – Miriam and Cathy especially – it seemed that what Jingkee had possessed was the invulnerability conferred by her sheer disregard of personal consequences, that and her maternal outrage, enough to overawe wild beasts let alone despicable men. She had worn a magic mantle.

The armed men turned and ran. What else could they do?

Stay and argue the toss?

"Those guys didn't have the orders to waste her. They were just goons. If they'd done that, they'd have been on their own," Nestor would tell his minions in the newsroom. "It was all of us or none of us." And if Boyet or Sherwin was there, they'd nod, implicating themselves in the danger, with the faint suggestion that Jingkee had been imperilling not so much herself as all and sundry, while the men had taken on more responsible roles.

At the time, watching wonderful Jingkee chasing the pistoleros through the trees it had felt – to be honest – like she was the US cavalry in the personification of a five feet nothing, ninety pound Filipina.

There was the flash of white as the men drove off in their car, then Jingkee came walking back through the grove. "Couldn't get their number," she said, "or their faces."

The men were too shame-faced to say anything.

Down on the beach Charina was breathing for herself, chest regularly rising and falling, normal-coloured but out, out like a light, out for lunch permanently, a non-inhabitant of the planet. Coma was the word for it, but a full stop in Jingkee's life. Period.

Who was the crazed grammarian, who had written finis on the face of the waters, revising, stuttering, repeating himself all the time, trying to rub out his errors? Young Darwin mumbled something about shooting in the water, film not bullets, but Jingkee said there was nothing on the roll when she developed it.

And there it rested, baffling for a while before resignation succeeded indignation. Nestor splashed the story – Murder on the Low Seas – too good a story to by-pass anyhow but it all petered out for lack of leads. Everything died the gentlest of deaths. Including Charina. Sleeping Beauty on Dextrose. She just wouldn't pass away. That kind of took impact from the story. It was like a victim-less murder. Visayan-style, things concluded without a formal ending, just wound down with a whimper.

Nestor said, his final judgement, "The guy would have got away with it anyhow. You could buy fifty judges for the price of that jet-ski. Or waste fifty witnesses. It's history."

Naturally, they didn't tell Jingkee.

Chapter Nine

CEBU WORE ITS BEST FACE FOR THE INITS. Going down Jones –
never mind it was renamed Osmeña, it would always be Jones for
Victoria – she was startled by the size and quality of the up-town
commercial buildings: the sawn-off replica of the Hong Kong
Connaught Tower, that gross colander, Asia's tallest building not
so long ago, complete here with ground-floor MacDonald's; the
mighty copper-coloured Metrobank Plaza, home of equally
mighty Atlas mining, detailed down to windstocking and heli-
pad on roof; the Babylonic Midtown Hotel, ascending like a
series of stepped glass cubes. She'd been impressed, and like her
to do so, registered it without qualification, the Congressman
rather more grudgingly. Downtown, the megastores apart, had
still been a noisome den – Colon, nation's most ancient street,
the aptly named, the filthy, its drains choked in garbage, still
flooding to waist height at the smallest provocation. But it all
only served as a massive material counter-point to emphasise
that great, that glitzy development of Cebu Uptown. The old
golf-course Papa had played on was no more: instead you had
the Business Park. That wasn't like the Visayas at all, more like
looking at the ground plan of a vernacular, revivified Versailles.
And in between, in the prolific interstices of the large-hewn
blocks of someone's vision, had sprouted the creative entrepreneurial spontaneity which alone could animate the big plans:
elegant little shopping malls, dinky hotels, their architecture
cute and original as marzipan models. She clapped her hands.
The Congressman's mood soured further. The Queen City of
the South, site of the slaying of the globe-trotting Magellan,

unhappy fate for Region VII's first European tourist, was nothing more nor less than his alibi. Taking Mrs there turned down the heat of her intention to investigate Manila. But every one of her exclamations of astonishment and pleasure was like a red-hot nail down the back of his shirt collar. The Congressman loathed Tommy O., the popular, progressive civic leader of the Cebu economic miracle, a man who was everything he wasn't and – worse – successful with it; a politician who eschewed assassination as a political instrument, well thought of in the US where he'd passed his twenties in a penurious exile, all the family property confiscated by FM (dictator, not radio frequency). This was in contrast to the Congressman who had been the next best thing to a presidential crony, not that it seemed to have done him any material damage. He was surprisingly sensitive to public opinion, though, and it was – Victoria calculated with amazement – more than three years since she'd been to Cebu.

They were there for a meeting of a Visayan representation group assembled under Presidential auspices, the Pres having promised a southern Malacañang palace. The equivalent, Victoria guessed, would be a Boston White House. It behoved Representative Init to attend, having switched horses with a bareback leap only at the end of the race. Never mind, changing political parties was about as hassle-making as sending colours back to a tailor. Silks would lost longer than a Philippine political formation too.

"We can be the new Cebu," Victoria told her consort in Room 312 of the Dynasty Inn, nowhere near so swanky as the Plaza but very adequate and well-populated by minor league Tagalog film stars and singers. Vicky's crowd, she liked to think. A few journalists wouldn't have hurt either.

The Congressman stared balefully at the dressing-table mirror. He found the room cramped and the town provincial after Manila. Being told to model himself on young Osmeña was the last straw. "Maybe we just want to be ourselves," he said to the mirror. This was their marital equivalent of screaming and banging each other's heads against walls. Mrs Init backed off for the moment. She began to unpack the Congressman's shirts, the delicate formal barong tagalog first that he would wear next evening. "Down the air-con," he rapped, pursuing a rare advantage. With dangerous meekness, Victoria complied. "I'll drink a coffee in the lobby," he informed her, picking up the Business Section of the *Star* which he'd purloined from the cabin of the Fokker Friendship, "That's if they have coffee in this place." Victoria was uncertain whether "place" meant the hick hotel she'd booked them into or Cebu itself. "It's all up to you," she said mildly, "just as you want it, you shall have it."

She occupied herself with a stroll to Robinson's Department Store – good as a trip abroad, all that marble and the escalators, not like the Philippines at all – followed by a manicure at Salon Rose. A Robinson's or Rustan's at home, that was when she'd know they'd put the town on the map; it was like an independent examiner coming to assess the grades. A Gaisano's didn't mean so much. An inveterate shopper, she contented herself with buying briefs for the Congressman and a Korean water filter for the mayor's wife, who was to be cultivated in the coming days.

The evening of the inaugural cocktail party found Victoria ready early, having passed much of the afternoon in the Maanyag Beauty Parlour. She had very good skin anyway but didn't scorn professional expertise. Every little bit helped. It was the Congressman who was rushing round like a headless chicken, looking vainly for the socks and singlet (vital under the transparent barong tagalog) which Victoria had given the laundry service (the tarriff was somewhat steeper than the reasonably priced rooms – the astute Chinese management clawing back where they could). "It's a good thing I went shopping," she told him. "You can take them to Manila. Green briefs are unusual even there. Who bought you those shoes, by the way? They're not your usual style, 'lin."

Did she know? He thought not. It wouldn't do to become paranoiac and give himself away by panicking. "I sent my secretary out for them," he said. "It was an evening like this."

"How lucky you are to have efficient women around you.

Your shirt is caught in your pants."

So, right from the start, things did not go the Assemblyman's way. Sitting in the lobby, watching Bush's rearguard reflex strugglings on CNN (the Congressman dispassionate, Victoria a closet Clinton supporter); then with growing unease outside the front door, they realised their limo was delayed, then not coming at all. Mrs Init, whose province was these matters, got on to the hire company on the security guard's phone. The Congressman was livid, made dire threats in the background as he caught the gist of things – there'd been overbookings, cars had broken down.

"Do they know who we are?" he asked Victoria.

"Of course not. If they did, this would not have happened," was the succinct reply, instantly mollifying though the Congressman had to bite back the pertinent observation she should have told them so in the first place. Thus they arrived somewhat later than polite even by PMT in an antediluvian, non-aircon taxi with doors that did not open well from the inside, if at all.

They discovered the ballroom door already closed – the Big Man had beaten them to it – and from the sounds of things the keynote address already underway. Punctuality was no particular virtue, tardiness no vice – except on this one particular occasion. What did he think he was trying to do? Upstage the President, himself famous for his lateness? Show the Tagalogs all those jokes about lazy Visayans were true? The Congressman was an unprepossessing figure at the best of times. Sweating profusely, blinking rapidly, he might have had his credentials questioned by the door personnel, had there been any. Mrs I. swept in serenely behind her labouring tug-boat. The Congressman would have liked to order her to keep a low profile but he didn't dare. Fortyfive minutes later he was able to merge himself in the general applause, clapping with the others, as grateful for the sound enveloping him as if the waves were the folds of a concealing blanket.

A Very Important Personage, not an elected representative

but a key Cabinet Member, an administrator, a muscle-man, spotted him. This kind of conspicuousness was OK by him.

"The President would like a word."

"An honour."

Magically, his Mrs appeared by his side. That was OK, too. She was the official Mrs. Approaching the spry, diminutive figure of FVR in the spirit of a flagellant drawing nigh a shrine, the Congressman looked for something respectful to say which would also establish common ground. Clearly, "I, too, also worked with your cousin, the late president Ferdinand Marcos," was not a great idea. Some backs blocked the way. The Congressman sidestepped adroitly before cutting in again with the aplomb of a Gobernador de Leon jeepney driver. He readied himself for his appointment with greatness. The Cabinet Member sheared him to the outside lane, like a patrol car a traffic-offender.

"You know Mr Dionisio Bugnaw III, of course? Mr Bugnaw, Representative Init."

Had the Congressman driven while he dozed into a flaming head-on collision with a petrol-tanker at a combined closing speed of 200 km per hour, awakening to disaster at the very last moment, he could hardly have been more unpleasantly surprised. Filling his windscreen, as it were, he discovered the unpleasant features of old man Bugnaw, the senior surviving member of the clan who were the hereditary enemies of the Inits. Wham!

A sickly expression of unimaginable ghastliness overspread the Congressman's face. When he looked at the President, at FVR, he might as well have been regarding the features of St Peter, split seconds after switching planes of existence, post-crunch. Bugnaw's face was also a picture of mortification. Since childhood (short as those grim and precocious childhoods had been) these two had had the genealogy, the demonology of the ancient feud relentlessly drummed into them, to the point where the other side had ceased to possess any human, still less amelio-rating, attributes. Dionisio III's great-uncle, Rommel, had personally shot the Congressman's grandfather, Wenceslao, through his open study window with his preferred weapon, a .45, hiding in the dark garden behind the trunk of a molave tree, still common in those days despite the logging already begun by the Bugnaws. Lolo Init had been in jeopardy of winning an ancient election hands-down, thanks to a bigger than usual distribution of douceurs following a bank heist his goons had organised. In turn Rommel had been sent to his Maker four years later on Thanksgiving (crimes going unsolved but not unavenged), his handsome face smoke-smudged and his moustache singed and tattered in a grenade blast which left his body as pitted with black metal as a wild turkey.

Things had gone downhill between the families from then, the feud blowing hot and cold but mostly hot.

The senior members of their generation, Dionisio III and the Congressman bore each other a personal enmity over and beyond the honour-bound ancestral vendetta which was largely waged without vindictiveness now, even if the ultimate sanctions tended to the terminal. Complex, shrouded in the mists of time, and not a little sordid, the affair was no longer quite transparent to even the major protagonists – not at all to even close insiders like Victoria – but suffice to say that both, in all likelihood correctly, had felt swindled by the other in an arms length third party commercial venture which could have been the bridge to a reconciled future.

Suddenly it occurred. The Congressman couldn't believe it, even as it happened, no one, but no one, laid hands on a guy in his position, but he could swear that surely it wasn't his imagination, he had got a push in the back which propelled him into Dionisio III. To stop himself tripping and going down he was forced to grab the other and ditto Dionisio, so that they found themselves in an embrace of passionate mutual distaste. The Congressman might as well have been holding the decomposing corpse he'd twice tried to make of Dionisio for the revulsion he felt.

Fish eyeball looked on bulging piscine eyeball. Horror on

both faces. The potential for embarrassment seemed infinite. The awful prospect – heaven forbid! – of naked personal confrontation! Blatantly expressed hostility! Each shuddered. Better almost to be struck down up some lonely road in an electric storm of muzzle flashes than endure that dire public mortification. It was irrelevant that FVR was there, the result would have been the same without him. Like zombies under the thrall of the necromantic current of convention, the two enemies bestowed a dreadful rictus on the other. In their bilious state words were for the moment beyond them. FVR's own utterances formed a kind of incomprehensible background scatter, to which they could only reply with inarticulate neutral grunts and sighs to signal that they were still sentient. The Cabinet Member joined the act – it was obviously a well-rehearsed piece of political theatre – and the Congressman and Dionisio III turned to him with grateful but glassy stares. National Reconciliation was the gist of the sermon – Government with New People's Army, Government with Rightist Rebel Soldiers, Government with Marcosistas. Something about healing wounds. How pointed was all this? Just a grisly coincidence or was the presidential intelligence network far better informed at the local level than one suspected? The Congressman and Dionisio III's minds worked in tandem for perhaps the first time in their lives.

A silence fell. And awkwardly persisted. Silence, terror of the cultivated Filipino. The Pres and the Cabinet Member wore broad smiles, perfectly at ease with the world and themselves.

"Aah," a sound like a death rattle came from the Congressman's throat. The Cabinet Member looked encouragingly at him, nodding the wretched man on. The Congressman writhed on the hook. Dionisio III said in a breaking voice, "How long the years since we didn't meet," taking twice as long to say the first half of his sentence as the last – the final words almost a sob. The Cabinet member made soothing clucks. FVR, bright, bespectacled, looking at the Congressman and Dionisio III in turn, as if he was a spectator at a tennis match.

"O-o, the years," croaked the Congressman.

FVR beamed. He could also have been looking at the parrot and the cockatoo conversing at the zoo. Never mind the sense. That there were sounds issuing was the amazing thing.

"It is, ah, hot," ventured Dionisio. "Outside, *di ba*, I mean. Hot the weather. But maybe you think it's cold, hah? Yes, certainly, I agree with you. Cold this month, if you say so."

"Ah, ah. Cold the weather," said the Congressman. "But, you know, you are right. Also it's hot. You are right, you are right the first time. Not disagreeing, not disagreeing you. Mmm, mmm."

Another pause fell upon the conversation.

"Your children know each other, too?" came the prompt from the Cabinet Member, who might have been better briefed. The Representative and Victoria were a famously childless couple. Dionisio III's youngest son, Rommel II, was however widely suspected of having been behind the bungled shooting of the Congressman's chief aide in 1986, bungled not in the sense of the aide having survived the hail of armalite bullets (he hadn't) so much as the Congressman having been the presumed target. Rommel II's own brother, Ian, a notoriously peevish character, had ordered Rommel's rub-out three years later (not for fouling up the hit, just sibling rivalry).

Both Dionisio III and the Congressman had to turn their heads to the side and look at the ground. Something inconceivable had happened: silence had become the more comfortable alternative.

"Well," said the Cabinet Member, sublimely unaware, "you've probably got a lot of local gossip to catch up on, Representative. We'll leave you to it."

Something close to panic appeared on the faces of Dionisio III and the Congressman, characters not generally known for proneness to that. The mighty prepared to move on; there was a lot of flesh to press in a short time. For the Congressman and Dionisio III it was like watching someone cut your rope on the mountain wall. At the precise moment the grandees turned their backs Victoria swooped in from a knot of wives ten feet back.

Plucking the half-full glass from Dionisio III's hand and both men from a dizzy pit, she said, "We'll just refresh your drink, Mr Bugnaw. For a while," and she favoured him with her most winning smile, as she retrieved her man. As grateful as Representative Init for remission, old man Bugnaw was sufficiently relieved to smile back, before he remembered who he was and replaced it with an expression of grim perturbation which actually made him look less frightening. As they moved away – all parties putting as much distance between themselves as quickly as decent, Dionisio III made a resolution to attend to the Congressman's demise in the near future, probably with a heist-style urban ambuscade – blocking cars front and rear and plenty of automatic fire – while the Congressman for his part considered the purchase of Kevlar armour and dreamed of his people finding Dionisio goon-less on a mountain road.

But Jesus, Mary, and all the saints, he was grateful to his wife, the indispensable, the proven. Going into the thick of the convention's fray, she squeezed his hand and he returned the pressure.

MIRIAM never had any symptoms at all. She wouldn't have known there was anything wrong with her. In that sense she should have been grateful to Boyet, at least given him some credit. They did say it was actually more dangerous for women, even though painless at first; there was that risk of pelvic inflammatory disease causing infertility amongst other things, although the last thing they wanted at this stage in their lives was a baby. In all their classic textbook glory Boyet had enough symptoms for both of them: the razor-blades and hot lead cascading down the urethra, the purulent discharge, the (he thought) six day interval between contact and development. He couldn't be quite sure of the timing because he couldn't pin down who'd been the one to give it him. It had been a colourful week, with two visits to Momo's and then an unlooked for opportunity with a normal girl standing by the Guava-

Breadfruit intersection waiting-shed. She'd looked fresh and natural in her city shorts, her real attraction being that she didn't look like a professional – far more attractive in her simplicity than any spurious glamour chick – but something about the way she was standing and her half-glance had alerted Boyet to the possibility that she was available if he persisted. Before their two hour romp in the Tintin Motel, she'd told him it was her first time with a customer. If it wasn't, it was probably only the second or third; Boyet could even now still believe her. Maybe it was her boyfriend who'd given her the dose and – of course – he now knew she wouldn't have been aware she had any unusual souvenir to pass on. He was nearly sure it was her – that was the paradox: you were less likely to pick something up off a well-trafficked pro.

All those early years of standing to attention at the urinal waiting for this very thing to happen, and then never getting it. Typical of life – things only hit you unaware.

Even before he got the diagnosis from the clinic, Boyet was aware he had a bigger problem than what was – basically – just a cold of the cock. He'd, against his will of course, and certainly his better judgement, had relations with his wife a day after the waiting-shed girl. Usually, he'd try to get away with a week's abstinence after one of his escapades, longer if he could wangle it. All the way home from the clinic it had been on his mind. Presented with the diagnosis of uncomplicated gonorrhea, he'd indulged in a species of venereal arithmetic. Clap incubated quicker than NSU, so probably it wasn't the first girl at Momo's or he'd have been struck a few days back, so the fact that he hadn't had sex with Miriam for four days after that wasn't material. He'd most likely been clean then. The question was – had he reached such a level of infectiousness a day after the waiting-shed girl that he'd successfully communicated the gonococcus neisseria to his wife? Maybe not. The doctor had broached the topic of subsequent contacts with well-practised tact. Probably saw these shifty, errant husbands every day. Boyet levelled with him.

"Better bring your Mrs," the quack advised. "Just in case," informing Boyet at this time about asymptomatic female infection and the consequences. "She'll come round to it," he added hastily, dispensing some non-medical exhortation now.

It was not a very comfortable trip home down Guava. Boyet even played with the idea of crushing some ciprofloxacin into Miriam's Milo. It wasn't so much the chicanery which led him to abandon the stratagem, so much as the fact that she only drank it at breakfast. The regimen was twice daily. Hell.

"Who gave you the disease?"

Boyet was a little disconcerted by the quickness and directness of Miriam's response. He'd expected immediate emotional upset, recrimination. Some tears maybe. But, no, she was getting right down to specifics and her eyes didn't look too watery. He'd sent the kids to their auntie as a precaution; maybe he'd been over-fearful.

"Well, I'm not too sure, 'day."

As soon as he said it, Boyet knew he'd made a mistake. He'd instinctively shied away from the direct, exact answer. You shrank from that – it was like taking clothes off in public and you committed yourself to a position. Now Miriam said, "Why? You lost count of the women? I hope it was women, by the way."

Boyet cringed. Sarcasm at last. Well, he'd left himself open for that one. His first words to her – how did you broach it out of the blue? – had been: "'Day, I don't know how to tell you this," which was only true, though he had spent the best part of three hours trying – longer than an *Up Periscope!* took, "but I have given you an infection." (Sounded a lot better than disease – you died of those, whereas your children got an infection if they neglected a cut knee). Miriam's next words (not quite in the picture yet): "What kind of infection?"

Boyet: "It's a sex infection, 'day." At this point he just wanted to get it over with, jump into the water and have done. But Miriam had then refused to let it drop, gotten sarcastic. She'd wanted all kinds of practical details (they were much more basic than men when it really got down to it), so much so that if she'd been a guy Boyet would have sworn she was getting her rocks off on it.

Naturally, he didn't reveal to her the full catalogue of his misdeeds: like how long it had been going on – over twelve years – and how many times (could you count the stars in the sky, the coconuts on the mountain?). How did you tell your wife you'd been cheating on her with prostitutes since six months after the marriage? That was when she'd been carrying Jennilynn.

A more traditional (e.g. less expensively educated) Visayan girl might have been more compliant. Women stayed at home. Men played around. That was the natural order of things. Females of Miriam's generation and social class didn't buy that one any more. At least, Boyet had decided, ideologically they'd cut loose, but in their instincts they were still tethered. Asians first, emancipationists second. That was the real problem – either as oriental females or as liberationists they'd have been uncomplicatedly happy. As both they were screwed up. Which was why he was now getting roasted at both ends.

Miriam was starting to lose control of herself. Her ironical manner had become too brittle, too light, and her eyes suspiciously bright. Boyet made no attempt to defend himself; his position was indefensible, and he knew it. Every instinct in him told him to lie, to abdicate what responsibility he could, those instincts ingrained from childhood, but he resisted their siren lure for every inculpated Filipino. In his present position he knew it would just make things worse. Only he made it a single occasion, an aberration on an otherwise unblemished record. He was tempted and he fell, he told Miriam. That was all there was to it. By implication, he hinted that one trespass – however aggravated the consequences – shouldn't take precedence over an otherwise unblemished history. He would take the rap on, as it were, second degree murder; murder one – and serial crimes at that – hinged strictly on self-incrimination, and more fool him if he indulged in that when there was no need to. Probably, he reckoned, Miriam would thank him if she was able to. Why hurt her more than there was need to? Just for the sake of his over-tender conscience? Much better to limit the damage.

After the words, silence. After the anger, hurt. Miriam was more Asian than educated. He had an afternoon of articulated reproach and resentment to endure, of "how could you?" (much more easily than you can imagine, he thought) and "Is that how cheaply you value our marriage and your family?" (my children and you, he answered with complete consciousness it was mere truth, are beyond price but – he didn't say – my little addiction has got nothing to do with that). Then she retreated into the ancient, non-verbal forms of expression of the Filipina, the extreme impassivity of expression, the tribal silence pregnant with meaning that still superseded the most polished expressions that modern education could bestow.

That was when Boyet knew he was going to get away with it.

Relief in a 3:1 dilution of remorse mingled to produce a powerful hormonal cocktail. Forty-three hours after first taking his deep breath, engaging super-ego, and operating mouth, he found himself on his knees before Miriam, making his contrition. "Never again," he promised, without a qualm or reservation, speaking the unqualified whole truth to her for the first time, his sincerity making his voice throb (somewhat, he thought, like the Rev. Jesse Jackson's) and redolent of a powerful self-belief. He was intoxicated with the force of his resolution. "Never again." And a third time, as if the words were a spell in themselves. "Never again."

"I believe you," Miriam said.

She believed him? Shit, *he* believed himself.

PART TWO

Chapter Ten

OF ALL THE AIRPORTS IN SOUTH EAST ASIA Professor Pfeidwengeler disliked Soekarno-Hatta the least and detested Ninoy Aquino International the most. The Jakarta airport didn't pretend to be anything it wasn't and Pfeidwengeler loathed sham. Soekarno-Hatta was low-lying (two floors, departure above arrival to the best of his recollection) and open to the elements. The soft, aperient breeze infiltrated the sprawling complex without let, other than the waist-high safety railing on each side of the covered walkways. The roofs were a pleasant, red-baked tile laid in a generally curvy oriental configuration that also succeeded in evoking medieval Heidelberg. As you strolled to your departure lounge, you had the comfortable feeling of being in a garden compound. There was no need at all for air-conditioning, even in the dry season.

Manila, on the other hand, was a monument to inappropriateness, to profligate folly and grandiosity. Blank walls with all the charm of a jail and such natural light as there was filtered through smoked glass of bullet-proof specification. Usually the air was stale and still. The frequent brownouts meant the air-con often didn't work at all, in which case the air-traveller was a piece of meat being microwaved in a giant see-through oven. Arrivals were exhorted to "accomplish" their customs and immigration forms in myriad notices – about the only thing that got accomplished in Asia's most racket-ridden and robber-infested airport, Pfeidwengeler would think as he contemplated the harrowing prospect of the scant kilometres to Makati.

Basically, the trouble was schizophrenia on the presidential scale. NAIA thought it was Changi Airport, Singapore – where Professor Pfeidwengeler now found himself in transit – in the same way that tertiary syphilitics thought they were Napoleon. He'd hummed along in Changi's electric cripple car, which felt like a hovercraft – drawing the usual stares, rather more open than in Europe – for what seemed like three miles but was probably just over one, through the huge halls, the gate numbers improbably increasing all the while. Before he had the satisfaction of knowing whether they exceeded two hundred or not, he found himself where he wanted to be. This was a quiet nook where there was a bar which sold his favourite Austrian (as opposed to Australian) lager – ugly scenes had been enacted all over Asia when the Professor had refused to drink or pay for the erroneously served Swan's or Foster's. The amiable Chinese barman, recipient of Pfeidwengeler's generous tips in the past, acknowledged him without obtruding. It was a far cry from the legendary barmen of the Cunard liners (which Pfeidwengeler was old enough to have travelled on) with their capacity to match names to faces anticipating the computer age but worth cherishing in the age of the anonymity of air travel. Beside this oasis of taste and authenticity was one of the chain of bookstalls to be found throughout the airport, and indeed island, and whether by chance or design this particular outlet did not sell the standardised range of mass market titles but a higher brow selection of travel, fiction, and biography in which the Picador imprint predominated. In fact, the stock would not have disgraced a university bookshop, in Europe. Pfeidwengeler, who was aware his mind worked unconventionally, had decided the stall was not frequented by the enlightened for whose taste the vendor might be supposed to have catered but by cretins, the larger portion of mankind, who – like ants scavenging rubbish – had snapped up everything except the worthwhile. Without entertaining very great hopes the Professor was hoping to find replacement copies of David Irving's *Hitler's War* which he'd pressed on his Singapore hosts and also James Hamilton-Paterson's *Playing with Water*, both in their very different ways models of the sturdily individual Anglo-Saxon brilliance Detlef so much admired. As he prepared to vacate his table – the barman dropping his towel and hurrying over – not easy for a man of Pfeidwengeler's bulk and disabilities especially with the redundant sun umbrella projecting from the centre, the Professor saw perusing one of the few magazines not to be shrink-wrapped (mind condoms against subversiveness) the man he thought of as the Jackal. The Professor quickly sat down again, waving the barman away, reaching into his case for the out of date *Frankfurter Beobachter.* Omar Hamid! Ruth Neumark's lapdog, sidekick, crony! The one human being he could say he actually despised worse than her, Hamid's puppetmaster. Technically the man from Niger, (although he invariably called himself a Libyan because that sounded more dangerous and more interesting and his mother had been born in Tripoli) legalistically, the Lib could describe himself as an author. This was on the strength of the skeletal volume of autobiography (in English), vers libre, haiku, and maxims (in French) which Dr Neumark had used her influence to get published on both sides of the Atlantic six years ago. She'd evaded writing the plug the publishers had requested for the book, disappointing them considerably with her dilatoriness after being so impressive with her enthusiasm. Although the book sold more or less no copies in the US or UK after securing respectful reviews, including one in *New Society* alongside the work of a poet from North Caicos and a Francophone Burkina Faso novelist, it had quite unabetted found a publisher in Italy which Dr Neumark considered a personal vindication. As a radical celebrity she possessed an iron-clad international reputation which nothing short of a torpedo under the water-line could damage, but she liked being contaminated by fall-out as little as anyone else. Professor Pfeidwengeler was one of the few people in the world who possessed a copy of *Dire Midnights,* remaindered and then pulped in short order. Pfeidwengeler considered it cruel and unusual punishment for trees but he liked to peruse Hamid's meanderings in some jaded hour in the same way that he might sniff a burnt feather for faintness, pick at kim chee after hepatitis, or inhale a young female's rectal odours for sensation. The fact that his drought-ridden country was one of the world's largest producers of yellowcake uranium had gone quite uncelebrated in Hamid's jottings. The Professor peered around the corner of his newspaper. It was unmistakably Hamid: tight woolly hair, tonsuring at the back with middle age, skin several shades darker than a true Libyan – *they* tended to milk complexions and freckles under the unquestionably African wire wool – which was an advantage to Hamid who could play the colour card as adeptly as any. It was often to his advantage to be considered an African, except in Africa. His wiry bicycle frame of a body, spry as ever, was that of a man half his age. Pfeidwengeler had seen him run like a gazelle in an intellectual's football match played under a bright Arctic midnight. He was reading the back section of *Time* Magazine, Pfeidwengeler could see, with some absorption. Perhaps it was a flattering review of his mentor, or maybe he was garnering clues as to what was fashionable at the moment. Pfeidwengeler saw his brown Levi jeans were heavily concertinaed at the knees, which might indicate a long journey passed in economy class. Hamid usually tried to negotiate a business class fare from the hosts of the intellectual's jamborees he was invited to – this on the strength of the arcane connections he would be making en route from conference to lectureship to workshop (all part of his attraction and credibility in any case – ANK-MOSC-DEL-VANC etc) where he would later issue from the rostrum thundering, unjetlagged denunciations of great power machinations and the racism that had blighted his career. He and Pfeidwengeler had met in the days when Pfeidwengeler still got invitations and before Hamid knew where Pfeidwengeler was coming from and before Pfeidwengeler had rumbled Hamid, in the smokers' coach on the way to Niagara Falls. Hamid had been bemoaning the cancellation of a piece commissioned from him on Chad by a prestigious American monthly but had been somewhat consoled by the fact that the fee had still been paid. Ruth Neumark had been in the vehicle reserved for non-smokers with the prissy, health conscious, non-Latin, non-Iron Curtain writers.

Where was Hamid bound? It had to be Gobernador de Leon – the only logical conclusion to draw, but the Professor prided himself on not jumping to conclusions, on not pre-judging (the true meaning of the word "prejudice", he liked to tell those willing to listen), on holding in his gut feelings as long as possible. So: there was Hamid who was a self-confessed writer and notorious attender, not fifty metres from the departure gate for the Silkair direct flight to Cebu City, the hub from which one might connect with the Short's Sunriser or Fokker Friendship to Gobernador de Leon where was to be held the convention on ecology and cultural diversity to which he himself had been invited. It was true Hamid had not been on the list of participants but then he wasn't too proud to turn down a last minute invite. "The following have been approached," the circular letter said, in the classic style of those documents, with the letter "A" in bold beside those who had accepted. These glittering lists weren't exactly fabrications. Pfeidwengeler never doubted all those mentioned had been sent invitations – what was the price of a stamp after all? The moot point was whether they would come. This list was as ambitious as any he had seen: the names of five Nobel Prize-winners had figured, none of them previously marginal figures writing in minority languages either, what Pfeidwengeler's former friend the alcoholic Oxford don Bilberry Edrich had called the "pools winners". Unusually, for such a heavyweight list, there had also occurred the names of an American actor and an actress (no connection between them, different generations entirely) known for their espousal of radical ethnic and ecological concerns. Perhaps they'd incite the laureates to attend and vice versa. The name of Ruth Neumark had not appeared which now surprised Pfeidwengeler, if Hamid had been invited in his own right. In those circles where reputations were brokered he had obviously been gazetted promotion.

Putting the *Time* back in the rack, Hamid bought a bottle of what Pfeidwengeler would find when he investigated was pink mouthwash or gargling medication. He was, it now appeared, definitely bound for the same destination as he sauntered to the Cebu gate for flight MI586 which would depart at its scheduled time. Professor Pfeidwengeler emended his own lifetime habit of extreme punctuality by entering a Duty Free to browse amongst the liquor and giant Toblerone bars for so long that he was among the penultimate group of passengers to board. He wasn't discomposed about Hamid's presence but he would like to hold the advantage of surprise for as long as he could. Two Australians in shorts, thongs, and singlets were haggling vehemently in this fixed-price outlet over the cost of a compact disc player. Australians, thought Pfeidwengeler, with mingled scorn and inspiration were just this: Texan Jews.

JACK Beaufort's routine called for light refreshment or *merienda* with family at around ten in the morning, earlier or later depending how work had gone that day. As the kids were up and running at 4 a.m. and Jack and Lilibeth by five, they needed something to take the edge off lunch at 11:30 a.m., otherwise this occasion and symbol of family unity and communication was in danger of being eclipsed by dire bodily need at table. Jack was a little stuck today, so he'd retired from the lists of self-expression prematurely at 9:30, or about the time Detlef Pfeidwengeler, still unaware of the presence of Omar Hamid, was checking in his aluminium suit case with the leather straps, like himself a survivor of the era of the great liners. Jack was working on a Compendium of the New Literatures in English, putting down on polished tablets of stone what had been the raw material of his popular lectures at his university in Australia. African, Indian, Burmese, Cypriot, Mauritian, Singaporean, and in one glorious instance, Kurdish: it was all grist to Jack's mill, so long as they wrote in some type of the Anglo-Saxon mother tongue. It had all been breaking new ground when he started, with risk-taking involved for his career. Now it was very worthy still and not quite at the point where it was all already old hat, but it had become a definite academic territory where the pioneers like himself were in danger of being evicted as squatters for having failed to register their claims early. Jack wasn't a sour man; he was enjoying his retirement and the writing in the mornings and most of all his second family. No matter that his Australian children, a merchant navy officer and a lady dentist, were probably laughing fit to bust behind the old man's back (if they weren't deeply ashamed), he knew he and Beth had a real love. So many of the Foreigner-Filipina marriages he'd seen had been a sham, a con-trick on the girl's side. He could hear Beth now, frothing the chocolate the way he liked it. The poor bastard foreigners just didn't know what they were letting themselves in for. Tricky wasn't the word for the girls. Wily as monkeys, they were Broadway-class actors with it. For a one-way ticket out of the country, any foreigner would do. No lie was too outrageous to sustain, no subterfuge too low. "I love you, vairy, vairy much *sirrr*," Jack had heard a girl say in Rosie's Diner, on one of his early visits (to red light Ermita, he was sorry to say). In his heart he didn't blame them. On the whole they were offered the male refuse of Europe and the Antipodes. Jack beheld the procession with pity and terror: the aged, the halt, the infirm, grey of skin, stumbling of gait; the mentally unstable, objectionable, or plain weird. Guys no self-respecting Swiss or Sydney girl would have gone near. Desperate, lonely men at the end of their tether. Jack had seen them with their weak faces and mad, rolling eyes, the huge, veiny legs they loved to bare in shorts, ankle socks, and sandals; he'd seen them meander to universal consternation in the direction of concert stages and grab the mike from entertainers too polite to resist before droning their mad inconsequentialities to a tolerant native audience; he'd seen them red-faced, shoving and abusing their consorts in public (only slightly less heinous than a discreet shooting). Could you blame the Filipinas? Sometimes their cranky spouses even murdered their wives or forced them to work the streets. Well, sometimes he could. The faces and bodies of angels (the beauty of the Filipina incomparable if you had a hankering for oriental women, and Jack had learned late in life he had) covering base and calculating souls. Not at Rosie's this time but in the lobby of the Philippine Plaza he'd heard a more up-market girl, her arms lovingly thrown round her swain, say in Tagalog to the waitress in the instant intimacy between her countrywomen which foreigners found so charming, a smile on her face, "God strike this creep dead." It was the smile which was chilling and the fact the bloke was quite human for a change. Jack felt for him. There but for the Grace of God. Lurking in the background as a major player without lines, an inane grin on his face, indirect recipient of foreign bounty, was Pepe Pinoy. In the absence of direct irrefutable proof to the contrary you had to assume he was there – presumption of parasite. Two free-size souvenir T-shirts from Puerto Galera? A pair of Boracay sun-visors? Allowance consumed at startling rate? Not a greater level of graspingness – though that was always there, too – so much as provision for the other, his price for her time. Jack had known of four girls who'd married foreigners who'd never realised their virgin brides were already mothers of two or three, bent on remitting every cent they could to kid and boyfriend. And *he'd* only known because Beth, bless her native love of gossip, had spilled the beans to him. He'd say eighty per cent of mixed marriages failed, the girls sometimes escaping the day after their residence or citizenship qualification was in. The guys who were rash enough to marry bargirls seemed to suffer a separation rate no higher than those who'd mail-ordered their partners, the "pen-pals".

Jack had made more than his fair share of mistakes in the archipelago, pre-Beth. A forty-eight-year-old widower off a wonderful marriage spanning three decades – young in the sixties, sharing tribulation in the sober seventies, serene in the effluent eighties – was a vulnerable creature, like a hermit crab which had shed its shell. He didn't even know how to ask a girl (woman!) out on a date. Forty-eight – that had been young enough to kid himself he wasn't altogether past his sell-by date (he still had a thirty-two-inch waistline) – but to have one foot in the grave so far as anyone manufactured after 1965 was concerned.

Beth was twenty-three years younger than him, which didn't sound too good and looked worse on paper, but he had no reason to feel embarrassed about how they looked when they were together. "Who cares age? Love the important," was Beth's standard reply. Actions spoke louder than words. They'd been together nine years, visited his relatives in New Zealand a cumulative total of nine weeks, and had two handsome mestizo boys who spoke perfect Tagalog and English with slight Irish accents. Jack could still get exasperated beyond endurance by the country and its inhabitants – generally the powerful; his conversion wasn't external: he scorned to wear a barong tagalog to his sons' prizegivings, preferring the blazer and silk square he always wore with his open neck Van Heusens, so that he looked like Pom gentry from the thirties. But he knew he loved the Philippines, loved it in the way the father had preferred the Prodigal Son.

"Dong," Beth called, she was a Visayan, "*Naglolo ka ba?* Come now. Waiting everyone."

Jack grinned as he always did. A stock accusation was that he took advantage of the privacy of his study to abuse himself. He had replied, "Only intellectual masturbation," the first time but Beth, bless her, hadn't understood. He hadn't any of the real stuff to waste, keeping up with Beth's demands. He'd been faithful to her from day one. She had told him foreigners made the better husbands. "Macho the Filipino guy, honey," she related as an incontrovertible truth, like sunrise was at dawn. "Cockfight, beer, chicks, hands spank wife easy-easy. Poor one or educate is the same." Jack wasn't sure about this macho bit. Observation taught him the *pinoy* was imbued with two normally contradictory qualities: gross recklessness and extreme cowardice. He and Beth enjoyed a frank communication; about the only relationship that didn't seem to rely on third party mediation and euphemism was husband-wife. When it was going well, that was. Beth was from the barrio; she hadn't graduated high school. She had not heard of the Greeks or Romans, or of Adolf Hitler. One day she had asked, "Dong, how far Auckland from Bethlehem?" but not carrying head luggage, Jack had learned, made you a lot nimbler around the posts on the everyday course. He was the one allowances were made for.

"Daddy," eight-year-old Leo said, "I've kept your chocolate hot, haven't I?"

"Attaboy," said Jack. "You can have half my puto bumbong."

"Do not drinking water Gobernador de Leon, honey," Beth said. "Have amoeba Gobernador de Leon."

"Sweetheart," Jack said, beyond irritation, "I am not a tourist. Neither am I an infant. I have lived in this country nearly ten years, time for the most delicate stomach to have acclimatised. And, may I remind you, you were the one who contracted Giardia."

"Huh," retorted Beth, "not infant! Big baby *ikaw*. Why you go so long?"

"It's not a long time."

"Three weeks long time. Maybe you got chick there."

"It's nearer two – weeks, I mean."

Although Jack knew Beth knew she needn't give herself the smallest concern as to his fidelity, he was equally aware she was in the grip of cultural paroxysm. Knife in her shoulder-bag, she'd followed his friend the seventy-three-year-old Boholana poet Milagrosa Gomez all the way home after he'd met her for lunch at Shakey's Pizza Parlour.

"Hoy! Stay away the chicks, or I cut your *tintin* off, pfutt! I am Filipina!"

"OK, OK," said Jack. "Have it your way. Just pack me enough briefs this time, will you."

"It's really very good of you to come, Dr Neumark," Carla Giolitti, the public relations person, had said in New York ten days previously.

"It's very good of you to invite me," said Ruth Neumark.

Her powerful ego often expressed itself in a form of Christ-like humility. A more modest or less socially self-assured person might have balked at the open reverence offered but Dr Neumark had encountered it so many times that she had a response at reflex level, in the same way that a veteran Springbok opening batsman confronted in the remote past with West Indian pace bowling might still be adept at ducking a bouncer.

"Well, I'll tell you frankly," said Carla. "It's an honour, it really is, both for me and for her." Then she changed the topic quickly because she really wasn't a toady and she was also very professional. Carla was a genuinely nice person, even if she did make her living out of that unfeigned niceness. "How's the new apartment?"

Here, did she know it, she was putting her foot wrong. Dr Neumark had in an unguarded moment told Carla, when she was giving her a contact number (direct communication without intercession of Dr Neumark's lecture agent being of the essence since it was getting late) that she was between places. Carla would have to try three numbers (old apartment, new apartment's business line and new apartment's private ex-directory number which Carla was sworn never to divulge). The old place was a block of service apartments which could be rented by the day or at a favourable monthly discount. Dr Neumark had rented by the quarter. The new was a sensationally expensive but, at the time Dr Neumark had bought, still tasteful and discreet owner condominium on the East side. Unfortunately, the developer had got it featured on *Lifestyles of the Rich and Famous* two nights ago. Dr Neumark was not keen on too many people being in the know as to in the first place how rich her third husband, the attorney and international tax adviser Gerald Goldblatt, was and, more importantly, just how much time she spent out of South Africa. The amount of time Dr Neumark spent out of South Africa – the passport of which Republic caused her as much inconvenience entering foreign countries as it might the most fanatical Afrikaner, she who had once been reviled as a "white kaffir"! – was not a trivial career matter.

There was a vital distinction to be drawn, between those white South African intellectuals and journalists who had emigrated, whether to Europe or the US, and those who remained. Unless actually expelled, in which case celebrity status attached for about five years, those who had left were regarded as not only morally inferior but also dimmer luminaries. In the minds of the humourless and parochial Scandinavian and American geriatrics and academics who controlled the intellectual foundations and award-giving bodies it was considered somehow less worthy to have strayed off one's patch. They were liberals, but imbued with a deep closet conservative dislike of gypsies. "You are the voice and conscience of your country, of the otherwise unspoken hopes and aspirations of the people," a Swedish Tweedledum and Tweedledee had eulogised her in tandem. She had a running feud with Angela Smith and Timothy Donovan, the distinguished actress and the writer in exile; Angela who had left Southern Rhodesia in 1951 with her baby and no husband, the homosexual short story writer Donovan who had fled Johannesburg over twenty years later, but the unlikely pair united in common detestation of Ruth. "I mean, who the *fuck*, the fuck, does Ruth Neumark think she is?" Smith had asked sympathetic hearers for more than two decades at her chalet in Gstaad, the Anglo-Saxon the more emphatic for coming from a woman rarely otherwise heard to swear. She and Donovan agreed it was the holier-than-thou aspect of Ruth which got their goat the most. As Dr Neumark had got more famous she had developed and projected the saintly aspect of her image, even at the expense of the sage. A recent twist noticed by Donovan had been the increasing use as theatrical property of the garment known in the West as the shawl. "Have you *seen* it, my dear?" he squawked, calling collect down the international line from London. Dr Neumark had been photographed in "it" by two rival London Sunday qualities for the same weekend and then worn a similar but light-coloured garment for an entire television interview. The aura in which it enveloped her was less of the colleen or the Zulu than the Mahatma, Ruth holding it tightly around her thin shoulders as she turned her face, with its rather oriental cheekbones, sideways and down to regard the interviewer with rapt humble attentiveness, then lifted that noble head to the artificial light with full consciousness of the seraphic glow upon it. "It was like she was reading the fucking beatitudes," Donovan told Smith, his voice tight with rage and jealousy, the satellite line afflicted with echo and repeating his statement for good measure, so that he heard it as from another party, the envy he had thought absent from his soul throbbing in the voice. Donovan lived in a mean quarter and had twice been beaten up by queer-bashers. Dr Neumark lived (some of the year) in what might be described as a palace in Cape Town, furnished in exquisite taste with the discounted wares of Barruch "Barrie" Goldblatt, gay younger brother of lawyer Gerald and interior designer and dealer of fantastically-priced bric à brac to the jet set. Smith and Donovan knew this, having been dinner guests in better times. Dr Neumark wasn't a liar by any means; on the other hand she did nothing to dispel the notion in some foreign quarters that she was more or less under house arrest. "Do you," an American interviewer had asked, breathless with respect, "do you get death threats on the telephone?" Dr Neumark had laughed at that as a good joke. No, never. But the mirth served only to reinforce respect for Dr Neumark's courage, her unassuming courage. "We do get all kinds of click-ings and strange cross-lines. And there are loads of wrong numbers. Loads," she would say, bestowing a complicit glance on whichever interviewer it was.

Dr Neumark had a genius for saying the right thing at the right time in the right place. Not even her sworn enemies, whether conservatives like Professor Pfeidwengeler, or liberals and radicals like Smith and Donovan, could say she wasn't quite talented. It was the way she fostered that ability that drove them mad.

So when charming Carla Giolitti made her diversionary small-talk about the new apartment she leaped in a sense from the frying-pan into the fire, had no idea of the history she was inheriting, which vibrations she was sending down what array of fine wire. However, Ruth Neumark was fully aware the remark was made in all innocence. She made herself smile and said, "Oh, shaping up, you know. It's very extravagant of us. We shouldn't really have done it, but it's granny's little indulgence. My son's children love the pool and the recreation complex. Grannies are like that, you know. Jewish grannies," and Dr Neumark smiled disarmingly at Carla and the very fat woman whose name she'd better get hold of again soon but who looked like a Jewess.

Without knowing it, Dr Neumark had in uttering her self-dismissive remark echoed a comment of Professor Pfeidwengeler's. He, too, as unbalanced here as in other matters, thought of her as the quintessential Jewish grandmother, redoubtable tyrant, maintaining her hold through emotional blackmail, guilt, and adroit alliance, with her opinions valued to the extent they were based on a distillation of life's rich experience and unassailable moral soundness. The shrewd Jewish granny but using a tried and tested domestic arsenal of megalomania and tantrum on a greater theatre of war.

This formidable hybrid smiled ingenuously again at her two companions. While not luxurious, Carla Giolitti's apartment was cosy, everything warm with the patina of use and in good taste, the cheap British computer – at the moment afflicted with the Leonardo virus – supplying the only jarring contemporary note. The combination of meticulous order and cleanness with the slightly frayed quality of the old but excellent furniture was indubitably appealing. It had put Dr Neumark in a mellow off-duty mood – her normal manner with new acquaintances in the professional line being one of quiet, correct evenness, with the hint of a chilly asperity just held in check – designed to let those unworthy of cultivation know that they were to be inferiors. Provided subordination was accepted and signalled – some kind of figurative buttock display requisite – Dr Neumark could go on to show her gracious side. When she wanted she could be very winning, but in an utterly dignified way that did both her and the wooed (whether audience or individual) a great credit. Both she and Carla were tall women, well over 5ft 10 ins, and slim as professional models half their age. Carla's black hair still showed no hint of grey, though Ruth had allowed traces into the glorious rusty mane that she'd inherited from her Russian grandmother, along with green eyes and freckles. Both also had the same sharp, delicately pretty faces – Carla's at forty-three still very pretty. So Ruth felt she had something in common with Carla without being in competition with her. Carla for her part, already overawed by Dr Neumark's reputation and now in thrall to her powerful personality, found herself (despite best professional and humane instincts) impelled to ally with the celebrated South African autobiographer to subjugate the third human being in the room.

This was Gracie Hipkin of the environmental pressure group Whalewatch. The first thing to strike anyone about Gracie – and this was unfortunate – was her extreme stoutness. It was unfortunate because it eclipsed her real qualities. Some people never discovered her attributes. She remained just a fat woman. Glandular problems left her weighing more than two hundred and twenty pounds and standing five feet six. In addition to being the butt of the usual cruel behind the back jokes she had an added cross to bear in being an officer of her particular organisation. Was it appropriate or utterly inappropriate? Big as a beached whale herself but then didn't ecology, environment, Greens etc include in their free association spectrum fresh air, jogging, aerobics, California, orange juice? Shouldn't she be, not necessarily svelte but a little fitter? Set the example? It was doubly unfortunate in this context that Ms Hipkin was a forty-a-day smoker, the insides of her fingers the colour of horse chestnuts. If you thought about it, the cigarettes kept some pounds off her and the strain of enduring other people's cheap witticisms did nothing to help her kick the habit.

She went for one now. Dr Neumark frowned. Carla caught the expression – part of her job, but she had also become unusually responsive to Ruth.

"Even Audrey Hepburn wasn't allowed to smoke here, honey," she said. "It's a rigid rule of the house. Do you hate me for it?"

"No, I hate myself." Gracie spoke a greater truth than the immediate context. She was unable to resist asking, "Was Audrey Hepburn really here?"

"Sure she was. We were trying to get her to do an ad but she never did. It was in Dr Neumark's chair by coincidence. That's a celebrity chair." Carla hoped she wouldn't notice the Groucho Marx ash-tray on the Moorish chest that served as coffee-table.

"Poor chair," said Dr Neumark, "but I'm in no danger of breaking it as you can see," with her ever so slight trace of flat vowels. "And you must call me Ruth. Both of you."

"Well, that's nice, isn't it," said Carla. Despite the half-hearted protests of her guests she went to get another percolator of coffee, sweeping up Groucho at the same time.

"That's an unusual sugar-bowl," Dr Neumark said. "Oh, keep it away from me then," Gracie exclaimed. She and Dr Neumark went on to discuss the merits and demerits of synthetic sweeteners while Carla was in the kitchen. Gracie was by way of an expert on these, both as dieter and consumer activist. She'd worked on a watchdog body monitoring the food industry before the whaling; again, Dr Neumark couldn't help thinking, not an inappropriate job, considering her own body. The poor creature!

"I shouldn't really say it," said Gracie, saying it anyway, "but I'd have gone on taking my chances with saccharine. I even got to like the bitter after-taste. But you can take nutrisweet with a clear conscience."

"Until the next report comes out," Dr Neumark said.

"Mmmm," said Gracie, sinking back into the sofa from her elbows on knees forward position.

"All the nice things are bad for you," said returning Carla. "That's just life. By the way, I'm afraid the tickets are only economy, with the promise of an upgrade from Philippine Airlines. The organisers will use their influence. We said we were a quasi-diplomatic group." She looked apologetically to Dr Neumark, who shrugged. She wasn't wearing a shawl, but a beaded black woollen jacket in a vaguely American Indian design. She had excellent clothes sense. This wasn't the time or place to kick up a fuss, but she'd raised blue murder in the past when not afforded first-class treatment. Strong men had quailed, women wept tears of rage and frustration. Her oceanic pity for the suffering masses in the abyss was matched only by the dizzy crest of her personal hauteur. There existed a history of automobiles booked on her behalf and forgotten, journalists left languishing, publicity assistants telephoned at 4 a.m., lunch dates missed but uncancelled. Like all the best radicals she was imperiously patrician at heart.

Or as Timothy Donovan had put it in the days of their friendship, with the vulgarity of the Union Castle steward he had once been, "Ruth's a typical bloody carrot-top."

Slipping into the role allotted her, Gracie said with a cheerful laugh, "That's more of a problem for me. I'm wider than two economy seats."

"I'll just give you an up-dated list of participants then," Carla said.

"All flying second-class," Dr Neumark said.

"Um," said Carla. "Well, new, we've got two Indians. That was my idea. Your hosts – I shouldn't be telling you this, but never mind," – in her extensive experience Carla had found it safer to be indiscreet in single-sex company. Men, and especially gay men, were actually bigger gossips; besides it was politic to give Dr Neumark a titbit just now and rope her into minor conspiracy – "took a little convincing at first. They're very anxious to make a big splash in the developed world – I hope that's not an impolite expression; it sounds so rude to call someone undeveloped."

"Evolving," prompted Gracie Hipkin.

"That was just the word I was looking for. They just wanted to invite Americans, Australians, and Japanese, and I think Taiwanese, with the odd European. But I told them, that wasn't the way. You'll get more attention from our media if there is, er, third world involvement. Otherwise, it's just another conference, isn't it."

"Positive discrimination," said Gracie promptly and comfortably. "And did they take the point?"

"Oh, yes, she's very sharp. You'll see for yourselves. So we've got Kumar and Mishra. She's a journalist. He's a diplomat and a writer. Well, of course journalists are also writers. I mean, not all journalists, but those who write are writers. Oh dear, I'm talking nonsense again. On course, Carla. OK, then there's Bob Richards, the Canadian poet – I don't know his work but he comes highly recommended from the other conferences he's attended. He writes on green themes, I'm told. There are the scientists – like you, Gracie. You'll find their names on your lists. Some very distinguished names there, by the way. I've got one of those cottonpicking viruses on my computer; otherwise I'd give you the details. We might have a French Admiral and some East Europeans, if we're lucky. Our journalists – I won't call them a necessary evil because they can be very charming..."

"When they want to," said Dr Neumark drily. The ensuing amusement was absolutely genuine. If you were on Dr Neumark's side of the line it could be a very consolidating and flattering experience.

"Yes, well it's always a little risky with journalists, but we need them as well, and the organisers are very eager for coverage. Actually I think ours are rather house-trained. There's John Hawkins, whom I've always found to be quite bright and very straight in his dealings. He'll be doing it for several of the Asian English language weeklies, the qualities, you know, not all under his by-line, of course. And there's a younger man from Britain, Rod Kienzler. There's the local people as well – one or two reporters and a professor. The Japanese delegation and the Taiwanese writer. And there's your friend, Omar Hamid, of course. That's the core of the conference, if you like. There are always changes and last minute dropouts. I don't need to tell an old trouper like you that, Dr Neumark," Carla waited for Dr

Neumark to rebuke her for not calling her "Ruth" but the remonstrance did not come. In truth, Dr Neumark did not like being called an "old trouper". Old she supposed she was at sixty-six but "trouper" she definitely objected to. It made her sound like what her enemies accused her of being.

Gracie Hipkin, who didn't just rescue whales, said, "It must be such a nuisance when they do that after all your hard work. At least you've got hold of us. We can't escape now!"

Carla looked serious. She was the kind of person who tried to do justice by her clients and wards. "It's just part of the job you get to accept. People have a perfect right to change their plans, and things do happen at the most awkward moments, children with chickenpox, grandmothers passing on."

"Oh, yes," said Dr Neumark, "burying grandmothers. I've heard that one." And, like the old troupers they were, she and Carla savoured the hoary old excuse with a certain stern cynicism.

Chapter Eleven

"*AND THE CHILDREN,*" SAID MRS INIT, wooing the microphone with the tone she knew to thrill. She was slightly husky with a virus at the moment, but she liked it. "*And their children's children, our posterity.*" She was answering her own question, borrowing the Congressman's favourite rhetorical device of their sala and bedroom conversations. She had just asked who they were doing it all for. She'd learned long ago you didn't go far wrong by adducing the children, God bless them. She didn't have any of her own, so nobody could accuse her of being partisan. "*They are at one and the same time the vanguard and the banner of our great battle against poverty, our unconditional war on want.*"

Victoria had slaved over her opening address, composed, discarded, re-instated; taken professional advice, heeded it for five minutes, then proceeded to ignore what she was going to pay (a modicum) for. She had maintained the same relationship with Nestor Chavez that Hitler had with Field Marshal Keitel and General Guderian. The Congressman, however, for his part, though not a subscriber to Philippine Military Academy values, still less to the Prussian officer code, had proved an invaluable sounding-board. From the start he'd complained about the entire conception's insubstantiality, its lack of relation to the concrete issues – being economic issues, of course.

"*Arte.*"

He'd used the expressive Visayan word, which by happy linguistic accident bore the same connotations as the English "arty-farty". What had it got to do with the real world? That was what he had wanted to know.

"Our combat, this great endeavour of ours," said Victoria, her voice rising and possibly causing a minor wail in the p/a system, which brought the audience to her side rather than jeopardised their attention, *"is not exclusively waged on the economic front. We must involve the marginalised,"* the last a signal word learned from Nestor, the labourer worthy his hire, *"women, children. We must uplift the poor. We cannot solve their problems with a hand-out. We have to reach their souls. We must empower the people to grasp their own destinies. How can we do this?"*

In his seat among the dignitaries on the dais the Congressman sweated. What the hell was she going to say? Break out armalites to the poor? Vic-Vic was so damned unpredictable lately.

"The weapons we shall employ" – 'Sus Maria, thought the Congressman – *"are the ones that touch the spirit: the arts, music, poetry, painting, culture. Debate, dialectic. We must inspire them to control their own destinies. The project involves the engineers of souls, not just the constructors of roads and bridges."* Coming to the end, Victoria allowed herself to look up from her sheet of paper. She was becoming sufficiently practised a public speaker to realise that it was easiest either to read like a robot from the printed screed without variation or simply to stand and orate without prompt as the spirit moved you. What was most difficult to accomplish was the half-way house method she was trying: referring to a prepared speech, ad-libbing, and then attempting to come back to it. Your eyes kind of lost the place and you hesitated awkwardly. At the moment she still lacked the nerve to throw away her crutches and just run with the words – she was left stilted.

The hall extended before her. She removed her reading-spectacles. It was hers, with the grace of the Blessed Virgin. From nothing she'd envisioned it. The lofty ceiling, the tiered rise of the seating, the handsome panelling, the air-con capable of cutting to the bone; then the marbled CR with its gilt taps and Rolls Royce plumbing, the water starting from the cistern with no more than the purring of a Corniche (the courtesy limo of the Gritti) and then the flow smoothly accelerating, carrying all before its irresistible passage round the bend. Impressive cornering characteristics. She'd tested it herself – only twelve seconds for the refill cycle to complete after flushing.

Victoria cleared her throat. The p/a system was karaoke class. She hadn't herself heard the minor feed-back distortion she'd caused by raising her voice too close to the mike. The beauty of the system was it sounded to you as if you were just speaking ordinarily – you weren't distracted by the thunder of your own reverberations – but in fact your voice was borne to all corners on an acoustical magic carpet. The place was respectably full. She hadn't taken chances. She had instructed Professor Benitez to have his students attend, but out of the university uniform; the girls had been only too pleased to get into civilian attire and they'd get a course credit for attendance. Probably learn more than they would at that rather stodgy, over-religious foundation. Young Vic-Vic certainly hadn't bothered to go to university. There they all were, eager young faces turned down to her, some bespectacled, none – she flattered herself – bored. The seed-corn of the future. The shallowly rising upper balcony was virtually empty, but never mind, no one in the audience would ever notice.

"And so with apprehension, a natural apprehension, but a still surer faith in the potentiality of Man under God, I declare open the VIP Multi-Media Resources and Dragons Convention Centre of Gobernador de Leon City, welcome you the delegates and press, our honourable guests, Mayor, Lady Mayor, Monsignor, Brigadier Nunao-as, and special guest of honour Senator Hercules Mijares. Our mighty themes shall be... Cultural Plurality in a World of Ecological Limits. I give you the Symposium."

Storm of applause. She was stunned. What had she said that so hit the mark? Shatteringly loud, rolling on and on. You would have thought it was the Sharon Cuneta fan club eulogising its idol. Her face flushed with pleasure. More hardened – though not necessarily more accomplished – public performers like the

Congressman had that knack of keeping wooden faces, so important for maintaining the vital veneer of professionalism and modesty. Mrs Mayor seized her hand as she rejoined the VIPs. "Wonderful, Victoria, so wonderful always." Victoria interpreted that as a more reliable augury than her subjective interpretation of the applause. The lady was the most notorious band-waggoner in the business. She loved a winner and she could spot them when they were specks on the horizon. And no one could put dissociative distance between themselves and a flopperoo so quickly as she. You could see her wondering whether to *kiss* Mrs Congressman. "Thank you, thank you," said Victoria to no one in particular. She took her seat by her Mister. "Why were they clapping so loudly?" she whispered huskily in his ear, with the kind of ingenuousness reserved for one's partner in life. His eyes narrowed. His mouth opened. As to what the response would be she was not yet cognisant but this she did know: the answer would take the form of an initial riddle to which he would supply the solution.

At this moment the Monsignor summoned them to rise for the blessing. Mrs Init had begun hinting to him several months back – one didn't instruct a Monsignor – that she'd prefer it quick and simple, not too florid, not too self-congratulatory, on the secular side. A little birdie had told her the Monsignor's usual style would not sit too well with the foreign intellectuals, many of whom she suspected of being agnostics if not outright atheists, the scientists especially. Everyone stood. As Victoria adopted the hands folded over groin, head half-inclined, looking through the eyebrows posture inculcated by the nuns (as if God the centre forward was taking his penalty kick and you were blocking him) it became apparent to her that everyone but one had stood. From her vantage she could see the shiny top of the bald head of the man she recognised from his photograph as Professor Detlef Pfeidwengeler. One of the first things she had noticed about him earlier, with some dismay, was that he had a bad leg. He either chose to, because it was more comfortable, or had to, on doctor's orders, wear shorts because of the undressed ulceration on his huge left leg and the terrible thrombotic veins like 1/8 garden hoses. The shorts were both voluminous and khaki. Nearly his whole left calf was black and blue, the healthy right leg looking about fifty years younger and the property of another person. The potential for cost had been what dismayed Mrs Init. If he had the bad taste to fall seriously ill the fees could be crippling to his hosts. Philippine hospital administrators – even her relations – surrendered nothing in point of business astuteness to any in the world. Really, the PR company should have checked the delegates out or got them to produce afffi-davits of sound health, especially as the (very) charming Mrs Giolitti had insisted that the hosts provide baggage insurance and underwrite medical costs. Why, you could get people coming with the aim of getting freely hospitalised!

The defiant smirk on Pfeidwengeler's face that was to become his habitual expression over the next several weeks told her it would have caused him no very great inconvenience to stand. He was originally a chemical engineer and something of an auto-didact in genetics and criminology but his fame rested on his non-academic views now, Mrs Giolitti had informed her. Victoria was supplied with a paper of his on inherited criminal tendencies, which she found largely convincing. John Hawkins had recommended him, for newsworthiness, the "big splash" as Mrs Giolitti called it. And in the circumstances that was well worth any extra trouble.

The Monsignor completed his model benediction, nodding to Victoria as he returned to his seat. Her first inclination was to give him a thumbs-up sign, but she restrained herself, even though he was probably sufficiently amenable to give her one straight back. Beside her, the Congressman was fizzing with the restrained desire to inform, to contribute something to the evening. Every time he bent across to get her ear, as it were, she was distracted – someone else, not more important, of course, but maybe more relevant to the immediate proceedings, would need to tug her sleeve, or the speaker at the mike would turn back to pay tribute to her or to make a quip which she would have to publicly acknowledge with a quiet and gracious smile. Poor Congressman.

Then at the reception cocktails she didn't have a moment to herself, or for him. It was one heady whirl to the next.

Not until she was in the sala with him at home – he'd left two hours before her – did he get his opportunity. "Inday, you know your question?"

"What question, dearest?"

"You forgot?" For a moment he looked annoyed.

"Tell me, I am all ears."

"You wanted to know why the applause sounded so loud? It's easy, 'day. It's because you already attended your functions outside – like skating, schoolsports. This was inside."

"Yes, so?"

"Yes, 'day." The Congressman started to look impatient. "It's like you're the one to shoot someone with a .45 outside in the street. Sounds only like a firecracker in the road. OK, a big one, an Original Thunder. Do it in a room? Shit! Like you let off a goddamned cannon!"

"So what do you make of it so far?" Rod Kienzler asked at those cocktails some hours earlier.

"It's only just started!" returned Jack Beaufort jovially. "In fact, it *hasn't* started!" Being the decent, fair-minded fellow he was, he fought to overcome the immediate and instinctive dislike for Kienzler which came over him. Bluff John Hawkins, the leathery Kiwi stringer, unafflicted with such scruples had also conceived an aversion to Kienzler but made no effort to repress it. Hawkins was the journalist Carla Giolitti had told her guests in New York she had always found straight in his dealings, which generally speaking he was. Kienzler looked round the hall with amused curiosity. "Well, it's all new to me," he said, with uncharacteristic modesty. "As far as I'm concerned, it began at Manila Airport, if not Terminal One. Cebu was a bit of a culture shock, though. What a tip! Talk about the Turd World!" He was twenty-eight-years old, with pale brown hair cut *en brosse*, the perky features of Harry Hedgehog underneath, round wire-framed spectacles and in a uniform Hawkins had never seen before but recognised as such: black jeans, the half dress, half-industrial shoes called Doctor Martens, and as concessions to formality, a white jacket and turquoise bow tie. Rod had been a lecturer at a Cambridge college before his present job with a television production company.

"I take it you've not been to these parts before?" asked Jack.

"The farthest East I've been is Crete," confessed Kienzler cheerfully, who had told them he had a brief to write an account of the proceedings for a London newspaper. Typical of today's brash young bastards already jousting in shiny armour without ever earning their spurs on a battlefield, Hawkins thought. Did absolutely everyone think they could be a journalist? "You're all right then, sonny," he said. "Wogs begin at Calais."

Rod Kienzler decided he'd better get a handle on the conversation. His normal mode of social operation was to "interview" the people he met in a non-professional situation. That was he subjected them to a barrage of questions about their livelihoods and personal histories without any real interest in hearing the replies; this put him in charge of the encounter and – he thought – was probably intensely flattering to the unglamorous recipient. He chose Jack to be the object of this exercise. The ploy tended to be less effective on journalists and was indeed often resented, while Hawkins had already given signs of proving unpropitious material.

"You said you'd been here how long? Twenty years? How long did it take before you felt you'd fitted in?"

"I didn't say how long," Jack answered equably, "but you're right, it's a long time, but nowhere near twenty years. And I've never felt I fitted in."

"Don't you feel you've lost touch with your own roots? And is that something you regret?"

"No, but it wouldn't be something to regret."

"Are you married?"

"Indeed I am."

"She's a Filipino or, er," normally fluent to the point of glibness, Rod stumbled (he didn't like to say "white" which was the word that came to mind) "European, a Westerner?"

"She's a Filipina, actually. Filipino is a male citizen of this Republic."

"Children?"

"Two."

"How do they feel about their mixed heritage?"

"I've never asked them."

Hawkins caught Jack's eye. The message in the glance was clear enough. Who is this idiot?

While fairly thin-skinned as regarded slights on himself, Rod's hide was unlimitedly thick where the sensitivities of others were concerned. He was quite happy to continue the interview; however, Jack said, "I would cite our present situation as a happy blend of the local and the international. I like the architecture a lot. How about you, Mr Hawkins?"

"John. Yeah, it's got a lot going for it."

John Hawkins and Jack craned their heads. Anything to put a sock in it, but the place really was nice. The main convention hall was nothing unusual in the eyes of a citizen of the greater world – though of the current trio Jack alone truly appreciated how amazing it was to find something like that in a provincial Philippine city. The reception hall was something else; it would have been special anywhere. Difficult to categorise. It was where you might kick your heels for a Borgia pope, but gone high tech. Not so much the churchy flagstones, which were actually marble joined with gold metal, as the three Renaissance pillars set off-centre and assymetrically in the – Jack checked – hexagonal chamber. These were white, ceramic covered, with the champagne-glass part on the ceiling actually glass, ornately frescoed and lit from below in such a way that they threw a second shadow-frieze inside the bowl. In one corner were cubist waterfalls and rapids illuminated by green filters. In the distance more green from lettering on PC screens, fitted with the vital new automatic voltage regulators. It was weird, could have been a disastrous monument to ill taste, but it worked. Sometimes Jack felt desperately proud of the achievements of his adopted country and countrymen in the way of the parent of a backward child startled by a piece of abstract art from the retarded hand. That someone could pull off something like this here, make real a vision like this out of the dusty, broken roads and black water drains, the third-rate and the makeshift – and he was often disappointed when visitors failed to share the appreciation afforded by his perspective. But he wasn't let down this time. "Benvenuto Cellini de-closets in Silicon Valley," Kienzler said. Not bad, Hawkins thought.

The three Anglos, otherwise so disparate, had unconsciously drawn together in the first place; other birds of a feather were also in their different flocks throughout the room. Jack felt he ought to be ashamed of his clannishness. A passing *pinoy* saw his roving gaze. "Not so bad, boss?" Jack thought the "boss" was ironic and liked the boy for it; he was just a stripling but endearingly confident.

"Actually we all like it a lot."

"Really? Then I'm glad. I'm the one who designed this room."

"You? You're just a boy." Hawkins laughed jovially.

Jack saw at once that the knockabout compliment had gone astray. The young Filipino kept smiling, but a little fixedly. Maybe he was getting fed up with seeing the plum projects snapped up by his seniors or, worse, the credit for his ideas stolen from him.

"We like the pillars a lot," Jack said. "Very reminiscent of Italian churches. Are they functional or just decorative?"

"No, they help support the weight of the fountain upstairs. Actually, it was the client who suggested the basic design. I was just the one to add some frills of my own. Madam has a lot of ideas from the places she's travelled to." The young architect grinned. "The problem is keeping up with her ideas. I tell her she should have been a designer."

"I take it, then, you're her regular architect?" Hawkins asked.

"Unfortunately not. I think Mum gave me the commission because I gave her a hat once."

"Well, I'd say you got the better part of the bargain. It must have been one hell of a hat."

The boy architect laughed but said nothing. He'd discussed superiors too much already.

"Where is Mum anyway? *Hors de combat* after that speech, I should think." This was Rod Kienzler, who was actually younger than the architect. The youthful-looking Filipino pursed his lips, inclining his head to point with his mouth to three o'clock, a gesture which appeared discreet to the point of conspiratorial to all but Jack who actually gave directions that way himself now.

"Oh, yeah, got her," Hawkins said. "Jack," he was discreet enough to enquire as a quiet aside, "who's the runty-looking little bloke on her tail?"

Jack wondered too. It was a perfectly apt description. Several inches shorter than the substantial and undeniably classy-looking Mrs Init, the runt of the litter had the worst of all worlds so far as hair was concerned, finding himself in a state of advanced balding but unkempt and uncomfortable with it, the long strands trained over his bare scalp forever falling into his eyes. He would probably have had the nervous blink anyway. The expression on his face was one of baffled venom overlaying relentless earnestness. He looked as spiteful and frustrated as a blind weasel. Something was plainly bothering him and he seemed to want to get it off his chest to the statuesque Mrs I. but every time he got near and opened his mouth she would engage another delegate or move off, the runt in vain, doggy pursuit.

"Young man?" Hawkins enquired of the architect, who had resigned himself to this address.

"That one? He is Assemblyman Init, the husband of Mrs Init."

Everyone digested this in silence.

The architect, whose name no one had got, excused himself,

disappearing amongst the great and good of Gobernador de Leon. At this moment Carla Giolitti appeared. "How's everyone coping? Are they giving you good quotes, John? We want acres of that lovely column space in the *Age*."

"Don't we all, babe. How about the *Hongkong Tatler*?"

Carla rolled her eyes. "How about canning it? Gentlemen, may I introduce to you Professor Adachi, Dr Enoeda, and Mr Hanabishi."

Hawkins bowed, forcing the Japanese to follow suit. Jack reckoned they'd been about to offer handshakes.

"Professor Adachi has the chair in English literature at Honshu," Carla informed them. "Dr Enoeda is an oceanographer and volcanologist, and Mr Hanabishi is an interpreter."

"And marine biologist," Hanabishi added with an impish and un-Japanese grin.

"Oh, I'm so sorry, Mr Hanabishi. I had no idea. Please accept my humblest apologies."

"Ah, no, dear Mrs Giolitti. The fault is entirely mine. I omitted to include it on the CV I submitted to you." He beamed at the Westerners, a bespectacled but thoroughly young man. Jack, who was resigning himself and Hawkins to the position of conference greybeards, asked with bright sociableness, "And what field of English literature do you specialise in, Professor Adachi?"

Nodding encouragingly, Adachi smiled at Jack who waited. No reply was forthcoming. Jack didn't think his question had been *that* asinine, for introductory smalltalk. Maybe the Japanese expected more precision from an academic, as well they should. He refined the terms of his inquiry. "Do you teach a particular mode or period, Professor Adachi? I mean like the Elizabethan dramatists or the 19th century novelists?" Again Professor Adachi bestowed upon him the smile of Buddha-like wisdom and benevolence but kept his counsel to himself. "Or," persisted Jack with growing desperation, "is it the *whole* of English literature?" Perhaps Adachi felt he'd slighted him by implying he didn't know his onions. Adachi nodded helpfully again.

"*All* of English literature?"

Hanabishi took mercy on Jack. "Professor Adachi," he said, "does not speak English." Hanabishi kept an impeccably straight face. Jack wondered if he was the victim of a bizarre Japanese cultural practical joke, permitted to be practised on *gaijin* in highly specific and controlled circumstances. Hawkins was first to conquer his incredulity. "You mean," he said, with mounting professional glee, "correct me if I'm wrong, but you're saying that the Professor of English Literature doesn't know English?"

"No, no," remonstrated Hanabishi, "that is not what I said. I said Professor Adachi does not speak English."

"What's the difference?"

"Professor Adachi has no command of colloquial English but he is a master of the texts he teaches. He is also a most distinguished translator."

Adachi nodded again, the short, all-comprehending nod, of, say, a pilot receiving orders on a windswept flight deck.

Hawkins said, "You don't understand a blind word of what we're saying, do you, Prof?" Adachi gave that helpful nod again. Rod Kienzler snickered. Carla said hurriedly, "I think it's not uncommon for oral language skills to be different from the written. I mean how many interpreters are also good translators?"

"Very few, in fact," agreed Hanabishi politely.

"Could you ask the Professor what authors he does teach?" Jack asked. His curiosity had been whetted; this wasn't just to make conversation. He really wanted to know. Hanabishi conferred in Japanese. Then he himself gave the pilot's nod and announced, "The Gawain poet and *The Cloude of Unknowynnge*."

Hawkins muttered something that sounded suspiciously like, "Bugger me."

Professor Adachi then endeared himself by bursting into laughter. "Very obscure," he agreed between chuckles, "very obscure."

Hanabishi said, "As you can see the Professor is not one to

stand on his dignity."

As Hawkins asked Dr Enoeda, whose English was nearly as good as Hanabishi's, if they were meeting near a major fault line, Carla felt able to detach herself from the melded group. These introductions had been no accident or spur of the moment thing. She'd devoted a lot of thought on the long flight over the Pacific as to which group of nationalities should encounter each other first, even to the extent of circling lists of names on the back of the first class menu card and then drawing arrows, sometimes in three or four directions, between the circles. A lot simpler than the data base programme, though she'd brought that with her. She'd heard you could buy virus inoculation programmes for a few dollars in the Far East.

She now saw something which she had not foreseen between the lines of lobster with mango and foie gras salad or raspberry tart in vanilla sauce: Professor Pfeidwengeler, standing quite by himself.

THE Filipinos, constituting the intellectual and academic elite of Gobernador de Leon, were standing in awe around a living legend in another part of this post-modernist Sistine chapel. The legend was Senator Hercules Mijares, the nonagenarian statesman and Philippine national hero, the worthy inheritor of the martyr's mantle of José Rizal in every sense other than that obviously he had succeeded in living well beyond his thirty-fifth birthday. This was not for want of effort on the part of either the wartime Japanese or President Ferdinand Marcos. The Senator was that seeming impossibility and walking contradiction: a traditional Philippine politician who had kept his hands clean of blood and out of the till.

It had been the whispered agreement of Boyet and Nestor Chavez to pay court to him when the speech-making was over. They vacated their seats immediately after the last oration, considerably disappointing the Brigadier who had thought they were about to give him a standing ovation, pushed through the

crowd at the back of the hall, scorned the refreshments table –
only to find Senator Mijares already surrounded by adorers.
Somehow Jimmy Boyar, Kamikaze Kelvin Fugoso, and – oh,
chagrin – many of the staff of the rival rag, were in front of them,
plus a contingent of local attorneys and officers of the student
debating society and Lex Circle who had also managed to beat
them to it. They discovered themselves at the back with
Professor "Saint" James Benitez of the city's major university, a
local figure naturally well-known to them but for whom neither
felt special warmth, Benitez an austere if not puritanical personality, tall and preternaturally young of appearance though
already middle-aged, the personification of pure, burning intellect, of no known sexual peccadilloes, and with a radical anti-
martial law past of which anyone could have been proud except
the slim and modest Benitez. Nestor nodded to him, Boyet
avoided his eye.

Senator Mijares was being assisted into his wheel-chair. The
lion-hearted old politician still insisted on walking and standing
without assistance for token periods of independence but the
small effort exhausted him quickly nowadays. He smiled kindly
at the reverent little throng, partly because he wanted to let
them know he was all there upstairs. His filmy left eye had been
ruined in the same bomb-blast which had injured his fellow anti-
Marcosistas, Osmeña and Salonga.

One of the students said, "Welcome to Gobernador de
Leon, Senator," and a reverent murmur, in which Boyet and
Nestor found themselves joining, went up. The Senator lifted
his right hand fractionally off his arm-rest, a tribune of the
people but never an ideologue, a man who had never told a
public lie without taking the trouble to recant it later, a sovereign nationalist of somewhat anti-US tendency – he had been no
little brown brother as a young man – but who had not been
selected by the embassy spooks for a dirty tricks campaign. (His
reputation proof against it and, besides, he had been expected to
drop off his perch at any moment for the last twenty years).
Conspicuous by their absence were not only Representative Init

and his cronies but also their mortal foes – flies were not attracted to the like of Senator Mijares, oil and water could never mix, the sky did not touch the earth. The nation's grand old man beckoned the student to him, with a gesture which plainly cost energy. He whispered in her ear. Then his own great granddaughter, herself a matron with children, firmly wheeled him away from what would prove his last public engagement. He was not irreplaceable. There were others like him, but they were thin on the ground and not guaranteed to get to the top of the pile in brazen times. In him were embodied dignity, courage, moderation, and intelligence. He had deserved a better stage for that exemplary life.

The crowd re-focussed on the girl he had spoken to.

"What did he say? What did he *say*?"

The student still looked a little stunned.

"He said, *Don't believe everything they tell you.*"

JUST as John Hawkins and Jack Beaufort were laughing with Professor Adachi over his choice of his life's work, the ice well broken, and as Senator Mijares glided out of the room and into the textbooks, Omar Hamid, "The Jackal", was saying to the Indian contingent, "Of course, the English are *so* racist." As a statement this was almost entirely blanched of emotive content. It was a password. First uttered by pampered intellectuals resident in the United Kingdom, usually with white wives, boyfriends or live-in lovers in tow, it had spread into liberal circles. Politicians, publishers, journalists, administrators seeking to curry favour with "ethnics" would do their best to get the remark in first themselves. It was becoming as formulaic as saying "Insh'Allah." Even Jack Beaufort said it; used to say it a lot in the course of his work at uni, but with a variation, "Of course, Australians are *so* racist."

So now Kamla Mishra and N.S. Kumar responded in their different ways sociably to this greeting, as they might to an observation about inclement weather, Mishra more vehemently by saying, "Terrible!" (as she would of snow blizzards or monsoonal rains), Kumar with more reserve, smiling faintly in what could be construed as agreement.

Hamid regarded it as important to establish common-ground with this pair. As Indians never tired of saying, they were Aryans. E.g., they regarded themselves as members of a master race, particularly a mercantile master race. Yet they were also unafflicted with guilt. They were unsentimental about negroes. In his sponsored peregrinations Hamid had come across a Trinidadian journalist of East Indian origins who actually made no bones about calling blacks "negroes", an unexceptionable, old-fashioned word, which did sound like "niggers". Blacks, in short, had reason to be wary of Indians. You didn't want them sitting on your jury, assuming you had the misfortune to be arraigned; whites were preferable, even skinheads or the mono-cled. It was an occasion, rare outside Africa, when Hamid would not be stressing his claims to negritude, so much as of third world mandarin. Kamla Mishra, who was environmental corre-spondent of a Bombay newspaper and wrote poetry in her spare-time, had met The Jackal twice before at conventions in Hong Kong and Prague. There was no special warmth between them – they had neglected to exchange addresses – but both felt it incumbent to give an exaggerated display of recognition much like people who only ever meet at the dinner parties of a mutual friend. As Kamla said, "Bunny asked me to send his best," and Hamid was left wondering who on earth Bunny could be, N.S. Kumar might have been forgiven for assuming the other two were friends or at least colleagues of long standing. He belonged to a much older generation which while not necessarily less guileful in its transactions was less ostentatious, e.g. more Asian. "And how is Bunny?" asked Hamid.

"Mmm," Mrs Mishra said. "Now this is the famous N.S. Kumar."

"No, no. Not famous, definitely not famous," remonstrated N.S. Actually he was. The protegé of J.R. Ackerley and E. M. Forster was no longer the slim, ingenuous, liquid-eyed young man of more than half a century ago but a venerable and distinguished figure now in his own right, as well as a grandfather. (Unfortunately for the Englishmen N.S. had proved as hetero as he was virile, but that had only made their worship the more ardent). They had lavished praise on his first, only, and awful book of poems but then N.S. had gone into diplomacy in middle life, very successfully, and on retirement had produced over a ten year period three massive volumes of autobiography characterised by a wit and an insight of which a Talleyrand or De Tocqueville might have been envious. Which went to show that Morgan Forster and Joe Ackerley might not have left their brains where their cocks belonged. N.S. wasn't being foxily Asian when he disclaimed his fame. He really was an unassuming person; it was his followers who were intemperate aggrandisers of his guru-hood.

"Very famous. I know," said Hamid, fawning.

"Oh, please," said the gentle N.S.

"There'll probably be other Indians coming," said Ms Mishra. "There was a last minute grant." She put a wealth of meaning into her glance at Hamid, the freemasonry of the third world bounty-hunter. Hamid widened his eyes politely – good luck to them, he signalled; he didn't begrudge the other man/woman his/her chance.

"The Goldenberg Foundation have been very munificent this year," Kamla said. Hamid made a mental note of that.

Both N.S. and Kamla were in national costume – what peripatetic Hindu intellectual wasn't? – N.S. also wearing a coarse white shawl reminiscent of Dr Neumark's London interviews. Four rolls of fat spilled through Kamla Mishra's sari – Hamid, who liked well-padded women, found it attractive unlike her gore-steeped daggers of toe-nails which would not have gone amiss on a griffin.

As earlier instructed, Gracie Hipkin came up to introduce herself. N.S. immediately made room for her with a spontaneously graceful gesture. As the pair of celebrated English authors had done nearly three-quarters of a century previously,

Gracie fell in love with him at once. With the foundation of his alliance system far from laid, Hamid was less keen to admit her into the charmed circle, but he was nothing if not supple. Besides, she was freakishly fat even by standards other than her own society's, which made her accessible – outsiders were amenable to recruitment. About the only sensible thing the Philippine lady had said. Hadn't the Russians seduced all those homosexual Englishmen? A saga of strangely recurrent fascination to Hamid, who chuckled over it with the right kind of American. What had some British fairy said – he hoped to have the courage to betray his country rather than his friend? Boyfriend more likely.

"Well, I just know I can include you on the side of the whale, Ms Mishra," Gracie said gaily. For a moment Kamla looked bewildered and Gracie wondered if she had picked the wrong person – which would be hideous, doubly embarrassing with a non-Caucasian. Then Kamla said, "Oh, of course," rather meaning she had deduced who Gracie was than that she would be enlisting. She was already on the right side of all the correct causes. N.S. Kumar said, "This is one thing Indians can have a clear conscience upon at least – they are not victimising the poor whales."

"Yes, that is all the doing of the naughty Japanese and Russians," Kamla said.

"Of course," N.S. remarked, "Indians are eating shark-meat but that's a different thing. Maybe it's a public service they are performing?" He looked for Gracie's comment but Hamid was quicker.

"I never knew that. They are the man-eating type?"

"Very large ones, anyway," Ms Mishra said. "you can see them wheeling the sharks on barrows in Bombay. They're brutes – the sharks, I mean. Enormous grey things – all bloody. Ugh!"

"Actually," said Gracie, trying her hardest not to sound snotty or too pedagogic, "there's no such thing as a man-eating shark."

"Oh," exclaimed Hamid, indicating disbelief for himself and

everybody else. "So what is eating all the people in South Africa and Adelaide? Sea monsters?"

"No – there are shark *attacks* but feeding on human beings is virtually unknown. They might make a territorial defence, or bite from curiosity, or plain mistake a human for something else. A feeding on our species would be something very rare."

"So, it's a case of once biting, twice shy from the point of view of the shark?" N.S. said. Gracie smiled brightly. "Too bad for the human being," Hamid said, just under his breath. He thought Gracie would make a good meal for the biggest shark; her proportions weren't human at all.

"How good it is to encounter to hear the voice of reason," remarked Harold Hanabishi, who had left Professor Adachi in the capable hands of Dr Enoeda and the congenial company of Jack Beaufort. Carla had enthusiastically acquiesced in his suggestion that he join Gracie with the Indians. Hamid gave him a neutral look, bordering on dislike. Hanabishi said, "It is very difficult to blame the shark if you ever looked up and saw a swimmer thrashing from below. The problem for the swimmer is that the single curious bite is likely to kill him. Or her, of course, as the case may be."

Gracie nodded gratefully. Help from the naughty Japanese quarter indeed!

"Then," continued Hanabishi, "most times the victim is not even swimming. The majority of shark incidents take place in less than two metres of water."

"The shark is more aggressive because it is out of place in shallow water?" asked Ms Mishra, who was a non-swimmer. You just weren't safe anywhere.

"Ah, no," said Hanabishi, "I think it is just the nature of statistics. Are there more sharks in shallow water? Are they fiercer sharks? No – but there are more people in shallow water to provide the statistics."

N.S. smiled faintly; he knew all about stats and what could be done with them. He refrained, just, from quoting Disraeli in present company. "So you, too, are a saviour of the seas, Mr

Hanabish?" he asked. As a career diplomat he'd mastered the art of reading lapel badges without seeming to break eye-contact, a feat akin to card-sharping or the Tondo knife draw. But, however ironic N.S. was, even when he skirted the sarcastic, no one ever took offence, his manner was so mild. Hanabishi smilingly disclaimed any such ambitions. Although his personal history made him a round peg in the square slot of his own society, the Japanese would also have made a creditable addition to his country's diplomatic corps; he, too, possessed imperturbability and adaptability to spare.

"You sound like a scuba fan," Gracie said.

"You guessed right." He clicked his heels.

"I thought so. Once you've swum with them you're never nervous again, are you?"

"Maybe we will have the opportunity to be regaled by you both from the lectern on the subject of the non-maneaters," said N.S., who had not the faintest interest in the subject. "That will be something pleasurable for us to look forward to. So *dull* to listen to figures from civil servants like me all the time."

Kamla Mishra rushed to tell one of her country's cultural assets that he could never be described as dull, or a mere civil servant, then went on to talk of another asset, threatened species, but quondam man-eater: the tiger. Apparently, the relatives of those killed were up in arms against the conservationists in Northern India. It was at this point that a restive Hamid, who had written a revisionist article entitled "The real Jim Corbett: Self-perpetuating myths of the White Hunter" about the intrepid tiger tracker's retirement years in Kenya, was at last able to rejoin the conversation. This was shortly before the announcement of dinner which, coincidental upon the previous carnivorous topics of conversation, sent them all to the buffet chuckling, even Hamid, so that the entire conference – mostly awkwardly new to each other – stared with mild hostility or interest as their dispositions took them at the laughing group of old friends and cronies. Carla Giolitti, who was in a position to be better informed, and had just failed to entice the thorn-stricken old predator Professor Pfeidwengeler to enter the company of his fellows, drew more encouragement from the spectacle than she should have done.

Chapter Twelve

BOYET WAS NOW DEPUTY EDITOR OF THE *CITIZEN*, Sherwin de Leon having died suddenly fifteen months ago. Poor Sherwin had been watching Darwin in an inter-academy basketball match when he'd keeled over. Young Darwin had done some prodigious growing in the eight months intervening between this and their ill-fated beach excursion and had made the team on the basis of his extra inches rather than any new coordination or positional sense. The coach hadn't interrupted the game's crucial last few minutes or substituted Darwin, for which he got credit rather than condemnation from all, including in due course Darwin. Sherwin had half-risen from his seat in the smoky gym, a notorious death-trap with bars over every conceivable window and bolt-hole to exclude non-payers, this being considered more important than saving life in a potential (e.g. unreal) disaster. It being known he was the skinny lad's pa no one had remonstrated over their blocked view. Then Sherwin had toppled a complete somersault into the lap of the proud father in the row below. He'd survived stroke and fall, with limited recovery to the right side of the body and a slight speech difficulty which, however, hadn't impeded communication when Nestor and Boyet had shown their blades in his private room at the hospital. "Never knew I had high blood," Sherwin said, speaking as if he was giving dictation which in a sense he was, both his visitors possessing excellent verbal memories and attending in full consciousness that they might be hearing their colleague's last words to them. "The doc says there are medications to bring it right down, but they've got to diagnose you early."

197

"Yeah," said Nestor, "just like it's always better to call the plumber in when the leak's small."

The three of them laughed, but not Mrs de Leon. They were glad Sherwin still had a laugh left in him.

"The doc," enunciated Sherwin, "says high BP is very common amongst Visayan males – it's the water or the diet, or heredity."

Nestor and Boyet each privately decided to get themselves checked out.

Darwin made his contribution, "The stuff Pa's on is rat poison – warfare." His mother looked as if she was going to cry.

"Warfarin," his father corrected him, still an editor to his bitten finger-nails.

Nestor and Boyet got up an office collection, more than a thousand pesos. With it they purchased the latest in Jap digital technology – the Casio BP, a watch which was an alarm-clock, stopwatch, and measurer of your systolic and diastolic readings at one and the same time. Before having it gift-wrapped by Jingkee's adept fingers, Nestor and Boyet took their own pressures – well within the normal range, Boyet's slightly lower than Nestor's, 120/75 as against 140/85. "I don't have your responsibilities," Boyet joked.

They never got the chance to make the presentation to Sherwin who died of a massive brain haemorrhage nineteen days later.

This was good in that their colleague had felt no pain, had suffered no degradation in his personality, and had enjoyed sufficient grace to prepare himself and say what everyone had felt might be good-byes. It was bad, or at least highly inconvenient, in that they were left with a gift on their hands.

"You can return it to the department store," said Jingkee, practical as women were, never allowing sentiment or fine feeling to get in the way of money, politely termed family welfare.

"It's no return, no exchange there," Boyet said.

"So?"

"No," said Nestor gloomily, "the sign says strictly no return, no exchange."

"Use a little *Citizen* muscle."

"I don't know if Sherwin would have approved of that."

"Just try."

It was no go. The watches were an expensive line for the store, difficult to move. They didn't like to give the watch to Mrs de Leon – an ugly black instrument even on a man's wrist, plus its tragic associations. "Like giving a pilot's widow the parachute he forgot to take," said Kamikaze Kelvin, surprising them all with his sensitivity. Jingkee had always wanted to give just the cash or a simple household appliance, but kept her mouth shut.

"Oh, hey, why don't you just keep it, boss. Advance testimonial from the underlings," said someone from the subs' table.

"No," said Nestor quietly but with a firmness they all knew was final. "I couldn't do that."

In the end they sold it to a pawn-shop for 65 per cent of what they paid originally and then divided the sum, not in the original proportions but equally. "That way, at least some people will get back their original contribution," Jingkee said, with a logic the men found warped.

It all left a surprisingly bad taste in the mouth.

Boyet hadn't even thought of filling Sherwin's shoes. Despite making a point of introducing himself to all and sundry, or at least those he wished to woo, as a journalist, he had no ambitions for promotion in that sphere. He was a lone gun, *di ba*, not an administrator. Maverick could be his call-sign. Overlaying this glamorous self-image, the one of Top Gun at the typewriter, was an incipient middle-aged complacency. He was quite content to jog along the usual routes of his life at the accustomed pace. Evergreen gave him a comfortable living with attorney's status; the journalism was the icing on the cake.

So when Nestor put it to him, it was like being propositioned by a superior's wife: intensely flattering but not terribly tempting.

"Think about it," Nestor advised.

He did.

The Deputy on this paper almost never became ed in the normal course of events. A George Bush/Ronald Reagan follow-on was unknown. So for a real journalist it was a career cul-de-sac unless you stepped sideways to another paper. Some prestige and responsibility accrued, but basically you were a burnt-out rocket. This Boyet didn't mind. He knew he didn't have the background ever to aspire to an editorship.

But.

Was Nestor choosing him out of liking and respect? Or because he didn't want someone good – in the, admittedly totally unknown event in the *Citizen*'s history, of the Dep Ed combining the roles of Lee Harvey Oswald and LBJ in relation to the editor's JFK? Was it just that Nestor wanted about him someone plump, figuratively speaking, rather than a lean Cassius?

But these weren't the kind of brutal questions that even Americans put to each other.

The subject lapsed. Their "interview" terminated without conclusion. Boyet didn't even want the responsibility and potential regret of refusing. No appointment to the post was made.

Then as time passed the position began to look more attractive to Boyet.

The thing was . . . home life had changed. Nothing dramatic. Miriam didn't throw pots and pans at him, subject him to the water torture of prolonged silence. It might have been easier if she had. You could take a deep breath, then address something overt. They still conducted what Boyet thought of as "marital relations" (and they were about as joyless as the phrase). There'd been no interruption to these, intercourse resuming only days after she'd completed her antibiotic course. Maybe she felt it took that to keep him on the straight and narrow. The form of the marriage was that she treated him with the respect he was due but it was the formulaic courtesy the probation officer extended her client when she addressed him as "Mr" John Doe. Boyet felt like crying out, "Look, Inday, it's the same me I always was. You loved me before. The only difference is you found out. Love me again. I'm the same guy I was then!" But the words stuck in the voice-box. Also he wanted to explain something. She seemed to think he was a prowling dog looking to slake his organ in something wet. That's why she offered herself, presumably. But "It's not like that!" he wanted to shout, longing to shake her by the shoulders. The last thing he felt when he used to pick the girls up was horny. He did it because it was an addiction, and addicts were long past enjoying what they were hooked on. Then he felt he was missing out on life if he didn't indulge; he wanted, with desperation, to add to his extensive stock of sexual experiences. He was like a collector of rare books let loose in an antiquarian library, except he was a curator of bodies, not volumes. He was scared to let a chance slip – he might never be able to have that girl again. It wasn't libido which drove him but a form of the acquisitive instinct. And he knew telling her, even if she understood the explanation, would just make things a thousand times worse.

Somehow she'd got to the kids as well. He'd already asked her, with dignity, to keep it between themselves. (Actually, he'd been ready to implore, to beg). With dignity, she'd told him not to give himself concern on that score. He trusted her to keep the promise, yet there was a distinct withdrawal on the part of the kids which went beyond mere adolescent alienation. Ilynn especially was not so close to her papa. She left the room to do homework when he entered in the early evening (since when had that become so attractive?), declined the trips to the skating-rink or cinema. The boy wasn't so pointed in his sulkiness – he was at the age when all he was interested in was firing his fat bamboo cannon every ten seconds, amazing the report a tea-spoon of kerosene could produce – but he'd certainly seceded to his ma as well.

What was it? Family telepathy? Pa was definitely in the dog house.

A Chinese would have found a new house for the family, changed his luck by changing location, varied the vibes; at least, re-arranged the furniture. Boyet felt the impulse to change career tracks. Maybe his kids would like him more for it.

"Sure," said Nestor, "I knew you'd come round to it. I was just keeping the seat warm for you."

Boyet tendered his resignation to Evergreen with due respect and consideration, always a tricky business this. He didn't want to make powerful enemies by appearing to snub the company and his superiors. He thought of himself as decent and responsible and the firm had provided him his salt for over fifteen years.

They were OK about it. Even congratulated him. "Don't put your old friends in the sticky stuff, hah?" said the chief of legal section, grinning and patting him on the back. As was etiquette, he kept his mouth shut to those he dealt with on the company's behalf. They'd only find out he'd left from his replacement. Even with his colleagues he was reserved, though of course once the cat was out of the bag even the janitor knew in two hours.

At *Citizen* he had his own private room, Sherwin's old pad. Nestor was out in the news-room, a visible king to his minions. To those who didn't know the set-up it made Boyet look like the big-time chief. To the insider, it made it seem as if the Dep was out of the swing of things (which was probably what Nestor had intended to do to Sherwin, à la Cory and Vice-President Laurel). But so what? Nestor was his friend. Nestor knew he wouldn't stick a knife in his back and Boyet himself was under no illusions as to his own editorial acumen – he was the new boy at school.

Yet early in his tenure, only the third week, Nestor held a private war conference with him. Management had told him to cut costs. Circulation was steady, maybe even on the up, but advertising had plummeted. Partly this was a reflection of the general state of the national economy – shaky at the best when everyone else was enjoying a boom, dire when the world was in recession – but it would, Nestor said wryly, be a mistake to look for the macro-explanation. Like any other small place, Gobernador de Leon was set in a wider frame, but it was the small, not to say petty, cause which had the most influence on your destiny. Their proprietor had had a tiff with his fellow plutocrats at the Rotarians, and flounced out of that worthy and laudable organisation. The owner of their rival had then picked up all the cinema and night-club advertising in Gobernador de Leon. Talk about a shot in the arm for a flagging patient. Instead of pocketing the extra cash, which Nestor had to admit would have been the national style, the guy had then put it back as an investment: they'd put on another few pages daily and beefed up on Sundays with a magazine. Their guy's answer? Fire journalists and save the money they'd lost on ads! It made you want to tear his hair out by the roots. "Shit, shit, shit," said Nestor, the first time they could remember him using that popular Philippine expletive in triplicate. Nestor said he'd fought for his staff. Boyet believed him. He'd told the proprietor they needed more people to fight a circulation war at a time like this, not less. But the guy was adamant: at least five had to go.

Nestor wanted Boyet to help him choose. It would have been bad anyway, but Boyet was being asked to select for termination those whose service was infinitely longer and probably more honourable than his. Shouldn't it be last in, first out?

"No. They stay only if they're good," Nestor said. "That's the criterion. No dead wood." Boyet winced. He'd been helping Evergreen fell forest giants for most of his working life; here he was cutting down trees again. They ran through the names. "What's young Cathy like?" Boyet inquired, still trying to operate on the principle of saving the long-serving (for Chrissake, those with families, kids).

"Great in the sack," said Nestor, absolutely straight-faced,

"Uh-huh?" said Boyet cautiously. You never knew when Nestor was joking.

"O-o," said Nestor. "So she's out of consideration. Take it from me, she's a darned good reporter, too."

'Sus Maria. He was serious. They both pondered. Nestor's finger stopped at Jingkee Zamora's name. Boyet had another moment of surprise. Surely not Jingkee, anyone but her –

Jingkee, the small but terrible. Apart from anything else they all owed her a debt of consideration.

"Jingkee's work has suffered," Nestor said, without emotion.

"Well, that's understandable."

"She's never here. It's not just lapses of concentration. God knows what she's doing with her time."

"Have you spoken to her?"

"I've tried."

"Do it again. We can't do it to her – firing her. It's not right."

Nestor grimaced. "You don't have to tell me that. But I was hoping you might take the opposite view. OK. We'll leave her out of it. Maybe you can take her aside for a friendly talk." Nestor visibly brightened. "Yes, that's a great idea. You speak to her."

"O-o." He'd heard Miriam advising Ilynn on an early romantic problem the other night – himself still excluded from adolescent confidences. Jennilynn liked a boy in the boys' school but didn't want to appear forward. "Send a bearer," Miriam exhorted her. "He's got a sister in St Monica's? OK, who's the sister's best friend? Chona? Then get Chona to mention your name – just to say you're a nice girl. Which you are." So – he was going to be Nestor's bearer, of a reprimand rather than puppy love. That was fine. He wasn't proud.

"Keep it light," Nestor said. "Hah?"

"Of course."

They ended up by putting four people on half-time, giving the effect of two redundancies. Nestor reckoned that would be enough, for the moment. It was his opinion that the proprietor's need to streamline his staff was pathological rather than rational. Inflicting economic distress on four members would give him the alleviation from woe he sought – the actual financial figures had more or less nothing to do with it. And, of course, the various irons Nestor had in the fire, his padded expenses, the ghostly contributors on the payroll who had no existence other than as front names for bank-accounts run by Nestor, the sales of purloined office stationery to the student middlemen – all these hallowed scams remained untouched.

The quiet word in Jingkee's ear belonged to an entirely different order of dilemma. Creeping up with a pistol to shoot her in the back of the head would have been less embarrassing. He was being asked to discipline Jingkee, a full-time professional journalist of more than fifteen years standing? On top of that she was owed extreme consideration for the tragedy, at which he had been a helpless bystander, politely termed principal eyewitness. Now here he was, Boyet Dinolan, tyro journalist and drinker of the cup of humiliation, assigned to rebuke the only one of them who had worn pants that awful day. It was obvious she was suffering from trauma. Give her time and she'd get over it.

He actually went to the subs table to speak to her once – all the others on the desk were to lunch – but his resolution faltered, and he exchanged a few inconsequentialities instead. He hoped she didn't think he was trying to make a pass at her. His whole life recently seemed to revolve around having to tell women unpalatable things.

He considered being totally negligent and dropping the whole matter. Nestor was never going to ask her, "Did Boyet scold you for me?" But then it wasn't Nestor he was really letting down so much as Jingkee. What if they fired her without him having given her benefit of warning? He'd be betraying his responsibility to Jingkee, no one else. Shit. Now if it was a guy it would have been so much easier. Take him out for a couple of cold beers. Tell him he was on his side. Drop a few indiscretions about management. He'd leave the guy with the feeling that he'd been enlisted into a conspiracy rather than reprimanded but still get the admonitory shot across. That just wasn't possible with a female whose superior you theoretically were. Probably women had an easier communication with each other.

Bing! He knew a woman. His wife.

Maybe it would even help their own relationship.

"You could mention we're having a management problem to her – tell her to get her head below the parapet. Maybe bring it up when you see her at that painting group you've all got."

"Sketching."

Silence.

"Will you do it? It's for Jingkee's sake. She could be out in the street if she's not careful. It's like she's got two jobs at the moment and we're the part-time one."

Silence.

" '*Day*?"

Eyebrows raised two millimetres, meaning yes.

"Thank you."

Delegation, that was the way to play it.

Boyet thought of them at their drawing class, sitting round a vase of flowers, bowl of fruit, or one of their number in the buff, in one of the university's dingy class-rooms; he'd heard they read their own poems to each other, too. Here they all were – him and Nestor included – trying to create their own little oases of culture and contemplation, or at least the framework for a secure and decent life for their children, kindness and consideration to their friends, in the middle of what? The Sack of Rome? The Rape of Nanking? The Valley of the Shadow of Death? Which was realer, the private life or the public context? You could to an extent insulate yourself from all the horrors going down around you. Just in terms of hours spent in the personal history that was your biography, you could cut yourself off from rape, brigandage, scams, hits; the world of syndicates and psychopaths. You could treat your colleagues honourably, more or less, in the six or seven hours of your working day – even if your nose was being rubbed in it by the nature of the job: what mining or logging companies did to minorities in the way or their own workforce, or reporting on such like for the edification of others. In the seven hours of your homelife you could be as evolved as your heart's desire. You could kid yourself that what defined your life and your family's were the terms you set. You didn't steal, you didn't kill. Then the walls you'd lovingly constructed came tumbling down, blown away by ravening Mr Wolf. Jingkee had built a charmed and consecrated life for Charina: the piano and ballet lessons, tennis, were only the outward and obvious forms of it, of the countless little sacrifices and civilities with which the mother had adorned the life of the daughter in which she had rejoiced. Gone. She might as well have planted vegetables, because that was what Charina was now. You laid shit on plants, that made them grow good as anything. Elegant roses and rank garlic alike. They should grow mushrooms in the blackness, in the moral brownout that was the totality of society.

"Boyet?"

"Inday?"

"Don't look so sad. It pains me to see it. Ilynn, hug your papa. We love you, daddy Boyet."

Boyet had to quickly go splash cold water on his eyes in the kitchen, before he came back – smiling.

Chapter 13

DR NEUMARK HAD BEEN SUFFERING FROM A HEADACHE on the night of the conference cocktails. She was relatively frequently incapacitated by these in the course of her career, her public life; although they didn't seem to occur so often, if at all, at home. Stress was a terrible thing, even contributed to cancer if you believed the modern scientific hunch. (Ruth did, with no reservations). Carla had been very understanding, clucked in excess of the solicitude demanded by her professional position. "You poor thing," she said. "I'll get some aspirin sent up to you."

"Oh, don't bother with that," Dr Neumark replied. "I carry my own stuff around with me. No fancy doctoring. Trial and error taught me what worked best." Typical of Ruth Neumark, Timothy Donovan would have thought – he'd witnessed the analgesic tableau several times in the past when they were still on speaking terms – in that she simultaneously laid claim to a martyr's crown with her history of migraine attacks, but bravely brushed aside useless offers of help. Carla felt a little frazzled herself by the long flight, never mind de luxe class and the glass of water she religiously took every hour to counteract the dehydrating climate of the cabin. "Just lie down and relax, maybe you'll feel better in the morning, Ruth." The first name terms sat easily with the advice, Carla thought, perhaps some personal warmth could even be said to contribute to the cure. Without in the least wishing to diminish Dr Neumark, Carla often found herself thinking of her distinguished wards and clients as children, needing feeding, tantrum-management, regulation of their interactive behaviour in playground as well as class. Dr

Neumark smiled thinly, then departed roomwards, leaving Carla with the feeling she'd said something gauche or even callous, one important mechanism of Dr Neumark's ascendancy being the ability to inflict guilt in matters large and small, abstract and personal; artistic and political. Once in her room – and to the relief of all the delegates they were very adequately appointed rooms – Dr Neumark fixed herself a large gin and tonic, found CNN though the reception was very snowy, and half an hour later bullied the hotel operator into putting her through to New York (Mrs Init having given strict instructions no long-distance was permitted) when she enjoyed a discursive twenty-six minute chat with Gerald.

One reason Carla didn't mind her star's late appearance was her own innate appreciation of the dramatic. Dr Neumark was entitled to some aristocratic airs, some differentiation. Carla herself couldn't very well bestow this – like giving her the presidential suite instead of the superior room – or there would have been a mutiny. So in a sense Dr Neumark was doing her job for her. After all, you expected a star to be late. Did Judy Garland come on first, before the warm-up act? Did she begin on time even? You created a feeling of anticipation – not that she considered her other distinguished guests as warm-up acts. And, of course, Ruth knew all about that world, about stardom and upstaging. Barely remembered now were her days as a "protest singer", before she'd published that first volume of her autobiography *Gazelle Morning* which had sold 15 million copies worldwide. But she had enjoyed a mild domestic celebrity with her guitar and long, flaming hair; the South African answer to Joan Baez, Françoise Hardy, and Peter, Paul, and Mary – or at least Mary – all rolled into one. One better than the Singing Nun – the strumming doctor. But as she had attained a fully fledged international fame as an autobiographer, or author as she preferred to be called, she'd dropped the guitar in favour of gravitas. Latterly she discouraged allusion to this phase of her career.

Even when Dr Neumark failed to show for lunch the

following day (Carla had already written off breakfast for her) she remained unmoved. She was confident Dr Neumark's sense of timing would prove nothing short of Napoleonic. The early part of the conference would see most of the ecological, which was to say scientific, discussion. The cultural stuff would follow that, interspersed with one or two technical disquisitions so that the segregation of topic wouldn't seem quite so brutal. Cultural apartheid, Carla was going to call it, but looking in the first class cabin at Dr Neumark's noble but rather hatchety face she'd decided to keep the thought to herself. In her fax Mrs Init had queried this, preferring what she called an "artistic spearhead" but no communication had followed Carla's despatch, pointing out the intrinsic news value of the harder-core subjects. Unprompted, John Hawkins had proved an angel when he'd congratulated her at the breakfast table in front of Mrs I. (who always seemed to be there at the crack of dawn with a raging appetite) on the structuring of events and how much easier it was for him to place his copy somewhere like *Newsweek* if there was something "solid" to start the flow. Carla had then noticed two things: Mrs Init had brightened visibly at the name of *Newsweek* – obviously an avid reader of the newsmags – while Professor Pfeidwengeler, sitting by himself three settings clear of anyone else, had opened his mouth – for some quip? – then changed his mind, grinning slyly to himself. John was a rock, a brick; behind that craggy exterior lay a big heart – not just thinking of himself like the other journalists: with them it was take, take and use.

All in all, it was probably better that Dr Neumark was withdrawn from the present scene and justifiably *hors de combat*. The last thing Carla wanted was for anyone to steal her thunder. Funnily enough, not one of the other "cultural" as opposed to scientific "educational" delegates had inquired after her whereabouts or well-being, not even her good friend Omar Hamid.

But when Dr Neumark failed to show for dinner by the third day, Carla was assailed by a strange and unwelcome feeling, a sensation she found difficult to identify because it was inconceivable she should have it. If it was actually possible for her to be miffed with Ruth Neumark (and she was sure it wasn't) she was miffed with Ruth. As had been the case on the two previous occasions, Dr Neumark's room phone gave the engaged tone. Carla therefore felt able to give her a knock on the door, ascending in the elevator, the occupants of which were visible from the lobby in a huge glass tube, much like boli travelling on the peristaltic wave. It had been Carla's assumption that the phone had been off the hook (she being far too scrupulous to ask the operator to eavesdrop and ascertain the actual state of the line) but when she entered in response to the peremptory but cheery "Come!" lo and behold, she discovered the long form of Dr Neumark perched on the bed in the middle of a conversation on the telephone. Dr Neumark nodded brightly at her (as if the last time they'd seen each other was half an hour ago, a sourer soul than Carla's might have thought). On entry Carla's expression had been slightly strained from all the things she wished to put on it and all those she wanted to keep off it: to wit, in the first category: brightness tempered by concern, optimism, cheery efficiency, sympathy, respect; in the second: impatience, irritation, frustration, disillusionment, inquisitiveness. Thus her actual appearance as she opened the door was that of extreme bafflement, shiftily darting eyes, and a glazed artificial grin overlying all.

Dr Neumark had the advantage of Carla. She had seen such an expression many times before on the faces of those assigned to deal with her. It was time to exercise charm. As previously noted, Dr Neumark had considerable charm. The impact on the recipient was largely a technical matter, the conclusion foregone; so it didn't matter that Ruth sometimes practised her charm in the spirit of a dancer performing callisthenics – if the faculty wasn't used it might atrophy. In this case she did make a large personal investment; it was important she didn't lose the allegiance of Carla, as she had with Angela Smith and other lessers in the past. So after a few seconds, doing justice by all including whomsoever she was talking to on the phone, she put her hand over the mouthpiece and whispered conspiratorially,

"Gerald does go on so!" Carla smiled back but very slightly tight-lipped. She had tremendous poise but she could never be a hypocrite.

"Well, I think that's enough for now," said Dr Neumark into the receiver, nodding vigorously to Carla. "Six thirty p.m. our time would be a better time for you to call next time." Hanging up, she smiled propitiatingly at Carla.

"Are you alright, Dr Neumark? We were starting to become concerned."

"Oh, my dear," Dr Neumark held out both hands, her head cocked to one side.

Carla's expression didn't change.

"I've been very . . ." Dr Neumark searched for a word, even inviting Carla to supply it. Selfish, irresponsible, childish, she would never have described herself as, still less a bitch, prima donna, flouncer, or cow. Nor, Carla found, did she herself wish to commit the offence of *lèse-majesté*.

"I've been very *difficult*," Dr Neumark decided on firmly. That was a good, non-pejorative description to admit to; she actually liked being described as such. It was what great artists traditionally were.

"Oh, but no," Carla remonstrated with a theatrical wail. "You're not, darling." Darling was not a word Carla had ever used, even to her late husband, the banker Gianni Giolitti. Such was the influence of Ruth Neumark: she had an ability to make people dance to tunes they weren't accustomed to, and if they got giddy they were all the easier prey.

"No, I've got to do better than that," Dr Neumark scolded herself. "A little headache shouldn't put an old trouper like me out of commission."

"Migraine," Carla rebuked her.

"Whatever. Well, dear. I'll just freshen up under the shower, gobble a Codi, and I'll join you downstairs for . . ." consulting her watch ". . . late coffee."

An hour and forty-five minutes later Dr Neumark found Carla in the Dragons Lobby with four delegates, six cups (five dirty, one clean), and an empty pot. "Ruth," Carla said quite crisply. "I'll order a fresh pot."

Uncoiling himself from where he'd been reclining crossways across the armchair, his elegant legs dropping over the armrest, Omar Hamid stood to greet Dr Neumark. He gave her the clenched fist black power salute, which she returned. Then they embraced, leaving an inch and a half between their loins, Ruth noting again the sour bodily smell Omar carried round with him in all climes, as of wood-smoke and fermenting beans.

"And how are the grandchildren?" Omar asked. He'd been a little disappointed when an ANC leader had stood godfather to the youngest.

"They're doing splendidly," said Ruth politely but firmly, who was in public mode. Carla introduced N.S. Kumar, Dr Enoeda, the volcanologist, B.K. Napoleon Wong, the Taiwanese dissident, Rod Kienzler, and a Dr Lubbers.

N.S. said, "I admire the work, now I meet the human being," with a courtly gesture of the hand and such sophisticated self-mockery behind the sincerity that even Ruth laughed with the others.

"We all hope you have recovered from your indisposition, my dear Mrs Neumark. The heat can be such a trial."

"Oh, it wasn't that. I'm accustomed to that."

"Oh, yes, one finds deserts in Southern Africa, doesn't one."

"I think New York in August was Dr Neumark's test," Carla interjected." If you can stand that, you can stand anything."

"Yes, it's that wet heat, isn't it," said Rod Kienzler. "It mugs you. Muggy. Everyone at Ann Arbour asks me to send their regards, by the way, Dr Neumark, and best wishes for your first novel."

"You sojourned too? That's very kind of them all." Dr Neumark had immediately marked down young Kienzler as useful. She needed to add a new system of cross-generational alliances to her network, otherwise so efficient over the years, if she was to stay in contention. "Have I missed anything terribly fascinating? I'm sure I'm going to be very disappointed when I know, Carla."

"Oh, nothing to write home about. We'd agreed on soft-opening. Oh, Professor Enoeda! What have I said! And after your fascinating lecture as well!"

They all laughed heartily at Carla's gaffe, Enoeda the most good-humoured.

"My consolation is for you to promote me from Philosophy Doctor to Professor, Mrs Giolitti. I know scientific lecture can be very dull and dried for arts people but I endeavour my best. I think cannot ask more." He looked around at everyone, shoulders heaving.

"What was the subject, Professor Enoeda?"

"Ostensible subject, Mrs Neumark, was science of prediction of volcanic eruptions but eventually discursive: interaction of natural disasters and man-made degradation of environment, ah, accelerated rate of lahar flows on denuded hillside and along line of clogged riverways. Also silted estuaries and so on, many serendipitous effects. Ah, eruption of Mt Pinatubo actually plus factor in delaying of global warming – industry putting TFC's into ozone layer but three billion cubic metres of ash in stratosphere dropped earth temperature one degree centigrade. Five year moratorium on greenhouse effect. Other things."

"Mmm," said Dr Neumark. "It does sound fascinating."

"Next topic: harnessing of geo-thermal energy for electric power needs. Very crucial for Philippines, Madam." Enoeda looked at them with his keen eyes. No one seemed to know much about the country they were in. "Power outages the big problem," he said. "Country is poor, sick man of Asia. Need foreign investment. But multi-nationals cannot relocate plant from areas of high wages if no dependable electricity supply here. Brownout lasting 12 hours sometimes, and every day in Manila two, three hours rotating brownouts."

"What's the difference between a brownout and a blackout?" Kienzler sensibly asked, voicing the thoughts of many of the foreigners.

"The same," replied Enoeda, "but sometimes here is voltage

fluctuation – we can maybe see the filament in light bulb turn brown from white. Technical term: Manual Load Dropping."

"Well, you are obviously the great expert on local conditions, Dr Enoeda," N.S. said. It was, he thought, probably not a very remunerative area of expertise.

"Of course," said Enoeda. "This country is a volcanologist dream, so I must be here many times. Maybe destructive potential of volcano can become national power resource. However, not to worry: supplied in this hotel with diesel generator. Never mind noxious emission from exhaust!"

By now Carla had decided the Japanese were going to be one of the great successes of the affair. Even Professor Adachi with his limited knowledge or, should she say, extensive knowledge but small command, of English was turning out a charmer for everybody. And as for Hanabishi, she could see why Mrs Init raved about him. It was like, of course one could never say it, like having snuck in one of one's own kind as a spy in alien skin. She poured coffee for Ruth Neumark in a happier mood. "What else?" Ruth asked, sampling a petit four that looked like a jewel and tasted like sawdust. Carla decided to have a mild bit of revenge. "Here," she said. "This is a transcript." As she passed it to Ruth, she said, "It'll probably only take you ten minutes to skim, then you'll be as well-informed as the rest of us, won't you."

"Or as confused," Rod Kienzler remarked. "It was a joint presentation by a Korean materials scientist and a very young local architect. Not the most compatible pairing – with your forgiveness, Carla."

"None required, Rod. You just go right ahead and comment freely on everything you see, that's what you're here for. In fact, in as much as that was a locally arranged thing, I didn't have a hand in it."

While the others discussed what the town might hold for the foreign tourist, Dr Neumark did her homework. Actually she didn't resent this. She was justly famed as a prodigiously fast and still retentive reader, though she gave her own addresses from a typed text rather than memory. So, cutting through the extraneous waffle, an act which was an intellectual pleasure in itself, comparable maybe in satisfaction to shaving one's legs in a warm bath, it came as no surprise to her that Japan was the largest consumer of tropical hardwoods in the world, with the Hong Kong construction industry also displaying a voracious appetite for the rainforests of South East Asia. To her surprise, she learned hardwood was cheaper than softwood (tell that to Gerald who, tired of rot, had at great cost specified oak instead of pine for the windows and sills of their own home in Cape Town). Cheaper from 50 to 100 per cent already! Get away – she didn't believe that, but the man had said it in public. They used it for falsework for supporting the forms for pouring concrete for the skyscrapers of Hong Kong and Singapore, for site hoardings (which seemed outrageous waste) and for pit props and shoring up trenches. Instead of using this exhaustible natural resource it was suggested that metal, softwood, steel sheeting, ply or chip wood composite sheets, or premoulded concrete should be viable alternatives, even if it added to the costs of building. Something on recycling construction materials which were filling landfills (God, the inelegance of the language) at an alarming rate. Suggested more permanent uses for hardwood: indoor decoration and formwork. Right on, thought Ruth. In the local context there was a suggestion that chronic shortage of cement might be solved by mixing the superabundance of pyroclastic debris with a revolutionary Japanese binding catalyst.

"Meaty stuff," admitted Dr Neumark, handing the transcript back to Carla.

"Would you like to keep it?"

"No, thank you, my dear." Something came to Dr Neumark's mind. "He didn't mention disposable diapers."

"What?" Carla was not alone in being unable to follow the logic.

"Plastic and paper chuck-outs for baby. You know, the ones that save the modern father from getting his hands dirty washing away the poop."

"What's that got to do with Hong Kong tower blocks?" Kienzler asked with mild amusement but happy to be Dr Neumark's straight guy.

"They take up more space in the landfills than building rubble and it's also inadvisable to burn them because of the plastic water-proofing polluting the atmosphere. They're an ecological nightmare. For Pete's sake, I'm surprised you didn't know."

"You are proving a better educator today than the lecturer was being yesterday, Mrs Neumark," N.S. said. "My Holmesian deduction is this: you have become a grandmother at the present moment?"

Dr Neumark complimented N.S. on his insight.

"Not so personally insightful. Passing through the different stages in life is a very Indian, if not Hindu, concept. But burning diapers is not a problem for India – the population cannot afford the plastic "poops"? They would be using cloth or leaves instead, or indeed nothing at all. This is a problem of affluence."

Kienzler decided a joke about burning widows would be in bad taste in present company, but he gave Dr Neumark some eye support. "What about the local architecture, Carla?" he enquired. "Will we be getting a wider acquaintance of it than our present surroundings?"

"You sure will, Rod. Mrs Init informs me she has very special plans for us. And you're at liberty to just take a cab in and walk around town for yourself."

"That's not dangerous?" Kienzler asked. It was his practice to make no bones about his physical nervousness; it was a kind of bravado in its way, queasy machismo that impressed educated girls.

"Oh, no," said Carla laughing, but not unkindly, rather indicating she would participate in the general relief of the knowledge. "Obviously I take your point, Rod. But Mrs Init was at great pains to stress that Gobernador de Leon doesn't share the problems of, say, Manila or the Muslim islands in the south. There's no kidnappings here. I think she said they didn't have a single bank robbery during the 1980's."

"Not like Manila," confirmed Dr Enoeda, nodding. "Peaceful."

"Well, she would say that, wouldn't she," Dr Neumark heard Rod mutter. She gave him the faintest of smiles.

"As much as everyone says it's a safe city – and I do believe them, Rod – obviously it is a poor country, so I think it would be inadvisable to wear very nice personal jewellery downtown . . ."

"Damn, I knew I was a silly bitch bringing my pearls," quipped Rod.

Laughing with everyone, Carla said, "... and of course flashing a big wad of bank-notes would be a real no-no in any city of the world. I think you can take it from a native New Yorker, this town's Disneyland compared to any American city. In fact, maybe we can all take a trip at, er, 5:30 p.m. That would give us a couple of hours before they serve dinner."

"More like two and three quarters," said Rod, proving a conference wit and, again, everyone laughed because with the best will in the world the service didn't match the splendid architecture.

"Do I have any takers?" asked Carla. There was a general murmur of assent but B.K. Napoleon Wong said in his grammatically superb but incomprehensibly accented English – the Adachi syndrome manifesting itself again – "If it is all the same with you, Mrs Giolitti, I would rather be left to my own devices."

"Why, surely, Mr Wong. Professor Lubbers?"

"I'll give it a rain-check, too. I may polish up my presentation. I can see the facts won't be enough."

"Okay, that's just fine too."

SECURITY had posed Mrs Init a few pleasant perplexities. She'd discovered, starting to organise the whole thing more or less single-handed at least from the Philippine end – a one-woman band, Vic-Vic – that she was the kind of person who actually thrived on what another might have thought of as stress. She was a brilliant organiser, with the correct balance between details and the big picture, meticulous but not so tediously fussy she missed the environmental wood for the ecological trees. As the time came to take on assistants, she discovered she could inspire her subordinates without crushing them, she was an energiser, she had charisma, unlike the Congressman who ruled with the dead hand of fear, his essential menace residing in his stolid ordinariness – but again, unlike her Mister, she was not frightened to delegate. Delegation in the situation in which she found herself wasn't the soft option: it was a risk, a leap in the dark, but she took it gaily. And the gaiety encouraged the creativity of her troupe, from her sound technicians and engineers, to the hotel's assistant manager, to the bevy of student girls assisting Carla, chosen for intelligence as well as extreme good looks, to the conference "aides". Yes, she'd gone to the extent of having yellow T-shirts stencilled with orange letters for them. And every day she drew these up in line, inspected their equipment, the twig whisks and long-handled plastic dust-pans, their attire, as if she were a general and they soldiers. No one's part was too small, she told them; no task so trivial it couldn't be done with pride. And then she despatched them with a new dignity to the four corners of the Dragons Centre, straight-backed, legs and feet turned out, marching like Soviet gymnasts.

And so to security. Security – she knew there was no such thing. It was a chimera. If you felt secure, then you didn't have security. That was its definition. It was permanent paranoia, institutionalised foreboding. If they could get to an American President, they could get to anyone.

In due course she was to amaze Crescente with this insight. How did Auntie know? he would wonder. Were there enemies or their surviving relatives gunning for that fragrant, distinguished lady too? Had she to live with it as well? he would ponder. No way. Surely? She looked too majestic, too calm. Like, he had power but he was tense with it. He did his best to exhibit control publicly, the smooth surface, but inside he was coiled up. He could recognise the palpitations in others, the slight surface quiverings from the terrible pent-up pressure below – *koan*, waddyamacallit, the high frequency harmonic tremblings – that was why when he erupted it was usually so fatal. But his seismic instinct detected nothing in Auntie. Who was a woman, too.

Mrs Init, who would have thought of herself as more of a typhoon than a volcano, even if they gave them men's names as well these days, had identified danger from the following areas: minor to non-existent risks – the New People's Army, the communist guerillas whose mail was franked No Permanent Address. Similarly, the Muslim MNLF. These were way off their home bases and there was no good reason for them to single out her and hers. Slight risk: political opponents like Dionisio III. But it was at once too large-scale for the Bugnaws and too small-minded. That was, to send every goon they had to machine-gun a bunch of distinguished foreign delegates, who'd never done anything to them, just to put the Congressman's nose out of joint. Moderate risk: crazies from the exterior, foreign fanatics. Hook-nosed, circumcised types – thought she – with a down on Uncle Sam, the British, the Germans, the Japs. She knew they constituted what the Congressman would call a "soft target" for these characters. There'd been instances – an Iraqi trying to dynamite the USIS library in Manila had succeeded in blowing himself up.

Certainly one couldn't totally dispense with security, as one might have for a lower key occasion. So who did you use? She didn't want to use the Congressman's own people, the body-guards the newspapers persisted in calling a private army. He'd argue he couldn't spare them. "You want to see my funeral advanced already, Inday?" Besides, this was her own thing and, in the unlikely event of trouble, she wanted the ugliness at arm's length. As for the official military, green army and marine uniforms all over the place would give quite the wrong impression. Besides, you were getting yourself into a whole favours and obligation network with the local brigadier. Ditto the mushroom-coloured presence of the Philippine National Police. That was taking a sledgehammer and a mallet respectively to an eggshell and finding the handles fouled with slippery grease. The ubiquitous blue uniformed security guard companies represented the correct teaspoon for cracking egg-tops. On the other hand Mrs Init preferred to confront the international terrorist conspiracy with something more potent than a teaspoon between her slim fingers.

In the way that her ideas came to her, not in a rash flash like they seemed to arrive for the Congressman and a lot of other – maybe all – males, this decision formed with relative slowness, stray notions wrapping themselves round a central point; it was like finding you needed to answer the call of nature. Suddenly what you hadn't been consciously aware of became the inevitable. It was, she thought, probably like a gestation.

Who was a relative – keep business in the family had been the most innocuous of Papa's sayings – and had an interest in the martial? Who retained his own model army, equipped with the latest technologies? Who had the clout to fear no repercussions? Who was the one so powerful and biddable withal?

Crescente A. Koyaw, of course. Her favourite nephew.

She'd always had a soft spot for him, even when he was just a baby and she was building up for her showdown with the nuns. As time had passed and it had become obvious he was going to be a difficult boy – those minor manifestations of temperament: slapping his yaya, kicking the chauffeur, hitting that other boy with the hammer, though, personally, she'd never believed the maid who'd said he'd raped her (not possible: he was only thirteen and three-quarters) – their relationship had grown sweeter in proportion to the bitterness the boy felt at the world's rejection. It seemed the lovely young woman and the obese lad had little in common but in maturity Victoria realised they sprang from the same mould of circumstance. The bus lines had shaped both their destinies, crossing Victoria's palm somewhat later on the timetable. Crescente owed his very existence to the decision of both sets of his grandparents to bury the hatchet, merging the rival fleets against Chinese interlopers, incarnating the alliance of old machinery with the union of the young bodies of Crescente's mama and papa. His conception could be said to be the result of the head-on crash between his father's sperm and his mother's egg, the by-product of the accident, Crescente, being delivered at his other grandfather's hospital. As for Vic-Vic, she'd been left, speaking figuratively, waiting at the stop for the Congressman's bus, when she'd boarded and he'd driven off into an orange sunset over waving palms for better or for worse, mainly better.

Crescente's face had lit up like downtown after a brownout. "You come to the right man, auntie," he said. He'd enjoyed scaring the Jap's *arte* sister-in-law for *Tia* eighteen months ago over in Leyte. He'd wished he'd had a video camera running; it had been a great piece of action theatre, taking lover-boy outside by the scruff of his neck, sticking a knife one inch into his thigh to get a howl, then rushing in with a plate of dog's guts to show *inday*. She'd passed out! But over five hundred people in a conference – that was even better, a whole different responsibility.

"Crescente," *Tia* hesitated uncharacteristically, looking to get the essential message across with tact. "This isn't like the other job, you know. It needs other, er, more discreet approach, *di ba*?

Crescente made reassuring sounds, holding up his chubby palm. "I understand, Auntie. Different ball-game, different rules."

"Correct, Crescente. I will be happiest if we never need you. You will be successful to the extent you are not seen." She was to rue this as soon as she had said it, for Crescente, no doubt wishing to be as obliging to his favourite aunt as lay in his power, said, "Yeah. Undercover, *di ba*?"

"No, Crescente. Absolutely not. Ordinary security guards. I mean, not ordinary security guards. But in a uniform. The delegates will be nervous if they see armed men out of uniform. A man in jeans with a gun is not a reassuring sight for anyone."

"In a suit and sun-glasses even worse," Crescente contributed.

"What I meant, Crescente, was your people will be invisible because no one notices people in uniform. They get used to them."

"OK. How about I'm putting my boys in uniform but I'll be the one to mix with the visitors? You can say I'm a professor from Mexico."

Mrs Init closed her eyes momentarily. She was imagining that. "No," she said firmly.

"OK, Auntie. You're the boss. But no uniform for me."

That she had to concede.

Crescente really gave it his best attention. Weapons first, then uniforms; he had to get his priorities right, the power of positive thinking. Go for essentials first. Ideally, the higher the firepower the better. But in the tactical situation there existed constraints – he recognised that, unlike the cavemen in the police who sprayed everyone twice, kidnappers and the rich schoolgirls they'd abducted. Machine guns were not the greatest idea. The Ingram MAC-10, superb in its proper context, was more or less uncontrollable the way the merrie men had taken to firing it one-handed. The good old Garand was more accurate, but the round had a nasty tendency to penetrate and kill anyone standing behind the target.

No, it looked like shot-guns, a homely but highly underestimated tool – except by the pros. No penetration but awesome hitting power with the right load, and a small spread with correct choke and again the right ammo. From the point of view of the protected, they weren't terrifying to look at either, while it gave the handler a kind of Wild West feel. Wild East, he should say. He had the Browning automatic, a fearsome, bucking beast of a weapon; the Mossberg combat shotgun, black and deadly as a mamba; a nondescript Spanish pump-action; then three or four high-class English double barrels and under-and-overs. The more responsible of the merrie men could carry MAC-10's as back-up to these. As for uniforms – he wanted them to look right (how you looked could stop trouble dead in the first place) but also he didn't want *Tia* having to pay too much. He was a considerate nephew. In the end, he went for American desert camouflage for their pants (great overtones of Desert Storm) and the same yellow T-shirts as the sweepers but stencilled UNTOUCHABLES after the film of that name, *di ba*? He would never understand why the old Indian guy would laugh so loudly every time he saw them. The Boss remembered Sean Connery as Eliot Ness had used a pump-action 12-gauge, the others Thompsons, Ness as lethal as a stagecoach guard blowing Apaches off their ponies. At their customary reveille, the chief goon told him: "We like, Boss."

Their morale needed boosting. He was darned if it shouldn't have been him who was pissed, but he was as cheerful for weeks afterwards as the merrie men were sobered. It had been an amateurish attempt, two idiots on a motorbike wearing crash helmets (the helmets alone should have alerted everyone) roaring up Guava as he came out of For da Guys, the fool on the pillion getting off three widely spaced shots from what was probably a single action .38 revolver (amateurs!), the driver jumpy as hell, swerving to near-disaster at the reports going off by his ear. As for him, he hadn't even ducked for cover, he'd thought it was a car back-firing or firecrackers. Give his morons credit, they'd realised at once. What was interesting, and he hoped ultimately instructive, was that of the ninety seven shots fired (calculating from the remaining shells in the MAC-10 magazines, the totally empty box in one lunatic's case) not one had hit the receding target. Not one! The merrie men had been crestfallen for weeks. As the focus of this murderous attention – however incompetent the execution there was no doubting the sincerity of the emotion – he should have been the one feeling pissed. But all he felt was joyful! It had been such a rush – beat running around on the jet-ski (which had languished in the garage the last eighteen months). In fact, he now knew being shot at (unsuccessfully) was a bigger high than successfully plugging someone. After the initial adrenalin hit he'd felt a wonderful relief. The boredom, the chronic boredom, had vanished. He just felt so glad to be still alive. He felt a real attachment to and appreciation of his mundane routines. It was like he'd had the toxin of tedium, the waste of his wasted days, everything that poisoned, depressed, and brought him down, rinsed out of him and he could see the world sparkling new again. Phewie! Thanks dong! he'd have liked to say to his would-be assassins – just to rub it in – before gut-shooting the pair of them. When the brakes on the BMW failed going down a particularly steep hill – so much for supposedly vauntless German technology – he'd just taken it in his stride, his new long, lean, stride. Naturally, the merrie men had redoubled their vigilance; they were scared the Boss was going to take it out on them. Naturally, he'd take extra precautions, not be foolhardy. But you know what? The thought that someone out there had troubled to put his name on a contract didn't faze him at all. Not at all.

He was too pleased with himself.

Chapter Fourteen

CARLA, WHO HAD SEEN IT HAPPEN BEFORE, BLAMED HERSELF. The problem didn't lie in anything substantive. It was just a loss of rhythm. That was the way people were, particularly artistic people (and she'd now learned that scientists could be even more temperamental than musicians or poets). If they got bored they became fractious, they'd manufacture unreal issues of contention. On the other hand, if they got too engrossed with their own current doings, the small, high-pressure world they found themselves in, they'd lose their sense of proportion and behave exactly the same way. It was a matter of balance. Intersperse the interesting and provocative with the not-so. Spice things up when it became necessary. She was the conductor, she set the pace, and she'd failed both the promoter and the orchestra.

Water had been the theme of the last three days, that after fire from Dr Enoeda and then hot air from others. Earth, she supposed, would conclude their discussions of the elemental. They'd been hectored and sloganised, mostly by Philippine speakers (National Discipline for a Green Philippines, Think Green Drink Clean), propagandised, proselytised, and actually – Carla flattered herself – in the end educated, even if the conclusion she'd drawn (and kept to herself) was that everything was so interconnected and the vested interests so powerful that change for the better was almost impossible. What was reform in one area would prove harmful in another. The lecture on controlled fission reactors by the visiting speaker, Admiral La Rocque, brought this out. The saga of the Marcos-initiated nuclear plant at Bataan seemed to encapsulate most of recent national history: the grants from the World Bank and the IMF, the accusations of bribing Marcos which the Philippine government had failed to make stick on Westinghouse in an American court, the successor governments initially taking environmental stances, then wavering as they considered the purely economic argument that the rickety conventional power stations left the country literally and figuratively in the dark. No one would invest in the Philippines, as Dr Enoeda had originally pointed out, if their factories couldn't run, not the Taiwanese, not the Japs, not even the Italians. Brownouts impeded the penetration of questing foreign capital and the smooth outflow of the country's own exports. Carla had seen Representative Init nodding vigorously at Admiral La Rocque's analysis, shaking his head equally vehemently when doughty Gracie Hipkin had heaved herself to her feet to ask what was better, sitting quietly in the brownout or watching yourself glow in the dark.

Professor Pfeidwengeler had then said panic was for the ignorant. Plutonium wasn't so terrible.

What, Gracie had screamed, unable to find her feet, such the shock. Professor Pfeidwengeler had smirked – Carla knew by now that he did love to get a result, did Professor Pfeidwengeler. Plutonium, Gracie told a hall which didn't know whether to be outraged or laugh, was the most carcinogenic substance made by erring, suffering mankind. And it retained its obnoxiousness for aeons. Carla had been distinctly impressed as Gracie got technical about the "back end of the nuclear fuel cycle" and the problems of high and even low-level waste management, reprocessing, and re-cycling (the latter highly inadvisable and dictated by weapons manufacturing).

Professor Pfeidwengeler riposted by citing statistics from Hiroshima and Nagasaki (the *only* ones worthy the name) which showed not only how thousands of Japanese had absorbed massive doses of radiation without harmful effect in later life but how the incidences of acute myoblastic leukaemias and melanomas in some sectors of the city population had actually been subsequently lower than the norm.

Gracie came back with the figures for Chernobyl, Pfeidwengeler only remarking she seemed glad! He then dealt swiftly with the environmental and economic arguments against atomic power (the old term "which was having the positive connotation, because nuclear is now being a dirty word"). He pointed out that coal and oil powered stations were notorious polluters. Carbon wastes and acid rain from *fossil fuels* were deadly catalysts for lead poisoning in the water table, with Philippine children already showing levels of 20-21 mcg/decilitre in their blood. That was as likely to produce cretinism and defects in posterity as radiation! Geothermal plants sprayed arsenic, lead, and worse into the atmosphere in the event of accidental blowout – look at what had happened in Hawaii. By contrast, the notion that there was direct causal connection between large quantities of the sub-stratospheric, wind-borne isotopes caesium-137, iodine-131, strontium-90 or plutonium-239 and the production of human cancers *without ingestion or inhalation* was not a closed and shut affair. Himself, he stopped drinking milk sixty years ago. As for the weak penetrating alpha particle radiation emitted by the heavy isotopes of plutonium – that couldn't penetrate human skin! Then on the other hand the effect of low dosage ionising radiation was a subject of great controversy. It depended how you used the data.

As for hydro-electricity – that destroyed whole communities, putting farmlands and habitations alike under water, then destroying aquatic life as temperature rose with the drop in lake levels, as it had at Lake Lanao in Mindanao. Regarding the argument that atomic power was uneconomic, that was a result of the gross construction over-specification forced on Western governments for purely political reasons, pandering to a paranoiac public. You could build reactors with millions of statistically accident-free years of operation for half the price. And then, said the Professor, even Filipino managers couldn't drive tarriffs up by pilfering rods of radio-active fuel like they had drums of oil. Balance the thousands of real children actually dying of the diseases of poverty, say from dehydration caused by simple diarrhoea, against the hypothetical hundreds who *might* die if there was an accident. Start the Bataan reactor now. He, Pfeidwengeler, would breakfast on it with FVR.

An awestruck silence followed. Then a firestorm of insult and counter-insult amongst the foreign delegates, Admiral La Rocque shrugging his shoulders and rolling his eyes, Gracie actually losing her voice, the Professor figuratively but visibly rubbing his hands in glee over what he'd done. Not one Filipino voice was raised. And it was for Bish Hanabishi to pour oil on the waters – if that was an ecologically responsible thing to say – to end the general Asian embarrassment in an explosion of nervous laughter with his well-timed intervention, that he'd been born in Nagasaki in 1956 (where his parents were already living in 1945) and that as they could see there had been "no problem for me to pass quality control, no defects."

The next day saw that ridiculous motion. While Carla could not directly blame Professor Pfeidwengeler for its passing she had no doubt in her mind that he'd prepared the atmosphere in which it was possible. The hysterical, self-important atmosphere of pent-up strain and inner regard; the hot air, that rather poisonous climate in which her regressing charges, forgetting about larger proportions, were concentrating only on their individual urges to assert themselves.

And it was her fault.

It was all a matter of rhythm.

Gracie Hipkin was the formal proposer, Kamla Mishra the seconder but – Carla knew – Rod Kienzler was the instigator, the mischief-maker who'd put the idea into their heads – that horrible British expression of his about stuff hitting the fan – and Omar Hamid his abettor. Just as the hall was settling down for the first session of the morning – Professor Pfeidwengeler always first in, way before anyone else, established in solitary, rebuking grandeur of the universal tendency to accommodate to Philippine notions of time – Gracie had pre-empted the chair, wearing a pleasant and self-dismissive smile, herself just the conduit of the motion, the general will. "Before we start the formal agenda of our day," she announced into the buzzing ether of general chatter, looking to front, sides, and as far as she could twist, which was not far, to back, "some of us would like to float a proposal. We think, from our informal canvassing, that it would find widespread support. In fact, we'd like to pass a motion and I'm mandated to propose it, and I'm seconded by our colleague, Ms Kamla Mishra in this. The motion reads as follows: *Conference, mindful of our duty to conserve all forms of energy and particularly of the difficult situation in which our host country finds itself as regards shortages of electrical power supply, is desirous to set a correct example. We therefore move for the air-conditioning system, which even necessitates some of us wearing extra clothing redundant to the climate, to be closed down sixteen hours of the day forthwith*.

All around the hall people looked at each other with polite, amused, querying expressions. A kind of humming replaced the aimless buzz. This was the sound of mild approval, of boredom moderately alleviated.

Mrs Init looked stunned. Her air-con! Her wonderful Japanese air-con! She fought for mastery of her expression, all the things that were second nature for the Congressman so hard for her. It was like, well, watching children throwing into the trash-can the sweets you'd just given them. Expensive, imported sweets. Ms Hipkin was asking if a show of hands would be in order. It was. They shot up, a Nuremberg forest. People turning, stimulated by the small physical excitement of the effort, giggling over their own solidarity.

"And the no's?" Gracie inquired to general titters, herself grinning broadly. The laughter lapped about Professor Pfeidwengeler like wavelets around a rock at low tide. "Motion passed, with one against, no abstentions," said Gracie to ironic cheers.

The two pre-luncheon lectures that followed concerned firstly the Asian Green revolution of the 70's – the doubling of yields made possible through new varieties of grain, principally

IR-8 and now IR-60 and C-4 cross-bred and genetically manip-
ulated Magic Rice strains created at the International Rice
Research Institute at Los Banos, Northern Philippines, and the
failure by the poorest Asian countries to invest sufficiently in
capital-intensive irrigation projects which had prevented the
most being made of the opportunity. This was followed by
presentation on the multi-million dollar Philippine Natural
Grade Carageenan industry, PNG carageenan being a substance
processed out of an edible seaweed consumed from time
immemorial in the Visayas but now capable of use in brewing, in
giving toothpaste "mouth feel", in extending the fresh life of
bakery products, in bulking out preserved canned meats without
recourse to water injection, in the aqueous vehicle of medical
suspensions, and as a mopper-up of waste in polluted waterways.

Nothing being without an infelicitous obverse side, they
learned of the cancer scare put out by the American competitors
and how the radical environmentalists had burned down the
farms in the Sulu Sea. (Big grin from Gracie).

The afternoon saw a talk on the degradation of coral reefs
from Bish Hanabishi and a paper on Pacific Drift Netting.
These passed without incident, barring relatively innocuous
comment from Detlef that one should not confuse economic
and moral issues. Fishing with poison or explosive was irrational
– it depleted stocks, it was not efficient, but it was not a crime
against humanity as such. Nor was there a provable connection
between the dumping of industrial wastes at sea and such
phenomena as toxic algae blooms. That was not a moral issue
either.

"It's a crime against posterity, surely, Professor," suggested
Bish Hanabishi gently, from the lectern.

"*Nein!*" bellowed the Professor, making the student Filipinas
in front of him jump, then giggle. "Stop this worry of the children – the generations will look after themselves. They can do it
better than we can. Our responsibility stop to ourselves.
Humankind tougher than you think. The children of Nagasaki
can survive atomic bomb, they can survive some few rubbishes

inside the ocean. Progress, *mensch*, progress – the environmentalist want to stop progress – that is their solution to all ill. But progress will providing its own solutions. You choose 20th century or you choose Stone Ages. Mankind have to trust itself."

"Sounds like moral argument to me, Professor."

Pfeidwengeler joined in the general laughter.

"WELL, it's really very kind of you all," said Carla. She meant it. N.S. Kumar and John Hawkins had just, in their very different styles, congratulated her on the way things were now going. She was surrounded at afternoon coffee, three days after Deadly Detlef Pfallout's pitch for plutonium by those she thought of as her stalwarts (Kienzler's nickname for the German which showed signs of sticking to the wall). Kienzler was not present. He was not a stalwart. But N.S. added to his earlier compliments another felicitation as to the variety.

"But that's just exactly what I'm worried about, N.S. It seems such a patchwork."

"Oh, no, goodness me, dear Mrs Giolitti. That is just the ticket. How deadly dull it would be to eat lentils every day, nourishing though pulses are. People want to be stimulated by the new."

"It's fine, Carla," John Hawkins said. "You can see the seams – you put it together. It's standard. And it helps me when I'm filing – something new every time. That's news values for you."

James Benitez, the nice Professor from the local university, said, "That's also the way Filipinos are. You will find we like to jump from topic to topic. Not one song. They like the three-tune medley. Always restless." He had a way of grinning broadly at what he was about to say that Carla found irresistibly charming, because most of the time – and certainly when others were speaking – he looked so terribly serious. She'd have felt a greater attraction if he hadn't also possessed that ambiguous quality Carla regretted in educated Asian men: in a nutshell, wimpishness. James Benitez, survivor of six weeks in the stockade under Marcos in 1972, and in 1984 of a faultily fused fragmentation grenade thrown by Scout Rangers in the pay of a provincial mayor he had insisted on testifying against in a separate murder trial, James Benitez, the incurably self-effacing, added: "The discursiveness of the topics is just superficial. Actually it's all connected – the volcanoes, the flooding, the logging, the water pollution, the dying of the seas."

Carla said eagerly, "That's exactly what I thought." She was surprised. Listening to the educated Filipinos was strange: what would have been perfect, even idiomatic, English in transcript but issuing in that heavy accent, all whirlpool r's and "th" soldered into "d", so that it seemed as if you were getting the gist of the statement from an echo or translation you were re-playing in your own head. N.S. said, "But of course: *only connect*." And he smiled wistfully to himself and quite incomprehensibly to everyone else. Coming back to the present with some small but still visible effort, he added: "It is the personal relationships which matter in this world and even the next. Never mind the visible agenda, that is illusion at its merest; it is the pretext of all our inter-penetrations. It could be anything, isn't it? Of course," he added rather more hastily and in a less ruminatory fashion, "that is not to say the speaking programme is unimportant."

Hanabishi, or "Bish" as he'd become to John Hawkins, laughed. "Don't worry about me, Your Excellency. It is my belief you are absolutely correct in your utterances. Who will remember what a lecturer said in five years time?"

"Next week," interjected Hawkins to general amusement.

"In my case I cannot even remember what I said five minutes ago, but we will all remember the people we met here."

"Well, if I can foster even some introductions I'll consider I've been successful," said Carla, fitting herself to the general mood. They were at that point where initial shynesses had been dissolved, people had more or less decided who they found congenial, but the conference still stretched pleasantly ahead without the sense of its culmination overhanging them. Carla always compared it to the fortnight before half-term at a new school. "I still get star-struck," she confessed. "Not very profes-sional of Carla, I know, but that's the truth. How often do you get to sit next to a Nobel prizewinner like Dr Lubbers?"

Hanabishi looked puzzled. "Lubbers, that's familiar."

"You didn't know he'd won the Nobel Prize for chemistry?"

"*What*?" shrieked everyone.

"Yes," said Carla, the imperturbable.

"*Who*?" exclaimed Dr Neumark, now dragged into circula-tion from her not unfriendly aloofness.

"Dr Lubbers. He was sitting next to you when we were at coffee on Tuesday. He gave the talk on enzymes cleaning up oil spills. Anyhow, he left yesterday for another conference, in Penang."

"I never sat next to him. In fact, I've never been anywhere near a Dr Lubbers," Dr Neumark said.

"My dear," Carla said. "You could have taken a biscuit from his plate. He was where John is sitting now and you were in Bish's seat."

"My dear," Dr Neumark insisted, with the beginnings of her famous asperity, "I was sitting there but there was no Dr Lubbers in the group. Otherwise I should have remembered him."

Carla held her peace and did not insist. Hanabishi said, "How remiss of me! Lubbers, of course. A very distinguished man."

N.S. was frankly vexed. "What an opportunity to miss!" He drummed his elegantly manicured brown fingers on the arm-rest. "Such a shame!" He was thinking how it would have made a good paragraph, or even sentence, in the next and possibly final volume of his memoirs. Lubbers alongside Francis Crick, Stephen Hawking, Fred Hoyle, Robert Gallo – all actually spoken to, N.S. was no bull-shitter, but the words carefully chosen so that the great man's sometimes two- or three-sentence reply could be inserted as what appeared a fragment of a much larger intimacy: N.S. stalking and then mounting these talking trophy heads with as much cunning and pride as native rulers of an earlier day might have tigers. "Carla!" he said sharply, and in a much more falsetto tone than normal, an authentic echo of exasperated Bloomsbury, "you are a very negligent lady! This must not happen again! We will not be denied our autographs!" Carla squeezed his hand and, to her surprise, found his thumb quite ready to stroke hers. "N.S., honey, you're the birthday boy. I think the memorabilia seekers would be after you, not poor Dr Lubbers. But –" professionals never too proud to accept a justi-fied rebuke – "I'll make sure it doesn't happen again. My over-sight, folks."

Chapter Fifteen

TRANSCRIPT OF A FORUM on the theme of "Asian Values in the 20th Century context: Assets or Anachronisms?" Moderator: Professor J. Beaufort (NZ). Panellists: Professor J. Benitez (Phils), Mr B.K. Napoleon Wong (Taiw), Professor D. Pfeidwengeler (FDR), Mr B. Dinolan (Phils).

Beaufort: Ladies and gentlemen, the best kind of chairman is an invisible one. No one looks at the referee in a boxing match, although I hope my fellow participants will heed my calls of "Break!" *(Laughter).* Our distinguished panellists are already well known to you, so we will not formally introduce ourselves nor do I feel the need for us to "warm up". It is already very warm without the air-con. *(Laughter).* Let me open by asking B.K. Napoleon Wong if he feels we can usefully talk of a system of supra-national Asian values as opposed to distinctly national or, indeed, regional or tribal cultures in Asia.

Wong: Ah. You catch me "cold", Professor Beaufort.

Beaufort: I'll count to ten. *(Laughter).*

Wong: I think so. Yes. Many cultures but a shared background. Just as European culture and therefore modern American culture share the common heritage to an outsider at least of the Judaeo-Christian moral system. That's fundamental. Then I think the Greek method of logical and mathematical inquiry. Roman law, Roman method also, the great law-givers and engineers. Now I believe both the Rome and the Greece of Asia to be China. For better or worse, China. Understand, please, that I don't speak in a partisan way. Now the culture of Japan, of Korea, Vietnam, is fundamentally Chinese. If Japan was not formally tributary like Korea and Vietnam, then the ideographic Chinese script – for instance – was wholesale adopted. A modern Japanese can read a menu in the Chinese language or vice versa can write a letter of complaint in Japanese to the management (*laughter*) and understand and be understood. I exaggerate very slightly. Korean, of course, is a 26-letter alphabetic language related only to Finnish and very distantly to Hungarian . . .

Beaufort: Of course. (*Laughter*).

Wong: . . . so China is giving the Latinity and, more, the value system of Confucianism, family solidarity, respect for ancestors and elders, subordination of the individual to the group, obedience to government, etcetera, etcetera to the rest of Asia for better or for worse. Sometimes, I think for worse. (*Laughter*).

Beaufort: Yes, of course, Mr Wong. I feel I should – despite my opening remark eschewing formal introductions – explain to today's audience that you have suffered imprisonment at the hands of Chinese governments of varying political hues at different times and different places for the expression of your views and your most effective satire. The very courageous expression of those views, I should like to say.

Wong: Not courageous. Stupid. But, yes, Mr Chairman, I have the honour to have been imprisoned by both Chiang Kai Shek and Mao Tse Tung. The Kuo Min Tang were just physically torturing their opponents, the communists worse – boring you to death as well. (*Laughter*).

Beaufort: Well, anyone who has read *The Dung Heap* knows your position on traditional China. But would you not admit what is certainly the most apparent feature to the outsider: firstly, the longevity and durability of that culture – whether one admires it or not – and secondly – as has become apparent recently – the extraordinary adaptability and flexibility of it in new environments.

Wong: Well, in evolutionary terms the primitive single-cell organism has proved itself the most successful. The amoeba is three billion years old, and it can still give you dysentery.

Beaufort: I'm thinking of the economic success of traditional Asian societies which have modernised in the material sphere but not the cultural – the dragon economies, Taiwan, Korea, Singapore, Japan, of course, and then China itself is enjoying prodigious economic growth. Twelve per cent with the rest of the world in recession? Professor Pfeidwengeler.

Pfeidwengeler: This should be coming as no surprise to anyone. Already everyone knows what kind of the society is economically successful. It gives discipline, collective values, and homogeneity. This is the simple explanation of the Japanese success and the German.

Beaufort: It's certainly a simplistic explanation. Don't both those economies require a substantial if concealed amount of immigrant labour whether it's Turkish and Yugoslav or Korean and Filipino?

Pfeidwengeler: Well, the Chinese gentleman talked of amoeba. I say the shark has its sucker fish also and also there it is the parasite which is dependent on the host for its survival.

Benitez: I think the interesting study is the point where this historically mythical, "pure" society has to acknowledge the extent to which it has been infiltrated and subverted by the alien – particularly in the case of, say, Japan.

Wong: The case doesn't arrive for China. That has been infinitely absorptive of all influences and conquerors: Mongol horde, Manchus, Marxism.

Benitez: I would propose that we can usefully distinguish between the blotting paper society of assimilated influences, such as China, and on the other hand the bastardised society such as, say, the Philippines (*laughter*) with a whole variety of fathering influences fighting for genetic supremacy: Malay, Chinese, Spanish, and coca-cola and Hollywood too.

Beaufort: You say Chinese, Professor Benitez, and in fact I believe the Sugbu junk trade considerably precedes the Hispanic conquest – the Chinese influence has been large . . .

Benitez: In all senses, not just cultural. Every modern Filipino owes at least twenty per cent of the blood in his or her veins to a Chinese ancestor.

Beaufort: And yet with the long Chinese influence, the ninety per cent literacy, the American bequest of widely disseminated English language proficiency and an overtly democratic political system closely modelled on the US pattern, the country is not one of the economic dragons of Asia. Why? Mr Dinolan, can you enlighten the foreigner?

Dinolan: Again, Professor.

Beaufort: I was reflecting on the many advantages of the Philippines' history and, not least, its geographical position, and wondering why it should not be a rich country.

Dinolan: I'll be the one to speak? Yes, well we are poor. We cannot deny that. No one has much money for sure except the rich. I don't know.

Pfeidwengeler: Dragon? It gives here the Sick Man of Asia. Since Independence the country has been a failure. Democracy not worked because the Filipino is a pirate in his heart.

Beaufort: Your comment, Professor Benitez.

Benitez: Let's hear the Professor to the end.

Pfeidwengeler: Two kinds of society only are existing, for useful purposes of distinction. The superior society and the inferior. What does a society seek to do for its members: prosperity to generate and freedom to guarantee. That is the two factors that gives the quality of life. But the freedom and the prosperity, they both go together. In the short term, the society of the drones can be prosperous – take Singapore. But on its limitations eventually it will under, eventually it fails. The expanding economies of Asia work on technologies they have borrowed or stolen – the inventions are from free minds, American or European minds. The Chinese, he is a good accountant. I remember at Cape Canaveral, my old German colleagues telling me: they use the Asian fellow to check their figures – but it's the old German von Braun or the young American Jews is always the originator. That's because in America it thinks free. You know we talk already of the Asian values. When Asian values is mentioned it usually gives the meaning of government values.

The West tell the East, we link trading concessions and loans to human rights and the Asian politician he says, democracy and human rights is not Asian concepts, not applicable to us. Security of group more important than rights of individual. You hear that one? But he really is meaning not convenient to us, the rulers. He is willing to steal the technology idea but not the idea of liberty. The ones underneath the government, they like to have their human rights, they don't think it's make insult of their heritage. My Chinese colleague agrees?

Wong: With qualifications, but basically yes.

Beaufort: I'm surprised.

Pfeidwengeler: Then you are not dead yet. We have to liberate our minds. So: you have to think for yourself, not think the thoughts of others. All this ecology rubbish – just clichés after the other. A mind builds its thought with individual bricks – the noodle takes the big pre-fabricate parts from others. I said just now: the superior society and the inferior society. But people, they're refusing always to admit the evidence of their own eyes. If one country have a superior way of playing football, of training the players, of plan for the game, then it's OK to say it, *ja*? But when one country have a superior way of organising its society – suddenly you cannot say it any more. You must spare the feelings of the black man, the brown man.

Beaufort: Different, Professor Pfeidwengeler, but not superior surely. Relative values . . .

Pfeidwengeler: It gives no relative values. Existing are certain absolute human goods and human bads. You know this is the problem: the black man and the brown man – he knows in his heart his society is inferior. But it is against human nature to confess inferiority. So he's full of hate and jealousy. But until he admits it he cannot improve himself. That's eventually the nub, so simple as that.

Beaufort: Really so simple, Professor? I think things are a little more complicated than you make out.

Pfeidwengeler: Ja, of course. I give you simplified model for clarity's sake. But you know it works. Look, you think the population of China would not jump on the first ship to America even tomorrow if allowed it is? They know the culture will let them live happier – not just the money. So OK, now it's OK to say communism is *scheiss*. Doesn't work. We are able – civilised, educated like us – to say one ideology is better than the others, open market forces is better efficient regulator than planned economy. What we cannot say: you losing your job, people throw you tomatoes, bad eggs – that one culture can surpass another. Even worse, one religion is kinder than another . . .

Beaufort: I would not have thought you a religious man.

Pfeidwengeler: Or indeed I am not. The great three bane: religion, nationalism, ideology. And in that order. You know, on these subjects disinterested scientific inquiry is made forbidden. My work on genetics in the 1960's – absolutely pure research. I had no preconception, no prejudices. I just want the truth. But even when it gives genes of flowers, you cannot present truth. The students rioting, breaking the meeting, singing to stop you talking. To say one culture is better than another – in their hearts people know the truth. Then to go on one step beyond: it gives superior intellect based on wider and better gene pool making that culture . . .

Beaufort: The battle over heredity and environment as factors in *individual* development is fierce and complicated enough. To carry it over into an entire culture is contentious and simplistic in the extreme. And, really, I think these race classifications are a century out of date, and as ludicrous as they're offensive.

Pfeidwengeler: It's not giving one factor only. OK, geography, climate, resources, interacting with genetic endowment of the folk. To rule out the last factor is more simplistic even . . .

Wong: I think anthropological and historical research is showing the persistence and stability of gene pools in even small regions. The DNA? The bones, colour of hair from grave sites in the remote past match very closely the traits of the modern population.

Pfeidwengeler: Exactly.

Benitez: So which societies in your scale are at the top and which at the bottom, Professor?

Pfeidwengeler: The bottom – the negro. Absorption of the negro is the big problem for the advanced society, I think, which finds them in its midst. They cannot rise from the bottom – I say their social specific gravity the highest. Take an Indian (very manipulative people these Indians), *ja*, or you take the Jew, the Chinese – the fellows can rise from the bottom even in one generation. The black man cannot . . .

Beaufort: My dear Professor Pfeidwengeler, he has never been given the chance.

Pfeidwengeler: You take your opportunity. It is not given you, like freedom, not given, only taken – except the black fellow didn't win his freedom – the white man ended slavery. OK, only in Haiti they win it. So why the black is already in the position when he can be denied? Because his culture innately inferior stands and maybe he himself. Africa – it's giving a disaster. Female circumcision. Obeah, tribalism. We examine the history of every independent black state there. I tell you, my good gentleman, it will give not one, I tell you, not one example of the voluntary and the democratic transfer of power. There, it's just to make money for yourself, then you look after your tribe also – that's being the entire history of their independence. White man's rule was better.

Beaufort: The present governments, one might say, are but continuations of the colonial power structures.

Pfeidwengeler: I know a good English word, Professor Beaufort: Tommy's rot. Now you and our Chinese friend talking of durable cultures. The culture of China is not so persistent as that of Africa. It survived ocean journeying, it survived slavery. You see the same negro vice in the Caribbean island and the American ghetto like you saw in Africa: dancing, raiding, drugging, mating of the animality.

Wong: These are sentiments I have heard issuing from educated Chinese mouths also, Professor Pfeidwengeler, and I also disagree with you. You have told us what you don't like.

Kindly inform us of what society you can admire. Maybe the German achievements of the mid-twentieth century?

Pfeidwengeler: Well, I tell you first, gentleman, you will not make me angry anything you say. OK? Clear all? I don't take nothing to be personal, so we are all happy. OK, the Scandinavian, the Anglo-Saxon society also. It gives perfected as possible political and social systems. It gives strong disseminated notion of justice and the social good – that is being the nub. Not the written laws – this doesn't matter. You can make beautiful written law and it's a society of pigs. The unformulated social culture of the folk is the factor prevailing.

Wong: I also admire the Anglo-Saxon political inheritance. I will agree with that.

Beaufort: So the Anglo-Saxon brain is the superior one? I think we can actually quantify the achievement and disprove that statement, and I'd like to steer us away from opinion to fact if we might.

Pfeidwengeler: No. The social culture is superior, which is not the creation of a single mind. The *individual* superior intellect stands clear: the Jewish. The Jew's intellect stands superior as well art as science; maybe even more science. It makes the funny situation. I find neither the Russians nor the Americans were trusting their nuclear scientists when together they were in one room. For why? All Jews were! The security men, as well KGB as FBI, all wetting their pants! Some KGB disguise as scientist – the Russian Jews helping the American Jew making a joke of them by asking the difficult scientific questions! KGB don't know what to do!

Beaufort: Well, they didn't make a very good job of Israel, did they?

Benitez: I am very interested to have an answer to this question. In fact, I am on tenterhooks. Where do the Philippines come on this social Richter scale? *(Laughter).*

Pfeidwengeler: I answer your question in all total seriousness. There is nothing so comic about our discussion. We are before saying the Filipino shares the general problem of the Asian culture: that is, traditionalist, family-based culture, the one that makes perpetuation of bad governments possible. It's the same everywhere: the Malay-type society, in the Chinese-type society, in the hybrid society. But the Filipino, he cannot get the advantages of this collectivist culture. Everywhere else growing five or seven per cent per annum for ten years more, until now recent the poor Filipino every year posts negative growth rate and even now though it gives growth, he's still in trade deficit, buys more abroad than he can make and sell to foreign. Now why?

So what is striking the European or the American about the country? Firstly, corruption, indiscipline, violence. But Thailand where I find myself living, so I'm speaking well, and Indonesia I can also say are more corrupt eventually. Indiscipline: OK, the Philippine citizen needs another police to protect him from the Philippine National Police. *(Laughter)*. The army, it's also gangsters: illegal logging, kidnap of citizens, gun-running for the rebels. But in Thailand also the big criminals are wearing badges. But Thailand is every year growing also. And the same level of casual and government violence. So it's none of these three factors . . .

Beaufort: Well, I find myself living here and I'd say the big problem is recovering from half a century of economic distortion when the Americans sat on any industrial development and ran the country as a gigantic plantation, followed by nearly twenty years of dictatorship during which a potentially rich country amply endowed among other resources with gold, copper, fruits, coal, fish, maize and copra was systematically plundered. They got rid of Marcos at EDSA – the dictator went but the debt stayed. Marcos deposited all the foreign loans in foreign banks and his hapless fellow countrymen are still paying it off. That's why there's no growth – more than a third of the budget goes on debt service.

Pfeidwengeler: I heard more than half. But you're the same again. The white man to blame for Africa problems today, the Americans and Marcos to blame for Philipinnen now. Where the buck stops? I tell you an Englishman's words: the people got the government they deserved. Marcos not an aberration – Marcos he was the *typical pinoy*. Inside every Filipino there is a little Ferdinand Marcos, inside every Filipina there is a little Imelda Marcos. *(Laughter)*. *Ja*. Do not laugh, you. It's true. This is a nation made of criminal and potential criminal.

Beaufort: Actually, I take your point. I really do. It's been a source of some mental anguish to me as someone who's made his stand here and loves the country. But I put it to you that poverty will make a man dishonest in ways both large and small. Often enough if he steals it's not for himself but his children – and is that totally ignoble? Take away the poverty and most of the dishonesty will go with it.

Pfeidwengeler: You are wrong. Not poverty make the dishonesty, dishonesty make the poverty here. The rich Filipino a bigger thief than the poor one. It gives one expression for this: moral *slightness* of the Filipino. It's a culture has no honour, no depth. A culture without commitment. You and I, we're coming from cultures where it's a big shame to tell a lie. We value truth, in other words. But the Filipino from earliest days is a liar congenital. He'll lie to his own – and to the white man, *liebe Gott*! When they hook their finger – make the Cross, you know it – swear it's the truth, well that's the signal comes a bigger lie. *(Laughter)*. Then every Filipino is also born a traitor as well as a liar. The national hero, it's Rizal – from José Rizal on it's traitors. Rizal change his mind, you know. He cut a deal with the Spanish to be an army doctor in Cuba, help the Spanish break the Cuban revolution, but the Church pull him back again half-way to Cuba and he's executed. But he was ready to cut the deal for his own skin. That's their idea of a national hero!

You know the Filipino is born informer. The Sicilian boy, the Irish boy, they also come from troubled society: rural, poor, by priest-ridden – but they've got honour. With mother's milk they take in honour and commitment: never to carry a tale, never to inform. The Filipino – he's Judas Iscariot. Even without bribe or threat – they'll inform. Cannot keep the worst thing a secret here. *Tsismis*, you know, gossip, the national pastime.

(Laughter). Well, sometimes that will give a good result. *Pinoy* know to betray an old friend to a new acquaintance just to enjoy it. They have no deep feeling, it's all on the surface, it's all new and shallow. Even run mad with a knife and killing, it's hysteria on the top, not deep like Russian. Having no memory, that's the national problem. Looking like big forgivers like Jesus, but it just gives the collective amnesia. The Chinese he didn't forget a favour; he have a long memory, looking the chance of requital the obligation you make him under. The Filipino, he'll forget your favour tomorrow – maybe undertake you something bad. So this is what, poor moral accountancy, *ja?* Cheaters also, using all ways fair and foul. So you remember the juniors baseball tournament? The Filipinos win the tournament in America for the best 12-year-olds in baseball coming from one town . . .

Beaufort: The Little League. I know what you're going to say.

Pfeidwengeler: . . . the Filipinos, what did they do? They forge their entries – boys coming from other towns. Over-age boys. OK, other Asia teams entering 14- or 15-year-olds. The Filipinos – one boy is 26! *(Laughter)*. And the serious thing? No one really thinks it's bad! The Filipinos, they think it's OK – only condemning the newspaper which made the exposure! *Ja*, OK. We laugh. But take this attitude, the opposite of the English fair play, the Asian playing dirty, to something bigger, take a whole nation like this, and it's not so surprising they rig the election or thief all the country's money if they ever get the chance.

Beaufort: Professor Benitez, your countrymen have been called thieves, traitors, Judas Iscariots. You sit through it with, if I may say so, typical Philippine tolerance and courtesy. *(Laughter)*. Will you now rise for the defence?

Benitez: I can't deny there is not some element of truth to all Professor Pfeidwengeler's charges, but they suffer from the weakness of all generalisation. Well, let's take South East Asia as an entity first: the big problem was that democracy – you know, multi-party system, one man one vote, civil liberties, separation of powers – was conferred with a stroke of the pen by the departing colonial powers, whereas Europe had centuries of social evolution to get there. Asia wasn't ready for it and, yes, I agree with the Professor and Mr Wong, the culture was unpropitious, no wonder there was corruption and authoritarianism. But the economic progress those countries made, the creation of middle classes and educated young elites – university professors playing their part! – *(laughter)* has put liberalisation on the agenda after more than thirty years. Now OK, here the prosperity hasn't happened, though we had the facade of it, with Marcos passing a law to legitimise his every act – and that is our unique problem now. To generalise myself, I'd say if the Filipino was asked to identify a national weakness it would be the tendency to divisiveness, to schism. You know the joke, put five Filipinos in one room for a meeting and two go to the comfort room, you'll have two factions before they return. I think it's this inability to present a united front to problems which is the nation's real Achilles heel, and it's the problem which this new presidential administration is addressing with the programme of National Reconciliation.

Beaufort: I think you put your finger on it. It's the incapacity to subordinate your family or clique interests to the greater good which prevents political progress and therefore leverage for social reform. OK, that's a highly abstruse way of putting it and this is hardly a scientific discussion. I mean, at the most exalted level we have crony politics and their inevitable corruption. But it could also apply to, say, college fraternities, or at the very basest level of the street gang, or – I've seen this – crew members off the same boat banding like a pack of wolves to beat an outsider to death. The notion of belonging to an exclusive group and enforcing its will against the world, and all the apparatus of group sanctions and Judas-hunting that goes with it. All that's very dear to the Filipino heart. Then if we take one admirable national trait – the pleasant management of face-to-face relationships it has a negative obverse side: this desire to call the stranger SIR – the Smooth Interpersonal Relationship – the desire to build consensus and avoid open conflict, all this undermines the workings of the country's overt political system. You have a modern system of open, managed, limited, abstract adversarial engagement and debate – democracy in other words – imposed on a society whose *mores* of favour-seeking and personal obligation are better adapted to lubricating the machinations of the feudal system. Then I think the astounding patience and tolerance of the suffering Filipino, while at one level very admirable, are also negative factors in themselves. As Professor Pfeidwengeler says, the national capacity to forgive is a great obstacle to reform – it's barely six years from EDSA and many of the Marcos cronies are now quite comfortably re-installed on the commanding heights of the economy. The Marxist-type revolution is discredited and obsolete – it's often worse than what it replaces. We see Vietnam winning the war and losing the peace, to borrow an expression. Yet it's tempting sometimes to imagine the Philippine dilemma as exclusively a ruling class problem and amenable to a, I don't know, a solution involving heroic surgery.

Pfeidwengeler: Well, you see the problem, sir, and you draw the wrong conclusions. Philippine politics – it's a cesspit. What we have now is the same *scheiss* only different flies. *(Laughter)*. All Filipinos have the same moral sickness. The humble, patient Filipino you so much admire, he'll also turn into a beast if you give him the chance. The CAFGU, you know them, they give the citizen a gun, make him a vigilante to kill communists: no gun, the man a lambkin is. With a pistol, he's Genghis Khan, he will kill his grandmother. You know, who's the dangerous one on the street or in America or in England? He's the young one, the poor one, age 15 to 25. I'm approximate. And very probable, he's black. *Ja*, I am not afraid to say it. Here in Philippinen? The young one, the poor one, not so dangerous. It's the middle-aged noodle, with a gun and money he inherit. They spoil him from a baby and he think his *schwanz* not so long as Vatti's was. *Ja*, he'll shoot you dead without thinking and afterward he'll buy his way out of trouble. And if they could, many more like to be that way. Give the Filipino a chance, he's not ashamed to abuse any advantage. I'm saying before: no progress unless you admit you are inferior. Now look at this I take from my pocket: Five hundred pesos, maybe 25 marks. OK, we all know you do a lot with it here: buy a boy or a girl, get your enemy shot. What it says here on the banknote: *The Filipino is worth dying for.* You know, you only have to say that when in your heart you know the Filipino is *not* worth dying for. All the big slogans, all the talk, it's a blanket over a big hole, and you put blanket on a hole, you fall in and break your leg. None of the big words, the fancy talkings got any connection with what really happen in the lunatic house. It's giving the big bullshit quotient here. Same in religion, same in politics. Can be the little housemaid makes her confession, *ja*, or the Senator making his big speech. Filipino thinks saying something is same as making it happen.

Beaufort: Well, I've more than once remarked on the Alice in Wonderland quality of national life to myself. But don't you think, Professor, that some things are better left unsaid? That rubbing people's noses in it isn't the best way to convert them? That the last thing the world requires now is ethnic differences pointed out and sharpened and that what we really need is fuzzy, old-fashioned tolerance?

Pfeidwengeler: Nothing is better left unsaid. You get the poison out. You don't leave it in the system. You pump out from force. Then health.

Beaufort: Mr Dinolan, a thought from you. Your fortitude under this onslaught has been exemplary.

Dinolan: O-o. Well, the Professor just gave me a thought. EDSA wasn't finished business? The cronies still around? Sure. We know the answer to that, *man.* Anyone going on the ferry knows it, hah? Filipinos don't flush. *(Laughter)*. I was just thinking, you know. You could call us the negroes of Asia. *(Laughter)*. No, really. What do we do better than anyone? We supply musicians all over Asia, *di ba*? Go to any joint that swings, I hear they got a Filipino band. Boxers? Filipino pugs scrapping all over Asia. And basketball, *man*? *(Laughter)*. Definitively, we have the tallest, the most skilful cagers in Asia. *(Applause)*. Thank you, my fellow countrymen.

Beaufort: Well riposted, Mr . . .

Dinolan: And the best-looking chicks. *(Cheers).*

Beaufort: Seconded, if I might say so. One could say the measure of a nation's political maturity was the extent to which it could shoulder criticism and still laugh at itself. From our side, Professor Pfeidwengeler, there is nothing I detest more than the expatriate who is forever carping about his hosts' shortcomings, real or perceived. The memsahib syndrome – and it's not confined to the ladies. And I'd just like to say it's a simple matter of perspective. If you're in your own place and a fellow countryman commits a transgression towards you, he's just an individual rogue. If someone does it in another country, he's a representative. An Italian has done it to you, or a Filipino, or whatever. It would be nice to get beyond this. Of course, I exempt your powerful critique from this. Surely we could end by sounding a positive note?

Pfeidwengeler: I think this would not be honest.

Benitez: If the guest has obligations, it is also incumbent on the host not to fish for compliments.

Wong: Most Asian hospitality is so overpowering as to closely resemble hostage-taking. And I speak not as one of the negroes of Asia but its Jews. Yes, the Chinese. *(Laughter).*

Beaufort: Look, Professor Pfeidwengeler, we've both chosen to make our homes in the East. I'm reluctant to argue *ad hominem* but, as in this case I'm in the same boat, I feel free to make a foul play. There must be something positive about Asia which attracts you, which entices you to spend your time here.

Pfeidwengeler: Ja, ja. Surely. I think it gives the old Chinese curse for an anti-enemy, May you live in the interesting times. But I'm the kind of fellow who likes the interesting times and places. Another way – the fresh meat is the most tasteless. Some like chicken – I prefer the English way – to hang a peasant until the maggots arrived. That makes eating. So as here. *(Laughter).*

Beaufort: Pheasant. Well, I'd really hate to leave our audience feeling that in any way I'd denigrated – I think that's a word that might bear some deconstruction – let's say slighted their – our – lovely country. I'm a Philippine patriot and I love this country warts and all. *(Applause)*. I think this is probably an opportune moment to close the forum and throw the discussion open to the floor. So if we can have a hand for our panellists *(applause)* we'll have I am sure, some energetic comments from the floor after our very contentious discussion. Don't be shy now. Yes, Mr John Hawkins.

Hawkins: Yeah, no. It's OK.

Beaufort: Come on, don't be bashful, John.

Hawkins: OK. If I'm not jumping in front of someone else with something more worthwhile to say. I'm only an observer really. What I was going to say was this. It's just something that's struck me in the course of my travels. Generally speaking, you often get a nasty government and a lovely people. I don't agree with our German colleague *(applause)*. The people *don't* get the government they deserve. In fact, often the harsher and more arbitrary the state the more charming the ordinary bloke on the street is.

Beaufort: Where in particular were you thinking of, John?

Hawkins: Well, a good case in point was Syria, and also North Korea. You had really quite vicious, rabid governments, very anti-Western – not that that's the definition of rabid – but quite ready to take it out on the nearest whitie in the vicinity, not to mention stringing their own people up on the smallest provocation – and the ordinary bloke who just took you on a personal basis. You couldn't have met kinder people.

Benitez: I've heard the sentiment before. Let's say we have personal cultures and impersonal cultures, or put another way, high context cultures and low context cultures, warm social temperature and cold social temperature. That's not just an Asian-occidental dichotomy by the way, Professor Pfeid-wengeler. We could say Italians belong to the first group. The greater the skill of a culture in negotiating personal relationships, smoothing situations, avoiding conflict, building friendships, the less capable it is of managing itself in the aggregate.

Beaufort: Interesting. I'm sure one of us possesses the key.

Benitez: Well, I'm purely tentative. I lack the Professor's conviction. Perhaps abstract concepts of civic morality – I don't know, corruption for government servants, payment of at least a modicum of one's taxes by the ordinary citizen, e.g. in both cases refraining from stealing from the common weal – are the weaker where a premium is set on the small and the concrete things arising from everyday face-to-face interaction. A degree of detachment or impersonality is required for action based on an abstract notion of honour.

Beaufort: To pursue the building metaphor, when all the bricks are smooth and there's no friction then the building will be inherently more unstable; it can all come toppling down.

Benitez: I haven't heard that before.

Beaufort: I think I'm only slightly developing your argument. And if we pursue the argument of individual Filipino virtues producing group vices we can run a control experiment by looking at the *pinoy* immigrant to other societies and – yes – what a model citizen he makes once removed from his own context.

Hamid: You are a racist, sir.

Beaufort: What?

Hamid: You are a racist, Professor Pfeidwengeler.

Beaufort: I don't think we need to descend to personal abuse, and it would be an elementary courtesy to address your remarks through the chair first.

Hamid: I have heard this man's poison all over the world and you others should be ashamed to share a platform with a man who is confirmed and notorious for his racist views. I repeat, his racist views.

Pfeidwengeler: And you, I have heard you barking at the lion in Africa and other places too. I hear that word racist and it's a word that stops thought. Rationalism stops when it gives that utterance. OK, you call me racist if you like. But a bigot is not I am, and that is what you are. Your mind stays closed all your life, but mine is always open.

Kumar: Gentlemen, gentlemen, Sophocles, the Gautama, these are surely our role models. This petty strife, this enclosed squabblings . . . what has this to do with the tranquillity of the sages which we aspire to emulate?

Wong: I, for one, Your Excellency, aspire to no such thing. What has the "tranquillity of the sages" brought Asia but untold suffering and the quietism which permits the hypocrisy of tyrannical governments?

Kumar: That is the fault of man, Mr Wong, for not sufficiently absorbing the lessons of the great teachers of the past. Can we blame Confucius or Mencius for the errors of Mao Tse Tung?

Wong: Well, I can, and I will tell you where it got me – jail. My theory is Confucius died of Hepatitis B and his teachings are as pernicious.

Kumar: No, no, Mr Wong. Please don't deny your nation's great heritage. Personal bitterness makes you speak mockingly of the great Kung Fu Tse. I beg you to overcome it. Most beseechingly, I implore you. *(Laughter).*

Wong: Not even with you as his proxy, N.S.

Hamid: We are diverging from the important topic, which is to condemn the transparent racist tenor of the preceding discussion. Please do not attempt to put red herrings across our path. I invite an apology of Professor Pfeidwengeler.

Pfeidwengeler: You will not get one, how long you bark.

Benitez: I really see no need for an apology. However much one may disagree with the Professor's views they are sincerely held and he should be free to express them. I, as a Filipino, was not insulted by his observations on my national culture; there were a few home truths in it. I wish that a meeting of this kind should be able to discuss any topic, however unsavoury or contentious, without heat. If we cannot then truly there is no hope.

Beaufort: A most eloquent defence from Professor Benitez of what, until recently, one had thought an unassailable part of civilisation: the right to free expression.

Hamid: Western civilisation.

Beaufort: Well, I'm surprised to find myself in the same camp as Professor Pfeidwengeler here. I believe this is a fundamental and not a tradeable or relative value. There have been previous civilisations, of course, some like Athens based on slave economies, but the characteristic of our technologically based civilisation, dating back to Protestantism and the seventeenth century scientific revolution, seems to me to be free thinking and free speech. They may be historically specific values as regards origination but not the less to be cherished for that. Diamond was carbon once but in its finished state is, as they say, for ever. Free thought and speech are the jewels in the crown of modern civilisation.

Wong: Well, God bless you and us, assuming he exists . . .

Beaufort: She does and she's black.

Hamid: I am leaving the hall.

Wong: There are, I am afraid, reviving Eastern civilisations which do not spring from the same notion of liberty. The last hundred years had been the century of America. The twenty-first century will be that of China and it will be predicated on values inimical to yours and the gentleman who has just walked through the door. For instance, it will not be sentimental about him and his kind. And free speech will be an irrelevance in a society where everyone bears the same prejudices.

Beaufort: What an unhappy prospect for teeming humanity.

Benitez: Well, the *pinoy* can add some spice to the rice porridge the world will be then. It will be difficult to make him into the efficient, character-less, feature-less ant of B.K. Napoleon Wong's predictions.

Beaufort: And would we trade that happy-go-lucky national character for a more prosperous but austere face? Actually, James, I ask that in all seriousness. The average citizen of Singapore is infinitely wealthier than the average citizen of the RP, in fact the average citizen of the island state often employs the average citizen of the Republic of the Philippines as his or her house-servant. But there's an interesting inversion of what

I'd call the felicity factor: the *pinoy* is far happier than the Singaporean perhaps because he or she is far freer.

Benitez: I think my knowledge of Singapore is too slender for me to base a generalisation upon it.

Pfeidwengeler: You are correct. *(Laughter). Ja*, apology. I mean friend Beaufort is correct.

Benitez: And I was, too. *(Laughter).*

Beaufort: Mr Dinolan, on that point would you regard the Philippine press in the post-Marcos era as a press as free as any in the world or, if not that, at least a useful watchdog of the nation's new freedoms?

Dinolan: Well, I have not been a professional journalist so long as all that, so if I speak of the late President's time, it's as a reader. The short answer is, yes, subject to the constraints of the libel laws, as anywhere else, and subject to the interests of the proprietor.

Beaufort: Speaking as a reader, two things strike me: positive and negative. Negative: the dearth of hard facts, the willingness to print rumour, gossip really, the plethora of comment and commentators and sometimes their venality. Positive: the extra-ordinary personal courage and integrity of a minority of those columnists – taking up the cudgels for the weak against the powerful. And it's dangerous – ten reporters killed every year?

Dinolan: Well, a newspaper basically gives its readers the fare they desire. Circulation is the important thing, as I am sure you would all appreciate. But within those limits, yes, there are some brave guys on the Philippine press. Especially the provincial press. Not me. *(Laughter).*

Beaufort: Generally speaking, the Filipino has found the English or American language a congenial medium of commu-nication, just as Indians adopted British English with fervour and, indeed, have produced users of it to rival any native-born writers. But in general the cultures of the orient, Malay or Chinese, have not taken to the Anglo-Saxon tongue – so admired of Professor Pfeidwengeler and Mr Wong *(laughter)* – with such readiness. Explanation, Professor Benitez.

Benitez: Well, to a certain degree the Filipino has. But the great writer of the nation remains José Rizal. There is still nothing in our literature to compare with *Noli me tangere* or *El Filibusterismo*, and Rizal wrote in the language of his Spanish masters. I actually would say Spanish suits our temperament better than English, which is a comparatively undemonstrative language. And we are demonstrative. *(Laughter).*

Beaufort: Go ahead, John.

Hawkins: Just looking at the average Filipino journo – I can't speak for writers because I didn't finish the two *pinoy* stories I picked up *(laughter)* – there seem two extremes they've got to avoid. There's the problem on New Year's Eve with the soldiers joy-firing their M-16's? One kind of hack is so intoxicated with the fact he can write a foreign language, it's like an advanced weapon in the hands of a peasant: the guy's spraying the biggest words he can find into the air, right? And the imagination's over-heating and jamming. It's the Wild Bunch with dictionaries. *(Laughter).* Yeah, Spanish would be better for a word-happy gaucho. Then there's the other extreme: the guy's so timid, it's like he's the only one turned up to a black tie reception in thongs and a singlet. *(Laughter).*

Dinolan: I'm wearing shoes today. *(Laughter).*

Benitez: The two best Visayans are a musical Monsignor and an attorney who looks like Shakespeare, Mr Hawkins. I'll pass their volumes on.

Beaufort: I can see Carla ready to fire a warning shot into the air. *(Laughter).* It's running well past the hour allotted us. I think I've been a Cory Aquino type chairman, rather than a Marcos, but it only remains for me to thank our distinguished panel for their contributions and especially our Philippine members for their kind participation.

Dinolan: Thank you.

Benitez: You are heartily welcome, Professor Beaufort.

Pfeidwengeler: Bitte.

Chapter Sixteen

JUN, THE ONE-ARMED BARTENDER OF FOR DA GUYS, had already thought them a strange group. You didn't often get Filipinos and foreigners together in his kind of place. Filipinas and foreigners together was another matter entirely, of course. Nothing more natural, like knife and sheath, pistol and holster, foot and sock, you name it. But middle-class, middle-aged *pinoys* and foreigners together in this joint was like an augury – of something bad, as most auguries are – like seeing budgerigars consorting with vultures, the foreigners in the old jeans that so belied their spending power (dirtier than shit some of their clothes but nothing wrong with the contents of the wallet), the Filipinos in their tailor-made pleated pants and paisley polos, shiny with jewellery and adamantine non-tippers with it. To top it all, there was an Amerikana with this group! Not the hippy type trailing after boy-friend, the girl malevolently comparing the dimensions of her big ass with the standard issue of the petite Filipina, the boy regretting he'd brought Erika, Kirsten or whoever on this trip. This one was a lady, someone to whom you said, yes mum, no mum, right away mum. She was well preserved but of a certain age. So why was she laughing louder than any of them, putting herself forward, behaving like a low-class Filipino tourist guide? The actual Filipinos with her were several layers higher than tourist guide, maybe big time robbers, Komander Kowatan himself, like attorney or licensed real-estate broker. The lady had looked him in the eye and said she'd like a Screaming Orgasm. Jun didn't know where to put himself. Then leered slyly at her.

"It's on the wall behind you," she told him.

"On the wall but I don't know how to do."

"At your age it's time you learned. Are you married?"

Snickers now, but Jun didn't mind. He knew he was going to get tipped like there was no tomorrow. The Filipinos in the background were not distancing themselves from their friends but from him.

"It's vodka, absinthe, blue Curaçao, and grenadine together. OK?"

"Again, mum?"

"Vodka. You know Vodka, looks like water? OK. Absinthe, that's the dirty bottle. Then the blue one and, let's see, the pink cordial there."

"Soft one the pink? OK, mum."

Carla was in a very good mood. All the groundwork had paid off. The conference was self-generating now: no more need for intros or mixing; they were as blended as the cocktail Jun was rattling with excessive histrionics in the silver shaker. No need either to keep certain parties away from others, jump in and pull them off, hover round the outskirts, ready with a drop of verbal oil to smooth the grinding of powerful personalities. In fact, the discordances formed part of the overall melody. Any community had its disagreements and characters. The argument over the smoking issue had given them all something to put in their pipes. Dr Neumark had been the influence behind that even if Kamla Mishra had been the formal proposer. It was as if she'd wanted to pay Gracie Hipkin back for the cessation of 24-hour air-con. Carla knew that Ruth resented that from the pointed remarks about non-opening sheet-glass windows in the rooms (since when had modern hotels had windows that opened?) and then a remark about the usefulness of deodorants in the tropics for some people who tended to sweat more than the ordinary. She didn't have to specify fat people. It was there for all to see, poor Gracie padding about in a martyr's pool of perspiration. Carla had been faintly disappointed in the remark – as she very occasionally was in Dr Neumark, such lapses however serving to show she was only human and not the ikon the journalists had made of her. And at least she hadn't singled Gracie out by name. Carla had discovered that Dr Neumark never descended to vituperation behind a person's back. In the sphere she moved in, a demi-mondaine of the worlds of academe and something akin to theatre, she was a rara avis in this where Carla had seen the mention of a rival or enemy's name send leading ladies, solo ballerinas, novelists, and world-renowned cellists into foaming-mouthed denigration. Ruth ignored it when a foe's name cropped up – so that you'd have never known there was bad blood – or just said, "Oh, that creature," with a quick smile at a third party. From Omar Hamid she'd learned not to mention the name of Angela Smith, so she knew there was bitterness there; yet when the name came up somehow, not a murmur from Ruth, just a face kept expressionless. Whether this was a species of massive self-control or just sheer magnanimity was unclear but either were equally creditable, Carla thought. And, in truth, it was exemplary. Of course, it also had the effect of heaping further glowing coals upon the heads of enemies when it got back to them, as it had to if this magisterial restraint was persisted in for a matter of decades rather than years, that Ruth considered them beneath consideration of vengeance. As regards the smoking issue, Omar Hamid had shown signs of recalcitrance, John Hawkins also. In fact the sharp things John might have said to Ruth would not have come under Carla's comfortable heading of constructive dissension adding to group solidarity (in the way that Professor Pfeidwengeler being conference pariah did). However, John was nothing if not a good sport, Omar Hamid (though still peevish enough to withdraw to his room for a thunderous eighteen-hour sulk) had moderated his opposition when acquainted with Dr Neumark's feelings, and finally all opposition had collapsed when amid applause crashing like breakers Gracie had thrown her Salems into the auditorium and announced her intention of seconding the motion.

It was Filipino values acting on them all, Mrs Init told Carla in all seriousness. "That's just wonderful, ma'am," said Carla bemused to the point of dizziness. She had taken to addressing her client as that, rather than the original "Mrs Init". Some form of development in the relationship had to be marked by a change in the address employed, and for the life of her she simply couldn't bring herself to call her "Victoria". Normally, a consolidating relationship with the client was cemented and signalled by a switch to first name terms but with this lady close co-ordination had meant a deepening into formality. In her way she was every bit as formidable as Dr Neumark. These two had by unspoken mutual accord decided not to contest the supremacy with the other, in much the same way as – granted the unlikely eventuality – a lioness and a polar bear might choose simply to sniff at and then walk by the unfamiliar but redoubtable creature. They gave the other the widest and most respectful of berths, with the result that they would leave the conference as more or less total strangers.

Of course, one could imagine Dr Neumark sitting quite happily in this particular dive over the stiff G & T that was her preference in these climes, one of Dr Neumark's sterling qualities being total sang-froid in any company – Greek and Belgian mercenaries, cannibal heads of state, princes of the church – but it took a gulp to conceive of Mrs I. ever wandering in here. Probably too near to home – she'd have been relatively unflustered during a 42nd Street mugging.

Boyet had no problem with Carla in this joint, nor did Nestor Chavez. It had been Nestor's idea to bring Rod Kienzler here, Nestor's happily deluded correlation being that Rod Kienzler was an Anglo version of him and he a *pinoy* version of Rod, so that 1) they were predestined to be boon buddies. 2) Kienzler could become an advantageous connection in the sense of supplying them with work on the vastly inflated foreign scale. (Boyet and he had been stunned when informed by Kienzler, amid some mildly patronising advice, of what American and British papers could pay per thousand words – about thirty times more than their own premium rate). Then, as an afterthought, they decided to invite John Hawkins (innocent of the antipathy between the pair), and Hawkins had brought Carla, who asked James Benitez. Benitez! Shit, they'd have hesitated less before inviting Pope John Paul. Benitez would depress the dead. Here the guy sat now, prim as Mother Theresa, with a Sprite before him, his back to the stage while the bikini-clad dancers bumped and thumped.

"They've got lovely figures," Carla said.

"Really?" said Boyet and Nestor together.

"Oh, of course. Don't you think so?"

"Chicken legs," said Boyet. "And her bust is very small." He knew it was OK to talk like this to Mrs Giolitti.

"I know a few who'd slay for legs like that. They look so young."

"Maybe seventeen," Chavez estimated, "but probably she's got a kid and a boyfriend with a drug habit worse than hers."

"What a shame. She looks so sweet. What do you think, Rod?"

"If you like simians."

"I'd say one in five of the girls I pass in the street here is pretty. And one in ten is really very pretty, beautiful."

"We'll tell our wives." Boyet laughed. He warmed to Carla. Why couldn't Miriam be more like that? Just then a girl arrived by Boyet. "Long time no see," she greeted him. "Now you see," he answered shortly. 'Sus Maria. Just what he needed. He'd had a nasty turn two days ago during his stint on the panel when he spotted the girl he'd used at the Breadfruit-Guava waiting-shed in the crowd of uniformed students at the auditorium. It had stymied him utterly, just before Beaufort had roped him into the discussion. The timing of it! This girl, a GRO here but whom he'd bar-fined as a dancer in a Pilipino-only joint downtown, had the sense to make herself scarce.

"Are the young ladies, er, available?" Kienzler asked. Boyet looked sharply at him; the guy was kind of tactless, *di ba*? Or wanting to make trouble? Hawkins asked drily, "Why, interested?" and made an appreciative friend of Boyet.

"Just academically," replied Kienzler.

"Customers can buy a ladies' drink here," said Hawkins. "That'll set you back all of, I'd say, US$3. You can do that all night. If the customer wants to take the girl out before closing time the management loses revenue from the drinks, so the customer pays a fine at the bar. Then he'll pay the girl a fee on top of that for sex."

"How much?" inquired Carla with the bluntness of the disinterested, thereby obliging Kienzler.

Professor Benitez said, "As of last March, the bar fine was 300 pesos and the girl would expect about 500 pesos minimum. Total, let's say US$30."

"Hey, that's cheap for a princess!" exclaimed Carla.

"My niece analyses the cultures in the City Health Lab," Benitez explained, quite superfluously as not for a moment had it occurred to anyone that he could conceivably have ever been the payer of a bar-fine.

"Not all the girls are dancing? I can see a few lonely wall-flowers."

"Those," contributed Nestor with ex-sub's relish, "those are the Guest Relations Officers."

"Oh boy, I like that," said Carla. "Bar-finable also?"

"Of course, babe," said Hawkins, "they're not here to admire the view."

"Mum, I'll be the one to give you your Screaming Orgasm," murmured Jun.

"That was quick of you," said Carla without thinking. "It normally takes ages."

They were all still having hysterics when an odd couple came in. Had they been Adolf Hitler and Eva Braun strolling through the door the impression could hardly have been greater. This went not only for Boyet, Nestor, and the foreigners. The consternation of the staff of For da Guys – dancers, Jun, GRO's, guards – somewhat exceeded theirs.

It was Gracie Hipkin and Crescente A. Koyaw. Gracie Hipkin and the Boss. The Boss and a monstrously fat Amerikana. He actually looked svelte by comparison.

They were holding hands.

"Sh-i-i-i-i-t," said Jun, not as under his breath as he might have hoped. "Porgie and Bess," thought Kienzler to himself, professionally a far less discreet character than Jun – a spiller of confidences rather than a retainer – but not sharing Jun's genuine and terrible shell-shock. The Boss with a chick! The Boss leading in the heavyweight chick to end all chicks, like their handlers led in Hulk Hogan or the Natural Disasters! Fortunately, the citizens of For da Guys were too stunned for the laughter which might have been terminal, even the giggling of the girls.

Crescente looked no grimmer than usual, which was already a very terrible sight for flunkeys. Gracie looked flustered, from unaccustomed attentions, but on fat girl's yummie Cloud Nine – happy with an embarrassing radiance. "Boss, Mum," said Jun, falling over himself to get to the Black Label, wipe the counter, get chairs out of the way, all with one arm. "Ah." He had a dreadful thought. Here he was ushering the Boss to his favourite cushioned stool at the bar, but *no way the rear end of the Boss's companion was going to fit on one!* He fought for control of his rebel face.

Surprise number two, which came actually as rescue: the Amerikanos already there waved to the Natural Disaster and, by implication, the Boss. The foreigners smiling welcomes, the three middle-class *pinoys* absolutely impassive, no clue as to whether they were the Boss's long-lost brothers or waiting assassins, about to hug him or shoot him, not that brods weren't known to shoot brods.

Carla tactfully vacated the sofa, into which Crescente and Gracie could just about squeeze. "Hey, neat! What a beautiful surprise, Gracie!"

"I guess great minds think alike. Crescente's been showing me town – places you and I couldn't go safely, you know."

"I'll say! Aren't you the lucky one."

Crescente nodded gravely. He and the other Filipinos estimated and acknowledged each other circumspectly. Everyone decided to treat everyone with consideration.

"Would you give me my third Screaming Orgasm, barman? Would you like to have one as well, Gracie?"

"This one has been giving you trouble, Mrs Giolitti?"

"He's been a dream so far."

"You can just tell me when he does. He's small but he's no good too. *Pagbantay, dong, mao ni ang akong mga amigo.*"

"What did he say?"

"He told him, take care, they're my friends," Boyet said.

"You're off duty now, old fruit," Kienzler remarked. The tone, the words, the attitude – better men had paid dearly for any of these, let alone in combination. "Old" was something the Boss particularly disliked. He was only forty-four. But different times, different places, different company, made for different consequences. He just pretended he hadn't heard.

"I think," said Nestor Chavez, "that the Colonel is not actually an employee of the Convention Centre as such, so he is never on duty and, by the same token, never off it. So we can consider ourselves protected. Correct, Colonel?"

Crescente forgave Nestor being what and who he was. He decided, however, to stick to the resolution – instantly formed on seeing the company he was to keep – of going easy on the Black Label. He didn't want his tongue loosened and it would just arouse curiosity if he was to go as soon as he had arrived.

"You didn't tell me you were a Colonel, Crescente," said Gracie, regarding him with glowing eyes.

The Boss gave a short bark. "Not something to talk about. Special Forces rank."

"Isn't it dangerous?"

"For other people. Change topic."

Gracie rolled her eyes at Carla. She had been told she looked like Diane Keaton in *Annie Hall* when she did this. Her expression, that was. They would have a good girls' giggle together at 4 a.m. in Carla's room, education, position, and intellect never ever having got in anyone's way where this was concerned. "He's quite a catch, honey," Carla would say, fishing images seeming to haunt a well-oiled conversation.

"Oh, he's a hunk. I don't know why I like that kind of man, maybe something primitive in me."

"It's a good local family. He's Mrs I's nephew."

"Oh, now why didn't he tell me that?"

"Call it modesty."

"I know he's an American citizen as well as a Filipino. He was very quick to tell me that. He even showed me his US passport."

"Maybe he wanted to let you know his intentions were honourable." They both cackled.

"There's something quite sweet about him as well."

"They're all little boys, honey, when it comes down to it."

"It goes with the caveman stuff, too, in a weird kind of way."

"Sure." Carla could see Gracie was looking for reassurance, help in stifling some of her own better instincts.

"You make a good pair."

"Oh, we're both fatties. You can say that to me, Carla. We're like two sperm whales together, I know that."

"Now, honey, stop that. You know you don't mean it. Let's have one more before we call it a night."

Many preceding drinks earlier in For da Guys, Carla had begun a regression into juvenility to equal that of her charges when she became acquainted with the name of the road they found themselves in. Chavez, the newspaper editor – who on earth did he think he was with the pony-tail at his age? – had attempted to deflect a barrage of personal questioning from Rod Kienzler with neutral counter-information about town. For instance, Guava Boulevard – now full of thundering trucks and fine dust – had been a tranquil thoroughfare lined with the fragrant, bat-haunted trees of that name and the indolent traffic of horse-drawn tartanillas. "And there were breadfruit trees in Breadfruit," contributed James Benitez, who welcomed the chance for some sensible conversation about local history.

"Ah, I didn't know you had those here," said Kienzler. "I think of Tahiti and the *Bounty* when I think of breadfruit."

"Do they really taste of bread, Crescente?"

"I never ate."

"They fry slices, just like potato chips," Hawkins said. He felt like Captain Bligh when he looked at the runt, Kienzler. "Quite a boring fruit."

"But they look nice, Mr Hawkins. A nice green colour. We call the fruit *culo* here, that's its local name."

"*What*, Professor Benitez?" asked Carla Giolitti.

"*Culo.*"

Carla looked around. Only Rod Kienzler seemed amused. "Breadfruit Boulevard," he mused. "I suppose it's the local equivalent of the Hershey Highway."

Carla's cocktail ran out of her nose.

"Is it a cul-de-sac?" Kienzler asked.

Professor Benitez sensed there was something in the wind. He smiled. "What does *culo* mean in American slang?"

"It's Italian," Carla said. "A rude word for part of the anatomy, but never mind."

"Well in pilipino *culo* is just *culo*," the Boss said in almost threatening tones. Gracie shivered with ecstacy.

"Let's change the subject, for God's sake," Carla said. "Is there another night club we could move on to? Where it's the customers who do the dancing?"

"There's Odyssey's and Mimi's Owlerie at the other big hotel, before they built the Dragons," Boyet suggested.

"Not those places," Crescente said. "You would not enjoy," he told Gracie.

"You're the boss, Crescente. This is your turf."

"I'm the Boss, but you can still call me Crescente."

"Then karaoke," Boyet said. He and Nestor had been wondering whether to take Kienzler to Momo's but still weren't sure of their man. There had been a sighting of Professor Pfeidwengeler there, according to unconfirmed reports which also said he'd been hit for a big bed-linen bill by Momo.

"I'm quite tired," Professor Benitez announced. "But don't let me be the one to spoil everyone's fun. Just go on without me."

"*Sige na*. OK," chorused Nestor and Boyet, without – they trusted – sounding too pleased about it. "I'll be the one to go and flag a taxi," Boyet offered. "For a while, hah?"

The Boss shook his head. "I'll be the one to drive. The ladies can ride the car. Maybe one of you doesn't object to riding with my bodyguards."

"Sure," said Boyet.

And, following in the Cherokee, he had no reason to regret being Nestor's subordinate, Nestor proving the one to get the worst ride – at about ninety miles an hour, straight through all the red lights. 'Sus, the fat one was a maniac, a public menace even by the Keystone Kops standards of the Gobernador de Leon utility drivers. Boyet was glad he'd never crossed a road while Mr Crescente A. Koyaw was in the vicinity.

For Jun, too, the evening took a nasty twist. Carla had, comparatively late, noticed his one-armedness. She'd already intended to leave a fair tip for his trouble. Now guilt prompted her into leaving an astounding 100 pesos for service, US$4, or twice Jun's wages for the night. Jun's eyes bulged. He reached for the note like Arthur reached for Excalibur.

Something like a manacle encircled his wrist. The Boss's meaty fingers.

"No tipping allowed here," the Boss intoned in a voice of doom.

"Oh, no, surely not, Mr Koyaw," said the Amerikana.

"Surely so."

"It wouldn't do any harm."

"Tell the lady, Jun."

"No tip allowed, mum."

"Is that the policy of the management?"

"That is the policy of me," the Boss said, sweeping the Amerikanas to the door and looking balefully at Jun. Talk about the Natural Disasters: the Boss was earthquake, fire, lightning, and volcanic eruption all in one.

THE last lap was in sight. But traditionally, or at least often, the penultimate circuit is run at a more leisurely pace as if the contestants wish to recoup their energies, avoid burning themselves out before the test of mettle on the final bend. That holds good for the school sports day as well as the Olympic final. And, if Carla was honest with herself, this event came somewhere between those two extremes of endeavour. They'd have a breathing-space – a drop in speed – with Bish delivering a pair of lectures: *On Japanese Forward Policy in the Straits of Malacca*, followed by *Spratlys – Regional Cockpit*, the good-natured young Japanese acting as the reverse of a hare in a running event, slowing things so no one felt they'd been pulled up short. His lectures had the desired effect.

The poetry reading was less successful. Carla didn't want controversy at this point, but it was supplied anyhow, or at least very nearly. Bob Richards, the Canadian who wrote on green themes, a late arrival and to prove an even earlier departure, was to lead a symposium which would give local talents a chance to bud as well. Mrs Init had promised a poem – considerable excitement had been aroused, though technically unwarranted, at the thought of this. In the event she had only proposed they all think a Green Thought three minutes each day. "That's the way to change our world," she told a respectful audience, sceptical only as to a stubborn minority. Kamla Mishra had been observed nodding vigorously, eyes flashing over her hawk-like nose. "Never under-estimate the power of thought," Mrs Init expanded her original exhortation. "A poem can bring walls tumbling down." The auditorium, unlike Jericho, withstood the crashing applause.

Then Richards, ginger-haired, balding, in embroidered muzhik-style blouse – recognised by the students as pure Jim Morrison – got up to say the only thing anyone would ever remember about him – apart from the extreme length of his 999 stanza composition on the dugong. Prefacing his reading with the standard remarks he used for non-European, non-North American audiences, he said, "Sometimes I am ashamed to write in the English language." The acoustics in the hall had remained

268

excellent, so that subsequently Jack Beaufort doubted whether he'd misheard. Certainly it was recorded in the transcript in its above form, but what Jack could swear he heard was: "Sometime I ashame write in the English language."

Richards waited for the applause which normally punctuated his address at this point, always polite, occasionally ecstatic, and on this occasion was extremely disappointed by the silence, broken only by the cry of "Shame!" from tiny Professor Adachi who had miraculously understood the sentence in the way that it might penetrate the dementia of a once great mind in the old folks home. "I think it didn't go down the way he expected," Jack said afterwards, Jack who liked to say, "Of course the Australians are *so* racist," to his third world friends, but drew the line at this. "He miscalculated the effect on a Filipino audience."

John Hawkins said, "Yeah, I don't think it was the first time he'd said it."

"Filipinos don't actually have a colonial chip on the shoulder. OK, the senators agitated over the bases but that was really a dollars and cents thing. The ordinary *pinoy likes* America and Americans, in fact there's nothing he'd like better than to be one. And as for the language of the oppressor issue, Holy Moses, they grow up speaking English. It's as natural to them as . . ."

" . . . taking a shit or thieving, if we believe deadly Detlef," observed Hawkins drily. "No, the rebuke came all the better from our pal James Benitez. What was it: *the tongue of Chaucer, Shakespeare, Milton is not a shackle on the spirit, it is a pair of wings.*"

Jack laughed. "I didn't think good old James had that much poetry in him." He hadn't laughed at the time. He'd been incensed. He'd barely been able to hold his tongue when Omar Hamid had said in a loud voice to all who cared to hear him, "The English language is a whore who will sleep with anyone. Anyone who wants to use her."

He'd just about retained his retort that some writers weren't good enough to get it up for her, but he might as well have spat it out. The rumour that was to get around his small world, spreading with the swiftness of the wings mentioned by James

Benitez, doing him untold damage with friend and stranger alike, the worse for his being the only one – of course – never to hear about it, was that Jack Beaufort was "a fascist".

"I had more respect for old Pfeidwengeler," Hamid would say insinuatingly on the circuit to all who'd lend an ear, before one day someone told him the story with the embellishments that had accrued and he knew that what he'd discovered was perpetual motion. "At least he was open. Beaufort's just a closet racist."

Carla thought of it as a minor piece of barging and shoving only to be expected during a well-contested race, not to compare with the fouling shenanigans of Slavonic ice-queen and Latin witch or the terrible moment when that barefoot South African wraith had de-railed the all-American Golden Girl, but then she – like Jack Beaufort – wasn't in the know. What she knew was that she'd reserved the lap of honour for her own South African star. And Dr Neumark had sworn to give it her very best shot, divulging the fact that she'd been working non-stop for the last ten days on her "position paper".

It was at this time that Carla heard the only conversation – if it could be described as that – between Dr Neumark and Professor Pfeidwengeler. Detlef's progress down the lobby had been signalled by the scattering of lesser folk, flight to other chairs, larger groups, the coffee-wagon, virtually any quarter rather than risk leprous contact. All that was missing were the bell and cloak. Making his fraught passage, limping, one foot in a tartan carpet-slipper, the Professor appeared innocent of the agitation he was causing on the flanks but then, naturally, it would appear entirely usual to him. At the end of the hall where she held her court, Carla, as she had to, it was what she was paid for, but she trusted she would have done so anyway, stood her ground. She found Kamla, Dr Enoeda, and Dr Neumark with her. Dr Neumark beamed at Carla: the prospect of sitting with a man known to hate her – whether this was reciprocated or not was a matter known entirely to Ruth – disturbed her equilibrium not one bit. And she wanted it so known.

"Coffee, Professor Pfeidwengeler?" Carla was about to offer only a shade more brightly than she would have done to anyone else, when Dr Neumark forestalled her. Blessed are the peace-makers, Carla thought, for they shall inherit the atrium.

"Hot chocolate, Professor?" inquired Ruth solicitously. "It's native chocolate, I believe. Spicier and thicker than ours. I hear you like it that way."

Pfeidwengeler glared at her without replying. Carla had judged him bigger than that. However, nothing deterred, she pulled up the biggest armchair available, into which Pfeidwengeler judged his fall with a "Gracious madam."

"Pass a stool for him, anyone," said Dr Neumark.

IT was Jack Beaufort who found himself sitting next to the Professor on the steep and serpentine ascent into the mountains of the hinterland. Carla had said, "Honey, would you? I'd be so grateful. I mean, I'm so grateful to you for everything already . . ."

"Then we might as well compound it," Jack said, smiling. He knew he was one of Carla's prefects, maybe even deputy to Hawkins' head boy. Carla had put up two blank sheets on the notice-board for them to sign on to – either the caves or the clam farm. Presented with the alternative of penetrating the devil's mine or plumbing the deep blue sea, Professor Pfeidwengeler had chosen the former. The sheets had remained virgin for some time, people wanting to see who was going on what trip. Pfeidwengeler realised this. He signed at the top of the list for the mountains, then switched to the sea, sending the minnows scattering in front of his pike-like jaws, before putting himself down again for what he'd always intended and sowing fresh consternation. John Hawkins and Ruth Neumark were the only ones to elect to stay, John to file more copy, Ruth to cope with a fresh attack of migraine and the final adjustments to her position paper.

Jack hadn't realised there was so much dust in the world. Even by rural Philippine standards it was something. They had wound their way through some perfectly unremarkable, scrubby foothills before finding themselves in this devastated moonscape. The larger air-con bus had gone to the group which didn't contain Professor Pfeidwengeler. Jack had thought this was going to be no hardship, what with the breeze of their passage coming through the wooden slats of the glass-less windows and the drop in temperature accompanying the rise in altitude. But it meant the white powder, fine as talc, wasn't filtered out. As they left the metalled highway the clouds rose. Within a couple of minutes Professor Pfeidwengeler, in what was to all intents and purposes an eighteenth century wig, had turned into Dr Johnson, while Professor Adachi, with his furry eyebrows, looked like that famous Chinese sage available by the thousands in porcelain. Enoeda shook his head at Jack, grinning, before passing a handkerchief to N.S. Kumar which was not spurned. James Benitez leaned over. "You can blame the Evergreen company," he told Jack. "Not so long ago, it was virgin forest."

"Logging?"

"No. Principally, this was where they mined the sodomite."

"Ah yes, happily named commodity, James."

Nestor Chavez bounced phlegmatically in his undesirable seat over the back wheels. One of the insights of Jack's decade of residence was that middle-class Filipinos were relatively doughty travellers. It was, strangely enough, the poorest of the poor, and mostly the females, who immediately clapped cloth to their faces under such contingencies. After half an hour they passed, with only mild exaggeration, from purgatory to paradise. The road became red earth, skirting steep ravines, with some forest trees, softer and more complex than the crude coconut palms. They passed a lonely settlement of seven hovels congregated around a gigantic banyan tree with what Jack knew were animistic fetishes hung in its aerial roots. A minute breezeblock chapel dedicated to Senhor San Isidro Labrador faced a doll's house sari-sari store selling obscure native brands of soft drinks and *biko* rice puddings. The coaster hove to for their comfort stop. Total silence. Of the foreigners Jack alone knew it to be unusual. He shared an unsuccessful imitation of Coke with Benitez, who commented how much he liked the spot and how, though born in Gobernador de Leon, he'd never known there was a place like this left.

"But for how long, James?" Jack asked.

Benitez shrugged. "Let's just enjoy it while we can."

"I think Pfeidwengeler would find that very Philippine of you, James."

N.S. was standing by the coaster, in some agitation. "What's wrong, Your Excellency?" Jack chaffed him. N.S. whispered in his ear, "I do need to jingle, old bean."

"Well, there's the whole wide world to do it on up here."

"Oh, noo, noo! Never. Not in public places, my dear Professor Beaufort!"

Jack noted this fastidiousness for future reference. Perhaps one of the minor tribulations of the upper-class Indian.

"There must be a *loo*, Professor Beaufort, in this forsaken place."

"Did they have one in Eden, N.S.? James?"

"I'll ask after the CR. Please, Mr Kumar, for a while." Benitez entered into conversation with the drinks vendor. He waved to N.S., who hobbled with grateful alacrity towards what Jack, even with the benefit of ten years residence, had mistaken for a chicken coop. After twenty seconds he emerged, smiling. Professor Pfeidwengeler wandered over, merely to peer inside, following which they all rejoined B.K. Napoleon Wong who had remained in the coaster.

At the mountain guest house they found themselves thrown into a greater intimacy than had been the case. It was to be dormitory accommodation. Jack thought it a tribute to the group that nobody whinged. Clean linen and blankets were on the bunks; in the kitchen were the constituents of a meal. Of staff, retainers, human beings there was no sign. "The *Marie-Celeste*," said Jack jovially, but only Benitez and B.K. Napoleon Wong got the reference. Those two volunteered to prepare the dinner. Wong was an astoundingly good cook in an eclectic

273

Asian stir-fry style; he disclaimed any attempt to produce Chinese cuisine of a given region. Amid mirth, in which Detlef Pfeidwengeler was able to join, they christened their creations as *coconut milk and snapper soup à la dynamiter* and *red-cooked garlic chicken and peppers à la Init* (motley ingredients well-mixed with plenty of sauce). Professor Adachi proposed a toast to the chefs in luke-warm Super Dry. He and Enoeda got drunk with remarkable lack of preamble. Songs of many nations followed.

In the morning a surprise: the arrival of Congressman Init with two Pajero 4WD vehicles. He had also brought a cave guide. When they got there the entrance to this seemed slightly larger than a dart board. "Detlef," Jack said, "I'm being entirely serious. Do you think you're going to get in?" Professor Pfeidwengeler's reply to this solicitous overture was a malignant smile which displayed his yellow teeth. In the event he was able to crawl through with no more apparent difficulty than anyone else, though the Congressman elected to remain outside. The chamber they were in was about the size of the lobby of the Dragons Convention Centre, but considerably cooler than that spot without the benefit of air-con. "Look!" cried Jack. "There's a stalactite!" He was genuinely excited.

"Before many more," said the guide.

"What happened to them?"

"Export."

That melancholy word, thought Jack. Explanation and exculpation of everything. The last refuge of a scoundrel.

"What is the smell?" This was Professor Pfeidwengeler.

"Guano," the guide informed them.

"Birds could fly in here, my man?"

"Living inside are bats."

"Ah. And, of course, someone make money from this side-line too, of course?"

"You are correct, sir."

Dr Enoeda shone his flashlight into the roof. "There they are." Everyone regarded the tiny creatures with a healthy respect. They'd heard the lecture on rabies control: the

Philippines seventh most endemic country in the world, the Visayas the seventh most endemic region within the Republic, South American vampire bats among the most effective vectors of transmission.

Chavez asked Enoeda, "We're not in a volcanic passage, are we?"

Enoeda laughed. "No, Mr Chavez. These are limestone caves, created by the passage of water over soft rock aeons ago."

"Maybe we can run a story on it in the *Citizen*. Mr Guide, there are any caveman drawings, *di ba*?"

"I never saw. I hear they take some bones and a pottery."

Benitez shook his head in despair.

Pfeidwengeler said, "*Ja*, the national heritage – that can be thiefed, too. No problem."

Chavez whispered to Jack, "I think there have been modern cavemen – not flint axes, *di ba*? More like armalites."

"NPA?"

"Just so."

N.S. had taken a stroll by himself in the darkness but returned just before Jack had opportunity to become alarmed. "Goodness gracious me," he trilled, "the system is quite extensive. One could become lost very simply."

"Mmm," reflected Jack, delighting the distinguished old diplomat, "it's a little like the Marabar caves and Miss Quested." Professor Adachi delighted him, and everyone else, even further with his, "Raping up in the cave, ah, Adela Quested?"

"You do surprise me, Tomoko," said James Benitez, Professor to Professor, "I would have thought Forster was a little late for you."

"Edward Morgan Forster," said Professor Adachi, nodding vigorously, "Edward Morgan Forster 1879-1970, the King Cambridge College." The cave rang with merriment, causing the bats to abandon the roof and fly around at high speed, emitting what sounded like squeaks of protest but Jack knew was the sophisticated radar of the animal kingdom. The guide took them in another hundred metres to where the cave narrowed to a corridor. This, he informed them in a thunderous whisper, started to branch off within another hundred metres but the main passage ran back at least five miles before emerging much lower down the mountain side.

"Most impressive," said Jack, who in his adoptive land was always looking for a chance to give credit where credit was due, even if it was only an appreciation of natural phenomena. He knew they wouldn't be going much further though pure mischief made him want to pierce the guide's merry bluff when he said, "We go?"

Leaving the cave proved more difficult than entering, even with Congressman Init acting as midwife on the other side. In fact Professor Pfeidwengeler had to abandon his clumsy attempt in order to allow the others through first, each of them departing with a heavy-handed attempt at jocularity directed at the German. Pfeidwengeler acknowledged all of them. Jack was last, and made a point of keeping his trap shut. The sunlight was even more blinding than he'd expected.

Pfeidwengeler had another attempt at squeezing himself through. They could just make out the pale disc of his face below. The Japanese, normally the most polite and reserved of the nationalities, proved the most appreciative of Pfeidwengeler's discomfiture to the point, Jack suspected, of abusiveness if you only knew the language. He didn't think it was specifically Pfeidwengeler arousing their genial sadism. It could just as well have been him or Benitez.

"Do not be concerned, Professor. We can pass you provision through," said N.S. Jack was unsure whether this was a joke or not. Chavez said, "Starvation rations would get him out quicker." It was B.K. Napoleon Wong who proved Pfeidwengeler's saviour. "Tell him to turn round," he instructed the Congressman.

"Hah?"

"Yes. Reverse. Look, he got in head and shoulders first. Now he must leave feet first. That's the way the hole is shaped."

"*Sige*! Now how you thought of that and we didn't?"

Privately, the Congressman's opinion was that it had taken a damn Chinese to come up with the solution. He relayed instructions into the hole. Professor Pfeidwengeler appeared surprisingly slow on the uptake, but perhaps that was because of the communication problem, neither being first language English speakers. At length the Professor's carpet slipper appeared. Professor Adachi pounced. Ripping off the footwear, he tucked Pfeidwengeler's shin under his armpit, and began tickling the sole in the manner of a man strumming a ukelele. The Professor's leg kicked convulsively. They could hear his shrieks, and their echoes, lapping below them. Pfeidwengeler's elephantine buttocks appeared, then his back. Professor Adachi relinquished the leg, grabbed a frond, and – jumping up and down on his bandy, bowed legs, both feet leaving the ground simultaneously – began to beat Pfeidwengeler on his backside without actually ever making contact. Steady Jack Beaufort, grave Professor Benitez, not one of the party was able to control himself. Only the Congressman stood there in mystification, his face as immobile as a dead toad. That only added to Jack's joy. And when Jack looked again, this time at Adachi's bared teeth, he had to drop, holding his bowels. Pfeidwengeler was now in the ostrich position. His head came up. Emitting a banshee rather than a banzai shriek, Professor Adachi pretended to belabour the German about the shoulders. Pfeidwengeler emerged to see his companions on their knees or on their backs, kicking their legs, some weeping, while a berserk Professor Adachi assaulted him with a Holy Week prop. It spoke volumes, Jack thought later, for the man's self-possession, his discernment, and his lack of amour-propre, his (strange word to describe Professor Pfeidwengeler) humility that he was able to sum up the situation in a glance, then proceed to pat the diminutive Japanese kindly on the head before disarming him. Pfeidwengeler threw the frond on the roof of the coaster, then mounted the narrow metal steps with difficulty but dignity. According to their varying degrees of self-control, later or sooner, the others followed, some with shoulders shaking yet or a sudden sigh escaping them. Adachi was still shouting into the hole, as if maledictions or a spell to bind a monster, in a language that didn't sound like Japanese to Jack's undiscriminating ear. After a while he recognised it as mediaeval French. Enoeda embraced Jack. "Professor Adachi!" was all he could manage. "Adachi-san!" Finally, Adachi entered the coaster to cheers and applause, Pfeidwengeler beating his own huge thigh in appreciation.

The trip back seemed to last all of five minutes.

CARLA was having a more tiresome time by the sea. For a start, she had a bad case of the trots. God knew what had caused it. She'd been careful what she ate and drank, and she believed Mrs I. implicitly when she said the water at the Dragons was quadruple-purified. Besides, she appeared the only one in trouble of the Caucasians – she didn't envisage N.S., Kamla, or Hamid's guts perturbed by the comparatively mild Philippine fauna. They didn't float corpses in the water-supply here, if that wasn't purest racism on her part. On the bus Gracie offered quiet sympathy and privately kicked herself for not bringing the Pepto-Bismol. Then the facilities of the Shahakwajee Marine Farm didn't match what the convention centre offered. Carla found herself thinking proprietorially and wistfully of the marble and gilt of her home of the last several weeks. Surprising how a tiny, trivial thing like that (certainly tiny – only viruses were smaller than bacteria? she should know that after the water lecture) could distort your whole attitude to life. Now, the $64 question was: did it affect Presidents and Foreign Ministers as well? She guessed it must. They were as human as she was. She'd just have to put a brave face on it.

Gracie's bliss was unalloyed. Her Friend wouldn't ride in the bus. He'd said there was nothing he'd like better than to sit with her, but his job was to be outside safeguarding them all. So he was spurting ahead and doubling back by turns, more like a destroyer with a convoy than the owner of a customised jeep.

Gracie felt nervous watching. Not of bandits or guerillas but the traffic, to the hazards of which they were substantially contributing. Every time Crescente changed down to roar past them, every time he came back alongside to take station at their rear again, it was like he was spinning the chamber of a revolver and putting the barrel to his temple. Sometimes it was a matter of a fraction of a second and mere inches, as he shaved past their bus, or a truck coming in the opposite direction. Gracie shuddered. And yet there was a part of her which found it thrilling, Crescente taking both hands off the wheel to wave to her. If it had been in his power to make the vehicle rear up on its back wheels and neigh, he would have done it. Once or twice, Gracie waved slyly back, but not so she felt it would encourage him.

Once they arrived in one piece, she had a room to herself, of course, as did all the foreigners; although by choice, they said, the Filipinos were sharing. Gracie wouldn't have minded, but she'd have hated to inflict herself on anyone, maybe they thought she smelled or obesity was infectious, or something. And poor Carla, probably it was as well; the poor thing might have expired of embarrassment.

The place was half-resort, half-factory, having commenced as pure clam farm. This proving insufficiently profitable, the owner had added a few cabins which had realised their cost surprisingly quickly. The giant clams — wonderful pollution-gobblers – were raised from tiny in glass-sided tanks, the black flesh – with purple or green dots – spilling over the lips of the shell. "Christ, it's like an alien's VD clinic," Kienzler had offered. Kamla Mishra had given him an icy look – both were in Ruth Neumark's orbit but they didn't like each other – and continued taking notes from the manager's technical spiel. Good for Kamla, Carla thought. She was always grateful for support and cooperation. Carla would be surprised to read Kamla's rather impressively detailed account in a Bombay magazine four months later. She'd assumed it had just been public relations, like Omar Hamid's interest in the pearl oysters.

Later, swimming costumes magically appeared for those

without, so they were able to slip in the water and cool off before a very passable "Swiss-German" meal which hit the spot after three weeks of sea-food. There was a floating wooden dock running into the sheltered site, so it was like being round a giant green swimming pool. No sand or tar to stick between your toes, the bane of Carla's Long Island childhood.

Mrs I. had mentioned the possibility of her attendance at some stage, but then let it rather hang in the air. Carla was not too concerned about this. Flexible Philippines etc. "Bish" Hanabishi was a good guy to have around for back-up; she planned to mention his name to a few people. The idea of a Japanese *on your side* would appeal to every captain of industry she'd ever worked for. He was surprisingly friendly with Dinolan, the tongue-tied gauche Filipino with the wonderfully appropriate name. She'd pronounced it in a French way at first to rhyme with Esmé before discovering it twanged with maisonette: Boyet, as in immature lad. In extenuation, James Benitez had said Dinolan was a better writer than a speaker. Nice of James, typical of James. Dinolan had a female journalist from his rag in tow for this trip, with an even less felicitous name, Jinky, which rhymed embarrassingly with Chinky and sounded like jinx. She'd noticed Dinolan leering up the woman's shorts, probably having something on the side with her, promotion dependent on favours granted. As someone with not much to sell in the way of qualifications herself other than her own personality, Carla had very quickly appreciated how difficult it was to land even a poorly paid middle-class job here, and what panic was aroused at the thought of losing one. It was virtually a charter for harassment in the work-place. She resolved to have a motherly word with the girl. She didn't look more than twenty-three. Carla could have been her biological mama, she thought.

Turning away from contemplation of this rather sordid state of affairs, it was sweet to watch Gracie. She was really blooming before Carla's very eyes. Carla didn't like to ask but it was fairly plainly first love. Getting away from the conference had done wonders. Gracie probably felt stiff about her ambassadorial role there – not to mention constrained by Dr Neumark's shrewd eye – but here she could kick her shoes off and let her hair down. In the nicest sense, she was like a very young girl. "Honey," said Carla, "it makes me feel better just to watch you." This wasn't quite true as she was now starting to get stabbing pains in the gut as well as the monsoon sheeting out of her bottom.

On the pontoon deck she didn't dare entrust herself to a flimsy swimming-suit, although normally she was justifiably proud of her figure, maintained by hours on the Nordic skiing machine. Gracie's guy went to find her a deck-chair – those strong but silent types tended to be the world's gentlemen – while she passed the time of day with Omar Hamid and Rod Kienzler. Not her first choice of company, but she had to keep lines of communication open to the potentially refractory, wild beasts often being soothed just by the sound of the human voice. Kienzler and Hamid had begun as allies, subscribing from opposite corners, as it were, to the same core values – both also living by their wits, Hamid with no institutional or financial safety-net – but there was an uncomfortable undercurrent of rivalry now. Hamid feared for his place in the sun. Kienzler made daily encroachments on his position. Kienzler basked in Dr Neumark's smile. The younger man was rapidly becoming a protegé whose usefulness to his patroness could well, Hamid foresaw, supersede his. Those flippancies which jarred on others he subdued in her majestic presence, while such as slipped through she forgave him. She knew the youth of the eighties and nineties weren't as single-mindedly doctrinaire as their counterparts of the sixties, those armies of the lecture-rooms and campus auditoriums of yesterday, whose appetite for striking gestures and flamboyant words she knew just how to stimulate and satisfy, sending them home in a delirium of righteousness and satisfaction from her stint at the microphone. Today's youth were at once more serious in their career-mindedness and less serious in their relative conservatism, felt Ruth. Kienzler was a useful bridge between these two eras, and Hamid knew negritude wasn't anywhere near so useful a play, there being no one quite so ready to stick a knife in a black intellectual's back as another negro writer or politician.

"*Gauloises*, Rod?" he offered.

"Cheers, Omar. Maybe later with my coffee."

Carla spotted in the far distance what looked like a speed-boat, closing at extra-terrestrial velocity; then as it neared, realised it hadn't been as far distant as she thought but merely tinier: a sea-scooter, whadyamacallit, jet-foil, rather than a fully fledged boat. It was still going quite fast, though, but with the steady plod of those machines rather than the wave-skimming bounds of a big outboard-powered boat. It was then that Carla saw Dinolan put his paw on Chinky/Jinky's knee. She noticed the girl's face tauten; a muscle throbbed in her cheek, or she was gritting her teeth. The poor thing looked under terrible strain, worse than the simple gesture, however abhorrent to her, would appear to warrant. This was probably just the tip of the iceberg, the least crude of his advances. The next thing, Dinolan had put his arm round her. Carla saw a tear run down the Filipina's cheek. A momentary flash of anger, very rare indeed for Carla in her personal let alone on-duty life, lit the scene for her with special clarity. Maybe it would pay to get mad more often, she thought. She saw Jinky put her face in Dinolan's shoulder and him pat her head. The other day Dr Neumark had said some-thing profound and shocking. They'd been talking about domestic violence, then Dr Neumark had said, "Of course, the sad thing is a few women enjoy it. They derive a perverse excite-ment from brutality. I've known one such in my life." Even from a woman, even from one as distinguished as Ruth Neumark, it was a scandalous thing. "I could never love a man who raised his hand against me," Dr Neumark added. "I simply couldn't." And, as if in proof of this terrible contention, here was this Philippine girl licking the hand that, figuratively speaking, abused her. That was why Dr Neumark was a world-famous writer and she wasn't, Carla supposed.

The Filipina recovered herself and wiped her eyes.

Carla moved towards her. "That looks fun," she said kindly,

by way of diversion.

"What, mum?"

"That," Carla gestured at the water scooter now going past them, with a cheery wave from the young boy steering it. Carla wasn't a vindictive person but she was not displeased by the look of cold fury on Dinolan's face. Some machinations deserved to have spanners thrown in them.

"What's that, Carla?" Gracie had come to tell her the deck-chair had arrived.

"The water-scooter, honey. It looks like the boat the golliwogs stole from Noddy. Oops!" she giggled, "Guess I should know Noddy isn't p.c. after all our discussions."

As it was just the two of them there – not counting the Filipinos – Gracie smiled complicitly. "Aren't they dangerous, Crescente?"

"Not so," said her strong but silent chevalier, whom Carla reminded herself to thank for his chivalry. "The motor cuts out if the boat overturns and there is no propeller to hurt your leg, just a hose."

Dinolan said curtly, "We'll be the ones to have another look at the clams."

"I didn't know you took such an interest in bi-valves," Carla said.

"Actually, Crescente, I meant dangerous for other water-users. You know, like swimmers."

"Ah, I don't know at all. Mrs Giolitti, I have something to arrange for your security. I'll be the one to go ahead."

"Sure, and God bless you for a sweetheart."

Carla settled back into her deckchair. The sun felt good on her stomach, though she knew exposure could get you diarrhoea as well. After a while she fell asleep, unfortunately omitting to dab sunscreen on to the bridge of her nose.

Bish Hanabishi had discovered the presence of a 7 cu ft per minute breathing air compressor and some heart-stoppingly rusty tanks with home-made backpacks. Jingkee and Boyet found him poking round this scrapyard trove in his vacation

Bermuda shorts and thick-soled flip-flops.

"*Uy!* Deep-sea diving equipment!"

"Not so bloody deep, boy-o." Whenever he spoke to Boyet Bish found himself using long-forgotten idioms from his student days as a mark of the camaraderie developing between them. "I would be too scared to more than quarter pump these bottles."

"No, not too scared for anything."

"Too sensible, then."

"They must use these to collect pearls," Jingkee said very brightly.

"I think so. You could never rent these out to customers."

"You could," said Boyet, "if you were a Filipino." He and Hanabishi laughed.

Jingkee said, "Hoy, proud to be Filipino, not like you and the German, sir."

Boyet thought how much he admired Jingkee's courage and composure. In the air Bish thought he detected something between them but minded his own business. He knew Boyet had the reputation of being something of a ladies' man. "I could be enough of a Japanese actually to put one of these on and encounter to have a look at the clams," he mused.

"It would be a change from pearls of wisdom," Boyet quipped.

"Did you encounter to see Miss Hipkin recently?"

"I think it would be difficult to miss her, Bish."

"She was on the floating pier with the others, Mr Hanabishi, I'll be the one to get her for you."

"Please, no. Ah so. Cannot stop her."

"It's difficult, the diving technique, *di ba*?"

"No, very easy. You just breathe normally, especially coming up. Ah, clear your ears descending, compensate for buoyancy. Very simple. Would you like to try?"

"No, no. Ha, ha. Water scares me. And to get inside it, no, no."

When Jingkee returned she had the resort manager, Gracie Hipkin, and Crescente Koyaw with her, and a look of implacable willingness on her face. "Arrival of everyone, Mr Hanabishi," she announced. Hanabishi bowed to Crescente, who gave him a brief nod back. Hanabishi returned him an even lower bow. He asked the resort manager, "Are you renting diving equipment to your guests?"

"Just for our own purposes, sir."

"Ah, I thought maybe Miss Hipkin and me could look at your underwater farm."

"But no one to escort you, sir, at the present. Our supervisor is absent."

"We are experienced divers, are we, Miss Hipkin?"

"Right on."

"I think no problem?"

"I would like to, sir. But I am not sure of the advisability."

"I am advising you to let them have the equipment."

"Yes, sir. Certainly, Mr Crescente. I will bring you the key to the locker, sir."

Gracie and Bish chuckled over the equipment's antiquity and disrepair. "Have you used a twin-hose reg before, Miss Hipkin?"

"There's always a first time. Uh-oh. Sixty bar. That's, Jesus, what's the conversion . . ."

"I think less than one thousand pounds. I can use it. One hundred bar in the other bottle."

"That's OK. I don't consume as much as you would think. Do you dive, Mrs Zamora?"

"Snorkel only."

"How deep are the beds? Forty or fifty feet?"

"Too deep for a beginner, Miss Hipkin, I think."

"I guess so."

Crescente insisted on carrying Gracie's equipment to the pontoon, although she insisted she was perfectly capable of doing it for herself. She wore orange overalls to go diving, not a swimsuit. This was a wise decision, Boyet thought, doubtless come to many years ago. But she was amazingly swift to put the equipment on herself, doing a forward roll into the water while

Hanabishi was still fiddling with the buckle on his right shoulder. She floated high and comfortably, despite the lead squares she had belted on herself. After Hanabishi had stumbled in, clanging his cylinder on the pontoon, Gracie said crisply, "Fifty-nine max for fifty-nine, with a one-minute safety stop at ten. I'll lead." She then startled Boyet by giving the thumbs down sign of a Roman emperor ordering the death of a fallen gladiator. Boyet could see her orange shape under the bubbles widening on the surface while Hanabishi was still struggling to get down.

"Do you know how to do this, Mr Koyaw?" Jingkee asked sweetly. She, Boyet, and the Boss were the only people at the end of the pontoon now.

"No, never tried it," Crescente patted his pockets for a cigarette but didn't have one.

"You must try to suppress the habit of smoking, Mr Koyaw. It can shorten your life, you know. Maybe you prefer surface water sports. Have you tried water-skiing?"

"No, never tried it."

"They say it's very exciting. For the skier."

Boyet had picked up a strap-less, perished face-mask. He lay on his stomach, his nose an inch into the water, and found himself looking at a second world, another dimension. Tiny blue fish darted in clumps of weed and broken rock. One inch into the alien element and the whole world above with its busy concerns became a vanished illusion. He could see the two divers moving parallel to him, Gracie not like the clumsy Gracie of the thin, unhelpful atmosphere but a being made agile and perfectly weightless by the abetting medium of water. Her roundness actually suited the element better than Hanabishi's thin, angular frame; she looked sleek and streamlined when she kicked her legs with casual, disciplined beats. Boyet lifted his head that inch, turned his neck to look for his companions on the pontoon and the other world was gone beneath its reflective lid. Jingkee was sitting on a mossy bollard by herself. Koyaw was already off the pontoon, walking quite quickly as if he was on official business. "Have a look, Jingk, it's a beautiful sight."

"Maybe later. I've seen it other times." She was smiling, perhaps a little abstractedly, but looking cheerful again. Women had rapid changes of mood, Boyet thought. A little while ago he had been very worried that she would break down completely. As one of the security people drove their jeep along the stony track to the cottages Jingkee aimed her forefinger and cocked thumb at it, swinging her arm to follow its progress. "Boom!" she said and laughed. Boyet found it in poor taste, especially for a woman, but made allowances. They passed the time discussing the newspaper, the fresh spate of anonymous threats Kamikaze Kelvin Fugoso had been getting, and the wisdom or otherwise of commissioning opinion platforms from Professors Pfeidwengeler and Beaufort, until Gracie and Bish surfaced right under their feet. Poor Gracie couldn't hide her disappointment that Crescente wasn't there to see her. Boyet didn't blame her. It was a shame.

CARLA had been back more than twelve hours before she found out. The problem now was constipation after the medication she'd taken. She was completely bunged up. The glistening porcelain of her suite remained unsullied.

There seemed even more giggling among the girl students than usual, if this was possible. (Carla hadn't thought it was). She still found it very charming. They were so much more accessible than American teenagers. "Hey, what's with you guys?"

More giggling. "You're not jealous, Mrs Giolitti?"

"Jealous? I don't understand. You mean of youth and beauty?"

Further tittering. "Maybe you're a fan of Roel Escarcinas? You know him?"

"Never heard of him, honey. He's a Philippine heart throb?"

"Maribeth going to bed with him every night, mum. She hugs his photo when she goes to sleep." Screams of protest.

Carla entered into the spirit of things, light-hearted banter though her guts felt like lead. "So what's the problem. Is Maribeth accusing me of seducing her picture?"

"No, mum. Maribeth can kiss Roel when he's coming here, day before yesterday."

Carla still didn't tumble to what had happened in her absence. In a way it was to her credit – not so much obtuseness as natural trustingness and a desire to think the best of everybody. "Oh, that's nice. Was he doing a promo? I mean, was he publicising a new film?"

"No, mum. Coming here. This place."

"Oh, I wouldn't have thought he'd be interested. And there was nothing going on anyway. We were all away." Her own words lingered in the air, began to echo and re-echo in her ears, with horrible insinuations. Nothing going on. We were all away.

"Also coming an Amerikano and Amerikana. Mr Bratt Allinson and Sylvia Dobbs."

"*What?*" This was like being told there was a stray cat in the yard and finding there were two lions. Bratt Allinson, the Hollywood idol of the Fifties whose recent reclusiveness had only added to his legend, friend of armed American Indians and the Black Panthers, who had given a cool million to the Brazilian rubber-tappers in their war against the road developers and beef farmers. And Dobbs, leader of the bitch pack, unfashionably radical but the face of the moment, two of whose releases were currently in the US Box Office Top Ten.

"Many photographers and journalists with them, mum. And also TV."

"CNN American TV, mum."

Their jubilation was so plainly unmalicious, so disingenuous, that Carla felt obliged to hide her own feelings. "Well, that's very exciting." Had she caught sight of her face in the mirror running alongside the escalators to the shops of the mezzanine floor where she would buy sennapod syrup and Whispers napkins she would have seen that her eyes glittered and her cheeks were taut with anger. She looked ten years older.

Mrs Init had plainly planned it for some time. And it had

been no coincidence that they had been away. In fact – a horrible thought crossed her mind – maybe they had all been but ancillary to this purpose. A side-show. The warm-up act. Bait for the bigger fish. Maybe all three at once. Oh, shoot! "Dumbo, Carla. Dumbo," she admonished herself. Then she thought again. They had not all been away. John and Dr Neumark had stayed. She'd get proper information from John. Going down the escalator again, she saw Mrs Init and her husband the politician, with some members of the cave party who had just arrived. They seemed extraordinarily cheerful, unless it was just relative to her own mood, chattering away, laughing. Professor Adachi even patted Professor Pfeidwengeler on his rump, which was enough to have them all in fits. Carla headed towards Mrs I. and N.S. Kumar. Mrs I. did not avoid eye contact with her on the way across, in fact she greeted her warmly. "How are you, Mrs Giolitti? How was the clam farm?"

"It was fine, Mrs Init. I understand there were visitors to the conference during our absence."

"That is correct. Your countrymen, or countrywoman, I should say, in fact. We were very honoured. I am told they are great celebrities in America."

"I knew nothing of them, Mrs Init. In fact, I don't remember ever being informed."

"I think I mentioned? You don't remember? In any case we did not wish to add to your work-load. You are already doing so much for us."

"It's considered professional etiquette, Mrs Init, to keep your organiser fully informed of everything that's going on. This was done behind my back."

Mrs Init laughed at the notion of this. "Not behind your back. We're just doing part of the work for you."

N.S. Kumar was not actually feeling uncomfortable; he wasn't directly involved in this, and behind the old school delicacies and politenesses, he was in fact exceptionally thick-skinned to the embarassments of others, as his great admirers of the past could have attested. But he had a lifetime's habit of intervening from the non-aligned position. His face creased in patrician distaste; he waved his elegant brown hands in deprecation. "So insubstantial this kind of tinsel fame, Mrs Giolitti. They are here today these people, gone tomorrow. Sophocles . . ."

Carla had sufficiently lost her temper to snub the courtly old Indian. Here today, gone tomorrow was also a peculiarly unfortunate expression in the circumstances. "I am very angry indeed, Mrs Init. And very disappointed."

Mrs Init smiled beatifically. It was the same smile Sister Annunziata had seen, did Carla – who was also a product of the nuns – but know it. She turned on her heel, tears starting behind her eyes (but never forming) as she waited for the elevator.

Who should emerge from this but John Hawkins. "Babe! How are you? Did they give the water baby a necklace?"

Carla smiled just to see dear old John again, but it must have been a wan one for, instantly solicitous, he asked, "What's up, Carla? Anything wrong?"

"No. Not really."

"Come on now, even I can see through that."

"Well . . . Oh, no. Maybe it's just me . . ." Then it all came out in a rush, a babbling rush. "If she could just have trusted me enough only to tell me I'd have kept the confidence," she concluded wretchedly. She did hate the sound of self-righteousness. "I don't know, John, maybe I'm too sensitive." She waited for him to tell her no, she wasn't. But John, who had kept a surprisingly – even for him – expressionless face during her recitation seemed unsympathetic. Hurtfully so. He then said, "Yeah, I'm sorry about that, babe. I really am. I wanted to tell you, but you know what they say, you've got to respect your source – and she really twisted my arm on that one. I guess she's the one footing my bill, so I went with it."

"You knew they were coming?"

"I did."

Carla also did her damnedest to control her expression, and succeeded admirably, though it didn't feel like it. So they both looked at each other with card-player faces. The elevator pinged. Carla squeezed through the closing doors and saw she looked OK in the mirror. But what was running through her mind was, *Oh, John, John, you betrayed me, too!*

Once in her suite the walls closed suffocatingly round her. Later, she liked to think that it hadn't really been her who had done the thing she would shortly do; or at least that the combination of illness, double betrayal and shock had exerted an aggregated influence in excess of the sum of their individual constituent forces. Because it was all, each by itself, really trivial, petty stuff. It should have been water off a duck's back. Hadn't they discovered those anti-cancer chemotherapies – which were nothing more nor less than poisons actually – were far more potent in a cocktail than neat by themselves? She had been festering inside, like Auntie Daphne with her colostomy. Probably the toxins locked tight and dry inside her by the chemical key she'd turned had also turned her brain. Could she blame Lomotil for malice premeditated? Was that all wickedness was? She'd like to tell it to the nuns.

Sitting in the close room in the intolerable interregnum between brownout and generator kick-in (it had lately been giving teething problems) she took leave of Carla Giolitti for a moment. Longing to express herself, to get the hurt feelings out of her system, she did something so alien to herself she could never feel ashamed about it afterwards; it was like someone else had done it. It was the first spiteful, the only really crumby, act she'd committed since the age of six.

Going to her brief case she took out her computer diskette – the one with the Leonardo virus inside – walked out the room and out of her skin, went to the conference office, put Leonardo in his slot, the narrow grave of warped genius, and tapped his infection home. Into the conference's records, into the centre's accounts, the Init files of deals done and funds diverted, the maze of foreign companies. She junked them all. And going back to her suite with head held high but a newly stealthy step, she acknowledged to herself something she'd found shocking from Gianni Giolitti when he'd been alive: the ladies really were more spiteful, she thought. We cry easier but we're more dangerous than the male. We have longer memories. And we repay what we owe.

Chapter Seventeen

THE PROP PULLED NESTOR IN THE DAY AFTER HIS RETURN from the mountains. He emerged, Kelvin Fugoso told Boyct, "looking visibly shell-shocked". In addition to his valiant quality Kamikaze Kelvin had a deadly instinct for the fitting cliché. Other expressions which came to mind (and indeed the first was the one used by the rival) were "a bolt from the blue", "a bombshell", "grim irony", and "sell-out". When he saw the proprietor's face, Nestor told Boyet glumly at Senhor Donut, he'd realised at once he was going to have to come up with a sacrificial lamb. The guy was so plainly bent on mayhem. He'd thought he'd throw him Boyar's columns; even, he had to admit, Cathy entire – with whom he was no longer having the thing – or good old Jingkee. Another look at the owner's face convinced Nestor he was going to have to jettison a lot more dead weight from the balloon than that. "Circulation," he was told, "has gone to an all-time low." The unspoken qualification to this was "under your distinguished editorship". The prop delayed getting the essential info across as long as possible, probably Nestor imagined, so he could inflict maximum humiliation. After all, a free agent doesn't have to eat shit. But Nestor wasn't being fired, not as such; he wasn't so much getting carpeted as having the rug pulled from under him.

The prop was selling his money-loser, his leaking rag.

To Evergreen Enterprises.

"Yup," said Nestor, recognising the aghast contortion on Boyet's face for the one his own had lately worn. "Same here, buddy boy."

"This calls for another coffee."

"Make mine a Chokko-Chokko." Nestor watched him go, still trim at thirty-nine in the jeans he was able to wear to work since he'd stopped playing attorney, but with the very noticeable beginnings of de-forestation on the back of his head. Poor guy – it was probably worse for him. He, Nestor, had further to fall but he was a trained journalist with cronies in the field to cushion the descent with offers of work. But Boyet must have been feeling he was in double jeopardy, having already jumped from the skillet and now on to the bars of a still fiercer grill. Evergreen. Of all the people.

"It's a novel line. They don't have Chokko-Chokko here in this outlet. You know, Nestor, it's not guaranteed they'll want a different ed." Nestor grimaced. He was under no illusions. "We'll just have to wait and see," and then he said the only characteristically *pinoy* thing Boyet ever heard pass his lips. "*Bahala na.*" *Bahala na, che sera sera.* Nestor's face suddenly became radiant. For a moment Boyet thought he'd come up with a life-, or at least career-, saving ploy, until he said, "Shit, no use wearing long faces. Let's go to Momo's."

Boyet looked at him with some admiration. He shook his head. "Couldn't get it up in the present circumstances."

"Says who? I know a chick would raise a dead snake. I'll tell you her number when we get there."

"I'm shot, Nestor."

"No, you just think you are. Keep me company, just."

"OK, I hear Momo's got cable now."

"Sure, just watch CNN. Maybe you'll see Dr Neumark on it."

JAMES Benitez gazed into the shimmering screen much like a Prophet of old might have discerned a sign across the mirage-strewn waste of pebble and sand that was the Lord's haunt. He was suffering unusual difficulty subduing the richness of his thoughts into the order of words. The cursor on the screen of the Dragon's CC micro-computer, as fanatically protected from spikes, surges, and fluctuations as FVR was from loopy head-shots, throbbed like a nervous tic. He mouthed his sentences back to himself, first scrolling the page up function to where he'd started but then finding he couldn't get there. The text performed tortuous callisthenics then began jumping up and down on the spot. James pressed another button and found his empire of words stable again. He settled for where he was, reading "... in 1926, the third child of poor Polish and Russian immigrants, who found economic success in their new land. She had, she says, 'a thoroughly ordinary upbringing', but excelling at school in the arts. This she doesn't say, but it may be deduced from the long list of debating and scholastic honours she acquired. At seventeen she conceived the ambition to be of service to her community and more pertinently to those who were not of her community, this sense of adolescent vocation being constructively diverted by her then mentor Rabbi Lionel Rubenstein into the study of medicine."

Benitez got the cursor, which seemed to have a mind of its own, under "adolescent" with surprising difficulty and consigned the adjective to scrap. He could always retrieve it, but he rather thought it could be misconstrued as offensive.

"She spent a total of seven years qualifying as a medical doctor, during which period she met and married her first husband, Leon Warshaw, a Polish pilot in the Royal Air Force. Sadly, he was killed in a flying accident in 1945."

On highlighting the redundant "and married" for scrapping, James found he had an entire page of some one hundred and fifty "and married"s filling the screen. This lasted about a second and a half, causing him to wonder if he was hallucinating.

"She met her second husband, like herself a doctor, at a small country hospital in 1952. In 1957, from what had been a hobby, known only to the friends she entertained at private events, she launched her musical career which was as short as it was successful." James felt it would simply not be honest to avoid all mention of Ruth the folk singer, though he suspected she'd prefer it. He was doing his best to see things through Dr Neumark's eyes, which was unfortunately not proving as difficult as it sounded. He had, on the other hand, passed a very taxing half hour with her in person, checking details, ascertaining what she wanted said and what left unsaid. She'd waved her hands, pooh-poohed his excessive regard for her sensibilities, then ten minutes later gone on to take offence in her frigid way over some emphasis that he'd failed to give – a raised eyebrow or tautened cheek, a half incline of the head, being the signals of his uncouthness. She was a damned difficult lady. Thank God, he wasn't running a conversation with her, just introducing her paper. She had read him some passages. To him, it had seemed a blend of sophomore Marxism and incomprehensible philosophical abstraction but then he was only a provincial Philippine Professor. It was what was known as a keyword presentation, on the same principles as Representative Init's foreign brandishings but, of course, of infinitely greater sophistication. Dr Neumark read at a brisk clip, business-like but strangely dramatic when heard in a hushed lecture-room, imbuing young minds with purpose all the more exciting for being unfocussed. Her tone, Benitez didn't fail to notice, was aggressively incantatory: the same rhythm Detlef Pfeidwengeler found not so much suggestive as ridiculous: the spectacle of a strong but unoriginal intellect masturbating in public. Acts of self-definition, vocabularies of transformation, identity moulded in the glare of burning Casspirs, post-revolutionary accountings, existential predicaments, creativity in the dimension of social apocalypse, the interaction between the private revolutionary gestures enjoined by conscience and the arena of the actual, the aesthetic of alienation – all these and more fell on Benitez's ears. What he didn't hear then but thousands had was the self-inculpating admission that charmed – the owning up to personal failing with a wan smile and the simple words, "My greatest regret is that I never learned an African language. Any African language." Which would always send the blood racing to Detlef's temples as he strove to prevent himself shouting out loud: "Start now learning, lazy sow. It gives never too late!" In fact, when the admission did come the way of James and the rest of the Philippine audience (despite the special circumstances of that morning which would turn Dr Neumark into heroine, if not goddess) it failed to charm in the way that it would have a monophone Anglo gathering since her hearers had been for the most part raised trilingually – which devalued the achievement. So the lacuna would appear not so much idle, as it did to Professor Pfeidwengeler, as simply bizarre: a personal eccentricity, like not knowing how to drive in America.

Now Benitez scanned the long list of Dr Neumark's achievements on his computer. She had actually won more awards than she had written books. There were six of the latter, if you counted separately the three volumes of autobiography and their prequel about her parents' experience of the pogrom, *A Blacker Hand*, which had sold even more hugely in New York than *Gazelle Morning*. Translated into nineteen languages, none (he would remember with a wry smile later) indigenous to Africa. He listed the grander sounding of her prizes and decorations or those in the languages more unusual to him – the two proving synonymous in most cases. She was An Illustrious Horseman of some mighty Latin sodality or other, which sounded queer to James until he started thinking of her as a literary Joan of Arc. Hadn't Professor Pfeidwengeler, to his embarrassment, openly referred to her as a witch?

Benitez decided this was enough for the moment – he was intending to follow Jack Beaufort's self-effacing example after all – and pressed "print". With that all the winged mischiefs in Carla's Pandora's box of Renaissance tricks flew their confinement to roost in the different files and sectors of his programme, leaving James watching the fountain of spinning, disintegrating meanings as much in awe as dismay.

His political past showed him resourceful and resilient as well as modest and sincere. He would, he thought, just have to find the guts to confront his identity on the existential plane, avoiding alienation like the plague, the plague, and mediate his own abdication from the process, whilst empowering Dr Neumark's assumption of role etc.

He'd have the guts to be himself – no one who simply did that ever dried up in public speaking. Ad lib, he'd do that ad infinitum. And he was starting not to like Dr Neumark, confusing the electronic bug and her for evermore in his recollections of those weeks, both equally efficient, equally opportunistic, and equal in their neutral indifference to their malign effect on human beings.

DR NEUMARK'S address was certainly not the last item on the conference agenda. Final motions would be passed: the end-product of whatever the general gut-feeling was on issues dirty, dangerous, or otherwise. Before this, there'd be a recapitulation for the record offered by N.S. Kumar, Bish Hanabishi, and Jack Beaufort. But there was no doubt Ruth Neumark's speech was the true grand finale, the one big one whose grandeur and finality would only be emphasised by the spatterings, dribblings, and short-lived blasts that were subsequent.

Representative Init, Mrs I. would be glad later, awoke earlier than usual, granting himself a bonus two hours of existence. Victoria, whose soul was not small, wouldn't have had it otherwise even had she been cognisant of the fact that the bird song reveille was to give himself opportunity to phone his Manila mistress from his surgery while the lines were still free. The sights and sounds of this, the Congressman cooing sweet nothings down the receiver, stunned, stymied, and amazed, in the way that the spectacle of a vulture squawking "Who's a pretty boy?" might inspire true humility in the heart of the learned ornithologist. The Congressman's facial expression didn't change – the same at the moment of sexual climax or his father's funeral, pulling down a commission or penning his signature on a joint Senate-Congress committee recommendation – but his vocal range registered an astonishing variation in expressing plea and endearment, baffled outrage, and endearment again, while his dead eyes looked coldly into the middle distance occupied by telefax and water-fountain. You expected him, Android-like, to peel off his face and don another as he put down the clammy receiver.

PROFESSOR Pfeidwengeler had dreamed a dream as charged as any while dawn broke, while the Congressman quietly put on his transparent socks and Victoria slept, while Jingkee's professionals – cashiered marines and defunct Scout Rangers this time, rather than junior Sparrows – primed their fragmentation grenades and saw to the M-203 combination 40mm grenade launcher and assault rifle, while Gracie Hipkin with lazy thumbnail back-flicked her clitoris in pleasurable delay of the circular motion of the index finger that would propel her into bliss as if she was scrubbing a recalcitrant dot of chocolate from her blouse. Still a virgin, she imagined riding pillion with Crescente and being penetrated on a floating Li-Lo.

Detlef Pfeidwengeler found himself a whale. He still had his own face, enlarged a hundred-fold, but the massive box body and flapping flukes of the gentle mammal. He was swimming placidly hundreds of metres down, still full of plankton browsed near the surface. The water caressed his flanks, supported his massive carcass as if he was flying in the stratosphere full of hydrogen or helium but without the obnoxious and dangerous properties of gas. He rolled in his slumber, winding the sheet around his legs so that they felt more than ever fused into a tail, mumbling about equal volume displacement. "Eureka," he muttered, and started to rise for breath. As he did so, the air-con kicked in, the brownout over, and he heard magnified and deepened by water which transmitted the waves of sound five times faster than air, the engine beat of the boat in which Dr Ruth Neumark sat in sou'wester bonnet, and of course shawl, behind the breech of the explosive-tipped harpoon gun that spelled his doom. He knew his spout would betray him but he also knew it was a necessity, inevitable. He had to flush his lungs with air or die anyway. He felt his back break the sunlit surface. He ventilated through the blow-hole sphincter behind his brain, knowing it spelled the end. *Boom!* With his 270-degree vision he saw the cruel spear fly towards him, streaming not rope but a long strand of spittle from Dr Neumark's mouth. Ach!

Unusually for him, Crescente Koyaw, for his part, woke without premonition at the precise moment the Congressman was saying for clarification to Manila, "So five weeks late your mens already, *di ba*?"

During his stint as conference security the Boss had shed the load of apprehension he'd carried with him so long he had forgotten its true weight. Overseeing the safety of others, taking proxy precautions, had acted as therapy. His detailed and elaborate arrangements for the protection of others had proved to be the singing of a lullaby to his own fears which, temporarily, he could regard as babyish. Also, being up and around at weird hours of the night while all were asleep had conferred upon him a sense of responsibility and invulnerability akin to that of the prison warder or airline stewardess. He felt full of confidence – confident enough to let people get away with over-familiarities unchecked – and a full decade younger.

He broke his fast on the hot water and squeezed calamansi Ms Hipkin had enjoined upon him, followed by the native chocolate and rice pudding that were his own idea. In the cool golden morning he drove his BMW to the Dragons Centre, a posse of motor-cycle-mounted Untouchables bringing up the rear with spit and roar. Having run morning parade, bawled out an idiot with a filthy 12-gauge breech, delivered yet another pep talk as to the extreme, the terminal unwisdom of relaxing just because it was all nearly over – received with idiot grins because they all knew how comparatively laid back the Boss had become – he was in the middle of checking under the lectern of the hall for an MNLF bomb – Gracie had explained how you could tell she and Dr Neumark were Jewish just from their names – when he was paged. Ping! Ping! Ping! There stood a boy in livery with one of those ridiculous round hats and a stick-mounted blackboard with his own name chalked up. He had a mind to shoot a hole in it. The reception girl pushed the telephone across to him with a simper.

"What is this?"

A woman's voice said, "Mr Koyaw, there are small boys vandalising your car in the park."

"What?"

"They are writing graffiti with spray cans and maybe also trying to cut the brakes again."

That "again" which he didn't register at the time was to haunt him later.

"You'd better be quick. Go now."

The Boss's eyes – he'd have been pleased if he could have seen, for there was no acting involved – went like El Jefe's in *Bring me the head of Alfredo Garcia*. Worse. Rushing out, 'sus Maria, not the BM – why hadn't he chosen the Datsun today? – he collided with Professor Pfeidwengeler who, despite sleeping badly, was unable to emend a lifetime's habit of ruthless, rigorously inculcated punctuality and who had descended half an hour early to secure his seat for the Neumark address.

"What gives, good my fellow?"

"Excuse. Sorry, no time. I am saving my German car."

"*Ja*, that's worth saving."

The Boss smacked into two Gobernador de Leon "Aides" who were sweeping the marble flags with one hand behind their backs, somehow got his foot into and then out of a bucket without falling over, and then hurt his shoulder on the swing door.

Forty metres away the BM sat there, no one in sight, but rocking furiously on its beautiful suspension from what was being done to it on its blind side. It was like rescuing a damsel in distress, saving another distinguished heavyweight lady, Gracie. As he got within 15 metres two things happened in quick succession. First, five men popped up – men, not boys, though at that point he still didn't understand – and four of them lobbed what he thought were their spray cans at him. As the fifth pointed the

M-203 at him, his uncle the Congressman's car, coming round the *fung shui* barrier of the Dragon's CC that preserved the building from evil geomantic influences, took a long burst from the combination assault rifle and 40mm grenade launcher all down its left side, bonnet to trunk. Representative Init saw the sparking out of the barrel a second and a half before a pair of terrible blows in the ribs – more like being hit by George Foreman and Sonny Liston with sledgehammers than a few grammes of lead – hurled him across to the right hand door. His dying thought was that Dionisio III had caught him at last with his pants down, a wall of darkness blotting out the corollary hope for revenge barely formulated. A second later the grenades went off, flipping the Toyota on to its side.

The Boss was already running back to the main door as the Scout Ranger with the M-203 fired, in his excitement pulling the rifle trigger at the same time as tugging at the launcher tube's lever forward and under – something not possible with the blunderbuss-like but formidably accurate earlier M-79 model – and sent the shell over the Boss's head, through the thick glass, and exploding among the bunching Untouchables. As he crossed the crunching glass shards in the lobby, the Boss saw Professor Pfeidwengeler heading into the gent's CR and followed, bursting open the door of the centre cubicle as the German was trying to bolt it. There was not much room inside for the two of them. Crescente changed his mind and dashed out, the door-bolt clicking as he hid under the wash-basin by the urinals, six cubicles down, and a Scout Ranger entered, saw feet, lobbed his last grenade over the partition, calling "Catch!" and ran out again to take an Untouchable's Browning blast full in the chest. Professor Pfeidwengeler looked at the grenade, dropped it in the pan, flushed, and was dead with no knowledge of his own extinction. Even one of the series of thick marble partitions would have sufficed to shield the Boss from the grenade's most lethal effect – wire and casing fragments – but the actual blast wave ran up the cubicle wall, down the other side into the next, up the opposite wall, and again up and down five times through the series of partitions before knocking him senseless for two hours with blood coming out of his ears and nose.

Half an hour before he regained his consciousness and saw Gracie's tear-stained, coarsened, pink features of Miss Piggy above his hospital bed – not his own hospital – Dr Neumark was concluding an even fierier than usual statement of position to rapturous applause.

She had categorically refused to abandon her speech in the face of "this outrageous piece of intimidation".

Epilogue

TWENTY-SEVEN YEARS LATER – when those born during the time of the conference's own strainings were already men and women, some with children of their own – a high-ranking officer of the Japan Strategic Materials Procurement Directorate met an equally distinguished environmentalist, now the Greenpeace Observer at the United Nations. The SMPD was a euphemism for the agency behind the nuclear re-armament of Japan. This meeting took place in Mexico City. They sat over the hot Aztec beverage of maize and the purple tortillas and nachos that it was the pleasure and inspiration of their (Japanese-chained) five star hotel to serve in its 24-hour coffee shop. It was 12:30 midnight and they had just met by chance forty-five minutes ago at reception. Although the different paths they had taken in their careers had put them on opposite sides of the fence (and they had actually crossed swords in personal debate twelve years previously) they were also old acquaintances as well as ancient adversaries, not to mention ex-companions under the diver's buddy system.

The Japanese, who was as bald as an egg, said to his svelte and elegant companion, "Have you ever encountered to come across any of the others who were in Gobernador de Leon with us?"

Gracie Hipkin shook her grey page-boy hair-do. "I can't say I have. I did read N.S. Kumar's obituary notices *everywhere*, as you must have done."

"Ah, yes. But that was just three or four years later," said Bish Hanabishi.

Despite the unwritten and unspoken verdict of John Hawkins – who like N.S. was long dead – that the personalities he had been reporting were mediocrities, essentially third- or at best second-division – many of those there had risen. Gracie, for instance, the new Gracie, was one of those who had changed their whole lives with Metabolhi – the Chinese drug, essentially metamphetamine hydrochloride without the addictive properties – which not only burned off fat but kept it off. Permanently. She now weighed 120 pounds, instead of 220, and was taken seriously. As soon as she had shed sufficient to stop being a grotesque she had started being commensurately successful. Hanabishi, who with his understanding and sympathy for the external world and his shaping by it, had been the equivalent in his own country of Gracie's circus lady, had found a path once his government had realised that rigid cultural chauvinism was as self-defeating in the battle for national survival against the stirring Chinese monster as stiffness in judo. (He could have done something about the lack of hair with another metabolic wonder drug but chose not to).

Now he said, "Mmm. How about Professor Jack Beaufort?"

"Never heard of the guy again."

"Ah so. Dear Professor Beaufort. A good man, I think. And Professor Detlef. A very sincere man."

"If you say so, Bish."

Amusement glimmered behind his spectacles. You could get a handful of Japanese who spoke English a little better than Bish, Gracie thought, but never find one who understood the nuances of communication as well as him. "But we all heard of the great Dr Neumark, Gracie. And our illustrious hostess, Mrs Init."

Gracie did her old Annie Hall roll of the eyes, which was no longer ludicrous but extremely charming. "Oh, yeah. Sure. Hey, what's this about NZG363 precursor being manufactured by the Self Defence Agency?"

Bish smiled but stayed silent.

"C'mon. It'll go no further. For briefing purposes only, non-attrib."

Bish's smile broadened into a grin. This was far too sensitive a topic. Instead, he told Gracie something he shouldn't have done about the Kuriles and hydrophones off the Nicobar Islands.

He knew he could trust her not to embarrass him.

AT this time Dr Neumark, in her early nineties and already very demented for the last ten years, was resident in her Miami sanatorium. Unfortunately there was no magic bullet for Alzheimer's such as existed for obesity and alopecia. In the decade immediately after the conference she had known unparalleled success: a one million dollar extraordinary award for lifetime achievement from the Goldenberg Foundation, the Semtex Award, and nomination for the Nobel Peace Prize. Contemporary events in Southern Africa had rather stolen Ruth's thunder in recent years, deprived her of her halo if not made her work totally irrelevant, and while not a forgotten figure, she had known some slight decline in her reputation, or would have known it had she been sentient. In the way that writers' statures are augmented by death and then suffer a devaluation, she was due for one more peak and a trough, but her biographer and the editor of her *Collected Letters*, Lord Kienzler, the former vice-chairman of the largest private television company in Europe, was confident that the eventual revaluation of posterity would be, as he put it, "both just and positive." Omar Hamid had met a bizarre and horrible end in 1999, the year Ruth received the Freedom of Lund University, when he fell foul of the central African dictator with whom his ex-mentor had actually once broken bread, and was tortured and then, in part, eaten. And, as naturally, later voided. As he had been one of the leading proponents of the theory that cannibalistic practices in Africa were but figments of the overheated racist imagination, he bore a major responsibility for the true details of his disappearance never being circulated.

Kamla Mishra met a very old and very rich Texan oil man – who had diversified into the chip – at her next conference but two, and became his fourth wife. She excused herself to the more radical of her Bombay friends by saying that she was in a better position to do something by working within the system. Anyway, being Indians they understood money talked.

Dr Enoeda tragically perished below one of the rims of triple-cratered, multi-coloured Mount Kalimatu in Indonesia without ever knowing about it, like Professor Pfeidwengeler under different circumstances. An unforeseen rain-storm had triggered a secondary explosion out of all proportion to the expected as it irrigated the hot pyroclastic deposits banked on the slopes the intrepid Japanese was scaling.

B.K. Napoleon Wong was imprisoned in Chungking with the connivance of both mainland and Taiwanese authorities in 1998, released two years later under an amnesty programme for the eyes of the outside world, jailed again in Taipei two years later, and died in prison as a man still free in his mind.

Professor James Benitez and Tomoko Adachi became firm friends, corresponding by turn in the Anglo-Saxon of *Beowulf* – in which James held the advantage – and courtly middle French – at which Tomoko held the palm. Tomoko secured an invitation for James to attend a conference in San Francisco, far grander than the Dragons, six years later and another equally well-funded (James's honorarium actually exceeded his annual Philippine teaching salary) in Yokohama eight years after that. Those were the only occasions on which they ever met in person again during their long lives, but the drop of envelopes on the mat in the familiar handwriting would always bring naughty boys' grins to both solemn faces.

Two days after the close of the Dragons' Conference Kamikaze Kelvin Fugoso was shot dead by assailants unknown. These were probably the bodyguards of the town's police chief who correctly surmised now was the time this salvaging would get lost in, or even be seen as part of, the bigger furore. He got two .45 rounds in the head on the way home from church, from a range close enough to cause powder burns to the scalp. "Very professional," as a surprisingly unshaken Crescente Koyaw made a point of stating. Nestor Chavez, who himself had three days of life left as editor of the *Citizen*, contented himself with the hoary remark, "Murders here are rarely solved but seldom unavenged. Hah, Jingkee?" Boyet was faintly disappointed he couldn't have come up with something more insightful and original than this, but then he knew Nestor was under pressure, like Hitler in his bunker.

On the day Evergreen formally took over the paper they fired him and Nestor both. The new ed was none other than – wait for it – Jingkee. "Good luck to her," Nestor said, without much rancour at Senhor Donut, "she'll be a loyal servant of management." Nestor reckoned Boyet had tightened the noose around his own neck with his enthusiastic pro-Green reporting of the convention. Generally speaking, this wouldn't please Evergreen. One spoke of Evergreen as an infinitely sensitive, infinitely irascible, barely dormant giant. Of course, it was but an institutionalised arm of an even larger impersonal Manila institution, but its nervous system was made up of a chain of insecure individuals zealous for their own personal advancement: thus the tiniest suspicion, nay the merest hint of non-conformity with company policy – still less outright disloyalty – would be seized, amplified along the line, and visited with awful repercussions. Then, slightly later, the picture grew even clearer. Evergreen had found a way out of its economic woes, what with the exhaustion of Sodomite and the shrinking lumber supplies. The company had done business with Welt Gruppe Tubol Farben of the Ruhr. Evergreen were to provide "docking and storage facilities". This was how the initial story appeared in *Citizen*. Innocent enough. That this presentation lulled any suspicions Boyet might have had was hardly surprising. That a hardened pro like Nestor was also deceived was tribute to the company's handling of the matter. Later, Nestor came to the conclusion the whole operation had been planned with meticulous cunning from Germany; at least, if the cunning was Philippine, the meticulousness was German-supplied, like the unwanted chemicals. And the money to buy *Citizen* had undoubtedly been Deutschmarks before it had been pesos. Yes, German toxic waste was being dumped on Gobernador de Leon – the stuff that was too dirty, too unstable, and too dangerous for greater German soil itself.

Citizen ran a story on "receiving and re-processing technologies" that would bring jobs and capital to the area. This was under Jingkee's direction, who had also gone bigger, much bigger, on Kelvin's death than those of the Congressman and Professor Pfeidwengeler. In fact, she'd dropped all follow-up on those after the third day. Boyet thought it unprofessional of her, never mind loyalty to a deceased colleague. She was letting what had happened to Charina influence her, he thought. By contrast, the rival concentrated on the survivor, Mr Crescente Koyaw, for human interest. (The dead didn't possess much of this).

The dreaded words "toxic waste" never surfaced in the *Citizen* but that was what it was, the orange-brown, sweating piles of barrels with the skull and crossbones stencils still visible. God knew what kind of chemical or radioactive crap it was, but it was never treated in any way, this end-product of German efficiency and prosperity, the poison of the perfected system that nobody could wash off their hands quickly enough. Turks were the ones at the other end of the tube from the Filipinos. The material sat in forgotten warehouses, under tarpaulins in the open, then not even under this flimsy protection, waiting for the day of admixture, of slow but remorseless catalytic conversion from inert to terribly active when it might explode and splatter, spreading fumes through the city where Mrs Init no longer lived.

Chavez went back to Manila and became chief sub on a national, finding all in all he preferred to be a medium-sized fish in a big pool.

Like the Sleeping Beauty, Charina Zamora awoke from her coma one day, but blind and with no idea of who she was. She never regained her eyesight but gradually reacquired full mental faculties and led a life of fulfilment. This was enough for Jingkee who immediately went to the Church of the Sacred Heart to pray for forgiveness, as she might bestow it.

Crescente Koyaw took a long vacation in the States and Canada along the North West Pacific coast, still somewhat awe-filled as to his own aplomb and presence of mind on that terrible final day of the Dragons. Then he decided he'd like to see mountains and snow for the first time in his life and headed for Colorado. After which he went up to Montana where he felt both uneasy and yet profoundly at home in a kind of cold and sparse Philippines, with all and sundry carrying deadly iron-mongery quite openly on the hip. A car back-fired on the main street of Helena sending him diving behind a fire-hydrant. This broke the ice and some good old boys stood him a couple of rounds in a nearby bar. All the time he was touring in his hire car – rigorously observing the 50 mph limit – Gracie was lobbying in Bergen, then in Tokyo, so they couldn't meet. By the time she got back to New York he was home again. They did exchange letters – she had asked him to make an artificial reef with old car tyres and to preserve it (he'd promised her "no one will fish it twice. Guaranteed."), and once at three a.m. EST she received a garbled telephone call from a Crescente she suspected of being drunk.

"It fizzled out," she told Carla with tenderness for the memory in the Russian Tea Room. She thought of it as her land-based shipboard romance.

Carla herself stopped freelancing soon after, went to work in public relations for an asbestos mining company at a vast salary ("we're probably the most sued company in the world," she told her friends cheerfully), then re-married only 18 months later, and went to live in Grenoble where she never saw any of her professional contacts or charges again, but did enjoy a bitchy comparison of notes with Timothy Donovan at a mutual friend's cocktails ten years later, the same month, unknown to her, that the Boss died of a massive cardiac infarction, his trousers round his ankles, of strain brought on in his own CR. A common occurrence among those males predisposed by heredity or their own lifestyle.

Boyet Dinolan went from bad to worse. He'd always been able to console himself that at least he'd never dabbled in drugs, holding those who did so in the same contempt that ordinary offenders held child molesters, he being an inmate of the prison of unsavoury desires. But now there was even an episode with shabu, "the poor man's cocaine". He first tried it in the company of a go-go dancer from the Pistol n' Holster, discovering that not most of the girls, not 99 per cent of the girls, but all the girls took it before work. "Otherwise, *naulaw*, ashame, sir," she told Boyet, the explanation necessary for the old or the alien. He had no inhibitions to dispel before he broke his promise and ejaculated in her mouth, but the ice-like crystals provided a euphoric smoke. He scored some more two weeks later from a pusher at the roller-skating rink. This inspired him to lay down a blanket prohibition on the kids going there. That also conferred a feeling of moral euphoria, taking the high ground as a father. He knew there was no good reason for it. "Pa, p-l-e-e-z-e cut it," Ilynn and Dexter had beseeched him with regard to his new pony-tail.

Without a regular salary he couldn't indulge either his old habit or his new quite as freely as he would have wished. In a way he was glad, but that didn't stop him asking Miriam for handouts. She had got a job selling Tupperware, before her brother in a wonderful piece of patronage secured her a position as a pharmaceutical company's agent: a fantastically well-paid job, with a car and the opportunity to sell samples of medicine and wholesale boxes of infant formula on the quiet. Two years later, Jingkee gave her a column – Women's Adze – and her cup flowed over. Boyet was big enough to take pleasure in it. He tried to think of himself as the retired champ – some of them bigger substance-abusers than him, if you believed the scandalmongers and funnily enough he'd started taking newspaper reports as gospel truth again. The odd bit of private practice came his way – wills, letters of intent, property transfers – and he contemplated writing poetry. That was it. He waited for the clarion that never called.

Jack Beaufort, too, for wholly different reasons, found himself less in demand on his particular circuit, though as the new century wore on the odd invitation arrived. Had he ever been aware of the reason he might have taken wry consolation from seeing the sententious old adage disproved about the good men do living on after them and the evil they do dying with them. Plainly, Omar Hamid's poison was nearly as virulent as when he'd been spreading it.

In fact, Jack had plenty to occupy him. Three years after the Dragons he moved south from Manila, first to Cebu, then Dumaguete, and back to Cebu. It was like changing countries. It wasn't just the different languages – "sweep", he told the teenage maid in Tagalog, inducing a fit of paralytic modesty for the word meant "lift your skirt" in Visayan – so much as the relaxed quality of life. Southerners, as it were, behaved twice as much like Filipinos as the Northerners. As others had done before him and more would after him, Jack fell in love with the Queen City and its gutsy, extrovert inhabitants, watched some small prosperity come their way and hoped it wouldn't change them. Many years later – in fact the year before Gracie and Bish's brief encounter in Mexico – as he lay dying in hospital in Sydney in the atmosphere of floor wax and Dettol, he would recall the odours of dust and of burning wood, with the fragrance of kalachuchi flowers nearly but not quite lost in the aromas of fermenting urine and barbecuing meat, that were the essences of the particular perfume of the city.

And he would often wish Professor Pfeidwengeler was still around, so he could renew his debate with him. Pfeidwengeler, he thought he saw now, had not been so much an instinctive hater of the alien as a disappointed lover. Jack's own mild dislike of the arbitrary power-wielders of his beloved adoptive country had in the years since the Dragons, fortified by a bitter personal experience, turned into unqualified loathing and contempt. He reckoned he could have out-Pfeidwengelered Pfeidwengeler on the subject. But he so much wanted to say to the rebarbative old German: "Look, the poor didn't pickle the rod for their own backs, you know. Don't implicate them. They're as innocent as can be." And he could hear Detlef's answering snarl: "Tommy's rot. It gives no innocence. They turn just the same if the chance they have."

To which he could say, pat with the retort worked on over many years, "People take on the ways of their masters to assure the survival of their families. Yes, it's a free for all. Corrupting bodies do have this tendency to poison the sweetest well – one arm will do as well as an entire corpse, but remove it and the water will spring as pure as Eden's. The people just have to know where the bodies are buried." He knew Detlef's scorn for the religious impulse, but he wanted to add, "It needn't be a mass deception. What other institution but the Church could work the transformation?"

He longed to know Detlef's reply but in all the years of their private dialogue he could never supply it, although he would have accepted its verdict as being beyond the appeal of any tribunal of his peers.

MRS INIT never looked back. It was as if she had reconstructed herself out of an heroic mould. Dignified, tearful Cory accepting Ninoy's martyr's mantle was nothing on this. She actually had no warning of the Congressman's fate, in the sense of preparation of a public face. She arrived in her own Toyota to find Representative Init's vehicle burning on its side and the entrance to the Dragons a gory shambles. People – students, surviving Untouchables, foreigners, hotel staff, newsfolk – were running round like headless chickens. She was challenged; she responded. Looking back, it all appeared as natural as it had seemed easy at the time, much like rushing to mop up a choco-late spill on an antique table in the sala. For that was how she thought of the Dragons, only much more expensive *di ba*? Within a minute she had taken control, supplanted panic with mama's purpose. Her pink hard hat magically appeared from nowhere, she instructed every gun in the place to be unloaded (brooking no male protest) and that was how she appeared in *Time* (Asian edition): pointing, helmeted not unlike Boadicea, with the 12-gauge cartridges strewn round her feet much like festival firecrackers and the English sporting shotguns lying broken open like the V's of twisted paper schoolboys of all nations fire from rubber bands.

Congressman Init became transmogrified into something rather more complexly formidable: namely, Congresswoman Init, there being no such provision for this particular contingency (far from unknown) as the laughable British institution of the parliamentary by-election. She was quite surprised how easily she coped, though her style was very different from the late Congressman's. For example, there was no need for a favour filter or request-bearer, such as she had been to the Representative – how could she approach herself? – and certainly she never put a contract out on anyone. One of the first things she did was accept Dionisio III's invitation to a daylight meeting on neutral turf, a Dionisio who – to be vulgar – looked shit-scared, arriving behind an advance party of about half a million goons and bowing and kissing her hand when she got out of her taxi quite alone to resounding subsequent effect. He assured her, with tears in his evil old eyes, that he'd had nothing to do with the late Representative's demise. She believed him, and then never wasted another thought on him, only using his great grandson Atty. Dionisio IV – who'd been bar top-notcher of his year – in a big intellectual property rights case early in the young man's career eighteen years later, the genuine ability of the great-great-great-grandfather at long last flowering four generations down the branch.

As for herself, Mrs Init veritably bloomed. She did two years in the shoes of her dead husband. At the end of the term, people suggested she should stand for Senator in the new elections.

She found she had no interest in that.

Spend US$40 million on what? For that was what it cost. No power-broker or speechifyer, she, but – well – an *artiste* of a special sort. Besides she knew she had no national name.

317

Probably she could have made Congress again in what was an area-based election. But to run for the senate on a nation-wide tally, it helped to have been a film-star.

What on earth could she do? She would have been the most brilliant First Lady in history – that was the role custom-designed for her, but she hadn't had the right partner in life.

Bingo!

She found she already had a character in that shadowy inter-national world, neither diplomacy, politics, banking, administra-tion, academe, nor footling celebrityhood, but a tinny amalgam of all, that enclosed mere sovereign national destinies: the civil service of global glamour. The Dragons – not a useless disaster after all – had something to do with it. But reputation, the equiv-alent of formal job references in less exalted careers, was not so much fashioned out of what one thought one knew about one's standing – the press-clippings, papal audience, ribands and orders, committees sat upon – so much as what one *didn't* know. Worth more than a whole fawning magazine interview that the egotistical might leave on their coffee table and the insecure in their ante-room were a few words of approval in informal conversation that the subject would never know had been uttered. Notable in Victoria's dealings had been the fact that she didn't have sticky fingers. It had impressed an old Dane with a UN aid agency so much – he was the warden of his enclave – that he bored everyone to death with his discovery, tantamount to finding a monkey that covered its mouth when it belched. Mrs Init wasn't obeying a private code of honour that you could wear like a hair-vest; she just didn't feel that it was very *stylish*. Anyway, as she wasn't planning to continue the voyage there was no need to salt away stock in the barrel. After she served three years as assistant to one of the medium-level luminaries of this world of ghosts (immune to the lets and checks to which the movements of ordinary mortals were subject, they floated through impervious barriers with ease, invulnerable to all conse-quences) she actually got a responsibility in her own right. Long ago, she'd decided the environment had too much talent devoted to it; the field bristled with competition. Children and their rights, that was also getting staked out. She started to specialise in the world of technology transfer and copyright, cruising these tricky waters for pirates, making sure parents got back their kidnapped brain-children (sometimes anyway), mediating between Professor Pfeidwengeler's admired creators and the lesser bred shoplifters in the world's bazaar. Lahore and Lagos became as familiar to her as Bangkok, Taipei and Singapore, as New York and Brussels. It was home that was a memory without lustre. As Jack Beaufort engaged in his obsessional mental mud-wrestling contests with the shade of Detlef Pfeidwengeler, so Victoria hovered on angel wings. For her the fray took place in a foreign country and a by-gone day, the era of the great demi-diurnal brownouts when she now inhabited the realms of light.